*Children of the World*

Other Fiction by Martha Stephens

*Cast a Wistful Eye*

# Children *of the* World

*A Novel by* Martha Stephens

Southern Methodist University Press
*Dallas*

Copyright © 1994 by Martha Stephens
*All rights reserved*
FIRST EDITION, 1994

Requests for permission to reproduce material from this work should be sent to:
 Rights and permissions
 Southern Methodist University Press
 Box 415
 Dallas, Texas 75275

Grateful acknowledgment is made for permission to quote lyrics from the following songs:

"It's Been a Long, Long Time" (Sammy Cahn, Jule Styne) © 1945 Morley Music Co., Inc. Copyright renewed and assigned to Morley Music Co., Inc. and Cahn Music Company. All rights on behalf of Cahn Music Co. administered by WB Music Corp. All rights reserved. Used by permission.

"You'll Never Know" (Mack Gordon, Harry Warren) © 1943 (Renewed) WB Music Corp. All rights reserved. Used by permission.

Library of Congress Cataloging-in-Publication Data

Stephens, Martha.
 Children of the world : a novel / Martha Stephens. — 1st ed.
  p.  cm.
 ISBN 0-87074-378-3 (cloth) — ISBN 0-87074-379-1 (paper)
 1. Middle aged women—Georgia—Fiction.  2. Mother and child—Georgia—Fiction.  3. Abused wives—Georgia—Fiction.  I. Title.
 PS3569.T3853C47  1994
 813'.54—dc20                                                      94-28704

*Cover illustration and design by* Barbara Whitehead

Printed in the United States of America on acid-free paper
10  9  8  7  6  5  4  3  2  1

*In remembrance of*
Evelyn Thomas Wise
1915–1992

# Children of the World

*Jesus loves the little children*
*All the children of the world*
*Red and yellow, black and white*
*They are precious in his sight*
*Jesus loves the little children*
*of the world.*

*"But didn't you know there was no Jesus . . .*
*and no one to save the children of the world?"*

# Part One

~

*Waycross, Georgia*

*Friday*

*August* 1979

## CHAPTER ONE

THE weather had said it would rain but they had been saying that for several days and it looked like the joke was on them again. No this would be another scorcher—she could see that, even sitting inside in the air conditioning, sipping her morning coffee in the amazing light of the bay window.

It was one of their worst Augusts. People said they had never seen it so hot, and of course no one could figure out how they had ever gotten by without air conditioning. Sometimes Margaret too would be surprised to think she had raised her whole family without it, and in this small house, on this sandy lot where they had had such a terrible time getting any trees started. Yet when she had first gone to work, she had always done the entire weekly ironing, for instance, on Sunday afternoon, no matter what the weather was, and had not had a heatstroke. And—*my lord,* she thought—by the time she had got to the ironing she had already cleaned up the house and gotten three children off to church and then served them up a whopping big Sunday dinner.

In the summertime the kitchen must have gone up to at least one hundred and ten degrees; she would have chicken frying and biscuits in the oven, pots on all the burners and other pots waiting their turn. She had cooked up a storm all morning in such a steam bath she could hardly see.

After dinner, Ruth and Laney would clean up—not very cheerfully . . . and in fact it was comical to think of the glum hurt looks they gave her when it was time to do the dishes. She herself would still not be ready to stop; that was when she would get out the clothes basket and sprinkle the pieces she was going to iron later on and roll them up in a damp towel. Only then was it time for something else—of an entirely different order. She shivered right now to think of the silly pleasure of it: she would go and lie down on her high bed with the Sunday papers around her, the afternoon sun banked pleasantly against the pulled shades, her shoes off and the fan on her. *Oh that was good!* and she was grateful for even thinking of it.

Of course hot sweating labor was mostly gone from people's lives now and she supposed that was for the best, but the pleasure of getting cool was gone too. Some people did not even know what it felt like to work up a red-hot lather and then sit down in a cool place and wipe your face with a cold cloth and drink down in one long drink a big fresh glass of lemony tea with plenty of ice. People thought it was wonderful *not* to know, but then they went out and tried their best to get back what they had progressed from in saunas and exercise rooms.

Margaret pictured herself up on her bed with her shoes off, years ago, and the fan blowing on her bare legs, ruffling gently the edges of the *Journal-Constitution*. Richy would come in, with nothing on but his khaki play-shorts, and want to crawl up beside her. She would make him go and wash his feet first. He would go in the bathroom and dab at the bottoms of them with a wad of wet toilet paper, and then he would come back and get up beside her and read the funny papers. He would not snuggle up to her like the girls did, but would lay one skinny leg along the curve of her hip, and *that*—why thinking of that this morning made her set down her cup as if she hardly had the strength to hold it. Sometimes she would lift up his knee and give it a kiss. He would not move behind his funny paper or acknowledge what she had done in any way and yet he did not resist her either. The wonderful truth was that all her children had loved her and they were all lovable children.

The despair in her life was not from them, it seemed to her, and yet when she considered this closely she thought that in another way perhaps it was. In an old snarled brain like hers, nothing at all could be remembered simply but always dragged in a load of other things with it. Good thoughts and dark thoughts, for instance, would not stay apart but seemed to develop all kinds of complicated connections to each other.

Tonight after work she was going out to a bridal shower with some old girlfriends and she remembered that the last time she had been to a party like that there had been something awful all over the papers that had happened in Atlanta or Savannah or some place like that, and that was all they had talked about, they couldn't get off the subject, and Margaret almost wished she hadn't gone. A woman had had some kind of strange breakdown and done away with her children and then herself . . . and the thing was this woman was not of the desperate class, her husband went to work every day like anybody else and they lived in their own house, and the neighbors had told the papers they had thought she was a perfectly normal person and a good mother; the women at the party said that that was the puzzling, the insurmountable thing, but Margaret herself had not wanted to discuss it, the whole business just made her feel peculiar.

There was something in her feelings about incidents like that that she could not possibly bring out into the open; in

5

fact the truth was that she had always felt a horrible fascination for such women, for ones who did what this one had done to their children. When she would read of such a case in the papers, she did so with great avidity and tension and almost strangling suspense, as if it were something that were touching *her*, or *might* touch her, as if she were expecting (half dreading, or half hoping even) that she would find as she read something that would touch her own life directly, personally affect or even change her. And when people said, "How could she, how could a person, how how how *could* such a thing be done," when they said, "Insane—insane, would have had to be insane," Margaret said nothing or she just shook her head and murmured . . . "I tell you."

And yet the secret truth was that there was something about it—about doing such a thing—that was not quite impossible to understand, not quite entirely alien, and something in it that overcame her more than anything else in the world with a terrible pity, and a grief, for all mothers and all mankind.


Perhaps her brain was nothing but an old bristly mass of half-sprung wires that could no longer make anything but wrong connections—but it seemed to her that this particular pity, this grief, was the same one she used to feel on certain occasions at church. She would feel it on Youth Night, for instance, when the Children's Choir got up to sing. When she would look around in the sanctuary, other people would be smiling, they would be happy, the very sight of the Children's Choir was something that seemed to simply fill them up with happy affection. They did not seem to be struck, as she was, by the glowering, almost angry looks on the faces of the children. For one thing, a lot of the children did not sing well at all and would not have even thought of standing up with the choir if their parents had not insisted on it. "Jesus Loves the Little Children" was the song they would sing, and in a way it sounded awful, it sounded like several songs at once, as if some of the children were singing another piece entirely—and perhaps they were. Margaret would look into their stern faces with a stern expression of her own and a definite antipathy—at that moment—for the song itself.

For here were listeners being informed by little children, in broken song, that little children were loved very much by Jesus Christ. ("Well I declare," she felt like saying.) And not just this child or that child but all the children of the world. And for instance, Jesus didn't care, they sang, what color children were; to him each and every one of them was precious ("Well I do know").

"Jesus loves the little children," sang the little children, in their ragged, wounded chorus, and there was definitely something terrible about it.

In the bay window Margaret raised her coffee to her lips and blew on it almost angrily. She hated to start the day like this, dragging herself down with discouraging thoughts before she had even gotten started good.

Yet even when she put down her cup and went into the bedroom, such a pretty, fluffy, good-natured room, deliberately composed to be an enemy of pain, her train of thought did not improve. She sat frowning on the edge of the bed, working a roll of hose up her leg to her girdle snaps, and thought ahead to herself arriving at work. She saw herself pull into the dirt lot of the old frame building which housed the Juvenile Court, sit for a minute in the car to get her breath, then mount the back stairs, that the fire department had made them put on, thinking—as she did almost every morning, at least momentarily—of the couple who used to work below her on the first floor, Colonel Clyde and Mrs. Clyde, who had committed suicide together, the only double suicide, as far as she knew, the county had ever had.

7

She didn't know why they called him Colonel. *I must ask Jim*, she thought, but she knew she would forget to ask him again, because ordinarily she wouldn't begin to think about the Clydes except when she was climbing the stairs. Of course if nothing distracted her when she unlocked her own door and went inside—a note, say, from Jim, on her type-writer, or the phone ringing—she might continue to think about them as she took off her coat. She would sometimes think about the note they had left. It was thoughtful of them to do that, she would think—for they were childless and they had no close kin to leave a message to. But of course the note itself was a puzzler, no one had ever heard of any-thing like it before. They said the reason they were doing it was that they were bored—bored was the word they used, and *tired of everything,* she believed they had said. They had worked for the government overseas and then been sent to this small bureau in Waycross. They were both strong and forceful individuals, very efficient, and they ran a beau-tiful office—their work was always caught up. Did not seem depressed, she would think. But then they had not *said* de-pressed, they had said *bored.*

Other times she would think of the way they had done it, so it would be a double suicide and not a murder-suicide— she shot herself and then with the same gun *he* shot *himself.* She had forgotten how that was known, but at the time it was. She imagined what the Colonel might have said: "My dear, I have never raised my hand against you and I don't believe I could, so you see you must take the gun yourself and hold it like this . . . ." And the thing was that though she had shot herself first and he must certainly have thought she was dead when he himself took up the gun, she was not and lived for several hours. The bullet that had entered her head had hit first on a metal hair curler and gone slightly askew. *So that hair curler,* Margaret would think . . . something else to ponder over. And then—so snarled was her old wiry brain-coil—that sometimes she thought then of mad killers

8

who had no special victims in mind but just ran through the streets shooting people down. Actually, she did not see why if a person like the Colonel could kill himself for no particularly good reason, except just to get out of something (this earthly life) that didn't seem worth the trouble—why such a person, if he were a public-spirited kind of man, might not decide to do the same service for others. Yet people that shot others were always said to have "gone berserk," whereas berserk was not a word that was ever used for someone like the Colonel who only shot himself.

She had had a dream once, where she was the victim of a berserk killer. She was drinking a cup of coffee in the drugstore, and a man entered a store across the street. In her dream she knew beforehand that he was going to kill her and she could also see into the store quite plainly from where she sat at the counter in the drugstore, and she could even hear what the store clerk said to the killer. "What you want," the clerk said, taking down a gun, "is a good Berserk, with a telescopic sight." Then the man, just as she knew he would, came out of the store, stood on the sidewalk, raised the gun and shot her through the telescopic sight.

That was all of the dream but she thought it implied that the man had gone berserk, was on a shooting spree, and that she was just the first of the victims of the telescopic sight. (She wondered if he had actually *needed* the telescopic sight to shoot her from that close.)

Margaret sat scowling on her bed in her slip and hose. Truly she wondered at herself this morning and her peculiar train of thought. Maybe today was the day something would happen to her and some little engine of her brain was trying to forewarn her. Suddenly she was very conscious of the nice soft bulk of the bed beneath her. She made a wry face at herself: if tonight was the night she would not turn these covers down . . . then covers would not be something that any longer appertained to her—and very little *would* appertain.

She wished, as always, she could be a person with a little

9

more good cheer, and she tried to make herself think ahead to what little pleasures the day might hold. If she were alone in the office this morning, she might get the watering can and water the hanging begonia in the window. That was truly a pleasure, for she loved to take care of things and keep them nice, and as she stretched her freshly groomed, smoothly begirdled body upward, rising a little on her toes in her spruce patent heels, carefully tipping, just slightly, the basket towards her, to hook over its edge the spout of her spotless can, she would feel—for that moment—graceful and serene, and would be thankful, for instance, she had not gotten stout and awkward.

Of course she was not skinny either and never had been—she had always been a little on the plump side. Her plumpest period had come years ago when she had first gone to work. In fact the day she had first met Jim, the judge of the Court (though of course at that time he wasn't yet the judge), she had felt absolutely fat and sincerely believed that everything about her was ridiculous.


MARGARET had stood up and slipped on her blouse but now she sat back on the bed and remembered a certain evening many years ago: the evening before she had first gone out to look for work.

*At bedtime that night she had been in the kitchen rinsing some dishes at the sink, clearing up where Leonard had had his snack.*

As always he had left everything out, had not even put the lid back on the mayonnaise.

She had heard him move in the living room, get up in his sock feet and turn off the television, then sit back down on the couch. He sat there, and she did not hear him move towards bed—a bad sign. It depressed him to sit in the dim gloomy living room with the television off just before bed. She herself had stood at the sink, her hands spread on the ledge, and in the other room Leonard sat on the couch. Of course, it was years before he had had his heart attack, but maybe his heart, even then, had been wrapped tight in twisted nerves. She had thought she heard him mumbling to himself. This was a habit of his, and then he would seem to wait for a reply. She had suddenly heard his voice work, strangely, in the silence of the darkened room: "My wife has not worked a day in her life since I married her." Wasn't that it, what she had heard? those old words of his . . . spoken so many times before in his little puffings of frightened pride?

She had stood at the sink, her hands on the ledge, her face deep drawn. It was time to move towards bed, but something told her to be absolutely still. From the living room she heard small raspings and clearings of the throat, sighs and low whispers, startled groans of surprise and consternation, and she knew he must be replying to himself in the voices of the town . . . "I see where your wife has gone to work. Bad times eh? Can't make it eh? Business is bad eh?"

Yes she had known, at some point, what the voices must have been saying to him, in his dangerous pricked pride. "Leonard Barker . . . his wife has gone to work. It's hard to make it on those selling jobs like he has . . . but just pay off some bills eh? Just for a few months eh?"

Then she heard the strained low tense voice of Leonard himself again, speaking to himself in the living room: "I've got a girl going to college next year." A pause. Then she heard him begin again: "See here! You know my oldest girl? The one that's going to college? Well my wife—"

Silence. Margaret stood at the sink. She knew that in Leonard's absurd brain the other sounds must be going on and nothing could stop them. *What was it that happened to those Barkers anyway? What was the trouble with them that got them in such a fix? Did they try to send one of them off to college, was that what they tried? Why you can't do that on a job like Barker had. At college they say it'll be just so much and then there's charges for things you never heard of and everything adds up, things nobody tells you about. He thought he could do it and of course he put his wife to work in a law office.*

Did he put his wife to work—was that it? . . . *his wife to work?*

When he had cried her name, in hoarse rage, in his terrible pricked pride, trembling to his feet from the sofa, he had turned and seen her, across the narrow hallway, at the bedroom door.

Of course she had wished with all her might she had made it to the bed, and that the door had been closed between them. For now the sight of her inflamed him. Again he cried her name, in that altered voice she recognized, that voice of trapped animal. "When I call you in here, *get in here!*" he screamed. "Get your fool face—IN HERE!"

She turned towards him, still in the little hall, and he had lunged up now from the sofa and begun his trapped-animal pacing, back and forth in the small room, for then his anger was on him like a beast—or he was caught in it, in the net of it, like a beast himself, like something desperate, wildly struggling; she saw him struggling against it—his own anger, saw his trapped animal pacing, his battle to escape it! But it was on him, it covered and trapped him, and when he whirled around to her, his face was gorged and bloated with flushed rage, almost crazed, and his arm shot out, one finger fixing her like a gun. "If-you-leave-this-house-tomorrow-I'll-kill-you-don't-you-think-I won't!" She was a goddamned whore, he said, and always would be. Then he ranted on in a high rapid rant, like an auctioneer's or a preacher's.

"If I didn't have these children to raise! I'd drive you out of here tonight! On the street where I found you! Where you belong! Because you are not the kind! that belongs in a house!"

He locked his eyes on her face. "Don't you try to fool me you old whore you can't fool me because I know you I KNOW YOU! I know you want to get out of here because you aren't FIT (or maybe he had said *ain't* fit) and you KNOW you aren't fit—to be a mother to these children!" He bent forward towards her, in an animal crouch, slapped one hand into the other as he cried hoarsely each word: "But-you-are-not-going-to-GET-out-of-here! You are going to raise these children! And you are going to raise them RIGHT! You're going to BE fit because I'm going to MAKE you fit!"

He waggled his head at her, rasped and sneered. "I KNOW you woman! And I know your goddamn tricks, so don't try your old goddamn tricks on ME!"

So it was that he ceased to struggle against himself and was simply lost in his rage and it tossed him blindly, shook and battered him. And of course her own emotion rose too, flooding her brain, running sharply into her eyes so she could hardly see. She felt her whole body like a weight on her heart, on her stricken lungs and heart, choking her breath so she could only hiss and whisper. "Devil! You devil! You know what you said! You know! We talked about it and you said—" She was still in the hall, and just before he pitched forward and raised his hand to slap her face and she held it up to him to slap, refused to hide or cover it, still she was able to close, with the hand behind her back, the door to where the children were sleeping . . . .


THE NEXT morning he had sat over his coffee with a black frown. Silent. He was utterly silent. It was as if he could not see or hear. She fixed the children's chocolate and went to wake them up. They came, frowning and silent too, knowing at once what was to be known, from her face and voice. They sat down and took up their cups of chocolate. They did not look at him or at each other. They drank slyly in small swallows, munched soundlessly their toast. They felt it would be a concession to him to let him hear them eat and drink. He himself said nothing, not a word. From the table he went into the bedroom to get his case, into the bathroom and out to the car.

When he came in that evening, she was setting the table. He did not come into the kitchen, but sat down with the paper in the living room. She went to the door and said, "I'm putting it on, if you're going to eat anything." He looked up at her with the slightly hangdog look that always followed his attacks, his mouth drawn down. He had a kind of blanched look to his face; he looked cleansed and restored, like one who had just gotten over an illness. His speech was quiet, deliberate, self-conscious. At the table he helped his plate. "What did you find out in town?" he said.

"They want me to start Monday."

"Oh they do? What is the pay?"

"Fifteen dollars a week."

The children had all retreated into the bedrooms when he came in. Now they came into the dinette and sat down to supper. Margaret was not sitting—it was her habit to stand behind the table, watch them eat, refill glasses. "Mama—why don't you sit down?" Leonard said. No, she was not hungry yet, she said.

Whenever Leonard had acted as he had, he sank into a mood of piety, of sanctimoniousness, where he exhorted others to be good, to do the right thing, to take moral account of themselves. He spoke to the children. "Did your mama tell you what she's been doing today?" Yes she had, they said, in polite, toneless voices. Leonard took a long, loud drink of milk, making a display of normalcy, of everyday gusto. "I tell you!" he said, looking at them almost darkly. "Your mama is not doing this for herself, she is doing it for you children!" They ate quietly, with a kind of formal restraint. "I hope you are going to appreciate it!" he said. They murmured their assurance, hating him, hating every word he said. He finished up his supper, took out his handkerchief and wiped his mouth with a noisy motion they despised.

He stood up and emitted a loud burp and went outside. Then he stood on the corner of the yard looking into the dirt street and talking to himself in a voice so loud they could almost make it out inside.

But Margaret went back to the morning of this same day. After the children had left for school, she had sat on at the table with her coffee. She had fixed her an egg and eaten it numbly, without tasting it, hardly knowing what she ate. When she thought of the night before, her husband's sudden animal rage, she felt worthless and small, and she thought remotely, almost stuporously, about various desperate actions she might take. But she knew she would find, as always before, that there was essentially nothing she could do. This was her life, would always be her life. Yet it was as if her mind still felt for something else, it was as if she were always feeling along a wall for a door, pressing herself against the wall, feeling and feeling up and down, all over, for a door. Of course there was no door, but that did not keep her from feeling for it, in her mind, again and again.

Washing up the dishes she had cut her finger on a knife in the dishpan; she stood thinking, pressing it absently, at the sink. When she got out the broom to sweep the kitchen, the blood ran down the handle onto the broomstraw. She could not find a band-aid, the children had used them all up, so she tied up her finger with a strip of old handkerchief. When the house was clean, she sat down in her housecoat in the living room; it was time for Arthur Godfrey on the radio, but she had punished herself that day for the failures of her life by not turning it on. She had wanted to be fresh for going into town, but she had slept very little and was already tired. Leonard, thank god, would be tired too, would have a hard irritating day on the road. She had slipped Laney in with Ruth and slept on Laney's bed, but of course she had not actually slept, her body was as stiff as a stick all night.

She was to get a ride into town with a neighbor, and when the time came, she was ready, in one of the new voile

dresses she had made at home for the specific purpose of going to work in, and in her patent heels, wiped off good with
a wet rag. Her hair was always a problem. She had rolled it
up but it could never be depended on to look good when she
wanted it to.

The neighbor had let her out downtown in front of the
town's one large office building. Going up in the elevator, to
Room 305, there was a moment, naturally, when she hoped
it would break down and she would not be able to get up
there to see the lawyers. She was thirty-six years old and had
never had any kind of regular paid job. This was only her
first try, she had told herself, so if she wasn't hired, it would
not be anything to be ashamed of, she would simply try
again.

She had no idea what lawyers would be like. Leonard had
never, thank god, had to go to a lawyer, would only have
done so in the worst extremity, because to pay them their
fee might cost you everything you had. He had said many
times that even if you went to them for some simple thing,
it would not turn out to be so simple after all and then they
would send you a bill that would pop your eyes out and put
you in the poorhouse.

But to *work* for lawyers—how would that be? That is—if
they happened to hire her. If they did, it would be because
they could not get anybody else. One thing she remembered—you could not fool lawyers, and they would probably
give her one look with their narrow eyes and know she
would not do. They would be able to tell by the way she
walked in the door, told her name, the ignorant things she
would say. She had had courses in typing, in shorthand and
in business English at night school. But if they gave her a
test she would be nervous and not be able to do any of that.
They would take one cunning look at her typing and say,
"We thought you said you could type."

She thought of a certain stratagem that relieved her mind
a good deal. If she did have to take a test of any kind and did

poorly, she would just leave before they had a chance to look at it. At least it would have been a try, nothing to be ashamed of, and she would try again later on, somewhere else.

The colored man on the elevator stool had pulled the door open for her and she got out. When she came to Room 305, the door was open and she was so startled that she walked right on down the hall. *There was a nurse at the desk.* She walked slowly by to look at the nurse again and then she sat down on a bench in the hall. The nurse, a stout gray-haired woman, came out in the hall, scowling. She spoke sharply. "Did you need any help?" Margaret leaned forward, then she decided to stand up, and it was strange that she could not even decide how to manage her own body. "I— you might can," she said. "I thought . . . I was looking for— an office up here, but I thought it was 305, but it's not, it's a mistake." The nurse looked at her watch. "Oh I know who you are," she said. "You're the one—you're that Mrs. Barker. You can come on in," she said.

They went into the office and then they heard voices in the hall and three young men walked in, talking and laughing. When they saw Margaret, they quieted down. The nurse said, "George, this is Mrs. Barker." One of the men smiled at her. He was quite young. He told her his name and introduced the other two men as well. "How are you?" the men said, and George said, "How *are* you today?" The other men went off down the hall. "Thank you for coming in," George said to Margaret.

He was smiling but his eyes would just graze her face and glance away. They might be expecting a younger person, Margaret thought. "Sit down over here," the nurse said, and George said, "Yes ma'am! You sit down now!"

But he turned his back to her and spoke to the nurse. "Where's Jim?" he said. "He said he would be right back," said the nurse. "If you want to talk in there—" she said, meaning one of the inner offices. "No!" George said. "I

17

mean, it was Jim who—you know it was Jim who wanted to—to see Mrs. Barker."

Margaret, sitting with her purse on her lap, looked at her dishwater hands, her cut finger. If he wanted her just to leave, what should she do? Should she just get up? What would she say? George stood at the nurse's desk, jingling the change in his pocket.

"That's Jim," George exclaimed happily, hearing steps in the hall. Jim was a young man too, though he was beginning to get bald. He was a tall rangy man. Both men had their coats unbuttoned, their ties loose. "Mrs. Barker, this is my brother Jim." Jim had a quiet, lower voice. "Oh Mrs. Barker!" he said. But both men looked away from her, oh it was the most awkward thing in the world. George said, "You know Mrs. Barker came about—the ad in the paper." —"Yes, the paper—" Jim said. "Don't let me be in the way," he said. He turned toward one of the inner offices, but George looked very distressed. "Well Mrs. Barker—thought you were going to, I mean she thought you wanted to—" Margaret was sitting on a chair near the hall door, her purse on her lap; in the small room she felt incredibly large and ridiculous. In the past year or so she had begun to put on weight; now she suddenly realized that she had not weighed herself in several weeks and was probably much fatter than she thought. She surmised that it was painfully obvious to all that there would not even be room for her in here. They were expecting someone young and slim, she thought. Now they just wanted to get rid of her, but each one wanted the other one to do it. She herself wanted to get up and go home. But she simply could not think of how to do it, what to say as she rose from her chair, so she sat still. She knew that as soon as she did leave, the brothers would flop down on the divan, laughing with relief. "The next time we put an ad in the paper—!"

"But who in the world would have thought somebody like that would turn up!"

They would ask the nurse to call up and have the ad taken out. "Good god!" they would say to each other. "And the way she just sat there—and sat there!"

Margaret was beginning to get a headache, and besides that when she looked down at her hands folded on her purse, she was appalled at the sight of them. She might at least have rubbed a little cream on them. Later, at home that night in bed, she had waked herself up laughing at a dream of herself sitting at a typewriter taking a typing test in her white gloves. The three of them, the two lawyers and the nurse, were standing sternly over her and watching her hands jerking and slipping on the keys, slipping sometimes completely off the typewriter, for she had indeed been wearing her white Sunday gloves.

The reason she had dreamed that dream was that sitting there, in absurd embarrassment over her hands, she had actually for a moment thought about taking her gloves out of her purse and putting them on, in case—in desperation because she wouldn't get up and go—they had asked her to type for them. And besides all that, was her hurting head—she really did not feel well at all, and she had an absurd image of herself falling over in a faint and the nurse administering something to her on the floor, since she was too fat for them to get her back up on the chair.

Then—exactly what had happened next she could not remember—she was sitting in one of the inner offices with the older brother Jim, who had not wanted to be the one to have this private talk with her at all but who had apparently been trapped into it by his brother George, who had simply run away to the soda fountain downstairs.

Yet the talk she had had with Jim that day was not at all what either one of them had expected. Somehow she had known, almost at once, even that first day, that he liked, he almost loved, her dishwater hands; altogether he liked her very much, was touched by her life and by the simple fact of her having raised three children and ruined her hands for them in the dishwater, then gone to school to learn to type—clumsily, frowning over the typewriter—so they could go to college.

And she on her part—she had known from the first as well that he was not much of a lawyer and that his brother was not all that much of a lawyer either; the thing was they were good, pleasant, well-bred boys, they had never had a secretary because they had hardly any business, and they were embarrassed to be anyone's employer; neither one of them wanted to be anyone's boss, and they were a little embarrassed, besides, to tell her that so far there was nothing to do anyway but answer the phone, which would mostly be their friends calling up or their wives, and that if any business did walk in the door, she would probably have to look for them at the drugstore counter downstairs, and that the nurse worked for a doctor in the office next door and just walked over now and then when he was gone to keep an eye on things.

Afterwards she went down to one of the drugstores farther down the street and sat at a small round table in the corner, thinking it all through, hardly realizing where she was until the girl came and took her order for a root-beer float, which was fattening enough for a little private celebration. She knew a new phase of her life was beginning, and it was beginning because she was ready for it to begin and had chosen this time for it to begin and it was the right time. She had thought it all out and had done the responsible thing.

Yet already the past was becoming the past, even as she sat there; already she was feeling a sad nostalgia for her life that had been. She had a vision of herself and her children, of bending down to their waiting, extended arms, to their expectant faces, composed and unafraid; she saw them all coming into each other's arms, their smooth bodies touching and holding. All of them were inside a circle, a mysterious bright ring, and outside there was nothing, nothing at all to beckon or threaten or distract them in any way whatever from the simple business of loving and holding each other in their ring of light . . . .

Yet something at last did stir in that blue distance they could hardly see; a long way off something was clearly stirring, then mysteriously approaching and beginning gently to pull. It was something they did not understand. No they had no way of knowing whether it was friendly and good, or evil and dangerous, but only that it was pulling them slowly apart and that the blue dimness of the beyond itself was drifting inside their circle, floating between them, and that without willing it, they were moving, being moved or pulled, as people may feel they are being moved by a tide though they may be standing stock-still in watery sands. There were times when this movement was a matter of pride to her and she was letting go and even pushing, gently pushing, and at other times she was afraid, she felt a desperate terror when their hands, extended, parted too soon—too soon!—and were suddenly beyond her reach.

But at last she was standing free, watching her children drifting into the dimness beyond; and so after a time, looking outward, peering out of the circle at last, she saw the faces of her children amidst the other faces *out there*, simply there in the throng.

Now of course all this had actually been happening for a long time, and though she had known it was happening, still, that morning she had seen it all as if from a distance—pure. But she had thought to herself, *Oh be practical!* and then she had been almost overcome with an enormous relief that her children would soon be safely raised and she had not inadvertently, as far as she knew, done them any irreparable harm . . . had not died, for instance, and left them orphans with nobody who could take her place.

Later she had looked at herself, solemnly, with interest, in the store windows as she walked along the sidewalks, and she had had a sense of space around her as she walked that was not unpleasant but was mixed, even so, with her sad nostalgia—a sense of space and a vague struggling sense of adventure . . . for herself alone.

AND INDEED the adventure of her little part-time job, such as it was, had certainly worked out, and for several years, up until the time when his tragedy had happened to the older brother Jim, she had spent her mornings, nine-to-twelve, rather happily and peacefully in Room 305, humming along on a small mild current of work as she manned the desk in the outer office that had been kept by the nurse, on the day she had walked so confusedly by, thinking it was all a mistake.

An office that had had no order, that had been all ragtag and harum-scarum, she naturally put very quickly to rights (her only genuine talent, she thought sometimes); she sorted things and straightened them, cleaned and arranged and stacked and stored—and now and then there was an actual letter to do or even a legal paper. But it was pleasant to remember that in the bottom drawer of the desk there had always been a bag of sewing and she had had plenty of time for that too, and for paying the family bills, and typing letters of her own, to her children, for instance, as they dropped one by one off the steep Waycross cliff (who would have thought it would have been so treacherous?) into the outer world called *college*, then *work, marriage*.

But the young lawyers had been right for her. Yes she had said that a thousand times—because so few things ever were right—and she had been right for them. For one thing, she was not a gossip; she was not obsessed with the little details of their private lives that she could report to her friends. And actually she wondered sometimes, even now, why she was not. But it was quite possibly simply this: she knew, without knowing, what other people's lives were like, she knew they were mostly pain and defeat and she did not need

22

to know the supporting details—she had plenty of that at home. But there was also something else: her own life was not an open book; there were parts of it she did not want anyone to know, or be inquiring about, and so she thought of others as being the same way.

Even when the tragedy happened, to Jim . . . when he was left by his young wife very suddenly, and was crushed and crumpled up by it (like the thrown-away sheets in the waste-basket), never to be smoothed out or quite pulled straight again . . . even then she did not perk up her ears, spread open her net to catch his private travail. When he and she had to turn to each other face-to-face, when he paused at her desk to hand her a sheet or be handed one by herself . . . she had tried to let him know by her expression alone that she was not oblivious to his pain, that she acknowledged it and took account of it. But again, she did not need to know the details of his ordeal, she felt she had always known them.

For truly she had passed through certain things as a child, in her *other life* (before she had come to Waycross as a girl, been married, had children, gone up one day on the elevator, with such fear, to Room 305), from which she had probably learned them once and for all.

But his tragedy had told on him, and what work came to him he did rather poorly, mostly he sat in his inner office with his law books around him, which possibly he was not even reading in, and so his brother and his friends, who had begun, even in the few years Margaret had known them, to succeed a little bit, to hand each other crookedly along over the power path of the town, began to whisper and consult about this inept and suffering comrade, this gangly fellow-lawyer, oddly bald before his time, and afflicted, perhaps, in other ways besides, and to save him from poverty and ruin were able to put him up for a salaried job, a very minor judgeship of a new court for children.

So she and Jim had moved together from Room 305 in

the office building to their old frame structure near the courthouse, and juvenile offenders began to enter sullenly their lives, to be brought up to them to be punished or let off or sent away, to have hearings held over them, awkwardly at first (but perhaps they were awkward still) in the dusty second floor room. "Let Jim take Mrs. Barker with him," the friends had said—it seemed almost Biblical now, it was all so far away—"since she will be his most fit companion for this gloom, and it will come to pass that she herself will keep the Court, keep *him*, and lo, all will be well with him, lo, it will be OK." And she supposed on the whole it *had* been OK . . . though of course neither one of them were cheerful people, and it was certainly not work to lift the spirits; and even today, many years later, slipping her heels on to go to work, touching her hair, pulling straight her dress beside her freshly made bed, her strength, her courage, almost failed her, and instead of starting out for the Court she just wanted to sit in the living room on the brocade sofa and breathe out, all morning, long ridiculous sighs.

But of course in the living room she occupied herself like a person who was normal, doing what she did every morning: putting things in place, generally picking up the room, knowing that she would need—absolutely require—its orderly solace at lunchtime, and stopping as she worked to gaze absently, even intently, at the family pictures ranged around the room, mostly her progeny . . . children, then grandchildren—three pretty little granddaughters, all of them smiling shyly, hiding a little bit from the camera. *Oh these babies were much too far away.* She could only grope blindly for them in their outer darkness, where she imagined them trying their best to shine their little lights all the way through to her—"*Grandma! Grandma! It's you we want!*"

When she had not seen them for a while, sometimes she

would be seized by a terrible need to know if they were happy, and she would take their pictures fiercely to the window to study them closely in a good light. Let them be happy now, she would think, for nothing can say, no one can know, what awful things may happen to them out here—out in the world. Today the pictures reminded her of something so startling she almost had to sit down: the smallest one had a birthday soon and her daughter Laney had not reminded her. Still, she knew what she would send—she would get the little thing a doll, for dolls were one thing little girls could never have enough of.

Oh the dolls that Ruth and Laney had had! Dolls all over the place. Dolls underfoot, dolls in your chair when you wanted to sit down, dolls trapped behind chests and under the steps, gnawed by the dog, squashed in the vegetable bin. And the dolls going through everything too: dolls with broken limbs and cut fingers; dolls with a cold having their noses blown; dolls getting their tonsils out, paid a nickel for swallows of water; dolls in a new dress going for a ride in the carriage, with a diaper over their heads to keep the sun out; dolls getting their hair rolled up for Sunday School, with a penny in their pocket to put in the collection. Dolls who cried when they had to get a shot. Stiff-legged dolls trying to learn to walk. Old dolls lying in heaps in the backs of closets, being rediscovered with guilty repentance and celebration. And sometimes, cleaning up the house when her children were little, singing something in her high soprano voice ("You Are My Sunshine" probably), Margaret would open absently a door on a fantastic, an overwhelming sight: a whole roomful of little school-dolls sitting in lines against the walls and chairs, little scholar-dolls taking down their spelling from the children's blackboard, staring oddly, their numbered pads beside them, their little pencil stubs and chalk butts propped in their fat clubbed hands. And where would their *teachers* be? Out swinging in the yard perhaps. Climbing the sand hill.

She thought of all the doll clothes she had made, Ruth and Laney standing by the sewing machine on summer mornings, when Leonard would be at work and the baby taking his nap. Just the three of them. And with something they all liked simmering on the stove for lunch—Spanish rice perhaps. *Children! Don't you wish sometimes you had never had to grow up!* Not that anything terrible had happened to them—not yet at least. And yet grown-up life was always troubled; it was her custom to think of their lives now as troubled, pressured, worried lives, no matter what they themselves reported to her. Her son-in-laws—thank the lord for this—were decent boys . . . at least they seemed to be, and yet she knew her children had a conspiracy not to tell her about the bad things . . . not wanting to upset her, and maybe it was just as well, but actually, who knew what they were really going through? Richard, for instance, still at the university at his age, hardly even knowing what for. And as for Ruth and Laney—she wondered what they really had to put up with, what secret cruelties their husbands practiced on them. In fact the more she thought about it the more it struck her, standing this morning in the middle of the living room with the wastebasket in her hand, that these husbands were not nice decent boys at all, and she had a picture of her daughters, or of a composite young wife that included them both, crying quietly in her bed at night, alone, thinking in utter wretchedness and despair, "This is all it has come to."

Margaret frowned darkly as she took the wastebasket through the kitchen; she narrowed her eyes almost menacingly on some vague vision of revenge against husbands, against anything that might dare to rear itself against her children, their well-being. She was angry to begin with, and opening the back door, she grunted with disgust when the humid air flew in her face like a slung blanket of fuzzy steam.

～

26

LATER, in the car driving slowly to work, scratching slowly over the gravelly streets of the neighborhood, Margaret did not fully remember taking up her purse and leaving the house, locking the door on the hot brick stoop, getting in behind the wheel, turning on the air conditioning.

Since Leonard had died and she had lived alone, a helpless prey to galloping thoughts of every kind, it was almost silly how absentminded she could be. She had come to realize how huge the human mind really is, what an immensity of things it could hold, all of them at once. She had never expected to be so awed, so amazed by her own brain, because after all it wasn't even a very good one, but even so—what a great big old business to be carrying around on one neckjoint. It could hold practically anything and yet one thing it could not seem to hold was the present. She was always behind herself or ahead. At home this morning, she had thought ahead to herself at work and yet as soon as she had started out, she had thought *back* to herself in the living room, waiting until it was time to go, settled formally on the sofa, her purse beside her, like a guest in her own house, sitting back to stare at her own memory-screen as you might at a movie in the theater. So she had seen Ruth and Laney lining up their dolls, misspelling the spelling words on the silly blackboard . . . and then she had seen one child, Ruth, coming home many years later, in springtime, sipping tea at the maple table in the dinette, not many months ago.

Ruth was over forty years old now, and time was touching her all over (for there is something that *wants* it to touch us all), and yet she was a handsome child still. Yes, Ruth was a lean and handsome girl and she still had her wonderful thick hair, and Margaret thought it was lovely the way she pulled it back behind her head, tied it in bright scarves. She had come alone this time and it was the right thing to have done, because it had rested her—the spring blooms were out and she took long walks down the blossoming, feathery streets, and in the late afternoons they had sat in the flowery yard, just the two of them, and oh that was good . . . and yet of course they had talked sometimes of certain things— terrible things of the past; of the husband, father, dead now a year, and how bad everything had sometimes been, how absurd to be married to such a man, and yet what deep, hopeless depression she had had when he was gone.

"Mother, you are better now," Ruth had said. "I believe you can be happy now."

They sat frowning in the lawn chairs, thinking, reflecting. "Yes-s . . . ," Margaret said. "I am happy sometimes . . . but I don't know . . . . "

"Your house is so nice now, your life is so calm. And in a few years you'll be retired and you can come and visit us more, all of us—Richard and Laney, and be with the children more . . . and you'll be happy . . . . "

"Yes-s," Margaret murmured, "I expect I will be . . . . "

"There is no reason for you to be depressed now."

Margaret stared forward, frowning. "No-o . . . no reason," she had said.

Then after a time Richard had come home too, from the university, and oh that was a marvelous thing indeed, and she had wished they had had Laney too. She had made biscuits, and fried chicken and gravy, and cooked the white-acre peas she had put up in the freezer—and a splendid pale slippery custard pie. Richard and Ruth had been so loving to each other, so full of teasing intimacy; stirring the custard at the kitchen counter, she had looked up and seen them walking in the yard arm in arm, smiling and content, and later she had seen them sitting in the glider, under the pine trees, in another mood entirely, forgetting themselves altogether in one of their serious, searching, sober talks, turning and gesticulating and shaking their heads, gesturing and frowning, rocking and pacing, then suddenly laughing, and she had thought *They care for each other still, and always will, and this is a blessed thing and I am a terrible person and full of ridiculous self-pity and blind self-torment if I am not grateful for it.*

Waking in the night she heard them still, for they loved this talking way into the night when other people were asleep, their voices languid, then rapid and intense, though never never loud (for they did not want to wake her), and she loved the man's voice and the woman's voice winding together, the soft harmony of that.

Of course as children, they had fought, but her children had always loved each other. The girls had loved the little brother like one of their baby dolls. It was amazing the way they would line him up, for instance, with the school-dolls, make him scratch little absurd scratches on his spelling-pad. Sometimes they had put him in the doll buggy and commanded him to go to sleep, and half the time he would too. They fed him little morsels of cracker off jelly lids. He hardly knew what was pretend and what was not. It was passing strange the way little tots would give in to big ones and do whatever they wanted them to without a murmur. His sisters had brought him in one day on a bamboo stretcher, mortally wounded on the sand hill, unable to twitch a toe, and then they had brought him back to life with the doctor kit, and as far as anyone could tell, he simply enjoyed it all very much.

Margaret, driving to work on this August morning, remembered Richard as a fat baby, swaddled in absurd bandages that day, safe in the care of his sisters. Then—distracting herself so badly she almost forgot to go when the light changed—she had a terrible counterimage of a child in true danger, of Laney caught in a thunderstorm, running home from the park in swirling wind and rain, great crashing boulders of thunder rolling down on her from fierce mountains of sky. Yes she had an image of Laney running hysterically through the storm that day, swept almost along by it, shrieking "Mama, Mama!" ridiculously, when she was still blocks from home, her face drowning in rivers of rain and tears, crying wildly, then collapsing in the yard, where Margaret saw her from the front window, and ran out to her

29

with a coat over her head, pulling her, taking her up under the coat, hauling, half-carrying her sobbing to the house, then once inside holding her soaked, sob-wracked body to her own, her head against her chest, stroking, consoling, working her gently, slowly, out of her drenched clothes, drying her little body, fluffing her hair with a towel, slipping over her cold limbs a clean dry gown, then taking her on her lap, choked spasms of diminishing sobs still convulsing her, holding a cup of chocolate to her lips, lifting her back to the bedroom to the warm bed, propping her on pillows, the other children kept at bay, pulling snugly a blanket round her, still stroking, soothing, so that finally, exhausted, her child fell asleep, in an ecstasy of safety and relief, the others coming round to whisper, touch, in awe (jealousy almost) of her ordeal in the danger of the storm.

Terror. Then safety. Peace. *Oh there is a taste of the divine in that,* she thought. And it seemed to her that there was for a moment a putting on, a simple grateful wearing, of immortal godship in that, and who would not cling to it and crave it, value it above all things?

So then she had heard, as from afar off—sitting on the sofa, her purse beside her—the voices of little children, singing of their love for her and assuring her most strongly that they believed in her and that therefore their hearts were not troubled, that even if she went away from them (one day watching television, at lunchtime, then simply not turning back up at the Court when they expected her), they would know she had done so in order to get somewhere ahead of them and fix it up (put a ham on to bake), prepare a place for them. They knew she would come again, and receive them unto her, so that wherever she was, there they would be also. For they knew full well, the children sang— or were they simply *reciting,* in melodious unison?—that neither death nor life, nor even angels, neither things present nor things to come, neither height nor depth nor any creature, would be able to separate her from *them,* her children . . . in the world that was and the one that was yet to come.

She was glad no one knew what went on in her brain, the hopeless nonsense she had to put up with there, for then it was not children who sang—but one child only. There had been flung onto the screen of her mind an image of a child—Laney!—rising from her seat in the choir to sing a solo (as she had truly done, of course, many times, in the First Christian Church of Waycross, Georgia), a skinny child, frail, her shoulders hardly even sketched under the folds of her floppy white choir-robe, her hands barely able to reach through its sleeves to hold her hymnbook.

And what was she singing? Why she too sang of her mother's love for her and of a gift she wanted to give her. Of course the rest of the congregation did not know she sang to the mother alone, they thought she sang to *them*, and they wept to be addressed in such beautiful song, but the mother had known, and on the sofa this morning she had watched herself turning slowly her head to the child in the choir, staring at her, almost blindly, through the light-filled glasses of her lifted face, listening to the old hymn (what could be more familiar?), suited so well to a young girl's thin soprano voice. *Oh love that wilt not let me go-o, I rest my weary soul in Thee-ee. I give Thee back the life I o-owe, that in Thine ocean depths its flow . . . may richer, full-er be.*

So in the spring Margaret, watching Ruth and Richard walking in the yard, in the yellowish bright-green of the early spring, walking almost sadly, it seemed to her, for a flickering moment, arm in arm against the streamers of bridal wreath, had had the image of Laney running in terror through the crashing storm, and then of her in church, singing a certain song about saving love; and stirring the custard at the sink, she had had a preposterous image of herself running out to the yard, crying "Children, children! I'll save you! I'll keep you safe and you know I will!"

MARGARET pulled into the dirt lot in back of the building where she worked. She sat foolishly with her hands still
on the wheel. She had always been full of clownish thoughts
like these; the trouble was that now that she lived alone she
could give in to them. She of all people to save anyone. And
when there was no saving to be done anyway. The hands
resting so absurdly on the locked wheel looked like very old
hands today and she thought, *We are all sliding. Sliding
towards death and no one can help anybody else, all we can do is
hold together as we go.* But she of all people to save anyone—
a case like her, a certified depressive most of the time
(though once in a while, rather cheerful) and no one with
the least idea what was wrong with her or how she could get
any better. Certainly doctors did not know, though for years
she had gone to them and demanded to be cured. But she
had distinguished in those days between bodily ills and ills
of the mind and spirit. She would suddenly come down
sick—she might not be able to keep a thing on her stomach,
or her head might pound like a locomotive every day, or one
of her eyes might cloud over and she would think she was
losing her sight. So she would sit frowning in a white asep-
tic room and a doctor would come in very happily and say,
"Mrs. Barker, we've got all the tests and I know you're going
to be delighted with this news because we didn't find a
thing." And she was not a bit delighted and they would say
*Something in the mind. Something emotional. Stress, worry,*
they would say. Or perhaps they would lean toward her,
touch her hand. "What is it that worries you so much?" they
would say.

But she had wanted to be cured of bodily ills.


GOING UP the back stairs to the office this morning (a
Friday, thank goodness) in the wilting heat, she thought
about the Clydes who had worked down below, and as she
entered the back hall and got out her key, she thought again

32

about the way they had done what they did. They had shot themselves sitting on the side of their bed on a fresh white sheet laid over the spread. (Maybe we should all shoot ourselves, she thought absently.) They had not seen any use in making a mess. Margaret hated messes herself and that part of it she could certainly understand.

No, one thing she did not intend to have was mess. She had her key now in the double glass doors to the office, but before she turned it in the lock she paused to enjoy the ship-shape look of the room inside. There is no reason why we should not be comfortable up here, she thought, thinking of herself and the judge, the court workers and attorneys, and then the others—the ones in trouble, children and families in trouble one way or another, the abject parade that passed through the double doors to those inside.

The hanging begonia in the window cast a morning shadow on the new linoleum. It was not standard office tile, she had made them put down something a little prettier and mellower with a slight gleam to it. They certainly needed any little bit of good cheer they could get, and she had gotten nice pillows too, soft enough to plump, for the vinyl settees. If she was not a very cheerful person, at least she was rational and she took great care to shore up what little store of good feeling she possessed and she tried to shore it up in others. When something made her laugh she was extremely grateful. Curtis, the court worker, made her laugh sometimes and so she liked for him to be around. She knew people thought she was glum; she *was* glum, she was not the type to greet people with a great big smile, and yet she hoped she was kind. *That kind, depressed woman up at the Court*—maybe this was how they thought of her.

The phone began to ring so Margaret unlocked the doors and went inside. It was the principal of the high school. A certain child had not been to school in some time, he had not been withdrawn, and the principal couldn't locate a soul who even knew him. Margaret checked her files but the

33

Court had no knowledge of this child whatsoever. Even in a town this size people could simply vanish into the thin air of the universe. Maybe they wouldn't have been here long and people would hardly have known they were here and then one night they would pack everything up and move to Florida. No he was not in detention, Margaret told the principal, and not down for a runaway. Just a plain truant, they decided.

By ten o'clock the phone really got going and some days she thought she would have to unplug it to get any work done. Most of the voices were full of woe: "Just want to tell you . . . Byrum done gone again." —"To his father's do you think?" —"That where I know he gone and I know he cooking on something and he want Byrum to cook on it wid him."

Once in a while it was good news instead of bad: "Just want to tell y'all Robert doing better and he going to school. Look like he thinking on what the judge tole him and it doing him some good this time." There might even be some good humor: "He say it gitten to where it ain't no use to run away nohow."

Runaways—and custody problems—were about half their business, and although the people that came up to see her and called her on the phone thought of her no doubt as separate from them entirely, thought of her as a person from the safe side of life, instead of the one that was always dangerous . . . still she knew the truth was different from that, and in all these years at the court she had hardly ever thought of runaways, for instance, without thinking *I was one myself, I ran away to my grandmother's when I was twelve. I ran out on the rest of them, you could call it running away, although I let my father take me to the train station and put me on the train.* Because that was all true, it had happened, and there had not been many days of her life since then when she had not thought about it.

Sure enough, when she looked at the hearings file on her

desk, to see what their business was today, it was another runaway case. Poor old Lillie Ringgold's boy. It was a bad time for a hearing—3:00 on Friday afternoon, and everybody would be irritable, but it had had to be that way because of the ones coming from out of town. Sometimes children that started as runaways were soon up for something else and this boy had robbed a store in a nearby town. Then they had said there was a weapon involved and wanted to try him in the regular court but first the juvenile court had to hand him over.

Margaret set the file in front of her. It was a particularly disheartening case. The way it all started, Buddy's running away, was the silliest thing in the world to have ended up the way it did. Somehow she was not in a mood to take things lightly today and she placed her hand on the folder before she opened it and thought *Buddy this is your life in here*, and the whole thing wasn't over a thing but this: a pencil to write with. She could have labelled this file The Pencil Case. Or—All He Wanted Was Something To Do His Homework With. The mother had told Margaret about it when Buddy had first run away. —"Now see, after this pencil fight." —"This what?" Margaret had said. —"This *pencil* fight."

Buddy had been given some homework to do, and his teacher had gotten fed up with him about homework and she had said that this time if he didn't get his work in she was going to see that he didn't get to march in the band the next night. The band didn't step near as high as it did before the black kids and white kids got mixed together a few years ago, she supposed it wasn't as much fun, but still Buddy Ringgold loved to huff and puff on his old trombone and he wasn't about to get left out if he could help it. So his mother said that that night he got out his book and he found him a piece of paper to do his work on but he couldn't find a thing to write with. He went through the whole house and practically under the house (in fact finally he did look under the

35

house); he looked in every crack in the floor and got his little brothers looking with him and Lillie too and there was simply not one thing on the place to write with. Margaret could remember just this same aggravation, especially when the children were little and would lose every single writing utensil she could come up with. In fact if she ever surprised herself by being taken up into heaven, she thought the first thing she would ask them was where all the pencils had gone to. (And the combs. With little girls around, there was never any of those either, and yet where in goodness name had they all gone to and where were they now?)

But anyway here was Buddy—trying to find a pencil. Finally Lillie had told him he had to go on to bed but that the first thing in the morning, before she started out for her white lady's, she would go down to the store and buy him a pencil and he could get his work before he went to school.

But about that time—Buddy's history took another turn. His stepfather came in. If only Buddy had gone on and gotten in bed . . . but here he was, his mother said, "still stomping and stepping around about he ain't got no pencil." And Bradford, the stepfather, had said, "Hush up right now," but Buddy would not hush up. "So Bradford catch him and he beat him pretty good," Lillie said. "And the next day Buddy gone."

At the time Lillie had first huffed up the stairs to see the judge, Buddy had been gone several days and she was not sure the police were doing very much to find him. One question in particular racked her mind. She did not doubt that a boy should be beaten when he was bad, even if he was fifteen years old, and she was clear in her mind that Buddy was bad that night, but what she was *not* clear on, was on who was permitted to do the beating and whether or not a boy should be beaten by his stepfather, even if the stepfather was a decent man—like Bradford was. "The thing is he done got so big," Lillie said. "If anybody goin to beat him now, he know it goin to be Bradford cause he know I can't beat him if I can't ketch hold of him and he know Bradford the oliest one strong enough to do that."

Margaret checked Buddy's folder to be sure the forms were all there. She had put in a bind-over form in case they needed it—turning him over to the adult court. If the police brought any proof there had been a weapon, Jim would not have much choice but to bind him over.

She looked at the charge on the police report. "Aggravated robbery." She wanted to write, "No—this is just a pencil case." She thought again about Buddy's search for the pencil; she saw him crawling over the peculiar dust under the house, his head stiff, just barely raised, feeling the ground between the crooked clusters of bricks that held up the house.

It was cases like this that made her wish she had another job entirely, and yet she never could think of any other kind she wanted. She could not imagine being in an insurance office, for instance, typing forms all day in a big room full of other women doing the same thing. Here she was the only one, and actually she ran the whole office herself and no one bossed her around. In fact Jim couldn't possibly boss a flea and she had to boss *him*.

And yet—this job was a hard one even so; if you already had a bad streak of depression, it would certainly bring it out. Besides, there was an awful irony involved that no one could feel but her. Even after twenty years she felt it. It had to do with the endangered life they dealt with up here. Most of the people that came up the stairs to the court were the kind that were always skimming along on the edge of danger. For them life was full of trouble and crisis, and when trouble came they had nothing to fight it back with. ("We got a little trouble over here today." —"Trouble is all he ever gave us." —"Well see now, when all this trouble started up last year . . . .") Trouble was about all they ever had and usually they looked like it too, and she knew that she herself, a rather nice-looking woman after all, in patent leather shoes, and stockings that fit and never had a run in them, was almost a symbol of well-being to the people in trouble who arrived at her glass doors, saw her working, gracefully she hoped, at the most orderly of desks in the middle of a little protective fortress of bright cabinets and stands. When she stood up to help people with their forms, they smelled her light toilet water, they brushed up against her firm, be-girdled skirts. And it was as if they knew as well as she did that she was a person with savings in the bank (something she never expected to have) and a house that was paid for and in good condition. Yes it was more than obvious how they regarded her. She had always been a good dresser, she never looked less than her best, and even now, at sixty-one, she had not given in to gray hair. She wore the best girdle she could find, price was not an object when it came to that, and good brassieres. She didn't look like the kind of person trouble would cling to—or maybe when she got her clothes brush out, she looked like she was brushing it off her with the lint on her skirts.

In this room trouble was something that seemed to pass in and out, to only be stopping by. When people laid it on her desk, she took it and typed it up and put it in the files. At closing time she might take a damp cloth to the vinyl settees, and sometimes she would suddenly feel that she was being spoken to by the ghostly voice of a departed guest, *That's right, lady, even when trouble has walked out your door, wipe off everywhere it's been, just to be safe.*

It was elementary, of course, that in this town, as in every other town, some people had old tires in their yards and sandspurs instead of grass and other people had fat green lawns, and mountains of azaleas in profuse banks of blooms, and pretty houses where everything worked, where when something broke a man came out the next day and fixed it on the spot and where if someone was sick they went to their own private doctor; where air conditioners hummed people to sleep at night, with a sheet over them even, and no one had rings of sweat under their arms; where the television never got stuck on purple and green—or even if it did, there was an extra one in the bedroom anyway and you never had to miss your favorite program.

*But listen!* Margaret had sat down, but now she stood up again at her desk to protest to the empty room. *I might have a pretty house all right—and a brocade sofa in the living room, but half the time I'm lying down on it with a wet cloth on my head and I've taken a nerve pill . . . because . . . because certain things are coming back to me that no one knows about . . . I was where you are, I'm just like you, I was never safe at all and never can be . . . .*

But she could not think this through, as much as she needed to—because what in the world was that on the stairs? Some kind of big commotion. The day starting in earnest now. The noise coming up the stairs was not black, no it clearly indicated a loud flock of country white people. She saw Curtis's curly head at the top of the stair-well. And my lord, not the Shegogs!

There were so many of them and they always brought the children and stayed half the morning. Every one of them was on some kind of assistance and had no place he had to be. They all talked at once, ate and drank and spilled Coke on the floor, and when they left she had to go in and clean the bathroom, for instance, from top to toe. But here they all were, crowding up to her glass doors.

And my lord here was Jim too—oh she almost had to laugh he looked so pale and unnerved, jostled about in this throng of fat Shegogs. Curtis was in there too, but his face shone, he was one big grin—later on he would be telling her what a trip the Shegogs were, because actually he liked coarse country people like that. But Jim looked simply baffled and unstrung; of course he never looked at all like a judge and this morning he had even forgotten to comb his hair. For a strange and very brief moment, standing in full view of them at her desk, Margaret hesitated, as if she simply was not ready for all this and might not go and let them in. But then of course she did go, and the morning began.

# CHAPTER TWO

WHEN she had walked back down the inside stairs at lunchtime, they had seemed to lurch away from her, and when she reached out to touch the wall, it wasn't where she thought it was, she nearly missed her step. She almost hoped she *did* fall so she could sue the county for all it was worth, for practically inviting people to break their necks on these bare, narrow stairs.

When she had found the message a moment before, she would have wished to have remained absolutely calm, but of course she was not the kind of person who could do that. And yet possibly there was nothing to it at all. Since no details had been given, it might conceivably even be a mistake—a message really intended for someone else, or if it *was* for her, some outdated matter of business some clerk had just never disposed of. Still, when she had read it, standing behind her desk, her hand fell roughly onto the typewriter and she felt that her heart might jump out onto the new linoleum. At the same time, she had had the feeling she could not put up any longer with her own absurdity and the preposterous way she reacted to things.

She had found the note slipped back behind the typewriter when she had pulled it out a little bit to wipe off her desk. (She couldn't stand a gritty-feeling desktop.) For a moment or two she could hardly realize anything, but then she did realize that it must have been left early in the morning by the girl down the hall, who sometimes let herself in to use the restroom before Margaret got to work. But what business is it of hers to answer our phone and leave us upsetting messages like this? she had thought. The girl had written it on a sheet from the memo pad. "Margaret. A woman called you from Jacksonville. Said she'd call back." Simply that.

What it most likely was, Margaret supposed, was some leftover detail concerning the absurd affairs of her mother. She hoped, though, that no one *would* call back and bring up the word *mother* to her. "I just want you to know," she might say, "that my mother has been dead eighteen years and I'm still not in any condition to receive any messages about her."

There was one other possibility that Margaret tried to keep from considering, and yet she couldn't help but consider it: there was at least one person still alive down there who could get on the phone and call her, but it was ridiculous to think that she would, and if she ever *did* do a thing like that, lord help her, because she would need all the help she could get.

THE NOONDAY heat in the back lot was something ferocious, in spite of the big shade tree, but Margaret stood for a moment beside the car while she thought about finding the note from Jacksonville, the city she had grown up in, and about how she had almost fallen on the stairs she was such a weak person, so easily alarmed and upset. After a time she collected herself and got in behind the wheel, leaving the door open while she started up so she wouldn't roast to death before the air conditioning came on. As she backed out of the lot, the day suddenly clouded wonderfully over, but then before she had gotten well out onto the road, the sun was back out again, pouring a fresh vat of fiery heat onto the noontime streets. The people walking on the sidewalks all gave the impression of trying to hurry out of the heat towards their cars and offices, and yet it was too hot to hurry too.

A colored boy with bare feet who didn't want to fry them to a crisp had stopped at the edge of the street to put his sneakers on. The air was so still that the trees along the road looked artificial. It was as if the engine of the universe had been turned off and nothing could move except the humans and their machines.

The Shegogs had thoroughly enjoyed themselves in the cooled offices of the Court; apparently they had found the room completely comfortable in every way. Thank goodness, though, Curtis had managed to walk them all back out as soon as it was feasible so Margaret could get a little work done. The older couple had come in to ask for custody of one of the children, and so the mother of the child had come too to say it was all right, and the rest of them had come as "witnesses." They all wanted to tell Margaret, and then Curtis, and then Jim, the many reasons why it was best for the child to move in with its grandparents. The Shegogs always enjoyed a discussion of this type; in fact they enjoyed all their relations with the Court. They had discovered the concept of custody several years ago and thought it was a very interesting and useful concept. A child could hardly go on a two-week visit somewhere without the Shegogs wanting to change its custody, and no doubt they would soon be coming back in to give this particular child back to its mother— or perhaps the father would turn up and they would give it to him, and the child would not even seem to mind.

*Margaret, when she was twelve, had had a custody change*

*herself* . . . and today, driving pokily home for lunch behind a line of other poky cars, she frowned over the wheel into the scorching midday light and managed to draw a dark little tent of thought over the whole subject.

She had gone from the custody of her parents, who lived on a dirt street in a bad section of Jacksonville, into the custody of her grandmother, who lived on a dairy farm of amazing beauty. As far as she had known, no forms had been filled out, people did not go as much by forms in those days, and there was simply no court or official notice whatever, and yet it had been a severe change in her life and something that had perplexed her very sorely ever since.

She thought of the silly innocence of certain kinds of conversations. —"Margaret, who was it you said who raised you?" —"Well, you know, when I was a girl my parents broke up and I went to live with my grandmother." (Hohum . . . .) It was almost amusing that she could speak of such a thing in ordinary words like that. For when she was twelve her father had betrayed her mother and herself, and the rest of them, and got this other . . . *person* . . . even the word *woman* was too good for her, and she might even be the one on the phone today . . . though where she would get the outrageous nerve to pull anything like that.

How anyone could ever have wanted her to begin with, even on a bet, much less betrayed others that loved him to get her—that was the primary mystery of all their lives. But in any case, after this betrayal, by the person she loved the most, Margaret had been put on the train, in a sullen trance of fury and pain, and sent to her mother's mother in Waycross and her grandfather had met her at the station in the milk truck and a new life had begun for her.

Of course she had thought about it over and over again through the years—this new life—and all the infinite changes it had wrung in her, and for instance, she had begun to work very hard at changing her love for her father into hatred. One thing she was capable of was hard work, that was one of her few talents, and so she had succeeded, on the whole, very well.

Of course it was no trouble at all to hate the person he had betrayed her *with*—it would have been just natural to have hated such a person even if she had not been as ridiculous as she was.

Margaret stared over the wheel into the blistered road, but what she saw was not the road but something else: her mother's thoughtful face the day her father first brought this other person in the door on Clark Street and showed them her round pie face and sallow eyes, her three strands of old stringy hair, asked them to please make the acquaintance of this lopsided person in a terrible dress, cast off by someone taller and skinnier than she was. Yes she remembered her mother's thoughtful silence as this woman was brought in the door and she recalled the peculiar agitation of the little three-legged dog they had, who definitely did not want this new person to enter the room, who flew back and forth at her feet trying to bite her anklebones. Silence was not what you would ever have expected from Margaret's mother and yet that day she was silent, and even when the three-legged dog set up a tremendous howl she did not seem to hear him at all; she just had this thoughtful look and this remarkable silence and even though she had been dead now many years Margaret would never forget it and it was just one of a thousand reasons why she did not want to get any calls from Jacksonville, today or any day.

Margaret herself had been shelling peas that day, or perhaps it was butter-beans, sitting at the kitchen table with an enormous tin pan on her lap. But she could see through to the living room and she had seen her mother's look, had watched the other children cease their ridiculous babble, and her father bend down to the three-legged dog.

She had an old aunt still alive today who never got tired of discussing it all. "When that old Nomey came along in Jacksonville and got hold of your daddy and you got so mad

45

about it they thought you were going to run away and you almost did run away and your daddy got Granny to say she would take you—"

"She *wanted* to take me; she said for him to put me on the train—"

"And you came in on the train and they went to meet you in the milk truck—" Nora's preambles were so long that sometimes she forgot what they were preambles to. She would have a cigarette cocked beside her face and now and then she would remember to take a pull on it.

"What *were* you—thirteen?"

"I was twelve," Margaret said. "Don't you know? You and Nolan had not been married long but—"

"This running away," Nora would say. "All these runaways. All this running that people do. Where they think it gets them. You and the judge up at the Court—sitting up there with all your runaways, or with the ones that have been run away *from*. And then the same thing in your own family. First your mother running away with your father from the dairy. Then your father running away from *her* . . . though actually he didn't run that far. Then you running away from him back to the dairy where it all started. And at the dairy Nolan not about to miss *his* turn. Running away from me, or at least they thought he did, although the one he actually ran away from was Granny because she wouldn't let him have anything to say about anything or even act like he was grown-up.

"And then look here—Granny herself running away from the rest of us to California, so we couldn't get hold of the dairy and she could sell it and have the whole hog and be richer than ever and have a wonderful time with her new California husband while the rest of us scraped along on nothing flat and it was depression and—"

Nora would have to stop and take a long hard draw on her cigarette, staring hard into the room, more or less in the direction of Margaret's chair.

"This running. All this running away," she would say, and perhaps they would not be in the living room at all; if it was one of those conversations they had had a long time ago (though of course they were still having almost the same one today) they might have been sitting in Nora's long old-fashioned kitchen, with its stale smell of damp linoleum, and perhaps Nora would have stirred them up some eggs for supper, and the almost comical thing was that Margaret might be a runaway herself at the very moment Nora addressed her that way, and Nora so obsessed with her theme of running away that she would be completely unconscious of it.

Certainly, on some of those occasions in years gone by when this history of running away and matters like that were being delivered by Nora, Margaret herself would have been a runaway from her husband on Suwannee Drive, and would have gone to Nora's, in preference to somewhere else, for the very reason that Nora would hardly know she was there and so it would be at her house that she would have the least explaining to do and cause the least disturbance.

It seemed to her now that she would no sooner have presented her face of consternation on Nora's porch than Nora would gather her breath for her first little launchings forth into the waters of her tale, a story for which Margaret had always been and was still the primary recipient, her simple presence, her face at the door, being even today the only cue her aunt required to take up her tale.

Yes possibly it was an exaggeration but it seemed to Margaret that in those days Nora, even while she was taking Margaret's bag and setting it down on the extra bed, had started down one of the familiar byways of her chronicle. And thus Margaret would begin to adjust herself to the room, and mentally to separate herself from whatever emotion-filled space she had left on Suwannee Drive; she would remove her wrap and set aside her purse and Nora might even absentmindedly assist her, but she was also strik-

47

ing out towards the highroad of her story, the heart and core of it: the running away from *her* by Granny's son Nolan, the whys and wherefores of that, and the whys and wherefores of everything that had come before, and especially of her prior relationship with Granny, and of their relationship during this brief marriage, and then the one they had had in the long years afterward and all the interesting particulars of it and the interesting particulars of the son's infrequent visits from the county he had run away *to*, the weighing and inspection of each and every known particular of his second marriage (the undoubted worthiness, for instance, if notorious gullibility, of his second wife) and so on and so forth.

This was the eye of Nora's tale, but in the important outer rings of it were matters just as germane to Margaret herself, all the relationships and affairs of her grandmother's dairy, of the courtship of her mother and father, for instance; of herself and Leonard, then of Granny and the new husband of her later years.

Of course it was repetitive, this narrative of Nora's—to the point of absurdity, she supposed; perhaps—some people might think—to the point, almost, of hysteria; but after all there were any number of variations to what people had to tell, to what they thought was the same story; and in Nora's case, for instance, there was the applying to the same scenes and particulars a whole spectrum of varying emotions, even to the furthest extreme of complete coldness and indifference, grim acceptance of *this*: that the choosing of her by the son was no more than an absentminded strategy for gaining the attention of his mother, a notoriously competent and commanding woman, of giving her the opportunity to see that he was grown-up, a man meant like other men for responsibility, and then when she would not see (because when had she ever seen *anything* about other people's needs?), he had drawn his own conclusions, "left out of there," as Nora might put it when she wanted to sound as rural as she could. "And why not?" she would add—and why would he have even remembered his wife and child?

"Because what were we anyway?" she would ask, and then she would answer herself—she was just country, she said, dirt country in fact. "Hound dogs and hog jowl," she said. "I was nothing," she would tell Margaret, "don't you know? A lowlife up at the big house. Or at least it was the big house to me, I don't know what you thought, maybe that was not what other people thought, but to me Granny was the most brilliant thing I had ever seen. And of course rich. And gorgeous. Why just to look at her! And so the big house was something I worshipped—yes ma'am, I worshipped Granny and everybody in it and I would have done anything she told me to, no matter what, that was how I felt about her, I loved her and worshipped her, yes ma'am. And then I grew up and all that other happened and her son ran away from her and she said it was from me—maybe she thought it was—and then I was just lowlife again."

Thus Nora—on those evenings years ago—before Margaret had even gotten through the door, would have assembled her smoking materials beside her seat, wasted no time in moving ahead to the urgent business of the evening: the divulging of a mostly ancient chronicle of family life, and a family she was not herself a blood member of. Margaret would adjust herself in a deep chair across the old-fashioned slipcovered room—just as today, on certain Sunday afternoons, she still adjusted herself in the same room, with no need to do more than swing her leg and stare forward to the chair of narration.

So on those evenings at Nora's long ago, her own memory would certainly have been free to slip backward to the hour before, when standing in the yard on Suwannee Drive, feeling for the car keys in pocket or purse, she had hardly known, for a moment, where in the world to set out for. And so would feel then, at Nora's, a slight disappointment in herself, for after all each time she had had to escape from

Leonard's rage, run off into the night, there was always—in spite of the horror, the disgrace of it—a pang, even so, of exhilaration!

The night air might be the same plain old air she had breathed that very night going down the back stoop to take out the garbage. But later on, when she flew out the front, with her deep-drawn face of despair, a disheveled bag in one hand and a child, possibly, by the other, if there was one who was not in bed, that air, the same old Waycross air, would surprise her with its moist smell of flight and adventure, its mysterious, quivery feel—of opportunity! To leave everything! Leave it all behind!

Who was there anywhere who did not wish for that at times—deeply, deeply? No matter who they were living with or where? To close the door and go! The power of that! To have that power in your blood would bear you onward to—who knew what?

And yet—where had she gone?

To her Aunt Nora's to spend the night.

Yes as she thought of all this now, driving home from the Court for lunch, waiting patiently for lights to change, for cars to move, she thought it had always been to Nora's. Though of course she might easily have gone to her in-laws, the Barkers, been petted and consoled, cried over even and grieved as on a virtual altar of lamentation and prayer, and all the blame laid where it should have been, on the wicked son and husband. Or she might have gone to Vivian's house, an aunt by blood after all, the sister of Margaret's mother, and the only one of Granny's children living in the town.

Or she could have gone to Granny herself, though as for that—it was confusing still even to think of it. It was not that she would ever have been turned away, *lord* no, she would have been made completely comfortable in every way, as you always were at Granny's house, because it was simply a very comfortable house, and it was not that Granny would have murmured a word of actual protest or complaint;

and yet there would have been, somewhere, a sly, shaded note of disappointment at Margaret's coming, at her *need* to come, her trouble, at her leading the kind of life in which trouble could make its appearance.

And so she would go instead to Nora's, and Nora would remember that other time when she actually *had* run away to Granny's, when her father had betrayed her in the city she had grown up in.

"THAT LITTLE stiff dress you had on," Nora would remember. "I know I was way out in the garden that day—*you* know, where I belonged . . . I was out there hoeing tomatoes probably, that morning you turned up. I know I saw Grandaddy Culp driving in with you in the milk truck. I saw him taking you in the back door. You had your long hair, almost to your seat, which you said your daddy loved it that way, and then I know we hardly got to see it again after that day because Granny took you to town and got it cut, she thought it was ridiculous. And then that little stiff fancy black and white dress, which did not look comfortable, although of course a father . . . a father might well buy somebody a dress like that—"

Certainly it had not been Margaret's mother that ever bought such things, what they bought her daddy bought and he had simply gotten whatever he liked or whatever she said she wanted, and he and she had gone to a particular shop where they had plump, friendly, cheerful clerks who always made a little to-do about things, and they would sit her father down on a bench at the front and he would hike up his trouser legs and spread out his stout legs, and oh it was strange how well she remembered it all—she remembered how he would lean his thick hands on his thighs, for instance, and the way there would rise, from one pulpy fist, the smoke from his cigar. In that little shop he was content, he sat quite contentedly there, and there were very few times when he could sit that way. The saleswomen would take Margaret in the back and put dresses on her and walk her out for him to see, for him to look her over in the pretty light of the store, and it was an experience that they valued and that went beyond the need of buying something to wear—and perhaps they hardly noticed *what* they bought.

"So when I saw that little stiff dress going in Granny's back door," Nora would say.

Her father had put her on the train. This was after the terrible advent of the person who might be on the phone today, who was still alive down there to cause a little more trouble and stress if she thought she could get away with it.

But in any case, her grandfather had met her at the station. At the dairy they had brought her in through the back door, into a half-screened back porch, a cool, shaded, dampish room that smelled of well-water and was a kind of adjunct to the kitchen. Of course she didn't know now if she had even noticed it at the time, but at one end it had a great deep metal double sink, for large-scale jobs that were too watery and sloppy for the kitchen itself. Granny cleaned her chickens there, for instance, and when she did this she wore a mannish, heavy-duty cotton smock that was never seen in the kitchen, not appropriate for any room but "the porch." The colored people kept their tin cup out there and it was as far into the house as Granny ever let them get; southerners could do as they pleased, but as far as Granny was concerned, black people were not clean and not suitable for anything but work outside. At the back of this narrow porch there was a certain corner with mops and brooms in it and an old rattan chair, and sometimes one of them would be sitting there hunched over his dinner, his plate on his knees.

But in any case it was through this porch that Margaret had been brought when she was twelve, carrying her clothes in a discolored drawstring bag, on a sunny morning in the summertime. They had walked her through the porch to the kitchen. And then, extremely shy and ill at ease, with a

52

peevish expression on her face probably, to hide her fright, already awed and surprised by what she had seen on the place as she drove in the gate, she had watched a tall, glowing figure, her grandmother, with waves of kitchen sun in her white hair, turn from the table where she was working with such authority, such presence and beauty, that it was as if in some remote but important area of Margaret's brain there began a slow, mysterious shifting of all the furniture. Today of course she thought it was almost silly to have been so bowled over, so carried away with everything . . . so overwhelmed by the glamor of the room, for instance, that later she could not remember any single detail of it—just an amazing impression of symmetry and order.

And yet it was not going too far to say that what she saw and felt at that moment had changed her life, the way she would want to live and what she would be interested in. Very few things in people's lives were clear but here was one thing about hers that was—that the whole effect that morning of a certain kind of domestic order and beauty spoke profoundly to something that had always been in her without her knowing it.

Then she had been taken to a small room in another part of the house, she did not remember by whom, but no doubt Granny herself would have been much too busy for such leading of people around, such simple jobs as that. Then in a while a bell was ringing—outside, it seemed to her, though she could not be sure—and she had no earthly idea why, so she was still sitting in the room on a small cot when someone came and got her to go to dinner. She went into the bustly dining room, to the long table where the family were more or less foregathered, and where the dairy men too were just sitting down, with washed faces and damp combed hair. Granny and her helpers were bringing in their steaming dishes and trays, and the unlidded smells of the kitchen smoked up more richly than before. She sat down where they told her to and Granny, or someone, tried to say who

53

she was, to introduce her to the company at large, or whoever might be listening, but hardly anyone was, they were
too busy scraping their chairs and passing the time of day,
starting the food around.

When her grandfather sat down, there was a sudden silence for him to murmur a blessing, and then the men fell to
and the various children of the place fell to, Nora and Vivian, for instance, and all the rest of them—but not as Margaret had expected them to, not with any special saved-up
hunger. It was amazing to think so now, but when Margaret
had first seen the table and the room, and in spite of the
working clothes of the men, she had begun to believe she
had arrived on some special holiday, celebrated only in
Waycross. But of course that was wrong, it was just a plain
weekday meal. And yet whenever she was handed a bowl,
she was shocked when she looked inside it, and when she
had filled her plate, she was stunned again by the fresh,
steaming, rich-colored splendor of it. And when she tasted
her grandmother's cooking—why that was a shock and a
half, she thought. In fact she could easily make her lunch
today, she considered, steering homeward from the Court
down midday streets, out of a half-dozen of her grandmother's yeast rolls and a little mound of her fresh butter.


MARGARET pulled up at home, churning the gravel in
the driveway, and sat absently with the motor on, staring
over the wheel into her piney backyard, where everything
was peculiarly, unnaturally still, and mottled now in partly
clouded sunlight. She imagined the angry August sun half
caught in a net of clouds, trying to flex again its terrible
power.

By the time she had crossed the yard and reached the
front stoop, held back with her elbow the screen door so as
to put her key in the lock, she was dizzy again from the heat
and she felt sweat collecting in her armpits, under her best

blouse and in spite of plenty of good deodorant. When she stepped inside, she paused for a moment, her purse still on her arm, in the lovely cool—just to look at the room, thinking *So this is my house, this is where I live.*

It was one of the pleasures of living alone to come home to a room that was just the way you had left it, with the light not streaming in raw and hot, for instance, but tempered and buffeted, pent up behind perfectly-tilted blinds and soft layers of drawn curtains. She loved this diffuse, glowing light, and with the air-conditioner humming along on low, the room had a warm-cool feeling she was truly devoted to. In the bedroom she took off her shoes. Then she padded into the kitchen to make her a sandwich, considered again her house, its neatness and order, its pretty flowery textures, its bright, cleared surfaces, and thought once more about *this:* how much like an immaculate Granny she lived now.

Yet of course her moods had brutal shifts to them and sometimes she turned on the house and did not like it at all, blamed it for her loneliness, seemed to sniff out behind the fresh clean walls a secret sick decay. Yes it sometimes seemed to her that with the children gone now so many years, with even Leonard gone now, the place was nothing but a ridiculous corpse of itself, grotesquely made up by her to look alive, a house that no longer had any place in the normal history of humankind, which for her always had to do with families, with people *together.*

She ate her sandwich at the bay window, looking out into the somewhat darkened day. Maybe the weatherman would finally get his rain this time. Of course it might pass right over them again, and the mood she was in today—nothing would surprise her.

Moods . . . moods were her downfall. No one understood them. They came over you sometimes in the twinkling of an eye. She might be sitting in the living room, for instance, feeling pretty good in that particular room, surrounded by the furniture she had carefully collected, saved up for over

55

the years, the pictures of her children on the TV, the things they had given her on the whatnot stand. She might think, *Sitting here today I feel rather cheerful and I blend comfortably into the room and the past that it holds and expresses*. And of course it was silly but she might almost feel that if she were to stretch out her arms, they would sink slowly into the walls on either side of her and she would hold and encircle the room the same way it encircled her.

Perhaps it was foolish, but she might think all that, just feeling very comfortable and lazy and calm, and yet, if she were then to get up, go harmlessly into the kitchen and fill the kettle at the sink, her stove burner turned up high, she might look down and see . . . in the bottom of the cup on the counter . . . or just beyond the kitchen door . . . something terrible . . . and would be suddenly down, defeated, as if she had glimpsed, in one innocent blink of the eye, a certain hideous truth she could not name, but which had to do with the utter pointlessness of life, so that even before she could put the kettle on the stove, she would have to sit down at the table and muse hopelessly and simply stare. The stove burner might blaze on ridiculously, and yet she might not even rise to turn it off, much less to heat the water and make the tea, because to do all that, stir in the sugar and the milk, to put it to her lips and drink . . . might seem like a refuge from pointlessness so weak she would have to laugh at herself out loud even to think of it.

But today, Margaret finished her lunch in the living room and got up in her stocking feet to turn on the television; then with the pillows plumped under her head, she lay down on the brocade sofa, something she always did at noontime, after she had had her a little bite to eat. She had trained the Court not to expect her to run right back up there after lunch—she took her time and got in a decent rest. One of her programs was coming on and she stretched back on the sofa to watch; and yet—perhaps because today she had received a message with the word Jacksonville in it and be-

56

cause this was a great dark pit of a word with things deep inside it no one should have to look at (though she knew that sooner or later today she *would* look at them, as she had on so many days)—what she saw on the TV screen was not the image projected but herself at age twelve again, an escapee from the white slums of Jacksonville, eating her first dinner at her grandmother's, astonished and deeply moved by the beauty of Granny's house and all her operations and affairs. She supposed she was as silly as the next person but she hardly thought she would have been surprised that day if someone had whispered to her as she stood in the kitchen door and first looked inside, "This is heaven and you are an angel."

And yet it was possible she had built the whole thing up over the years. For of course in one particular way it was not heaven there at all. In one way it was one of the cruellest times she had ever had.

In fact it was a genuine question as to whether or not it was this early period at the dairy, rather than the terrible things that had happened beforehand in Jacksonville—dire and shameful things, brutal, brutish things—that were the reason that now, at sixty-one, living what ought to be a calm, smooth life, a safe and almost prosperous life with money in the bank, with all her children safely raised, that even so, to keep from becoming a nervous invalid, a blight and blot on the lives of her children, some days she had to take fifty milligrams of Sinequan and twenty of something else, sometimes a sleeping pill besides that, and many shots of B-12 . . . and still suffer days in bed when she could not move her neck . . . still have to endure bizarre reactions to things she read in the newspapers.

It would be curious indeed, she thought (and she had tried over and over, lying with a wet cloth on her head on bed or sofa, to think it all through, though she could never think it *completely* through, to what she thought of as the other side) if the deep cause for all of that was not Jacksonville itself but her first weeks and months at the dairy.

~

SHE SAW THIS: in Jacksonville deep evil to begin with, that in a way no one could help; then her father's betrayal; and after that, a second betrayal just as incredible, and in fact her grandmother's worse, in a way, than her father's, since it was completely reasoned out, had nothing to do with any emotion, even a perverted one—her decision, that is, not to offer her help to anyone but Margaret, to save from the Jacksonville fire and flood only her granddaughter, ignoring and abandoning the rest, even her own daughter.

"Of course your mother—no one wanted to hear a word about her," her Aunt Nora had said, not many Sundays ago, "after she had those afflicted children. They were just thankful she was living off in another town. If something like that is way off in somebody *else's* town . . . the sensible thing"—Nora had pursed her mouth hard on the word sensible—"would be to let well enough alone and hope you never heard a peep out of them and not do a thing that might make them turn up in your town and you might have to help them out."

Nora considered carefully the little coil of smoke from her cigarette. "Families are not something I care for," she said. "I don't think they're worth much. You might not agree with me but I think the whole idea of family life is this: 'Let's all race along together, but if one of us falls down—too bad.' Who do you think's going to slow down, who do you think is going to sweat and haul to pick them up? Not families, no ma'am. Not in my experience. I don't think families have that much to give, real help is not something they think they can spare each other, although they might feel they can spare a little advice. And you know what that would be: *don't fall.*" Nora made another little face. "Not *if* you fall, do this or that and we'll help you out, but—*don't fall.*

"So your mother . . . let's say she had already fallen—don't you know? Or let's say this—she wasn't in the race to

58

begin with, and then she had those children and how was she going to drag them along when they didn't even know what race was?"

In that time at the dairy years ago, when Margaret at twelve years old had taken up her life at her grandmother's, letters would come, separately, from her mother and father. At first it was only her father's letters that would be held back—her grandmother would go through the mail and if there was a letter from Margaret's father she would simply put it in the pocket of her apron. Later, when they were burning trash down by the shed, Margaret would know that his letter was burning too. Then after a time, she realized that Granny's program for her separation from her former life had entered a new phase and that even the letters of her mother were being kept from her.

She remembered this: a sea of morning sun, she and Granny in the kitchen making pies, Granny rolling her dough with glowing arms, Margaret slicing apples into a tub of streaming light.

Nora had come in in her grubby work clothes to bring the mail. Granny had looked at her in exasperation, perhaps just for her raw country face, and stopped her in the doorway, not to have her tracking on the waxy floor. Nora did not pretend to have ever had Granny's affection. "Of course there wasn't anything that said she had to love me," she would say, "just because her son married me." That day Nora had given Margaret a quick harsh look . . . of resentment, Margaret had thought at the time, though probably Nora would say it was pity, a look that meant—how can you sit around in here with her all day, when you could be outside with the rest of us, breathing your own air?

Granny had wiped her hands to take up the mail. She thumbed through the pile, and Margaret had caught a slant-ing sidewise look that made her put down her slicing knife. "If a letter . . . if one from Mama comes . . . ."

Granny had murmured to herself, probably counselled or questioned herself as to some matter in the mail, gone back to her ball of dough.

But Margaret did not take up her knife. "If a letter comes . . . from Mama and them . . . be sure to give it to me . . . . "

Granny did not like to let herself become annoyed, she had kneaded, she had rolled, had worked on as she began to speak. She said that Margaret must not let herself be the worrying kind and that she was the kind of person that if she wasn't careful she would be, and that she should always remember that cheerful people were what made the world a decent place to live in, and that all she needed to do was to stop all this frowning, this worrying, this thinking about things that no one could help. *(Don't let me have to say any more.)*

"But from Mama," Margaret said.

Then Granny looked at her hard, her aggravation rising suddenly into serious displeasure. And there had been that day, indeed, a letter—addressed with a vague smudged pencil on a square envelope probably meant to hold a greeting card. In the bottom Margaret could see, folded narrowly, a sheet from an old-fashioned lined tablet. This was her mother's letter and of course she had been duty-bound to read it, and yet it was agony to do so. She thought of the big inept letters, laboriously drawn—not by her mother, but by the old neighbor down the street. *Dear Mar-grett . . . .*

Here Margaret, lying on her brocade sofa many years later, closed her eyes and tried to avert the words that followed, turned her head on the pillow as if to fend them off, but they would not be fended off. *How are you we are all fine but your mama wants you to come home now and so does Riley and Barba and George . . . .* At the bottom her mama's own hand. *love mama.*

Margaret would write back, now and then, a short obscure reply, and then the little neighbor began to take liberties with the text and to put in things of her own. "Your mama is always trying to get your daddy to say he will send you the money for the train but he says no. He says he has wrote you and told you how it is and so it's up to you what to do and it might be best for you there but your mama says it's best for you here where she can take care of you."

These lines, even after fifty years, made Margaret snort with amazement, stretch up on her elbow in sudden indignation. "Her take care of *me!*"

*Years later she is married and in her mama's house again. Her mother has just given Bobba two pieces of baloney—Bobba loves baloney and raw wieners.* But Riley has put Bobba's baloney in the toilet and George is as mad as fire. He stands by Margaret's chair while she tries to talk to her mother, tapping her arm relentlessly every few seconds, saying, "Maga, Maga. Ri'ee took Bobba 'lone." The dialect of this house is one that is understood by only a few people in the world; Margaret is one of them and yet sometimes she feels that she too is letting it get away from her.

Finally she gets up to investigate George's charge, and even though in this house she is used to feeling nothing but anger and despair, still, going through the smelly rooms, she discovers something that makes tears come to her eyes: the door to the toilet is missing and someone has hung up a crooked sheet in the doorway. Now, lying on her brocade sofa at lunchtime, staring forward through eyeglasses she cannot actually see through at moments like these, she can remember no farther than this crazy sheet draped in the door. *But how had that happened?* she asks herself.

Her brother George had a temper like a bear and he was as strong as one too and he might very well have broken off a sticking bathroom door and thrown it in the back yard (where it would have felt right at home with other torn-off things). And she could imagine this: her mother chattering on about it like a voluble child, almost cheerfully, then rigging up a clumsy sheet.

From this many years off she was able to feel that there was a kind of outlandish humor in a Jacksonville scene like that that people stronger than she was might almost enjoy remembering—perhaps it would amuse them to think *Well at least they had put up a sheet*. But a sad-sack person like she was could not appreciate an angle like that.

In fact she did not want to remember any part of it. No she did not want to have any memories of her mother today, she was going to make a conscious effort not to. And yet of course you could not control such things, and she had no doubt but that sooner or later it would all start rolling towards her again—her mother's life, *all* that Jacksonville life—and she would be powerless to stop it.

AT THE DAIRY, in the language spoken there, her mother's name, and the name Jacksonville itself, were words that had not seemed to exist; for all she could remember, the whole state of Florida might have been missing from the dairy's geography. If she had wanted to measure her grandmother's force in their lives, she might have measured it by this: by the fact that her disapproval of certain subjects, life on Eighth Street in Jacksonville, for instance, was so strong that even when the others might quite safely and privately have gone against her, they did not. Oh it was such a pity that even when she and her grandfather were alone, and might have touched, healingly, this broken bird, this secret subject of Jacksonville, spreading it between them in awe and pity, still they did not. If only he had ever said, drawing her close in some private place, on some quiet afternoon, soothing and calming her child's fears and constraints, "Margaret . . . listen child . . . tell me about your mama . . . because she is my daughter and I have my rights too and even if we're helpless to *do* anything we can at least do her the honor not to refuse to speak her name for she has not done any wrong and cannot do any." But these words were too grand for anyone to say and Grandaddy Culp had not said them. Sometimes Margaret imagined that later on she had said them herself, to Leonard, before they were married, and yet actually she had not, any more than her grandfather had.

Yet she believed that her grandfather wanted—always—to go against her grandmother with respect to his daughter Emma in Jacksonville, a person, after all, who was not competent for normal life—but he was not the kind to go against anyone, she supposed he was actually a coward and that possibly it was his cowardice that made him drink. Drink was his "weakness," and like any other weakness, Granny had nothing but towering contempt for it. Nora had said, "Margaret, didn't you know? Don't you know why he drank himself to death?"

It was one of their Sunday talks. Margaret had been sitting back in Nora's big chair, across the small, old-fashioned sitting room, and she had frowned and said nothing. Nora did not necessarily expect her to reply. She would be busy rubbing out her cigarette or lighting another one up and though Margaret might murmur some little something from time to time, Nora would not let it interfere with her line of thought.

"Those gre-eat big old flower gardens," Nora had said, "that people rode by just to say they had seen them. Those old canna lilies in front—as big as trees," she said, pulling a long face, as if canna lilies themselves were disgusting. "Why they were nothing but a danger to the people on the road . . . trying to slow down to see what in the world they were. And that old silly table as long as the house, about to break down under all that crackerjack food. All those rolls, for instance, that Granny had pulled them all off with her own hands. Those truckloads of fine sewing. All that brilliant business-work building up the dairy and the Stand. None of that was for him. It had nothing to do with him and he knew it. Oh he-e knew it—yes ma'am. They would talk about how wonderful Granny was, all her wonderful achievements; they'd say *Don't you know Mr. Culp is proud. He must be a proud man.* But listen—this is how proud he was . . . he would have loved to trample that whole garden underfoot. Didn't you know that? Nothing would have done him any more good than for him to stomp down all Granny's flowers and take an axe to those canna lilies. Plow all those wardrobes of crochet into the corn patch. That was all that would have helped him—except for getting drunk all the time. So he got drunk."

Nora had paused in the darkish room to cock her cigarette by her face, address a long stern look towards Margaret's chair, towards her expressionless face, the glinting lens of her glasses. "He didn't have all that talent and genius Granny had, he was just good . . . and that's nothing, that don't count.

"Of course everything about Granny was tremendous and she was a wonderful wife, o-oh *yes* ma'am! Anybody would have told you what a wonderful wife she was—except her husband. But what does that count?

"Now this is how much she cared, how much she even knew about him: she was the last person on earth you could complain to about anything because she hated complaints and any kind of weakness or sickness. And so here was a man that she slept in the same room with him all his life and she didn't even know he had what he had—a bad case of varicose veins. And of course—around there—he was ashamed of it and kept it a secret. And he had a worse secret than that even. Those veins would hurt him and when he had a lot of work to do on his feet, he would want to wear something on his legs to give him a little relief and he would wear a pair of Granny's old stockings under his socks— garters and all. Granny never knew a thing about it, she didn't even know he had this affliction and he couldn't let her know because she didn't believe in afflictions and he would have been ashamed of doing anything at all about it . . . not to mention what he did do."

*Oh Nora, Nora.* It was not that Margaret was ever relaxed in Nora's house, and yet she would let herself settle further and further down in the big chair, as if she were trying to sink beneath the level of hearing and sight; but after all she did not go out to Nora's under any compulsion, no one dragged her.

Leonard was dead, she had nobody to run away from now, no need—for years—to run *anywhere*. And besides she had always known about ninety percent of what would be said when she came in the door and was already half prepared for it, with her habitual expression of crossness and gloom.

"These people that never have a thing wrong with them, that nothing is ever the matter with them," Nora went on, "that don't have a nerve in their body, who never let anything bother them. You just want to shake them. I wanted to *take* that woman! and shake her! so many times! I wanted to say 'Listen I don't care who you are! Because I want to tell you right now you better open your eyes and look at people, because if you don't hurt some people do and I just—I just think . . . . '"

Nora's voice had risen higher than she had meant it to that day and so then she had lowered it, remembered to pucker her lips again with scorn.

"These people," she said, "that don't know what it is to have a headache."

Margaret had murmured softly, almost to herself. "I don't know . . . there must have been a few times when Granny herself . . . ."

"No," Nora had said. "No ma'am. She didn't know what it meant. Don't you remember? You could turn the whole dairy upside down and you wouldn't find a tin of aspirin even. There wasn't one aspirin on the place. She hated all medicines—and all doctors."

That was the truth, Margaret knew it herself. And she knew what Nora would say next. "The reason I know this for a fact was when Grandaddy Culp died."

"Yes," Margaret said. *She and Granny and Vivian had been just inside the gate, starting up the walk after church, when*

*Granny had stopped and held out her arms to hold them back.*
Then they all looked in the living room window and saw the
heads that should not have been there. Granny tilted her
wide hat towards the house and raised her head, as if to sniff
the air, catch the scent of the particular danger that lay
ahead. And it was in this same second or two that she must
have gathered herself for what was inside, completely prepared herself. (And that isn't normal, Margaret thought—
and yet she still didn't know whether it was good or bad.)
Then Granny strode forward, tall and lean in her fashion-
able white Sunday dress, with its tiered waist of homemade
lace, her long skirts riding gracefully back in the splendid
wake of her motion to the door.

Inside they had Grandaddy Culp on the couch and the
room was full of whispering and crying, mixed strangely together, a primitive sound that Margaret could hardly bear to
remember. And apparently she had not stepped forward to
see and no one had urged her to and in fact she remembered
a terrible fear that she would inadvertently glimpse his face.
She had stood near the back of the room, seized by this great
fear—and yet also, it would seem, since she did not actually
leave the room, by something else just as great: the need to
study the face of her grandmother as she stood over the
couch, making her own diagnosis (not trusting anyone else
even to know if he was alive or dead), the need to seize this
opportunity to find out something about her grandmother
she might not find out any other way. And yet—what had
she found out?

For then people were being sent away—perhaps to their
surprise, perhaps they had expected to stay all afternoon to
give their support. She remembered Granny walking them
to the door, thanking them for coming, and doubtless this
was another one of those times when people shook their
heads, and far from being put out, said they had never seen
such courage, such strength. Yes it had been Granny herself
who did what was needed, made certain calls, sent certain

66

people away and had certain other people in, more necessary to the business at hand.

Nora was describing all that. And how she herself had wept and grieved so bitterly, how beside herself she was and how she almost told Granny to her face that it was she who had killed him by breaking his heart, making him drink himself to death until he had had a heart attack. But of course she had not said anything remotely like that, any more than anyone else ever had.

"So the aspirin," she was saying now. "I know there wasn't a single one in the house—because the day he died Granny did not even miss her nap, things went right on, except that when she went to lie down, after doing certain things and talking to certain people, having dinner put on (I won't say she put it on herself but of course it was made before she went to church and I know that it *was* put on, by someone), she got ready to take her nap, and she sent somebody down to the neighbor's. *To borrow two aspirin.* I don't know who it was who went . . . but—"

Nora had looked up. "Margaret. Maybe it was you who did that . . . for all I know."

Margaret had hesitated, but only for a moment. "Yes," she murmured, "I was the one she sent."

So on that afternoon at Nora's she had raised her head, turned it, her glinting eyeglasses, towards Nora's face so that she—Nora—could have the pleasure of seeing her acknowledge her aunt's look of vindication, as if all she had needed was this one detail to bear out all she had said.

"So when her husband died, of thirty-eight years, she did take two aspirin—I want to be fair, you know that—and *felt better.*


"AND OH how people admired that, they just admired the way she put all us weaklings to shame, how she did everything herself and never shed a tear. I still hear about that to this day. How strong she was, in her widowhood—in both her widowhoods, in her grief. And I say to myself, 'What grief?' and I still say, 'What grief?'"

Yet as for fear and grief, Margaret thought, as for worry and alarm . . . there are more ways than one to show that you feel such things. She considered Granny's flower gardens, full of heavy blooms most people did not even know the names of, laid out almost like show-gardens that charge admission; she thought of her drawers and chests of fine needlework which no family could have ever actually used; the immaculate, beautiful rooms . . . and not just the main rooms of the house, not just that *they* were immaculate and beautiful, but that the porch and shed were too, and the milking barn, the lots and walks, the attics and stoops. What did all this mean and what did it show? Nora said it showed Granny's contempt for everything but her own works, for people's human needs, their need for *other* things, that could not be seen or felt or admired. It showed, Nora seemed to say, that Granny herself was simply not acquainted with certain fundamental things that other people had always known . . . darkness, weakness and fear. And yet what it really showed, Margaret thought, might be completely the opposite of that. Granny's gardens and doilies, her stored canisters of sweets, her beautiful plants, always dressed, always trimmed and turned, her bright, clean, almost engraved-looking dairy books, her order and account books—what was all that but her "weakness," her liquor, her aspirin and Elavil, her migraines and nervous breakdowns? What she had to build (like her husband had to drink) between herself and her dreads and fears? "And yet I don't really know . . . ," Margaret thought, "and Granny herself didn't know . . . and so how could anyone else . . . one way or the other?"

Nora was still running on about Grandaddy Culp. "What he wanted was not drink, drink didn't satisfy him for a minute, he wanted *her*, a little affection and consideration, but she never let up and gave him any, no ma'am."

"So he drank," Nora had said, as if she were making a large concession for the first time. "All right—he drank. But she was the one who drove him—"

"I don't know," Margaret said, almost sharply. "I wonder . . . who drove who . . . was driven to what."

Nora's eyes circled Margaret's chair. She smoked her cigarette and her eyes moved rapidly around the room, as if they were absently seeking out the source of some mild disturbance. Then her thoughts went on down their regular track, and before long she came up to where Leonard had entered the picture, not long after Grandaddy Culp died. "Of course Leonard didn't really court you," she said. "He knew who to court—he courted Granny." Nora leaned forward. "But Margaret, did you know, when you and Leonard got married, that Granny was going to California, sell the dairy? Did you get any clue about that?"

Margaret could not remember that she had.

"Because I believe she had made up her mind before you got married to do just what she did—sell the dairy, go to California to her sister's and get her a husband, come back and run the Stand, and that was one of the reasons she didn't want to hear anything against Leonard, why she liked him from the start, the minute he started coming around . . . moony-faced and in love . . . on the drink truck. Because you were the only thing on her hands. She certainly didn't count me and my little brat—because her son had run away from me and so of course there was something wrong with me . . . *and* him, although the main person that something was wrong with was her, she was actually the one he ran away from and I should have told her, I should have said, 'Slavery is over, you can't do people like that anymore, even your own son, you've got to let him get down from that truck, down off that load of milk-cans, sign papers himself sometimes . . . .'"

Here Nora finally had to stop, and when she tried to light her cigarette, for a moment her hands would not cooperate.

*These old griefs—hers and mine so intertwined this way.*

"But the way she did things," Nora said, after a while. "She just *decided* to find her a new husband in California at her sister's. So look at what she does. Sells the dairy right out from under us, as soon as she can get you out of the house, and without as much as a fare-thee-well to a living soul even though some of us had expected to get a living from it and it was depression and there wasn't that much else you could get. Sells the dairy and puts her money in the bank and goes to California before anybody can turn around. Then—how long was it? Six months before she came back? opened back up the Stand? And then the first thing you know Mr. Wallace turns up from California to marry her. Which everybody thought was wonderful. A sixty-five-year-old woman starting her life over like that, and I mean the smoothness, don't you know, of the whole thing. What was Daddy Wallace? Sixty-five, sixty-six? Just retired and in good health, with money in the bank, just the right amount to suit her—not so much that he could lord it over her but not too little for her to have to worry about hers. It was such a neat little deal, wasn't it?"

But of course nobody knew what was in Granny's mind when she went to California—it may have been just to see her sister. In her spare time her sister was a painter, a talented person like Granny was, and at the dairy they had always had a lot of her California ocean scenes on the living room wall. Granny and her sister had a lot in common and they admired each other. But even if Granny had made up her mind—to the rest of it—and found just what she had started out to look for . . . *don't you admire that in a way?* Margaret had started to say. But instead, she had simply said, "I know I liked Mr. Wallace a lot"—which made Nora very cross.

"Everybody liked Mr. Wallace. I didn't say there was anybody who didn't," Nora said. "But people felt sorry for him too."

"He was so good to me during the war," Margaret said. "Fixing things on the house, for instance."

He had kept things in wonderful shape at the dairy—although the dairy now was just the main house and the ice-cream-and-dairy-goods shop, the Stand. Margaret had always had a sincere respect, almost a love, for men who "fixed things." She loved to have things in good repair—nothing worried her and pulled her down as much as a sticking drawer or a cracked pane, a rusty screen or bulging concrete, a door that wouldn't shut right. With all people had to worry about, she thought they ought to at least be able to count on their windows and doors.

"Oh he could do anything," Nora was saying about Daddy Wallace, "and he was a gentleman besides."

A gentleman who could fix things—yes that was a wonderful combination of qualities, Margaret thought.

"Which was just luck," Nora said. "On Granny's part. And didn't you feel sorry for him?"

"He and Granny had a lot in common," Margaret said. "They both liked things to be clean and in good repair." She had paused, getting up a mental list. "They didn't like to argue and they wanted life to be calm and organized. They both liked to travel and when they went somewhere they had it all planned out."

"*She* had it all planned out," Nora said.

"I think he thought Granny was a remarkable woman."

"He was too polite to assert himself," Nora said. "The way Grandpa Culp was too weak."

"I can't think of any time he needed to assert himself," Margaret said.

Margaret knew that what Nora was implying, what she actually wanted to say to Margaret was this: "You didn't love Granny, you really hated her, and it would help you if you could admit it—like I do." And Margaret thought: No. I hated her *and* loved her, and I certainly don't mind admit-

71

ting it—but I can't see where it does any good. Hate and love are still there.

"Margaret," Nora was saying. *"One thing.* Because if you understand this I want you to explain it to me right now, I want you to tell me how you can have a person that has reduced her husband, a perfectly good normal man, to drink and depression and giving up on his life . . . who has driven off her only son and has given up one of her daughters to— what she gave your mother up to in Jacksonville . . . and not even to mention whatever she did to a silly person like me and my silly little brat (because we didn't even count to begin with) . . . who has gotten ahead and made a fortune by never letting one single human consideration stand in her way . . . if you can tell me how a person can do all that and not even be thought bad of . . . in fact be loved and admired for it—then you're a whole lot smarter than I am because I don't get it . . . *no* ma'am, I just don't."

Nora let the smoke curl out of her mouth as if she didn't have the presence of mind to exhale it properly. "How people can admire people for doing things they themselves are too good to do," she said. "There are certain rules of life that people try to go by and then somebody comes along and breaks all the rules and the people love and admire them for it."

Margaret murmured a reply, absently, without raising her head, as if she had no idea whether her words would reach a listener. "I don't know . . . Granny didn't come from around here for one thing. People knew she was different and maybe they thought she had her own rules that came from somewhere else and that she wouldn't have broken for love nor money."

"I know she wouldn't have broken a thing for love," Nora said.

It had grown chilly by then in Nora's living room, almost cold. She got up to light the heater with her cigarette matches. It was getting on towards dark but they could still hear children running and calling in the yard next door.

"Coming ready or not." At the dairy, out in back by the milking barn, Margaret was it that day, she was the new girl running to find them and she didn't even know all their names yet. The well had been filled in and planted in petunias, and the well-curb was home base. She ran to find them over by the wood-house, crept softly up to the open door, waited for a moment, soundlessly, behind it, then suddenly looked inside. Then she had screamed—and she didn't think she had ever run before in such a wild, galloping, jerking run. The children ran out from the places they were hiding in and other people ran out of the back door of the house and she was still screaming, and crying too, and they all began to say "What? What is it? What in the world?" And she had said "dead man"—"dead man in the shed."

So they all began to turn and look toward the shed and then the children began to giggle, and all of them walked in a troop, grown-ups and children too, out to the shed and looked inside just to be sure, and then the adults were smiling, a little oddly and ruefully, and shaking their heads, and the children were laughing, teasing and taunting, doing cartwheels on the grass for sheer delight.

But Margaret had to give Nora credit—it had only been her face (freckled and splotchedy) that had been serious, disapproving that day; only she who had not wanted people to behave the way they were behaving and who had set off roughly down the yard to the shed (her big knobby shoulder-bones working comically under the straps of her bare-shouldered sundress) to pull the door to, out of respect, so that Grandaddy Culp would not hear anything he shouldn't have to. Although what could he have heard? He was lying crazily on the floor with his mouth open . . . horribly . . . one palm outstretched under the neck of his jug, one foot hung-up under his chair, under the old armless rocker he kept out there just to rock himself drunk in.

But Nora was driving something home. "Margaret, look-a-here, what rules did Granny have? I can't see where

73

she had *any*. No ma'am. Where we have good and bad, right and wrong, she didn't have anything." Nora's eyes stared emptily for a moment and then she said, "No, that's not right, I don't want to be anything but fair, she did have *one*, she had one rule and it covered everything, everybody she knew, including her own flesh. *You* know—my lord—you know what Granny's rule was. *Don't ever get in trouble, and if you do, keep it a secret, don't ever come to me for help.* Because trouble was something she couldn't stand, and she didn't think it was necessary.

"She didn't intend to put up with it," Nora said. She sat forward, straining her face insistently toward her visitor. "Even with your father," she had said that day, and inwardly Margaret had stiffened as if to receive a blow, though she made no outward sign, did not even sit forward in her chair, but swung her leg in the same narrow arc. "It wasn't what he did—to you-all or to Emma. That wasn't it. It wasn't that what he did with Nomey was bad or wrong. She didn't care about that. She didn't care how pregnant he got anybody or what kind of old somebody it was or whether he ran off with her or not and left the rest of you high and dry. That wasn't what finished Raymond off, don't you know?

"As far as Granny was concerned, what finished him off was that actually he *didn't* run away, he didn't cut off from a thing, on one end or the other, he just took one great big old mess of trouble and piled another one on top of it. So what Granny couldn't stand was not that he was bad, it was more that he wasn't smart—because it's not smart to get in trouble. It wasn't smart to leave one woman—or not leave her, don't you know?—just to get the old thing he got and then not even go off with her."

SOME OF all that was certainly true, Margaret considered today, lying down in her stocking-feet at noontime, remembering—unable to stop remembering—that someone in

Jacksonville was trying to communicate with her again after all these years. That old Nomey, for all she knew. That-Nomey . . . that-old-Nomey . . . . She almost smiled to think that these were the only names she had ever given this particular person and the only ones she was able to give her now.

But some of what Nora had said was true, and yet at the time it was happening, Margaret had not quite known it, and when she had begun, at twelve years old, her new life at Granny's and seen what beauty, what near-splendor she lived in, at first she had believed (though it was pathetic to think she *could* have believed) that she was only the first to be saved and that when Granny knew how the others were living, realized the full extent of the trouble that had come to them, she would make a plan to rescue them too. Maybe she had even thought that sooner or later she would open to her grandmother her whole exhausted heart, say certain things that possibly she was rehearsing all along in the back of her mind: "Mama needs help, she always has, and something has to be done about it, especially now that my father has this other person, although of course he is trying to take care of the rest of them too but as you know there were already three children, people, in the house that were not . . . competent . . . even before this other, this extra one turned up, and so I guess you can imagine how it is around there and although I know you probably think that in certain ways Mama has refused to help *herself* and that she should not even have kept these children, for instance, to begin with—or no maybe you don't think that but just think no one can really help her because she is so stubborn and for instance would not even obey you yourself years ago when you probably did not want her to run off from the dairy to begin with to marry my father and just won't do what anyone wants her to and so people should just—"

Margaret tried to adjust herself on the brocade sofa, and yet it was not just her shoulders, her hips she really wanted to realign, but certain tracks of her old memory-bed, so that a certain appalling train of reminiscence could not go down it anymore. She closed her eyes—it was a part of memory she was determined to block today as long as she could, she was always determined to block it one way or another, keep it from giving her a massive migraine headache . . . and yet when it was a question today of messages being sent, phone calls coming in, others waiting at the office for all she knew, sooner or later it would all burst through again.

But truly she had thought, when she had first taken up her life at her grandmother's, that her grandmother would rescue the others too. And in the meantime, she had begun to try to train herself not to frown and worry, or at least not to frown, but to smile and look the way Granny wanted her to—pleased with herself and with her new happy good life. So she had given herself up to tubs of sliced apples and embroidered cushions. In fact it was a simply accidental—and in a way confusing—fact of the case that it should have been she who was naturally inclined that way, who had a special aptitude for her grandmother's arts, for being her good child, when so many were not good at all, when her Aunt Vivian, for instance, would not learn a thing but only wanted to do frivolous, trivial, wasteful things with young men and women in town, people who had no desire but to go to the beach, to ride in cars and have a good time—although actually you could not *have* a good time, her grandmother said, if you had no pride of achievement, no sense of accomplishment and personal worth.

And truly, whenever Margaret thought—in any connection whatsoever—about personal pride, about inner peace and the satisfied self, the picture that came to her was indeed of her grandmother at rest, a woman who had worked all day like a dog (and not even mussed herself) taking her midafternoon nap, lying up—as if on a downy cloud of her own labor—over the hand-crocheted white bedspread, her head perfectly straight on the lace-fringed pillow, her hands in her tatted cuffs folded on her stomach, snoozing gently, even snoring a little whistly contented snore perhaps, her figure altogether a symbol for Margaret ever after of strength and repose.

*But so little in life is ever clear*, Margaret thought, *and no memory is ever as simple as that*, and she would no sooner have thought how good, how wonderful that was, to work so hard and then rest so well, when something dark rolled down on her, making her think *But no one should rest like that . . . and to work well for your own ends is not enough . . . not as long as people are suffering, in Jacksonville or anywhere else, and it is simply wrong to rest that way and maybe none of us should ever rest at all.* Of course even as a child, she had known that there was more than one way to feel about her grandmother's repose, and she would peer around the doorway to look at her on the bed, and then peer around again, and think one thing and then the other, and what was more, allow herself to frown *(while she's asleep I'll frown and worry all I want to)*.

At certain points her mind's angles could be laid perfectly over those of her grandmother's, but at other points they could not do a thing but intersect. Children, after all, were not like clean sheets of paper that you could just roll in your typewriter, tap out on them anything you wanted to. *Certain things cannot be written on certain people—every mother, for instance, knows that*, she thought; and sometimes she wondered whether anything was ever written at all. A child goes along, trying to break the code of her own character, and always recognizing, with a shock, that messages she is learning to make out on the characters of certain adults are the same ones dimly forming on her own self.

Did that explain, in fact, her own shock, her fright even, when she first came to know Leonard's parents? Such sad and woeful people. So grotesquely exposed. Their feelings had stuck out all over them and they were not even ashamed of them. No they were always giving in to gross emotions.

And yet, had she recognized, possibly, that whereas there was one projecting plane of her grandmother's that fit perfectly onto a plane of her own . . . for other connections she would have to look elsewhere, even to the likes of her in-laws?

Leonard and Margaret had met at the Stand, had courted and become engaged, and then, as was proper, the Barkers had called on Granny Culp. They had looked awkward, almost ridiculous, in Granny's living room, could not strike the tone of the fringed footstools, the satiny cushions.

In fact the Barkers were not the kind of couple who normally made calls on people other than relations. Though before the depression they had been a family of some means, they were not people of fashion but of rural background, had never lost their country ways. Some years ago they had come in towards town from a dirt farm on the other side of the county, not all the way *into* town but only to the outer edge—got that far down the big road from the old place to build a small store, and then a larger one, which prospered surprisingly, almost mysteriously, and their customers came to them from both directions, from the country behind them and the town up ahead, and they built a house on a freshly-opened-up street across the railroad tracks from the store, and the town soon came out to meet that street and envelop it, and they sent their children to the town school and could even start to think of sending them to college, when the great grief, the big trouble of the depression, had driven down on them.

In the living room at the dairy, the Barkers had looked as if they did not want to sit too hard on Granny's furniture, or as if they were actually prevented from sitting comfortably back in a room like that by the particular kind of rigid limbs they had. Since they hardly knew what path to take, with this fine Mrs. Culp, they set out at once on the one that was always safe, the mourning path, the one they always felt equal to—and so they mourned Grandaddy Culp, and asked

78

to see his picture, exclaimed over it with approval, grieved and commiserated some more.

Mrs. Barker had already had (perhaps had always had) her thick snaky reddish-gray bun and she wore no makeup whatsoever, looked old and plain beside Granny with her short, stylish, curled white hair (or would it still have been finger-waved?).

"These children—I tell you, Mrs. Culp, getting married in times like this, trying to get started . . . they're the ones it all falls on." Mrs. Barker shook her head in grief.

"I told Leonard—" Mr. Barker said. "I said 'Ask the Lord and do what he says.' I said 'Son, if I tried to tell you, it would be wrong.'"

Granny had an amused look on her face. She looked to Margaret as if she might be about to make a bawdy joke. "Some things," she said, "boys and girls going after each other, don't wait for good times. Some things go on—no matter what."

"That's right!" Mr. Barker said, as if she had been speaking of the holy ghost.

He reflected darkly. "Leonard's a good boy," he said. "I don't mind telling you that. He's not bad."

Granny said, "Leonard's going to do fine, aren't you, Leonard?" He and Margaret sat on the far side of the room. Granny could not see any reason not to be cheerful. "He and Margaret will do just fine."

Mrs. Barker drew herself up and made a show of speaking her mind completely out. "I said 'Son, if you love her, you know we'll love her too'—and we do, don't we, Will?"

"Leonard don't drink," Mr. Barker went on, "and never did. No woman will have to worry about *that* from him. Thank the blessed Lord."

Mrs. Barker said a mournful amen to that, for Mr. Barker himself had been a terrible drunkard in his time—and Granny, Margaret saw, did not let her good nature slip for a moment but joined very happily in with a merry amen of her own, and there was nothing to show that she even remembered the special weakness of Grandaddy Culp. (And possibly, since there was no *use* in remembering it, nothing to be gained but a decrease in happiness and an increase in fretting distraction and regret, she really did *not* remember it, Margaret thought. As far as Granny was concerned, people did not have to lose control over their own faculties, they did not have to let their minds, their memories, for instance, get the upper hand—*they* had to be sure and get the upper hand.)

Whenever Margaret thought about the drinking of Mr. Barker, it always brought to mind something else, a primary cause, as everyone knew, of the Barkers' mournful dispositions, a great trouble that had come to them long before the first crack of the depression, and had opened up in them an actual river of melancholy where before there had only been a healthy stream.

In old age you have time to think about your own thoughts, and Margaret could see her mind as a thick latticework, herself stepping gingerly across, never knowing when she put her foot down in one place what might be tripped, what loose plank of memory somewhere else. And so Mr. Barker's drinking brought to mind something else of a different order entirely that chilled her brain, threw a black shivering chill over her whole brain-field—something horrible, the heart of all horror she suspected, and although she had thought about it for many, many years and even read, with a certain terrible avidity, accounts in newspapers of parents who had taken certain matters into their own hands, still the experience itself she could never think all the way through to. It was as if it lay way up on a very remote place on her brain-peaks and she could only think up to it on a clumsy slant and always fell back in time not quite to catch a glimpse of it. Or sometimes it seemed to her this way—she was staring hard into deep dizzying darkness, where she could see a certain dread outline, a shadow . . .

even in the darkness, darker than the darkness itself . . . and she was reaching towards it, thrusting her hand into it, this darkness, and yet she could not thrust it far enough. Of course it was the greatest blessing of her life that she could not, that nothing had come to her, as it had come to the Barkers, and so many others, and taken her hands, pressed them around that chill horror, curled her cold fingers until they had slowly, horribly, taken hold . . . .

Yet it seemed to her that possibly all people are born with a certain perforation down their middles and the knowledge that they may someday be torn in half, and then some people were, and lay stunned in two ripped parts, one dead and the other still alive to know what death was. But this did not satisfy her and sometimes she thought it would be more like this: you, in the death-room, have watched your own self die and yet you are not dead exactly, you move, you walk on your legs, you squinch your mouth, you slice lemons for the tea, wipe your palms on your apron, thinking yes these are still my palms flattened on this damp cotton . . . yes I can still feel its dampness and through this dampness the taut muscles of my stomach . . . yes this is my stomach which can still fill and be emptied, fill again.

No she had not known what that was—to have life torn from her while she was still alive (for that must be what it meant, what it was like, *to witness the death of your child*), and of course she did not want to know, and yet not to, she could not help but feel, was to be deceived about some fundamental quality of the universe, to go through life stupidly ignorant of the innermost nature of the world's depravity.

Sometimes it was as if a light were trying to shine for Margaret on this depravity—and it was the light that was shed from Bright's Disease, a name that whenever it shot independently into her consciousness brought flying with it the same set of thoughts as the ones evoked by "Mr. Barker's drinking." This Bright's Disease she always saw as a glaring ring of light holding in place inside it a certain dreadful scene—a child's sickbed, in a dim room of dark wood, parents in attitudes of bowed grief. It was a malady that had a modern cure for it, people no longer died of Bright's Disease, and yet that could not alter the picture Margaret always saw inside its glaring ring.

When she was first married and had gone to live with the Barkers, in those very bad times when a place of their own was something new couples hardly even hoped for, and was making the astonishing discovery that she was to be more their bride than Leonard's, that it was as if he had brought her there for *them*—their way of drawing her close, of entering and possessing her, was to give her daily instruction in the history of their forsaken lives, their fallen state, and specifically in the death of their youngest child of Bright's Disease at ten years old. *No one can know us without knowing this about us, putting their hands in these wounds, feeling how thin our heartbeats are—how thin they have been ever since. Understand this: the pall, the black curtain of eternal gloom that dropped down forever over this house, and even this if you possibly can: the fear forevermore, the waking terror in the night that the others would be plucked as well.* Leonard's cringing cowardice and fear—where did she think it came from? Why it was the same fear bred in the bones and brains of them all. The fear they were all washed in as in the very blood of their lost lamb. See it, hear it, they said, know and understand within your ignorant duped powers to understand. Hear the father saying, "Rosella, Rosie, Rose! Tell your papa what you want, anything you want, anything in my power to get or give."

Then her reply: "Papa, don't drink. For Mama's sake, don't drink whiskey any more."

And listen to the father, twenty years a drunkard, no not exactly a drunkard, but a binger, terrorizing the house when he went on one, saying "I won't take another drop, I never will again." And then did not. Even after he knew that that was not enough and that history would go on and did not hear vows like that, and would pluck her anyway.

Mrs. Barker was still exclaiming over it, her husband's sobriety, half a century later, still marvelling over it in her ninetieth and last year, and telling still the death of her child (*Margaret, if you could have seen that little thing . . . if you could have touched, have heard, have watched . . .*), as shocked, as floored, as if it had happened last Monday and Rosella still fresh in her grave. "Why to think that Rosella . . . that little Rose—that we would lose her like that, to think that that old Bright's Disease would get hold of her and ruin her little kidneys, and wear her down to nothing, until I could feel all her little face-bones when I bathed her face, until it was almost a blessing that—no I won't say it *was* a blessing, no I still can't say *that* . . . and I've told the Lord I can't."

*A whiner. That woman is a whiner if there ever was one. And why does she want to look so old?* This in Granny's voice, or at least that was the way Margaret heard it, and yet it was not at all likely that Granny had ever actually said such a thing, and certainly she had not said it in the presence of Margaret. Nora, though, might have *said* Granny said it, even claimed to have heard her say it.

"Now as far as the Barkers—you know Granny couldn't stand them. Old down-in-the-mouth people like that. Old whiney-piney down-on-their-luck people like that. You know how much that suited *her*," Nora would say.

"I don't know . . . I don't say they were Granny's type . . . but she never said anything against them, not to me."

"Why no ma'am, of course not, why she wouldn't say that to *you*, why they were just what she was looking for to take you off her hands."

Mrs. Barker never forgot a thing or any of her feelings about things, in fact her feelings actually rose and billowed over the years, whereas Granny's seemed to curl vaguely away. Granny felt it was healthy to get *over* feelings and go on and have other ones, but Mrs. Barker never had an emotion that she let get away from her. But as far as health was concerned—both of them had fabulous health and lived to be ninety-odd years old. Neither one ever went to the doctor for a shot of B-12 and they wouldn't have been caught dead taking a tranquillizer or a migraine tablet, not to mention a sleeping pill. In other words, Mrs. Barker thrived on lamentation, and Granny on absolute abstinence from it, on cheerfulness and positive thinking, and the only weak and unhealthy one was Margaret herself, with nothing of her own to go on but confusion.

What with all of it together (with Jacksonville too blowing behind her still, a black wind always gathering secret strength), how could it be otherwise? She was a person for whom lamentation had been forbidden by her grandmother, and who had learned to do without it and almost despise it, but whose internal arrangements, after all, were what they were, and were not in the direction of cheerfulness and positive thinking.

*And yet—all of this is an exaggeration,* Margaret thought. For surely no two people could really be as different as these two women had seemed to her to be, in her still almost adolescent need to distinguish among adult possibilities.

But living at the dairy, long before she had met the Barkers, she had made certain determinations and perhaps they were wrong but she had made them: *There are those who do not feel what I feel. There are those who feel it and do not show it. There are those who feel it and do show it—and they are the ones Granny does not like to come to call. Granny herself does not feel it and she says that even if you do feel it you must not show it and it is best not to feel it to begin with.* In fact Granny must have thought that even in this last Margaret had made progress, but she herself realized, when she had married and moved in with her in-laws, that she had probably not made any progress at all, for what she saw all day, at breakfast, dinner and supper, on the open, childlike faces of Mr. and Mrs. Barker she immediately recognized as the same emotions she herself had hopelessly failed to stop feeling. It almost seemed, in fact, sitting across the oilcloth table from them in the dark-walled, old-fashioned kitchen, with its dampish well-water smell and its smell of half-stale food on the sideboard, that her own personal stock of primary feelings (fear and pain, worry and regret), which she had learned at her grandmother's not to let pass to her face, her lips, seemed to pass instead to the faces and lips of the couple across from her.

Everywhere in the house she turned was this—headlong, rampant emotionalism. As well as a constant foreboding that the occupants could relieve only by incessantly speaking about it. *We are accursed*, they seemed to say—*did we not lose our child, then our livelihood, everything we had?* Could they doubt that even worse (yet what worse) was still to come?

On the wall was an object to which, at bedtime, the old man lifted mournfully the kerosene lamp: it was a brown-tinted photograph of the stricken store, with Mr. Barker and his brother posed almost handsomely on the steps . . . a brother long since dead now of the shock and despair of it all.

By the time they had gained a daughter-in-law, the Barkers had lost everything but the house they lived in, and what could they assume but that they would lose that too? They half-believed, in fact, that the whole world was cursed and coming to an end, that they would all end by starving to death. Margaret, in the meantime, they worried over as one of their own, regretted daily, continuously, that they could not do better by her than they could, described to her life before the depression, never went for a walk but that they took her up the street across the tracks to The Store, sold for future use as a warehouse but meanwhile boarded carelessly up and weathering badly, desolate, bereft. More than once they walked her to the back yard, showed her the old wooden sign removed from the front gable, leaning now against the back wall, its elegant letters—Barker Brothers General Store—turned inward in decent respect for the living dead.

Mrs. Barker would spit on her handkerchief to reach inward and wipe clean the dusty lettering. She would notice signs of rot on the rim which rested on the earth. "Why Will! Look at this! Why this won't do! Will!"

And Mr. Barker would shake his head, grieving not only at his loss, but at his wife's mad grief, sighing "Mama . . . Mama . . . ."

A little way down the same street was the other place of business, the new one, about one-fifth, perhaps one-tenth, the size of the old place. It was a little icehouse, newly built out of the cheapest lumber, not a plank more than was necessary, and with no personal letters at all, just a severe, pentitential ICE HOUSE painted in black on the red wall—for an icehouse had to be red or people would not know it was an icehouse. It consisted of nothing but the one small cold-room and the thin narrow porch for Mr. Barker to sit on, leaning against the wall on a straight chair, to wait for business. What had been the prices? Two pounds for a nickel, five pounds for a dime, Margaret thought, the blocks of ice dragged with prongs out of the cold-room and onto the porch, then onto the beds of wagons and trucks or onto fresh newspaper readied in the trunks of cars.

Once the Barkers' fortunes had turned, their bad luck come on them with the death of Rosella and all that followed, they knew it would never let up. *And my lord! when Ruth was born*, Margaret thought. They *knew* she would be sickly and would not live. And of course they had a premonition, even beforehand, of danger, of terrible risk, and had been astonished and full of thanksgiving when she had not been born dead to begin with. ("And there was Granny in California," said Nora, "having a wonderful courtship with

Mr. Wallace, not giving you a thought while you went through all that.")

Margaret had lain up in the front bedroom at the Barkers' and the labor had gone on all day, with Mr. Barker groaning and worrying, mumbling over and over like a drunk man, "It'll never make it, nosir, it never will, God be praised if this is his will," pacing up and down in the doorway, or in the living room; and when the doctor came in to examine her, Mr. Barker came too, bent over her in a prayerful swoon of alarm and would not be sent away, until finally she said, almost whispered, to the doctor, "I can't have it here, I want to go to the hospital."

Leonard was rocking on the porch and every now and then he would get up and walk around the house and then sit back down. In the kitchen Mrs. Barker stood over the cold stove and wrung her hands, said, "Oh-h Lord. Let this poor little thing live, oh-h Lord"; fixed glasses of iced tea, stopped to wipe her eyes on the hem of her apron; and every so often the three of them, happening to meet—in their distracted wanderings around the house, in the hallway or outside her room—frightened each other afresh, each one certain that the other had bad news, said to each other in terrified whisperings, "What is it? What's happened?"

Then the doctor finally understood that the child might not be born if it had to be born like that. Margaret had heard him go into the living room, and then there was a sudden wail and swell of agony and pain, and she knew he had cracked with one word-blow—*hospital!*—all their thin hopes for this grandchild's life, even for hers.


BUT IT happened that Ruth *was* born, and that they both lived, but by the time of all that a lot of water had passed under the bridge—whole rivers, in fact. Yes, though it might not have seemed that way to anyone looking in on Harrison Street, great rivers of change had swept her again. She had passed quickly through another stage of life, possibly the shortest one of all, and somewhere along the way, perhaps only in old age, she had even come to have a term for it in her own mind (or had she read it somewhere?): *the stage of hopeful bride*.

Margaret, on her noontime sofa, almost smiled. She nearly forgot, sometimes, that she was still alive and that there was no reason to think there were no stages left. She hoped one of them—*dying grandma*—would be even shorter still. (*"Didn't you hear? Margaret Barker has had some real good luck. Didn't you know she fell over dead the other day, watching television? After lunch, she didn't go back to work and they couldn't understand it. Then the neighbor went in and found her. I'm just so happy for her I don't know what to do. I just wish she knew she'd had this good luck."* Couldn't it turn out that someone would say such a thing? Wasn't it possible at least?)

But that first year at the Barkers she had been altered forever by a terrible knowledge—revealed to her little by little, a word here, a word there, her new husband's tone of voice sharper by a hair each day, yes by a whole collection of words, acts and gestures which slowly paid out a current of what had been, in this husband, carefully pent-up rage, against what she could hardly guess, but which she knew, somehow, even at the time, had nothing to do with her and so was completely beyond her doing anything whatever about it, and that she was simply there to receive it like a random piece of furniture that could be incidentally pounded on or cursed when anger rose . . . . Yes the terrible knowledge was coming to her that the fundamental error, the one mistake, that a person hopes and prays they will not make had already been made; there came to her—as to so many before—first the cruel intimation, then the growing certainty, that whatever she had hoped to build in her life of good and beauty would have to be built on a no-good base (*oh it wasn't worth two cents!*) and so could not be built at all.

Yet when Ruth was born she began a stage which was in

88

itself one of amazing happiness—*the stage of loving mama*
. . . and perhaps her emotion for Ruth was all the more
fierce because of her terrible knowledge, perhaps she was
prepared by that to have a rending pity for all little girls, for
their little innocent dreams, nurtured all their young lives in
soft dreamy hours with picture books and dolls, and in smiling, smug imaginings of safe, contented futures (full of love
and gentle pleasures and soft pride), little picture-book
lives, with no trouble and crisis but just small problems tenderly, demurely overcome with patient applications of gen-
erosity and love. Oh she hated for little girls to grow up.
Yes even now. Oh when she even thought of little girls, all
over the world—dreaming, smiling little girls—growing
up, ready to love, then setting cruelly out on a wrong road;
little girls bewildered, little girls (even if they were big girls
now) losing their way, lost and crying even; little girls that
had believed, or felt, that someone somewhere in the universe was protecting them and planning for them, knew
what they wanted and needed and was getting it ready all
the time, getting someone—The Someone—ready, growing
him in another house on another street to be chosen by her
when the time came, grooming and training him for her to
choose him . . . . Then, when the one-to-be-chosen had
been chosen, boy for girl and girl for boy, daddy for mommy:
then the fundamental miscalculation made known. The
horror—the absurd horror of it!

For courting couples, it seemed to her, were no more to
each other than dolls. My lord, the dolls they had been to
each other, Leonard and herself. And it was a terrible irony
that each of them had needed for their secret cowardice and
fear someone brave and cheerful, calm and strong, someone
to say, "Hey now! What in the world! Hey come on now!"

Neither of them knew that inside their little doll faces,
with their fixed plastic smiles of courtship forbearance, was
the same quivering pulp of hideous fear and trepidation . . .
and shame. Oh when she thought of Leonard, coming out to

the dairy after work, freshly shaven and in a nice clean shirt, so easy and relaxed, chatting so naturally, so freely with Granny, full of such casual, earnest, unstrained solicitude and charm, calm, imperturbable, calling a greeting to this one and that one across the yard, a slight boy but good-looking, with thick brown wavy hair, a slender but manly almost athletic body, a person with certain boyish ways but still perfectly content to sit chatting with women and children. In fact this was just the way Granny always saw him ("she *wanted* to see him that way," Nora said) and she never believed he was any different from that.

Margaret, lying down on her sofa at noontime today, taking her a good long rest before going back to the Court, remembered her husband's young easy boyish ways when she first met him at her grandmother's dairy, and then . . . the absurd aftermath of all that.

She closed her eyes on these scenes that had oppressed her so many times. She wished she could doze off a little while, before she had to get up and put her shoes on, go back to work. But possibly, wherever she was today, no matter where she went, there would be a sticky hedge of tension that would go with her and surround her, the way it was surrounding right now the brocade sofa—now that this message had come from this other world, that other life she had had long ago in Jacksonville.

This evening, before she went to her bridal shower, she might call Nora.

"Nora. I think that old Nomey called," she might say.

"I want you to know!" Nora might start to say, but she did not like to be surprised by anything. There would be various eccentric noises of lip and throat, and then she might say, "What in the world would she be calling *for?*"

"Oh she never could get it through her head how disgusting she was. You never could get it across to her."

She thought of what she might say to Nora about all that. Maybe she would let off a lot of steam she had rarely let off before. Of course she might not get to say all that much, because gradually Nora would warm up to the subject herself, and then she would take it completely over, her whole chronicle would begin to ravel out, and finally Margaret would be ready to drop at the phone, and she would be glad she could say, "Oh I wish you'd look at that time!" for of course she would have to be ready when her ride came.

But in the meantime it was as if Nora's voice went on . . . "when that old Nomey first came along and you couldn't stand her and wouldn't even sit in the same room with her and they thought you were about to run away and they might as well *send* you away before you could go and your father took you and put you on the train to Waycross and your mother didn't like it one bit and Grandaddy left that morning in the milk truck and I saw him from out in the tomato patch and then he was bringing you back . . . and I saw your long hair, your little stiff black-and-white dress going in the back door—it seems like the next day almost that Leonard came around to the Stand in the candy truck, that Leonard was the new candy-man, and was starting a courtship with Granny and Granny courted him back and just thought he was such a friendly, nice-looking boy and we didn't hardly know *what* you thought but the important thing was what Granny thought. Then there you were over on Harrison Street in the depression with those old moony Barkers and Nolan had long since done *his* running away and Grandaddy Culp was dead of drink and depression and Granny felt so good she got her a beautiful new suit and went on a long trip to California—on what she sold the dairy for, so nobody else could get hold of it . . . and Ruth was born and—"

Margaret closed her eyes. Memory, she thought, sleepily . . . beckons and we cannot but follow . . . oh it sounded so much like a hymn in church . . . memory . . . like death (though why did she say death) . . . like a shepherd . . . leads us . . . and we go . . . .

# CHAPTER THREE

MARGARET sat up sharply on the brocade sofa and saw by the clock on the mantel that she had caught her a little snatch of sleep. Good. It would build her up a little for the hearing at the Court this afternoon and then, after work, the bridal shower. Still, she had the kind of brain that hardly ever gave in to sleep completely and part of it had gone right on conjuring up that very strange life on Harrison Street.

Could anyone at all, today, fathom the life of that depression time? Reading by candlelight, going to bed without heat, afraid to stick your toes under the bedclothes?

Mrs. Barker had sewed on an old treadle sewing machine, and fitted up practically everything they all wore out of the outgrown clothes of neighbors on the street. Mr. Barker had got his shoes secondhand, and it was a comedy to even think about: the old brogans he bought would be too large for him to begin with, and then when it rained they would warp and the toes turn up. When he stepped off down the street to work in the mornings, he looked like a little duck of a man with thick turned-up feet.

All these scenes, funny and sad, rose up in Margaret's brain today, and in fact the whole history of her marriage rose up, and she had to ask herself, point-blank, whether women like herself were not obsolete. Were women different today or was everything just the same? Her whole marriage rose up in great flashing contours—and she almost wished people could study it and learn from it. *Little girls . . . women and men all over the world! . . . learn from us if you can.*


AT NIGHT she had sat in the front room with Mr. and Mrs. Barker. Of course they had to worry about electricity, so they sat together in one room and the rest of the house would be dark. Mr. Barker had sat by the radio, full of foreboding when the news came on, hunched over his chair, murmuring "Lord help us . . . ." Leonard would be at the pool hall every night. As soon as he had seen the awful strain and ordeal of the courting game through at last to a successful end, her company had ceased to interest him.

It was not actual strategy, outright deception, Margaret had realized, but simple male courting instinct that had inspired him to keep his real habits a secret from her until after they were married. Not one single game of pool had he played during their courtship. No, every night they had been together and she never heard a word about any pool. She had not even known that he hunted and fished, that it was his full intention never to miss again a local basketball game, that when it was football season he would go to that, and in baseball to that.

Before Ruth came it had been slightly different, but only slightly. Margaret had had no reason, after all, to have to stay at home, and now and then, perhaps once a week, they went out together like a normal man and wife. And yet for Leonard it was a duty, a trial—all evening he had a dark, sullen, aggrieved look on his face. He would rush her out and rush her back in. "Let's get this over with"—that was the way he felt about it. It began to seem as if there was really nothing for them *to* do anyway. Once in a great while they went to a movie, but that was awful, for him it was just agony; movies were so "slow," he told her, they never got anywhere. He said you could always tell in five minutes what was going to happen and then you just waited—in torment—for it to finally happen. When they walked out, he was beat, he looked like a whipped dog, and so finally he just laid down the law—no movies, he said, he couldn't take it, his nerves wouldn't stand for it, and in fact he said he would not go anywhere where he couldn't smoke and move around. So going to church, for instance, was out as well.

So it came to be settled very quickly between them that there were certain things impossible for them to do together, and they never went again to a movie all their married life, to a play or a meeting or a speech, and they never went to church together—*she* went, with the children. Almost the only events he went to, in all those years, were the children's three high school graduations and Laney's wedding—not that the children *gave* a toot, by this time, whether he went to things or not.

He had also gone to a certain small number of funerals, to those of his own parents of course (not to any of her people's, not even to Granny's), and to a very few others where he was asked to be a pallbearer and couldn't get out of it. But he hated a coat and tie, hated passionately his old cheap blue suit and kept it scrunched way back in the closet where between-times he would never have to look at it. It was almost as if he had deliberately bought the worst thing he could find—an old square-looking, styleless thing that didn't even fit him, was too big. The pants were even a little long and he refused to have them shortened. It had seemed to be an actual principle with him to look as bad in that get-up as he could, to justify his self-pity when he had to put it on. And he would sort of hunch and slink around in it, with only one button actually buttoned and with both hands plunged deep in the pockets of the coat, dragging the thing down on him until it was a sight, and letting his starched white shirt stand ridiculously out around his neck.

What he liked, as far as dress went, was to go off to a game of some kind in the same clothes he had gone to work in— cheap slacks and a sports shirt—and no matter how cold it was, no wrap but his beat-up coat-sweater. At the games he would not go up in the stands and take an actual seat, he would stand up the whole evening, watching the play from down by the railings or the entranceways, huddled with some old buddy or other, his hands in his pockets, jingling his change to steady his nerves, smoking cigarettes, ducking back and forth to the concession stand for peanuts and Coca-Colas.

All in all, wherever he was, he had to be moving or at least ready to move when the need came on him; he liked to talk to people from doorways or on the street or from the wheel of his car with the motor running. All the jobs he ever had were driving jobs—the candy truck and drink truck, then his own car in route-salesman jobs, selling from catalogues his "general merchandise" to small stores around the county and in counties nearby. He loved the motion of boats, running them fast on south Georgia rivers, and he loved tramping hard through quail fields. It was odd, Margaret thought, but it seemed to ease his vaulting nerves just to be in the presence of things that were moving fast; she herself could not understand it, but it seemed to absolutely rest him to watch the swift rushing flight of birds, the surge of players on a field, the exploding crack of pool balls.

But where had that left *her?* His old bird dogs had seen more of him than she had. What does such a man want a wife for? she would ask herself in those days. Home was nothing to him—just a place to eat and sleep, and take care of another need a man happens to have. So actually it was as if she had married his mama and daddy instead of him. After Ruth came, he never had to think about his wife at all; he just thanked his lucky stars that she had something to occupy her and keep her from being able to go out with him at night in case she still wanted to.

People said that in time he would wear himself out and his nerves would let up on him. But when they moved into their own house a few years later, they had not let up a bit. When he got up in the morning, he would sit down at the table and drink three cups of coffee and smoke a chain of Lucky Strike cigarettes. By the time he got up to get ready for work, he was as high as a kite, his nerves stood out all over him and he could hardly get his clothes on.

He was a person who simply could not relax. The harder he tried, the harder it was. She remembered him sitting in the stuffed chair in the living room after he had got that chronic bad throat and had to give up cigarettes (my god, what he had put them through then), his body breaking out in all kinds of new tics. His fingers thrummed furiously on the arm of the chair; he strummed, tapped and drummed all over everything, shuffled his feet, blew his nose for no reason, crossed and uncrossed his legs. People said, "All he needs is a tail to wag."

It was not difficult for Margaret to understand, after they got married, why Leonard had dropped out of school—she saw that the type he belonged to was not a type that could withstand much education. She could imagine a doctor examining him and writing a notice to the school board. *This boy is afflicted and not medically educable. I have checked him and found him lower than anyone I have ever examined on the sit-and-listen scale. Anything of that type longer than four minutes in his case would be dangerous. He should not be in a schoolroom unless there is one where he can stand up at all times—I would not want him under any circumstances to be assigned a desk. In fact my prescription is that he pace up and down the room as fast as he can while lessons are going on. Otherwise I cannot take any responsibility.* Yes she could actually imagine some sort of paper like that.

For years Leonard had played hooky almost as much as he had gone, and he was always being dragged in to his father's store by the visiting teacher. When he did go to school he would be almost ill, whipped nearly senseless by the drone of the boring, old-maid teachers. He hated everything about them, even their miserable, sick humor; no matter what it was that made the other students laugh, let loose a little bit, it did not make *him* laugh. He would sit in the back of the room with a glaring, eye-popping scowl, leaning forward on the edge of his seat as if he were about to get up and run, bristling all over with bursting nerves.

Margaret was not sure how she had known all this—but somehow it was all very clear to her. Some of it Leonard had told her himself, when they were giving each other the things that passed for courting confidences out at Granny's, but of course he told it with a genial, mature, easygoing humor, reflective and self-scrutinizing (a tone she rarely heard again after they were married), and he said that it was not so much that he hated schools, hated teachers, although he supposed he had hated a few of them, as that he just wanted to get out on his own and be his own boss. Some of the teachers he described had made her laugh, and she still had a clear image of Leonard's jerking face looming darkly in the far back of the room as old breathy, fat, blubbery Miss Brown (with a piggy face and pink eyes) introduced herself to the class. "Now I'm your history teacher (blubber-blubber, breathe-breathe), Miss Brown, but I always tell people that they needn't to ask me (breathe-breathe, choke-choke) if I have any brown relations!"

People said she had heart trouble and that her heart might stop on her any minute and Leonard had fervently hoped it would, and had been full of shame years later when

97

it did finally stop, since he had wished it on her every day he was in her class.

At fifteen Leonard had left school for good. He said that it was what happened to his sister that had made up his mind. His sister was as smart as a whip and she had graduated with straight A's. She was a good, practical girl besides and had taken all the business courses the school had, yet the depression had started and she couldn't get a job, finally had to take a position with no pay—that is, she had to work six months, on trial, for a shrewd lawyer, as a kind of apprentice, just because it was the depression. "When I saw that!" Leonard said.

And yet what had *he* done? Margaret knew this: he had gone on a wild playing-spree with his pals for a whole year, and later he was ashamed of it, almost terrified of his own behavior. For it was only the daughter who had saved the family. That was the year Mr. Barker lost the store, and the house would have been lost too but that the daughter persevered at her "training" and then was kept on by the lawyer for seven dollars a week, which was about all the cash money they had, the whole family, and yet it kept them from being thrown on the street, and after a time even got the lights turned back on.

When Leonard left school, his mother had cried hard into her apron. The father defended him, asked what good was school anyhow when there were no jobs, and blamed the school for being dull. Leonard, of course, told his tales on the teachers, the older women who manned the school; he had made his father weep with pity to hear how trying they were, how arbitrary and unfair, how full of spite because they were old maids and didn't have a lively boy like him at home, with a real boy's needs and sensitivities. They didn't give him credit, Leonard said, you couldn't please them no matter what, they meant to take it out on you—their resentment of the male sex—one way or the other . . . and it wasn't his way, his papa knew, to let himself be trampled on like that and treated like a child when he was almost a grown man, with a grown man's nerves, that people had better start paying attention to and giving him credit for . . . .

After Margaret and Leonard were married, young men and women they had met at the dairy (standing in line for fresh peach milk shakes at Granny's stand) would stop by at the Barkers, cry out from the porch *y'all come on and do so and so*. It was a wonder they had even tried it, but then they were not acquainted with Leonard's nerves and what they would and would not let him do, had known him only during his courting period when he had carefully hidden them, kept them pulled in, no matter what, like terrible claws. When the friends appeared, Leonard would talk fast and make a good excuse, and no doubt fear alone had shot his heart rate up to about two hundred beats a minute . . . horrible trepidation that he might have to spend a whole evening coupled off, doing what *women* would want to do, knowing his nerves would not stand for it.

Later when he was his own householder, when Margaret had had the effrontery to have caused him to build a small frame house on Suwannee Drive (and in wartime at that, when something might well have struck them down for even trying it), certain hard-to-discourage friends still came by to pay calls, stopped by with their children for actual visits.

When this would happen Leonard would be caught and there would be nothing he could do but get up his act, meet them at the door with a happy burst of chattering welcome, talking louder than anybody else, like the original good old boy. In fact she was the one people thought was glum, a hedgehog of nerves and worry. But after all, it was she who had known what it was costing him to be nice to them, and she would hope and pray they would get up and go *(oh lord don't let them stay long)*, while Leonard went on like a crazy man and couldn't help himself, for of course there was a rebel part of him that wanted to be a generous, genial host in spite of everything, and the horrible fact was that it was his nerves themselves that drove him on . . . to a breaking point she knew would come as soon as the guests went home. But in the meantime he couldn't stop himself, and his voice rose higher and higher; he would be so absurdly beside himself that even when the company were actually *ready* to take their leave he couldn't let them, and would shout, "Hey where y'all going off to?" and begin to holler and cry about giving them a meal (*God save us all*, she would think), thrusting a red, glowering face into hers, barking out to her as if she were deaf, amusing them all by pretending to be stern: "Margaret! What have we got in the house to feed these people?"

My lord, it was enough to make her tired all over again, just to think about it, the whole scene, Leonard's race against his nerves.

Then there was something else. She had never been north before her children grew up, and yet she thought she might have picked up a touch of her Grandmother Culp's outsideness, her un-southernness. It was not that Granny was not friendly, not cheerful and outgoing—she would not have been glum and sad for anything. Certainly when people came to call on her she made a proper little fuss over them and gave them a due amount of smiling hospitality— and yet when someone said something, for instance, Granny listened, and she waited until they were through to answer back. Whereas *these southerners* (for that was the way Margaret thought of them sometimes, when Granny's ways superimposed themselves on other people's) were shouting and screaming before they could get out of the car, and the ones they were calling on starting hollering from the front porch, and none of them had the least idea what the other ones were saying for at least ten full minutes. Then finally they would all wear themselves out, just from saying hello-how-are-you, and would have to sit down and get their breath.

Margaret was not one to carry on like that; even if she was glad to see people, she couldn't make over them that way, she didn't have one of those high, wafting, singing voices so many people had, she didn't blubber and bluster over people, and sometimes, when one of them came on at her like that, she just gave them a stern look and they began to settle down. For herself what she liked best was a nice quiet easy talk—she would like to have known a few couples that she and Leonard could sit down with like that but of course it couldn't be that way, not unless Leonard had had an operation on his nervous system.

So in any case, she was married, and the most serious and important part of her life was beginning. She had finished her strange, split growing up, with its two parts that she had never been able to sew together (the one on Clark Street in Jacksonville and the one at the dairy in Waycross)—that there was probably nothing strong enough to sew them together *with*; but anyway she had grown up, she was nineteen, it was time for a husband to appear and so one *did* appear. And Leonard—nice-looking, cheerful, easygoing, devoted, hardworking—had all but moved in with them out at the dairy, had put on his act for six months. It was a truly amazing performance, and none of them could see through it, not even Granny. ("Granny didn't want to see through it," Nora said.) In fact it was so unnatural a part and Leonard played it so well that it took him years and years to get over the strain.

The one and only time, before they were married, that she had almost begun to catch on to Leonard's act, to see something odd poking through . . . the only time—as it seemed to her now, looking back—that she had almost heard, faintly ticking, the time bomb of strain running down inside him, was in the candy truck on the drive to Jacksonville, when she had been trying her best to explain to him what they were going to meet at the other end of the road.

As she had spoken to him that day in the truck, she had had a dim, disturbed sense that he wanted to stop and burst out of the car. He had a crouching, beleaguered look to him, he looked like a cat about to leap out of a pen. He certainly wanted, at the very least, to turn around and head back home. It looked as if he couldn't bring himself to urge the truck on, that he was actually trying to pull it backwards with the wheel rather than urge it forward, and that yet it went forward in spite of him while he worked to subdue himself, to tame, for instance, his voice, make it say things ("What about that?" —"Is that the truth now?") with at least a semblance of considerate reflection.

People had not necessarily approved of what she had done that day. *Here this nice husband appears, to help get you out of something, and yet you could not let well enough alone, throw off that old mess you had left back there in Jacksonville. No—you had to take him straight down there and introduce him to it.*

And yet she could not say that she was sorry, even as badly as it had turned out. At least she had had, all through the years, the great satisfaction of knowing that, unlike him, she had not hidden herself in any way. As far as Granny was concerned, going down there was one of the most childish and repugnant things Margaret had ever done, and in order even to do it, she had had to tell Granny a deliberate untruth: "Sunday Leonard and I are going to the beach in the drink truck." (Or was he still driving the candy truck?) But in any case she had thought: *I will not start this marriage with a lie, a secret that amounts to a lie. Granny did not dig me up, a twelve-year-old girl, in her flower garden. I was not brought home with the cows one afternoon. Granny didn't find me under the Christmas tree one year, a present that had come her way just because she deserved to have one child around who wanted to learn how to knit and make doilies. No, I was actually born, like other people, and once had a mother and a father, grew up in a house that is still standing (such as it is) in a town that is actually on the map.*

As she had begun to speak in the truck that day, in serious, self-conscious, halting tones, Leonard had kept his eyes on the road. She did not sit close to him. She felt it proper that she sit formally on her own side. She had spun her awkward tale, and he had begun to say appropriate things.

"Oh is that right?" he would say. "Well I do know. Well what about that?"

But the more she told, the more necessary he had found it to keep his eyes strictly on the road, and the more peculiar his face began to look to her. They were not going fast—in fact they went more and more slowly, until it seemed as if they might not be able to get there, that he did not *intend* for them to get there. It was probably the longest ride of both their lives, and surely he had never forgotten it, any more than she had, and yet afterward they never spoke of it again.

She still had not quite known him, had not felt, on that occasion, "So *this* is the way he is." For of course all of that was an extraordinary circumstance, and she had taken him completely by surprise and it was a lot for him to take, it would have been a lot even for someone calm and reasonable. It must have been as if a whole shotgun full of perfectly just and frightful questions had gone off at his head. No doubt the twitching antennas of his brain had been feeling and testing over rough lumps like this—"If this is what she comes from, what the others, the rest of them . . . *are* . . . what would hers and mine be like?" Wasn't it true, in fact, that in spite of certain vague, discreet assurances Granny had had from a physician acquaintance of hers ("Oh Granny," Nora said . . . "well, Granny knew that if any of *yours* came out that way, you could just write it off and get rid of it the same way she did hers")—wasn't it true that Margaret herself, when Ruth was born, had been suddenly and unexpectedly overcome with quaking fear? To the point that later on she even thought it had been a factor in the way Ruth was born, as if Margaret had been afraid for her to *be* born? And was that not also why, when Ruth had turned out to be not only normal but smart, and as little more than a round dumpling of a babe had started to chatter and converse, and at the age of three to be taught by her granddaddy to write her name, that Margaret had been so moved, so unreasonably pleased and touched?

So after all, Leonard, going over in the truck that day, could not know all that—how things would work out that is, could not know the answers to any of the questions he might reasonably be posing to himself. Still, it might certainly be supposed that at that callow time of his life, and considering that he was not a reasoning man to begin with, he had not had the clarity of thought or even the presence of mind to raise to himself any very specific questions, that his mind was simply full of vague panic and alarm and that what he saw before him was just a dark funnel of trouble, mysterious, like so many human troubles, hard to fight or understand.

Though that was all guesswork. How different it might have been if he had only said a word out loud—one word—of what he felt . . . his resentment, his confusion and fear, instead of battling on to conceal them all, an effort which cost him so much that by the time they had drawn up at last on Eighth Street, they could not get out of the truck, for the reason that Leonard, saying politely that it had gone to sleep, could not move his leg, had to concentrate hard on trying to rub it back to life; and then it would not rub back, and when he finally did get out, he could not put his foot down properly and walked like a lame man.

Yet when Margaret's mother appeared on the crooked porch, he stumped on, grinning, almost shouting a roaring greeting to her, and she in utter delight sang and shouted it back to him, and so the whole blubbering household took to him at once; but when they had settled him in the living room, wiped an armload of junk and trash out of a lopsided chair for him to sit in, he was still rubbing his leg . . . or was it, this time, his ankle? Then later in the day when she had watched from the cracked window Leonard and her brother George going to the store for a carton of Coca-Colas, holding hands—a scene of surpassing strangeness—Margaret had seen that Leonard's limp had not left him, and she thought she had crippled him for good.

THEN AFTER they were married, or *she* was married—to his mama and daddy on Harrison Street, and Ruth had come (and he had no reason, for instance, to think twice about leaving her mateless night after night) . . . then his nerves broke through, and Leonard burst out of himself altogether and she saw what he was.

She thought of herself sitting, a prisoner, in the gloomy house on Harrison Street, looking in terrible discouragement at the rough, scarred wooden floors, worn almost black, full of splinters for people walking barefoot, absent-mindedly wishing for something at first she could not name, thinking vaguely *I want out of here*—until the idea of her own house had finally come to her, though sometimes she did not understand how it had come, and would try hard to puzzle this out, scowling, trying to peer through the veil of the past. How had she had the nerve? It was as if it simply came out of staring so long at rough dark floors, thinking: *I would like to have a floor of clean, new, smooth, light-colored wood, sanded and stained a color of honey . . . which you could see yourself in when you waxed it.*

So little girls must grow up, Margaret thought. And so what? What of that? But she could not help but think there must be certain little gods of life who were glad they did have to and couldn't wait to get their hands on them and give them a nasty shove. She thought of all the dirty deals these little gods cooked up for people and how it just tickled them and made them feel good to see people with their heads sunk under black clouds, crawling under iron lids of defeat. *They love for people to be miserable and afraid*, she thought, *and yet we foil them sometimes, we get the better of them—for a little while.*

For after all they had ruthlessly taken Margaret herself, when she was little more than a hoping child, and deliberately put her in a bad predicament, caused her, by gross deceptions, to marry the wrong man, set her down—when she especially needed somewhere bright and cheerful—in a gray worn house where they were saving electricity, even more than was necessary, and things hardly ever had more than a thin woolly light on them. And yet even at the Barkers, in that dark, suffering, depression time, something good had happened. Ruth came.

*My child was born*, Margaret thought, sitting halfway up, suddenly, on the sofa, as if even forty years later there was still something surprising, unusual, about it. And the little nasty gods, little demons, or whatever they were, were used to having things mostly their own way and had planned for her whole life to be full of gloom and regret, and they were furious, no doubt.

She pictured Ruth at one year old, in her stroller. She and Margaret were going for a long stroll downtown. She was a fat baby with a face as round as a pie and absolutely no hair, even at one. It was almost alarming, but people said not to worry, that all babies grew hair sooner or later. But this little being was Margaret's precious revenge on everything that had wanted to betray her and spoil her life, and it was absolutely necessary that she be properly adorned. So in order to put a bow-ribbon on this child, she had had to take the ribbon—and with no hair to pin it to—tie it around her head, under her chin! Yes there were pictures of her like that and Margaret did not remember that anyone had thought it was comical or out of place, though perhaps they had.

So when Ruth was a year old, in any case, with little legs like stuffed sausages, and this ribbon tied, absurdly as it seemed now (though not entirely so), around her face so that the bow sat on top of a completely bald head . . . something else had intervened as well, to get the better of the vicious little gods.

It had had to do with their stroll downtown.

This was the part of the day that Margaret most looked forward to since it got her out of the old dark house into the sun and fresh air and gave her time alone with her child, with no grandparents hovering over her, finding signs of illness, of peculiar distress that could only be known by grandparents.

First they had breakfast in the kitchen at the back of the old house, with coffee-water pumped from the well on the back porch. Ruth could spoon her own pabulum, and sometimes she would put the spoonful in her mouth and sometimes she would dribble it, in a careful, studied way, down her arm in a neat rope. They had their breakfast, and then Ruth would be dressed in one of her many handsome little dresses of soft batiste or dotted swiss or silky sateen, each one with little panties to match. It was their main revenge against privation—they were all of them determined that Ruth, if no one else, should always look simply beautiful, depression or not, and with two seamstresses at work for her (mother and grandmother) she was a baby who did very well; for after all, you could buy a little piece of cloth for a baby's dress for very, very little—for twenty-five cents, she supposed, or perhaps less, perhaps fifteen or twenty. In fact these strolls with Ruth downtown (that Margaret loved and looked forward to so much) often had, as their excuse, the buying of another smidgen of material for yet another frock for this child who was already the height of fashion. That might be their mission, or it might be simply to bring back for Mrs. Barker a packet of hairpins for five cents (which she used all her life to keep her plaited coil stuck tight on the back of her head) or some other little dime-store affair for housekeeping needs.

In those days many people still walked everywhere they

went and thought nothing about it. From the Barkers' house it was three full miles and more to town, and yet they covered it almost every day. Besides being such an enjoyable walk, on wide sidewalks down treelined streets, with Ruth so manifestly glad to be out of the house, all her senses open wide to the various and astonishing outdoor world unfolding for her personal entertainment beyond her stroller bar, there was a spirit of enterprise and efficiency about it too; for they had their little shopping missions to take care of, however small—or they might stop at the post office, or at the light company to pay the bill.

Mrs. Barker saw them off from the porch, and would kiss Ruth over and over until she began to shake her bald head in annoyance and Margaret thought they would never get away, and then just when they almost did, Mrs. Barker, no matter how warm it was, would run back in the house to get some little gear, a knitted cap, perhaps, for Margaret to stick in the back of the stroller in case it suddenly blew up an arctic storm.

Even then Margaret and Ruth were not free, because they had no sooner gotten down the block and out of sight of Mrs. Barker, who would be waving at them with her handkerchief from the end of the banistered porch, amidst the great heavy rockers that Mr. Barker feared would soon be going for firewood, "if things kept up," than they came in view of the little red icehouse just across the railroad tracks. The icehouse had a very narrow front porch with thin rails, and Mr. Barker would always be sitting on this porch, leaning back against the wall in a straight wooden chair.

Mrs. Barker worried and wept sometimes with frustration, feeling strongly that her husband would catch his death of cold out there, or in summer from heatstroke or heart attack, and she pled with him as much as she dared, and begged in private her only son Leonard to try to reason with him, persuade him to build a separate shelter to sit in and wait on business—or at the very least to get the little porch itself enclosed. Didn't her husband know full well, she said, that if he only wanted to, he could just stand up and holler from his porch and colored people going by would stop at once, in times like these, and get to work for almost nothing to find some old lumber and close it in?

But Mr. Barker meant to punish himself one way or the other for losing his business and ruining his family; for forfeiting—as he saw it, as peculiar as this was, since a whole lot of *them* were in exactly the same boat—the respect of all his friends; for not even being able to buy his grandchild a nice play-pretty when he wanted to or his wife a good pair of shoes from a proper store such as he himself had been the proprietor of. His only personal luxury was his tobacco and the rolling-papers for his cigarettes, and even these he would turn on in disgust sometimes and threaten to foreswear.

Yet now and then the time would come when he would have given himself all the punishment he could take for a while, and then he would turn a sudden mean little temper on his wife and daughter. Never on his son, Margaret recalled—and yet it was the son who had had the genius to take these little sketches of temper and to create from them those great monuments of his own wrath. Why, though, were tempers rained specifically on wives and female children?

Possibly there was in any male fraternity, even of two, enough co-pity and co-awe to explain any and all of the blind ways they spared each other. "We may be *lowly* males, *defeated* males, but we are still males after all, as witness these fits that we throw at the heads of women."

Or possibly Leonard was spared because his father felt that it was his son who had borne the brunt of his own failure, that just when the time had come, after years of struggle and then of triumph and success, for him to do for his boy those things that are the crown of a father's fatherhood— take him into a thriving family trade, or start him off in a business of his own, or at the very least send him away for a proper education, he had instead fallen like a shot into childlike helplessness himself, been brought down with a thump, by the depression, like a winged quail. In fact Margaret never quite understood how it was that Mr. Barker, in his last doomed days behind the handsome wooden counter in his store (supplier of every need, from shoes to nails to well-ropes, from soap to paregoric, men's needs to ladies' needs) had been able to read, trembling, in the papers about men being ruined and throwing themselves out of windows, and not himself have gone stealthily upstairs, on the morning of foreclosure, and opened a window in the dry-goods room over the back lot, turned to this final advantage the mark of his special prosperity—his two-story building, the tallest general store on that side of the county, the only one high enough to be worth anyone's trouble to jump out of.

But Mr. Barker had not jumped out of his window, and he had had to fall back on the icehouse for punishment, on deliberately putting it up in full view of the ruined boarded-up store down the street, and then sitting down in all weathers behind the railing of its absurd porch, waiting to sell an occasional customer a nickel or dime's worth of ice.

When she thought of Mr. Barker taking revenge on himself, there was another image that came to mind: she saw him in the front room lighting the old oil lamp at bedtime, taking it with him to his room to save the half-penny of lights he might have turned on in the hallway to see him to bed. *How mad that was*, Margaret thought, and she pictured him stopping on his way to the hall to cast the lamp's glow upward on the wall, to the framed photograph of himself and his dead brother on the steps of the store, standing so imposingly for such small men, with such neat mercantile poise and assurance, their shoulders set to the lens.

But they had learned to say nothing, she and Mrs. Barker (and what could her bridegroom have said from the pool hall downtown?), not to resist Mr. Barker in this—they just paid it no mind but lit their own ways to bed with the lights, and Margaret, in fact, had even read in her bed once she got there, by a small lamp on the wall behind her, with a very decent bulb in it of perhaps forty watts. The season was late winter, mild enough for midmorning strolls, often beautiful and balmy in fact, but at night quite cold, so that sometimes she had made her a hot-water bottle to take to her bed— that did not have a husband in it. And she remembered this so very clearly: spreading around her on the bed, under the forty-watt bulb, the thick envelope of papers, pictures, plans and designs which she had acquired, almost by accident, on one of those morning strolls.

Yes, it would be late at night that her chance would come to take out the brown envelope from the bottom of the drawer and read and study the papers in it, think about them very sharply and practically sometimes, or dream over them at other times absentmindedly, while the Barkers snored in another cold winter room and Ruth's flannelled bottom reared up in the crib across from her.

It was natural that in memory she would connect the brown envelope and the morning strolls—because for one thing they were both things that had made her happy in the midst of unexpected sorrows, and also because the brown envelope would not have been there *to* study except for the fact of the morning strolls, as well as another coincidental matter or two, a detour on the strolling route, for instance, on a certain day, and on the detour street the raising of the blinds in a certain storefront window, revealing to passersby—to strollers-by—a person of her acquaintance working at a desk; also of course it was necessary that Leonard stay late every night at the pool hall so that she could *study* the brown envelope in private once she had gotten it, through the woman in the shop. And of course she could go on and on. Except for a thousand things that came after that, perhaps millions of things if she could only sort them out . . . she would not have progressed from study of the contents of the brown envelope, from absentminded, unhopeful calculations on the back of the flap, to . . . all that she had progressed to . . . lying here at noon, for instance, at the beginning of old age, on a brocade sofa that rested on good pine floors.

So there was more reason than one to remember so well, so fondly, on the whole, the morning walks to town .rom the Barkers' house on Harrison Street, the only time in the day when she would almost cease to be afraid of all her prospects, and would escape for a while the oppressiveness, the ignominy, of her situation, the peculiar spot she had landed in, the unlikelihood of her ever being able to think of herself as a normal and successful person. Pushing her crowing baby down the long wooded, flowing blocks of Bainbridge Avenue, across Elizabeth, with its island of chinaberry trees, waiting, in pine-flecked sun, for the light on Payne, she had not felt her defeat to be so final as all that.

It was only just then, at Payne Street, that she would truly have begun to get her breath and to have piled behind her enough lines and shapes, enough sheer space (only partly filled with trees and buildings and fences and poles) so that she could no longer see, when she paused to look back, the crossroads way down at Harrison Street; and thus the daily struggle of breaking twice away from a crazily doting grandparent—once at the house and then again at the icehouse—would have been survived once more.

For when Mrs. Barker had finally conceded her own defeat, had no more admonition to give, nor any other last-minute irrelevant item to fetch for the back of the stroller, Margaret and Ruth would set out down the block at last towards the railroad tracks, where rolling over the crossing would be bumpy going indeed and Ruth, who always did the intelligent thing, would get very quiet and concentrated and squeeze tight with her chubby hands the front of her stroller bar. The minute they were over, Mr. Barker, on the lookout, would see them from the icehouse porch and he would rise from his chair and begin to wave—a great big sweeping arc that Ruth would be sure to see, and Margaret would say "See Granddaddy?" and Ruth would rise a little in her seat, trembling with amazement, crying, "Gan-da, Gan-da," and they would see Granddaddy springing down from the narrow porch down the way. Margaret remembered how rapidly he would materialize, advancing upon the stroller before they were even well across the tracks.

Today, these many years after his death, after the end of so many things, she could see, imagine, him again, striding hard across the icehouse lot in his brogans and his loose short cotton coat, a small thin man like Leonard was, a Barker-sized man, people said, since history had not recorded any Barkers over five-feet-five, a thin and yet not a skinny man but a *sturdy* thin man—still waving as he came and already smiling that teasing smile that only his grandchild, who had no knowledge of depressions, of lost worlds of power and pride, could evoke.

Then the show they put on, the two of them! It was not as if—*my lord,* Margaret sighed, a grandparent herself now—he had not seen his Ruth at breakfast not two hours before and given her a smacking, teasing, jostling good-by as he had left for work. But now here was Margaret left to roll an empty stroller down the block while the two of them crowed and gurgled and hooted at each other like crazy people, and Gan-da carried his baby girl in his arms to the icehouse yard, where they could just walk around and around and act silly and he could tickle the top of her bald head with his bearded chin—and muss her ribbon badly and make it fall down around her ears.

At last Margaret had to intervene, beginning simply with a murmurous supplication, but gradually raising with increasing urgency her plea that she and Ruth had been, after all, on their way somewhere, had set out for a specific destination, were going downtown. *It's time for you to hide the nickel,* she would almost have to say—and finally Mr. Barker would proceed to the final rite, take out a coin and hide it under his arm or about his clothes or under his cap, so that Ruth could find it and explode in mirth, later be bought something with it downtown, an ice cream cone perhaps.

For what else could the crushed grandpa bestow? A nugget of ice from the icehouse? The nickel games must have made him cast a glance every time down the road, imagine himself carrying his baby up and down the incredible aisles of Barker Brothers Store, which had probably had two dozen kinds of hard candy, for instance, in fat shiny jars. She could see Mr. Barker in his suit, white shirt and suspenders, choosing from a rack, for his baby, a card of huge golden buttons. (For of course children love buttons and lids and spools and cans—they know they are really toys, usurped by adults to do things they were not meant for.)

*But the store would have been too much for a child, overstimulating, as people would term it today*, Margaret thought, *and I would have had to put my foot down sometimes.* Yes, the rich funny colors and smells and shapes would be too much, the queer, tickly feel of certain commodities, the soft, *squishy* feel of something else; *big* things on the floor that were too heavy when you tried to push them (she saw Ruth squatting over them in embroidered pants), smaller things that rattled when you picked them up. She saw Ruth tasting peas from a croker sack and someone putting his finger in her mouth to get them out. She saw her banging in frustration on a huge glass case studded with bright spools of thread.

They had said that Leonard as a boy had banged on cases like that, and when they would not open, had had kicking, squalling fits on Barker Brothers' floor. In fact it was her husband Margaret most often pictured in his father's store, even though it was already closed down and boarded up before her marriage to his mother and father. She had a mental picture of Leonard opening a box of One Hundred Assorted Screws, taking them out in dark concentration, lining them up in rows by size. The store had definitely played a magic on him too, for he had spent his life in stores, or going in and out of them with his catalogues under his arm. He had never *owned* a store, or even dared hope to own one—not with the store-ruining demon of his father's tracking him all his life, ready to pounce given the least chance. No he would never have tried to buy a store, or *run* a store (which was just what the store demon was waiting for, no doubt)—and in fact he was not an "inside man" to begin with.

She had a fierce vision of Leonard closed up in a little store of his own, pacing fiercely up and down the walls like a frantic beast. Even when customers came in, he could not stop, and would simply cry out to them, "No, no—don't you see?" and wave them on. No, it was not precisely "store" that he yearned for and dreamed of, though he dreamed mad dreams, no doubt, of the magnificent importance, the respectability and financial well-being that "store" had once brought to his father and the store-demon of the great depression then taken away. But the drawers and drums, boxes and kegs and jars, cases and cabinets—all the sundry goods of stores—had played on him all along their assorted charms, so that it was out of the same stock that he was later to make his own livelihood, selling it to small-time storekeepers mostly out of catalogues, working for companies in Atlanta or Jacksonville as a small-time jobber of bobby pins and safety pins, work gloves and fishing twine, ladies' hosiery, and ball-point pens.

But in any case the grandfather's rite, on those mornings years ago, his ceremony of play and affection, would be over at last and Ruth would be settled back down into the metal stroller, her ribbon pulled straight, her dress brushed off and spread down on her chubby thighs. She would seem to mentally prepare herself for the ride to town and then she and Margaret would stroll away, wheels lightly clattering, across the intersection and up the rising sidewalk of Bainbridge Avenue, crushing under them like hapless bugs the little demons of despair. Then Margaret, with certain rattling things in her head smoothing out and lulling over as they glided, began to be happy, and by the time they had come up to the bustle of town, the movement of people on the streets towards banks and stores, buggies and cars, she *was* happy.

It was true, nevertheless, that she could see down a certain short street, snuck off the way it ought to be, the weathered ugly wooden sign of the pool hall, despoiler of young husbands, devourer of the innocent dreams of hoping young girls. Yet she did not quite believe that all life meant her to have was lonely nights in old sad houses where they did not even keep the lights on. No she could not believe it . . . as she and Ruth clattered on so companionably, looked in their windows and crossed their streets, spoke in passing to people they thought they knew, turned the corner at the picture show.

*Oh children*—Margaret thought today—*remember the old library over the police station?* Up the back stairs they would go, Ruth in the mother's arms, leaving the stroller under the staircase. Or Margaret would lead her very slowly by the hand sometimes, a short-legged tot just able to stretch her legs from step to step. And then—*how nice up there.*

They would find themselves in one very long bright room, with great arched windows in old-fashioned, elegant rows. Mornings so much the nicest time to be anywhere— and crazily, in spite of everything, the slow partings, for instance, from almost aggrieved grandparents, it would still be morning. They would have risen very early, according to the harsh custom of the house, for the Barkers were much too ashamed of themselves for being ruined ever to lie in bed past the crack of dawn.

Margaret considered how quietly, how almost dreamily, people go about their tasks in the morning, with what pleasant little sighs and yawning murmurings, their minds not yet drawn tight with the accumulating business of the day and all its aggravations. She remembered the barely-sketched sounds of someone in the back of the room filling a coffeepot, tinkling cup and spoon, inquiring before long whether she herself wouldn't like a good fresh cup ("Yes I believe I would").

Ruth, very satisfied to be still now, after the long breezy ride, would be sitting in a miniature chair at a very low table with big picture books spread richly all around her, while Margaret examined volumes from the shelves, or was handed new ones in bright covers by the librarians. At the far back of the main room, there was a small alcove of books of the kind Margaret liked, and whenever in her pleasant wanderings down the rows she would arrive at this hidden alcove, she remembered that her small daughter would know it at once. No matter how occupied she might have been with her own books, Ruth would sense at once that Margaret had disappeared from her field of vision, was not to be found in the back rows of the main room—and just as Margaret, in the alcove, would stretch forward her hand towards a title on a shelf, wee running steps would sound. Ruth would turn the alcove corner and when she saw her mother, suddenly stop stock-still and give her a good serious searching look to be sure she *was* her mother and that she did not intend to disappear from the premises—then just as quickly, she would run back to her books. *Yet Ruth does not remember any of this*, Margaret thought. For after all it had all stopped—the morning strolls, the visits to the library and the shops—a good while before Ruth was four years old.

It was such an obvious thing, and yet very curious, always, to think about: the fact that parents knew children in lives children could never know they had even had and had only other people's words for them; and that yet the children were the way they were partly *because* of those early, lost lives of theirs. It seemed that people only began to exist for themselves, in their own minds, at about five or six—though of course there were spots and streaks and little pinpoints of memory long before that. For instance, she knew that Ruth remembered her grandfather Barker's death when she was four—or at least she remembered this: herself sitting outside the door of the front room where they had his body, sitting all dressed up in her little cane-bottomed chair, being noticed and kissed and cried over *(oh you poor darling little thing)* by everyone that came to look at him. In fact she thought she knew—somehow—that that was *why* she was sitting there: for this prodigious chance for attention and sympathy, not for grief, for she could not remember her grief at all and had no memory whatever of seeing his body, though it had lain only a few feet from where she sat at the door, and did not remember his dying or being told that he was dead . . . .

Indeed Ruth had said many times that she knew nothing whatever of the morning strolls, though there were several years of them, or of the way she and Margaret both lived for them at the time, the profound importance of them.

She had one dab of memory about the icehouse. She remembered being passed across a car seat (yet whose car would this have been?) from her grandmother to her mother in the icehouse lot, and then held partway out of a window to receive a bristly kiss—and a nickel—from an old man with a white beard. She remembered being made happy by this old man's affection, and how mischievous it was, and yet how much she had felt it as a perfectly ordinary thing in her life and simply no more than her due. Other "memories" Ruth could not be sure about. She thought she remembered being held by her grandfather late one night in the kitchen on Harrison Street, and being fed by him, with a spoon, something good from an old-fashioned, bottle-green, spiny glass—she thought it was leftover cornbread gibbled up in buttermilk. "Because for one thing—I feel I know how it tastes," Ruth would say, "even though I don't have any other memory of tasting such a thing."

～

IN THOSE DAYS, in any case, when she and her husband and child had slept in a back room in the cold dim house on Harrison Street, when she was already long past the stage of hopeful bride, with the single pleasure of strolling each day her bald, fat, intelligent baby to town—on one of those days something rather important had intervened in her life.

She did not doubt that some of the friends she would later meet at the First Christian Church would have said that what had intervened was *God*, for they were always saying that. "We just don't know, do we, what He has in store, what He's planning for us, what He thinks is best." And perhaps it *was* God—she supposed one might as well say "God"—that had surprised them as they started down Bainbridge Avenue from the icehouse one morning . . . and saw up ahead workmen in the street drilling and hammering, saw city trucks all around and red flags, the road completely blocked. They had turned away and taken another route . . . though naturally babies do not want to turn away from motion and noise, they want to turn directly towards it; and Ruth had poked her finger, in a very awkward little beginner's point, a crooked amateur point, towards the animated scene up ahead, and rising in her stroller seat, said *Go!*

But on this fated day, Margaret had turned them off onto the narrower street behind, so that clicking along in the mild soft sun on a day in early winter, not long before Christmas, her long skirts swishing pleasantly against her legs, they soon came up to the familiar intersection at Richmond and Elizabeth, where they would have met themselves if they had travelled their usual route. Now this was the fateful thing: leading up *to* the intersection was a last short block of little stores and shops, and as they strolled past this block, Margaret chanced to see, through a wide, rather smeared window (almost too smeared to have seen what she saw—and what if it *had* been too smeared?) someone she knew sitting at a desk. She had stopped at this window, looking in in surprise, though not necessarily having decided to go inside, when the person chanced to look up and see *her*. And this woman who had chanced to look up had been silly old Mary Bloodworth, who had just gotten married to a big stout boy who loved to drink milk shakes at Granny's dairy stand.

So of course silly Mary had pulled Margaret in, stroller and all, pleased to death to see her, moving her mouth as fast as it would go, and hugging Ruth and chattering in her face until she got upset and had to be rescued by Margaret and petted and kissed. But being with Mary was almost relaxing because you hardly had to say a word yourself—Mary said it all for both of you, and while Mary talked, Margaret had had time to look around her at the cluttered room, where blocks and strips and squares, samples of this and that, were strewn about on the floor and on heavy, listing racks, and enormous books and notebooks and catalogues were tumbled in piles in the corners.

This was the office of McDaniel Construction Company. On the walls pictures of new-built houses hung rather crookedly. ("I couldn't just sit here, I would have to straighten this place up if I worked in here," Margaret had thought, "and I *know* I'd sweep the floor.") But in the pictures and pamphlets, the new houses sat smartly at interesting angles on rising lots, and Margaret wandered around the room, nodding and murmuring while Mary reminisced and carried on, and rendered in a high singing voice little modern histories of people they had known. Margaret had drawn close to an inside view of one of the new houses, and suddenly a beautiful pine floor shone up at her—the color of rich honey in its coat of golden shellac.

What all had Mary said? "Are y'all going to build a house?" Yes she had said that. And Margaret had almost laughed. "*Oh no!*" Well she thought they might decide to *rent* a house . . . whenever they thought they could. A *house of our own*, Margaret had said. And Mary had said yes yes, oh of course, a house of your own, because with a child now, of *course* that is what you need don't you, that's what people need isn't it? a house of their own.

No one but Mary was in the office that day; the builder, Mr. McDaniels, was out building. Mary's job was mostly to answer the phone; when people called to say they wanted to build a house, she took their address and sent them a big brown envelope from a whole crate of brown envelopes down by her desk. "This tells them all about it," she said.

So that was how Margaret, taking a detour, had strolled right into a brown envelope of her own, whose contents she then would study in her bed late at night . . . in the beginning just out of idle curiosity . . . and yet no, had she not, from the first, kept the envelope hidden in a drawer, under her slips? And didn't that mean that she had had, all along, rolling around in a little remote corner of her head, a little marble, a little loose pea, of secret surmise and prestidigitation?

Yes it was true that from the first day she had brought it home, the brown envelope had been hidden—it had not been openly and honestly shown about. While she was quietly putting it away on that first morning, the midday dinner had been simmering on the stove and the Barkers had been administering to their grandbaby her elaborate welcome home. They had been close to tears with astonishment and prayerful thanksgiving that she and Ruth had not been killed by flying rocks at the road construction site (*to tear up Bainbridge Road—why think of it,* they said—*and to make people take a detour that they aren't used to and that might be dangerous, oh what will happen next, Lord help us all*); and indeed, thanks be to God, they had found, with worshipful relief, that neither could they discover on the body of their precious love any sign of her having fallen ill since the morning—when they had examined her from top to toe—from any wasting, crippling disease.

So while enormous amounts of grateful cooing and hugging, of crowing and kissing were going on in the kitchen, Margaret had slipped from the back of the stroller a paper bag containing a brown envelope (as well as a wee smidgen of silky cloth for a tiny frock) and taken the envelope to the drawer in the bedroom and slid it under her slips. So there must have been a little pea of hope and calculation pinging about in her even then.

Then in the nights, alone, with Leonard at the pool hall and Ruth asleep in her crib, she would spread on the bed the papers inside the envelope and look them all over; and though very possibly she had tried, at first, to restrain herself, still she was immediately transported by these papers to a spanking new sun-bright house with honey-colored floors and a huge picture window. Old houses, of course, did not have picture windows—only clever, pretty, new houses. Margaret saw in her mind's eye a brilliant picture of Ruth playing on the honey-colored floor and a river of sun pouring through the picture window into the bright clean sea of golden pine.

Clean, bright, fresh, new. This is what she wanted—a fresh start, a new life in her own house that no one had ever lived in but her, a house absolutely blank with no memory of anything, a house thought up, planned, and signed to by her, she to be finally mistress of her own place, with no father, no Granny, no Barkers to have any say whatever—she to put the meals on and call people to table, she to say what went where, she to invite people or not invite them, she to fix things up, every crook and cranny, to suit no one but herself.

Was this not the idea—to get that child, that bitter marriage, out of that dark defeated house, take up the little dream-dress of her girlhood, brush it off and try to put it on once more? For she must have thought that if at night in the new house, there were only herself and Ruth—no old father, for instance, the picture of ruined pride, groaning over the bad news on the radio, in a ghostly room where even at six o'clock on a winter night shadows were almost scary . . . if there was only herself and Ruth in a house that was miles away from the pool hall downtown . . . might there not be in that exquisite picture of the sun-drenched child, a hand stretching forth, a young father's, young husband's hand? to smooth, in satisfied ease, the down at the nape of a little girl's neck?

MARGARET had sat down and then Mr. McDaniels had gotten up to shut the door. When he sat back down, she bent forward from the edge of her chair, almost crouching towards him. If it was futile, she wished to be told so at once and save her nerves. She said, "My husband only drives a drink truck. He only makes eighteen dollars a week." Mr. McDaniels did not look up, but he blinked, tapping his pencil on the desk in front of him. Perhaps this disclosure had embarrassed him. (My god, woman—then what in the world are you coming around about a house for?) But no, perhaps he was as shy as she was—when it was a question of the opposite sex . . . . When he did look up, toward the window, as if still thinking, calculating, she thought his eyes looked canny, shrewd. (But that would be good, she thought, wouldn't it? if we did business? And yet maybe it would not be.) Oh this was hard, a hard thing to do—a terrible thing. Bad times still. And you could not tell whether things were getting better or worse—though it did look as if people were beginning to take a chance again.

Margaret hid her hand under her purse that day so she could clench and unclench her fist. The fundamental horror of her position in regard to Mr. McDaniel was this: there had been no prices on the houses in the brown envelope.

Then Mr. McDaniels wheeled around to her. "Is he steady on the job?" he said. "Your husband?" Oh yes. "Yes," she said. "Of course I don't know a thing about loans," she said.

Mr. McDaniels studied again, frowned at his desk top. "Do you want a big family?" he said. Oh this was very diffi-

cult for both of them. She murmured, "No . . . not *very* big
. . . ." Suddenly he opened a drawer and took out some
sheets, rifled through them, squared his eyeglasses on his
nose. "I can give you . . . let's see . . . frame house with three
bedrooms, eleven hundred feet, thirty-years loan if the bank
clears you, and it would cost you nineteen dollars a month."

Margaret emitted a little sound of emotion. This sum,
brought so nakedly, so suddenly forth, stunned her, made
her feel—for a moment—almost ashamed. This was a lot, a
lot of money—more than she had counted on, and yet less
than she had feared. One whole week's paycheck. And yet
wasn't it worth it—for a house that meant so incredibly
much? Mr. McDaniels went on. "Then—this might not do
you—you could go down to two bedrooms, nine hundred
feet, and that would only be thirteen dollars a month. Taxes
and insurance—everything is counted in that." Thirteen!
Now surely, surely that was possible.

Margaret had the brown envelope on her lap, and when
she pulled certain papers out of it, to show them to Mr.
McDaniels, something awful was interposed. There came
from beyond the closed door a high piercing scream of pain,
as if from one who had just received a mortal wound. Mr.
McDaniels rushed to throw open the door, and just inside
the front entrance he and Margaret saw a white-faced staring Mary gripping the handle of the stroller, and a red-faced
Ruth, bawling at a preposterous volume and pitch, raising
her contorted body up from the seat of the stroller. When
Ruth saw Margaret, her screams seemed to cease in midair—
completely.

For a moment the room was utterly silent. Then Ruth
smiled, she gurgled quietly through her tears, put out her
arms, and Margaret picked her up. For a moment they were
all shaking hard, they could not stop. Mary could hardly get
her voice. "Outside—she was the best thing—and then—
when I strolled her in the door—" —"She expected me to
be here," Margaret said, "and when she didn't see me—"

—"I thought she had hurt herself—real bad," Mary said; "I thought it was a terrible pain."

*In fact she did have a pain*, Margaret thought. And after all, the pain of mother-loss (or father-loss, if that is the kind of child you are)—there's not much that is worse than that. *And child-loss.* She had known what that was. Sometimes, especially when her children had first left home, she had hungered for them, and ever since, once in a while, she wanted them back, she needed little ones round her neck, ready to shake the heavens with their grief if she should ever be withdrawn from them.

But that blistering yowl of pain from the wee mouth of Ruth in the McDaniels Construction Company—why remember it, why think of it at all, since it had nothing to do with anything but a tiny girl's mortal, irrelevant fright, left motherless in the strange world of babbling Mary Bloodworth? But it had stung her, Margaret, with a small special guilt, as if she had deserved, just by being there in that particular place, discussing what she was discussing, to have this protest lodged against her; and so this cry of Ruth's, just because it had let loose its roaring terror in that particular guilty place, came somehow to be connected with another outburst of pain and fear that would ensue from the morning's talk with Mr. McDaniel—that of her husband Leonard . . . so that later on, whenever she would think about getting the house, of having first laid the plans, then of the entire ordeal and triumph, sometimes this cry of Ruth's of terror and alarm broke again in screeching silence (like sounds in dreams), foretelling what would come.

AT TIMES she imagined herself sitting across a desk from a sterile-looking man in a white jacket. "Mrs. Barker, we've got everything back now and there's not a thing wrong with you but some overactive memory glands and actually it's no wonder you're anxious and depressed and unable to live in the present and enjoy yourself—we think *anybody* would be that remembered as much as you do. So we're going to have to do something about that. We're going to give you some anti-memory shots to bring things under control."

Oh in a way it sounded like a wonderful idea—and yet as she thought about it, very quickly, she was not so sure. "Well, I know that I remember too much but everything I remember is not bad and in some ways I *need* to remember and otherwise I might lose things too terrible to lose."

The man looked slightly exasperated, but she went on. "I mean, I don't see how I could separate the things that are bad to remember from the things that are good and the problem is that even if I could divide them and just get rid of one and not the other I don't know if it would work at all because then the things that were left would not make any sense and I would probably have to imagine anyway and make up from scratch the ones I had gotten rid of."

The man shook his head, he had never heard of anything so foolish, he did wish people would not try to doctor themselves this way.

Then she felt bad about it, she knew he could not understand. "Well there *are* a few things," she said. "If I could forget just one day or two, I think I know which days they would be."

"I don't know," he said. But he took out his pad. "But why don't you tell me—what you have in mind."

"Well there was one night," she said, "when I was still living with my husband's people on Harrison Street."

"What was the date?" he said.

"Well I couldn't give the exact date—"

"Now we would have to have the date, Mrs. Barker . . . ."


SHE MIGHT not know the date but she did know that the Barkers had gone to bed that night and she was sitting alone in the dim front room trying to baste a hem. Then she heard the candy truck pull up outside and the heavy door of the truck crunching shut, Leonard's hard rapid steps on the porch, the front door rattling, banging, the scrape of his feet on the mat in the hall.

How many times, through the whole length of all their married days, she wondered now, thinking it over once again, had she listened, waiting somewhere in the house, lying or sitting, or at other times awakened from sleep, to her husband coming home in the night? In fact how many times over those years had she and the children remarked on this, the wonder of it: that a man so slight, that so very small a man, could make so much noise, gather such force, shake and stir the air with such violence around him.

Years afterward, in the small house on Suwannee Drive—for this dwelling was, after all, destined to be built—the rest of them would lie in their beds and they would hear Leonard jolting like a small train through the tiny hallway (Mr. McDaniels's joke on her, as it turned out), rocking against the narrow walls and doors; they would hear his bare feet on the kitchen linoleum, slapping down on it like the flat flapping feet of a duck almost; yes certainly by then they would all be awake, lying in their beds with their eyes open, waiting for him to have his milk, perhaps a mayonnaise sandwich, and a stomach pill to go with it . . . for they would hear him open noisily the kitchen cabinets, the refrigerator, hear the milk being plopped hard on the table, then more hard flapping steps, water rushing at the sink, faucets wrenched with a sudden whine.

Yet, this was what was so peculiar, beyond ever puzzling through: this loud, rackety, clamorous man, wracking them all, the whole house, with his clumsy, violent, indifferent motion—could not bear any noise but his own. He was as sensitive that way as a baby. Or put it this way: he had the fine-tuned hearing of a fragile invalid with sick invalid nerves. Other people's noises made him jump like a cat, writhe and suffer. Let someone rise in the night, squeak the bathroom door, for instance, with ever so slight, so meager a guilty squeak—and his cry of outrage, of injury, would tear through the house, stun the quaking villain in his tracks. "Who *is* that? What's the matter out there?"

A small sleepy voice would sound in meek reply, then the father bleat again, "I've got to work in the morning!" And of course his booming plea for quiet, in the name of rest and sleep, would snap them all wide awake. So actually, all those years, even in the night they could not relax but were tense in their beds—they lay as if trapped in their own beds, afraid they might have to rise and wake him, knowing he slept with one ear cocked for a squeaking board, a whining tap.

And the point, she supposed, was this: other people's sensations were never real to him—only his own; he was trapped in himself as they in their beds at night. *He never knew us,* the children would say . . . . They said all he did was live with them in the same minute box of a house, come and go, bring them food and keep, watch them walk, eat, talk, read, study and play, but that he did not *see* them. When he moved, it was as if he moved in the center of a small whirlwind—no a blizzard—of himself, of his own feelings and sensations, thoughts, worries and plans; the blizzard moved ahead of him wherever he went and he could not see through it to those beyond; through the pelting stream of his own tense and heightened stream of thought, of springing and careening worries and fears, he could not see them, could hardly make them out, glimpsed them as moving blurs. Yet how was it that through the whirling sound of his wind, his blowing blizzard, there came through to him somehow, to his raging nerves, the thinnest thread of unwonted sound—the one wee *point* of sound that, added to the thousand points that raged inside him, was finally too much for him to bear?

But the children—how could they have loved this whirling nerve-storm with a father inside it, who scowled and paced, muttered to himself and answered himself back

. . . but who wanted sometimes—suddenly, in a peculiar mood—more than anything else, to be loved and wanted, valued as a father . . . and of course was always repulsed, in subtly vengeful ways sometimes. Even with Ruth, a baby at the Barkers, Leonard most of the time had ignored her; had never rocked her or fed her, burped her, changed her, never took her for a walk, brought her a toy—no, Margaret thought, almost with surprise, he never once did a thing like that that fathers do. Yet if she was sick, he was smitten, struck to the heart, just as the old Barkers themselves, and full of cursing rage and blame for the rest of them. Yes, he would be sick with fear and anger and it was almost the only way they had of knowing that he cared for her at all, or even knew he had had her.

And once in a rare while there came on him a mood of playfulness; something in him let up on him, goodness knows why—some little nasty thing that had hold of him forgot and went to sleep . . . and he would want to carry her about and make her laugh, to look at her baby's feet and hands, to hear the words she had learned. Yet just as later, with all the children young and old, he could not please her, he did not know how—he was too loud, he shouted in her face; he frightened her, was too rough, tossed her up too high, did not know how to speak and soothe like her grandfather did, tease and play. Finally he would make her tremble and cry and turn away from him, hide her head from him, and then he would put her down, give her back, leave her alone, turn with an absent, baffled look on his face, leave the room, or even leave the house . . . and this was his fathering, that was his fathering all his life.

So the barkers had gone to bed that night and she was waiting in the front room, trying to stitch a hem in the poor light.

On this particular evening her husband Leonard, who

was driving the drink truck, had promised to come in early so they could talk in private about a certain thing—in spite of the more than obvious fact that she was not actually married to him but to his parents and had no reason to be alone with him or to have private things to say to him.

Very likely she had been thinking, that night, waiting and plying her needle in the dim front room, of Leonard at the supper table on the same evening, wolfing his food, and of what had transpired when she had informed him of her need to speak to him about *a matter of concern only to ourselves*. He had bent over his plate, wolfed down the plate of greens and fatback piled on the slab of cornbread, and gotten up wiping his mouth with a flapping noisy flourish of his handkerchief. It was not his habit to sit at table after his food was down, but to chew the last mouthful standing up, just before he swept the white handkerchief out of his back pocket. That night he had walked about the house for a while, opening doors and absently looking into rooms—he himself could not have said why. He had had a hushed muttering awkward consultation with his poor father, about some matter of family finance, Margaret assumed, a purchase to be made, or a repair, perhaps, that could no longer be put off, the father grieved and repentant, always, where his only son was concerned, full of sorrowful patience for a boy too much put upon at too young an age, with too much on him.

Perhaps that night when Leonard came in, she had looked up from her sewing, remembered how, earlier, after his talk with his father, he had walked aimlessly through the house, as if even *he* had had a sense that being married carried with it certain duties and obligations which could all be discharged, even so, by not going immediately out after supper, but wandering absently for a while in the house, more or less in the presence of one's wife and child. He would soon be setting out after all on the strictly male adventures he had been anticipating all day as he made his rounds to his stores, assessing the contents of cold boxes and drink shelves, then putting his small brawn—alongside his black helper's—to crates of Nehi Orange and Coca-Cola, Dr Pepper and R.C.

But on his tour of the house, he had paused in the kitchen. The embers in the stove were beginning to die out. A few covered dishes had been left on top, and a pie plate or two in the oven to catch the last heat, help them stay good until later in the evening when someone might very possibly want another bite of this or that, a saucer of greens or a piece of sweet potato pie, perhaps a hunk of hard cornbread broken up in their milk or in a bowl of pot-liquor. His mother had been hanging her apron on the nail in the pantry, and in the middle of the kitchen floor Ruth, holding onto Margaret's hand, was just stepping into her hot tub, filled from the last kettle of water from the dying stove.

This round, chubby Ruth, with no waist whatsoever but girded round the middle with a wide belt of flabby belly like someone of middle age, was tipping one toe very gingerly, very tentatively in, to test the water which Margaret herself had certainly not failed to test beforehand and which Mrs. Barker too had checked and doublechecked, naturally assuming that only a grandmother could be depended on to keep from burning a little girl's foot in a scalding tub. So Ruth was being given her bath, in the kitchen still warm from supper and smelling of greens and tea and soap and other mingled after-dinner odors connoting, for this night at least (who knows, ever, what will come on the morrow?) the relative well-being of the house, where so far people could at least be decently fed.

On this night Leonard had paused in the kitchen, on his walkings around the house, to pay his fatherly respects to the scrubbing of his daughter, to smile a wide, ridiculous, preoccupied smile over the tub, to holler—too loudly— "Daddy's girl—that's what she is, yessiree!" which simply made Ruth stop washing the corrugations of the tub with her baby washcloth and turn an alert look on her mother's face. The grandmother got her wrap and went out the back door for a turn in the yard, with a chilly dusk beginning to fall, a chicken here and there pecking at her feet; and in the kitchen Leonard lingered, standing in the doorway jingling his pockets, thinking ahead, no doubt, to the night's activities in town.

Still, that evening he had actually sat down at the enamel table, strumming on it sharply with his nails, making a few commonplace remarks to his wife, which she returned with no outright challenge of rudeness or sarcasm, but certainly not with any warmth, but just a deliberate, untoned perfunctoriness, which she was never sure whether or not he caught, or whether he just determined—in a half-conscious, self-protective way—*not* to catch. And so he was getting through rather well the hour he seemed to have allotted himself "at home," a terrible impertinence, of course, from her own point of view, so he could enjoy in good conscience the important part of the evening yet to come.

But it was then, in the kitchen, sitting by Ruth's tub with the towel on her lap, that Margaret had had her chance to put to Leonard her request, to ask him if he would come home early to discuss with her a certain important thing. Naturally he had frowned, been aggravated—he did not want to come in early, and he had no wish to have a talk, and without question he would have felt that if there was anything really important to talk about, she would not be the one to talk about it *to*.

She was spreading Ruth's towel now on the kitchen table, getting her baby powder out of the cabinet. Leonard scowled and fretted, thinking, his head bent. She had begun to know him and she knew that somehow the reality of her despair, of her waning hopes for this marriage, that he could never discuss, never listen to in words—that nevertheless this knowledge peeped inside him, peeped and blinked like a small bulb of trouble through the dark curtains of his blind self-occupation and unconcern.

THEN THAT evening when he had at last come in from town, he had walked right past her to the kitchen and poured himself a tall glass of milk—she heard him gulping it down in one long thirsty drink. Milk was his major drink all his life; he drank no liquor, not even beer—that was his father's sin. She remembered the long loud drink of milk, but then when she would try to think what happened next, her thoughts would go all ascatter—they flickered and jumped, skipped and slanted like film in the theater out of control. At some point she had opened the brown envelope. At some point she had followed him through the living room into the dining room back to the kitchen—at some point he was refusing to look at what she had in her hand. At some point he was hollering furiously and saying for the first time certain incredible things, and she was setting the terrible precedent of being shocked and shattered by them instead of laughing at them for the jokes they were.

Yes, this had been the first statement of the Leonard doctrine. He said this: that he had earned every red cent they had had since they were married, that she had not brought in a single penny and that until she did, it was not up to her to spend one, it was up to him—because it was his money, all his, since he had earned it by the sweat of his brow, by breaking his back every day loading drinks while she had nothing to do but go to town. He said ever since the day they were married he had paid for every mouthful of food she had put in her mouth and for the clothes on her back. He said it was already breaking him to begin with, all this going downtown shopping every day, buying up all the stores, bringing home great sacks of expensive cloth, for instance, and he didn't know what all else. Whatever it was, he said, they could not afford it. And now on top of this (which most women would be ashamed of if their husbands were working as hard as he was for the few dollars he was able to get for it), she had now pulled this crazy stunt, had played him for a fool in front of the whole town, put him in a position of having to go down to Mr. Tom McDaniels and tell him what he made on his job and apologize for wasting his time (since they were not the kind of people who could ever have anything or buy anything, go into any kind of debt); tell him that his papa, when he had lost his store, had taken nothing out of it whatsoever—except that about once a year a farmer who had owed him a big bill came by with a load of wood or a bushel of corn—and was a pauper and would be a ward on the state if anything happened to *him*, Leonard, or got him into debt.

He said to think that he had married an insane woman and a common whore! And yet he *had*—as could clearly be seen by her attempts to ruin him financially, her persistent attempts to ruin the whole family, to see them all out on the street. Everyone in town knew what she was trying to do— she might as well have had it announced on the radio. Her entire behavior, every word she had said, every move she had made since she had moved in there showed, he said that night, without a shadow of a doubt that she had come with the single purpose of seeing his mother and father in their old age forced out of their house into a room somewhere. He knew she wanted to see them living in one room (which was what a whore *would want*) and that deep down she was jealous of his family's good reputation and the decent clean life they led, in spite of losing everything they had; and what made her so mad she couldn't stand it was that they didn't live like her mother and them in Jacksonville.

Yes this was the first night, the first time, he had used this name against her: *Jacksonville*. (To even speak that word.) He said he knew that what she was hoping and praying for, behind his back, was that he and his parents would end up in a filthy broken-down place like the one *her* people lived

134

in—with steps you could break your legs on and smelly messes that made you sick. *My lord!* Margaret thought, dredging it all back up again. *He never gave such a show as he gave that night!* Yet wasn't it too bad . . . with nobody watching but her?

To think, he had said, that with everything else he had on him, he had had to be fooled into marrying an insane person, someone crazy enough to try to plunge him into a mortgage debt to the tune of thousands and thousands of dollars, whereas anybody with normal sense could see what terrible trouble they were already in . . . and here he had tried to take out his wallet, but his hands were jerking and shaking, and his overall condition was so bad that for a long time he couldn't even work it out of his pocket and then could not get it right-side-up in order to open the fold and show her that right now for instance he did not have a thing in the world but two dollars and some-odd cents— that was all he had! To last them to payday! But of course you could not show a *thing* to a whore, he cried hoarsely (his words choking and scraping in his lathered throat) because to a whore nothing like that mattered or made any sense.

So that night the demon of his wrath began to ride him and whip him on, and it was as if he could hardly see out of his own eyes or speak with his own voice. Yet his curses had been rasped out, nevertheless, and he said it drove him wild every day to think that he had ended up with someone who was off her rocker and who might be carried away to an asylum any day, leaving him to care alone for a motherless child and to apologize to the whole town, to all his friends for instance, for letting himself be played for such a fool, letting his family's name be dragged in the mud by a person who was a whore *and* insane, when one or the other would be bad enough.

This was the doctrine he was putting forth, or something extremely like it that Margaret did not even need this particular memory to supply, since she was to hear it over and over again, with nothing very original added on, for years to come.

Then they were in the kitchen, had arrived there somehow without even realizing it, because by now they hardly knew what house they were in or on what street, and the whole enormous fight blew on, with Margaret lashing out too at first, but then gradually reduced to something else: astonishment and profound incredible hurt, then to weeping, choking, driveling delirium; and then all at once Leonard had completely *blown*, swollen cords of rage working up and down his face, his fierce eyes fixing her in a bulging stare of maddened hatred, and she was springing back, her hand up against his blow, then was crying out and holding her face, weeping hard but still in a kind of choked hysteria. Then he had pulled himself up, still staring, out of his animal crouch, and was suddenly silent, except for his loud horrible breathing, as he tried, like a dead man, to suck up air from his strangled lungs.

It was just at that moment that they had become aware, in the relative silence, of this: the mother and father behind the kitchen door, murmuring, moaning their lamentations, Mrs. Barker crying a little—softly—and being restrained by her husband from opening the door. But then from behind the wall came the mother's *voice*, a small, infinitely sorrowful voice, a tenderly cajoling voice like one might use to a small boy: "Son, do right now. You do right by Margaret now." And even more softly: "Oh Will! Will!" But the father was silent. *He cannot bring himself to reprimand his son. He is hoping that somehow his silence will say what he cannot.* And indeed Leonard, listening to see if his father would speak, was stricken, visibly, by his accusing silence.

Yet there flushed again, rose again in his reddened face, hatred and bitter anger at his wife. For now he hated her not just for her original sin—trying to ruin and destroy him by tricking him into debt for the building of a house—but also for his rage, then his shame and guilt. He hated her equally for them all.

IN THE morning, when Mrs. Barker rose in the cold house, her old long robe about her, the thick braid down her back loosened more than usual by restless sleep (or utter sleeplessness), Margaret heard her lighting the fire in the kitchen stove, and she rose from the couch in the front room where she had lain all night, in her clothes, and slipped into the hallway, leaving no sign, and went into the bedroom where Leonard and Ruth were sleeping, and stood over the crib, her hands on the rails, staring hard at her child, placing her hand, in sober reflection, over the minute round hand of her child's.

Margaret, remembering all this in old age, lying on her own sofa at noontime, between stints of work in the Juvenile Court, thought *Oh children, children, why do we even live and what is life . . . what is the meaning of it? I hate to think of you grown up now, finding out how things really are . . . because even if things in your house are not too bad and there isn't too much meanness and cruelty and despair . . . sooner or later, after all, something else comes—death!—more and more, even if only—at first—in your mind, taking up all the empty seats there . . . so that no matter where you look, there he sits, sitting and sitting.*

*And you look at him. And he looks at you—and you don't know why or what this life is or why it is taken away from us.*

THEN LEONARD'S amnesia. By no visible sign whatever did he betray that he had been the one—himself the one, none other than he—who had come home one night and battered and abused his wife because she had made inquiries, been given information, about the building of a house. No sign whatever that he knew he was the one—un-

137

less it was his exaggerated calm and courtesy, or his pale yet fresh look, like one who had been through something but was getting over it, his strength coming back, the signs of recent suffering receding in his face.

Margaret bore a bruise under her eye. But Leonard never noticed or acknowledged this bruise in any way, nor did his mother and father, though they wept, no doubt they prayed about it in private. As for Margaret's silence and sullenness—that too, though it grieved them profoundly, they made no outward sign of observing. For days and days it was only when she spoke to Ruth that Margaret's voice rose and vibrated; at all other times she spoke a leaden monotone in a voice broken and out of tune, off-pitch, but no one seemed to note such a thing . . . nor did Leonard respond in any way if she herself made any mention of the evening in question.

The brown envelope had been put back in its place. Margaret did not throw it away, yet she hardly thought about it or she thought of it as dead and irrelevant. She fell back on a smaller plan, the barest irreducible minimum plan necessary for their going on. She thought about it without pleasure, her mind cold and clear. She would wait a few weeks and then she would say, "Find us an apartment that you can afford, where we can live on our own. Or I will take Ruth and go."

Then Leonard came in one day from work. He came into the bedroom, pretended to be looking through some things on the dresser. He said, "You had an envelope—a big square one—with some things in it from the builders."

She answered him severely, in her toneless voice. "Of course I had it, but you wouldn't look at it. When I tried to—"

"I thought I saw it out here on the dresser," he said. His back was turned to her. He spoke lightly, calmly.

"Did you think I would leave it around so you—"

"I thought I saw it."

Then she opened the bottom drawer of the chest and took it out. She put it into his hands and left the room.

Later, she was making biscuits at the kitchen table. She could see through the screen door into the yard. Leonard was talking to his father. Such thin small men, such little weak, worried men. They paced about on the packed dirt of the yard. Behind them the garden was freshly broken where the father had been plowing with a borrowed mule.

Then they were all at the table in the dining room. Mr. Barker held Ruth on his lap and fed her a drop of this and that from his plate. He and Mrs. Barker were speaking of life on the street—an old neighbor had moved back to the country, people had come to get her in their wagon. Leonard was not listening, he was eating fast, his head bent over his plate, eyes sunk on his food. Then without warning, he looked up. He said, "I'm thinking about building me a house. I been telling Papa."

Mr. Barker's head dropped. He held Ruth quite still on his lap, and she turned around to look at his face. "The Lord knows I can't tell you what to do," he said. "He knows I'd be the last one to have any say."

Mrs. Barker began to cry. She took a big handkerchief out of the pocket of her apron. "O son, son . . . you little things. Will . . . a thing like that . . . don't let them, don't let these little things . . . ."

Leonard stood up from the table, the white of his hand-kerchief flashing as he wiped his mouth. He said, "If I want to build me a house I will and you better hear me—what I'm saying to you." For a moment he stood by the table, did not walk away, his eyes lidded, scowling, but he was listening to the tune, the special quality, of his parents' wail and lament ("Oh son, son") as if he could tell just by its particular tune what it boded, what substance of just complaint, forewarning, was there, and what sheer fright.

In time the Barkers knew that it was Margaret too—or perhaps Margaret especially—who wanted to do this frightening thing: build a house, go into debt in the middle of the depression, without a penny in the bank to fall back on if Leonard, for instance, were to lose his job, if he were to get sick. Where would they be then? There was much whispering and shaking of heads, private lamentation and carrying on, almost as if death had struck the house. Yet towards their daughter-in-law they were just as gentle and loving as before; it was not that they were angry, they were truly not angry, but just mortally afraid of her innocence, her innocent hopes, doomed to get herself and Leonard and Ruth (oh poorest little thing, poor darling thing) trapped and ruined completely unawares.

In fact it was finally, as much as anything else, their fright and despair by which (though he himself had felt them too, just as keenly) Leonard was driven to forge ahead, by which his delicate little pride was pricked. Did they dare even to suggest that he, father and husband who never missed a day's work, could not put up his own roof over the heads of his family?

Then, fortuitously, and as if to settle the whole case, a small raise was tendered—could it really have been, was it in actual fact, only four dollars a month?—by the slave-driving, penny-pinching boss of the drink company, and then Leonard paid a pale, scowling, wary visit to Mr. McDaniels, and then Mr. McDaniels and Margaret began to study and figure and plan, and the house began to be built.

Not the nineteen-dollar-a-month house, but the thirteen-dollar house. And—*such is human history*, Margaret reflected, *for our lives are such a matter of petty economies*—the six-dollar difference had affected their lives in the most profound way, would end up cutting years off all their life-spans, she did not doubt. Five of them in this little shoe-box house. Five people to live in two bedrooms, a kitchen, a living room, and a miniature dinette into which nothing would fit but a table and chairs. No porch at all, back or front, nothing but stoops. Everything smaller, the whole thing smaller scale, somehow, than she had figured on. And on some of it Mr. McDaniels had simply fooled her and betrayed her.

When she thought of the linen closet in the hallway! The whole hall in fact. It really looked like a practical joke in there. The entire hall was no bigger than a small bathroom—one step across and two steps long was all it was. And it was the matter of the linen closet she had always expressly inquired about, expressly made known her wishes about; she never, no she could never forgive Mr. McDaniels for the linen closet, which was nothing more than a narrow strip of doorless indentation, ceiling tall but no wider or deeper than a good-sized book. She had given it to Leonard for his shotgun. He could prop his gun in it with a few inches to spare and put his boxes of shells on the one ridiculous shelf. So she had had thirty-six years without a linen closet—no decent place to keep her towels and sheets. No, she could not forgive it ever. Even when Mr. McDaniels died, she could not help it, it was the first thing she thought of. "He did me wrong about the linen closet," she had thought. Why in the world didn't women build houses instead of men?

But taking the house all in all—and even though they had gotten the one that was too small, because Leonard had been almost too afraid to get even that—still it had been the right thing to do and she had done it. They had their place that was all theirs, and no one could tell them what to do with it or how to live in it, and at least what there was of it was clean and new and full of light and the floors were pine and the color of honey; when she waxed them, down on her knees, she could see herself in them as in a mirror.

Still, her mind always went back to the thirteen dollars a month, the house's cursed smallness, the closeness. As the other children came along, it oppressed them all more and more, living as they did practically in each other's laps. When it was time for Leonard to come home from work, they didn't have to look at the clock, something would just come over them. The whole house would get still and tense. The children's games, whatever they were doing . . . stopped. And it was not that anyone spoke to them, warned them, referred in any way to their father's coming home. Something just came over them at that time of day. They would quit whatever they were doing and go in the back room, just lie on their beds perhaps, with the door closed, for all the good it did in a house that size. For no one could fail to hear him come in—hear the door bang, his loud voice, hear him stamping and blowing, his case flung against a chair.

Oh the difference in the house when he was there. The amazing difference that a single presence can make if it is alien, unwanted (possibly dangerous), putting everyone on the alert . . . if it is something that cannot be removed but that everyone has to watch out for so it doesn't get them tangled up in it, go off in their face. A presence (like that of a fierce dog, perhaps) known to be vicious at times, though pliant enough on most days, downright cheerful when it was going fishing. (*Still, don't let down your guard!*) When Leonard was in the house, all banter, all light talk, all gay teasing talk—along with any talk that was earnest and seri-ous—ceased among the children; it was not for him, not for his alien ears.

Why Laney grew up without Leonard even knowing she had a sense of humor! One Saturday she came in from a spend-the-night, and it was unusual but two of her friends came with her. Leonard was watching the ball game on TV, something none of them would dare to disturb for a minute, but when the friends came in, he sprang up and grinned and shouted at them to make them feel at home, and they said oh we had such fun, oh we had such a good time, because Laney—and here they just burst into giggles and helpless laughter—because Laney is such a character, such a funny girl, and you know these little crazy acts she does? these acts that she gets up where she—

But Leonard did not know what in heaven's name they were talking about, although of course he pretended he did and began to laugh and shout some more, until they thought he was a terribly jolly person. That night when he climbed in bed, rustling and pulling on the sheets, waking her up, he said to Margaret, "What did they mean? Laney's acts? She's not that type of a person . . . is she?" There was a plaintive tone to his voice that Margaret would hear more times than one as the years went by.

For Leonard, after all, was blind, he was deaf and dumb to other people, and there was a grotesque pity about it that she felt more and more as the years went on and as her own regret became such familiar furniture in her soul's house that she could almost forget it once in a while. He was blind to his children, his wife, though they lived all about him, with him, all of them lashed together on the little narrow skittering boat of a house; half the time he did not see or hear them, feel them or know them.

Though in the years at the Barkers she had just begun to know it (and needless to say she had not known it at all when they were courting, she and that relaxed, smiling, good-natured, normal person that had won her for Leonard, disappeared on her wedding day), she knew in time that the trouble with Leonard was that he himself had contracted the dread Barker-family disease—of merciless and ceaseless inner terror and alarm. The fact that, unlike his mama and papa, he could conceal it so very successfully at will, that it was with him a secret that outsiders rarely even intuited, that he could have hidden it, for instance, for the whole five months of their courtship . . . all of this only meant that it possessed him in a particularly virulent form. She remembered that even after the contract had been signed and Leonard had his finances laid very carefully out and had borrowed the two hundred dollars down-payment from his company and knew how he was going to pay it back—even after all that, his fright came back on him from time to time and he would have a relapse of quaking fear. One day he suddenly had a terrible thought: it struck him, as if for the first time, that in order for people to live in a house it had to have furniture in it; the people had to sleep on a bed and eat at a table. Unless they planned to stand up all the time they had to have some chairs, even a couch; and the food eaten at the table had to be cooked on something—ah-ha . . . a stove . . . and where would all this come from? Who was going to make them a present of all this?

Of course in the end they did what all broke young families do, they begged and borrowed, bought a few pieces secondhand and began to save a few dollars a month for something special; they had saved that way for the maple dining room set, for instance, which they were to eat on all their lives.

But Leonard had shocking premonitions about such things. And for instance, on Harrison Street one day he had said—for no reason and not because anyone had yet even mentioned such a thing to him—"Don't you ever say the word *shrub* to me." She said, "What . . . ?"

"There's not going to be any bushes around that house!" His voice rose. "Don't you ever"—fixing her with his finger, thrusting it almost into her eye—"let me hear that word. And I better not hear anything about any trees or any lawn or any azaleas or camellias or abelias or whatever they are." But she had not said a thing about any work on the yard. She had more or less planned to do it all herself with whatever she could throw together—maybe it wouldn't be a thing but grass seed or cheap plugs of centipede.

Then, from something he said later on, she knew that a certain word that for him was a word of terror—like so many other words—had sprung up in Leonard's mind, and something that had been ready all along to click on in his brain had suddenly clicked on and he had thought, *Yes they have a word for it—for what they do to the yards of new houses—landscaping.* And just thinking of the word for it, this extra, unanticipated word of just the kind he had feared, threw him into a fresh spasm of outrage—it was as if all ruin and starving poverty, all poorhouse beggary and shame was in that word. For had he not known, all along, that in spite of the fact that the whole affair—the building of a thirteeen-dollar-a-month house—sounded so utterly reasonable and possible, so innocent, that there was still a trick in it some-where, a trap that he had walked right over as he had stud-ied his figures, trustfully done his arithmetic . . . ?

Yes there was a catch in it all somewhere and now he had suddenly thought he had seen what it was: it was this *land-scaping* work. And it was as if someone had said, "Well, of course the house itself isn't that much of a deal—it's the *other* stuff, the landscaping and all *that*, that puts you in the poorhouse. It's those bushes around the house and all that sort of thing—and the contract says you've got to do it too—that'll sink you down."

And so naturally in his fear he came down on *her*. And thus it was to be through the years, and as the children grew up, he came down on them too, snorted fire on them all—and though no doubt there were always reasons, fairly spe-cific fears that churned his innards until he had to spew out a stream of burning bile, half the time they did not even know what these reasons were. *No wonder,* Margaret thought, *that today, even all these years later, I can hardly get off my couch to go to work.* She thought with disgust of peo-ple with steady nerves, people that admired themselves for being sane and sensible . . . who would say, "Oh I just don't think it pays—do you?—to let yourself get upset." *You peo-ple!* she thought.

Yet as for Leonard she could not help but pity him for those other, rarer moods of his, when for some reason that dense streaming fog that he lived in seemed to spread away from him, blew wispily away, and squinting and straining, he was able to catch a glimpse of the rest of them. But when he looked into his children's eyes, it was not faces of natural

145

affection and repose he saw, no, he saw no smiling, playful looks of tender interest and regard, but faces banked over, emotions kept away, behind, out of his reach, in reserve for others. There was nothing for him to see—on those infrequent times when he actually *could* see—but eyes that were cool, on sly guard, and he hated to see that, he resented it profoundly.

"Unfair! Unfair!" she knew he would think. Meanspirited, ungenerous children! Coldhearted children without love! Children not normal, mother-raised in some queer, devilish way—to be like this to a father that loves them . . . loves them by god!—and never misses a day's work for them, out on the road rain or shine, no matter what, bringing home the bacon for shoes and clothes, fried chicken and tapioca pudding, gas to drive around on; a father worried sick sometimes that there wouldn't be enough for everything they needed (though thank god so far there *had* been enough—just barely) to live a decent life in a house of their own, have decent friends, look like decent people when they went out the door; a father (amazing, Margaret considered, that he could actually believe it) with no life but his family, who would lie down and die too, for instance, if any of them ever got sick (*lord keep us from that—lord! don't ever bring that on us*), who would not be the same person if anything ever happened to them, who no one would even know for the same man.

Did Margaret realize that? he would demand to know. That he could love them that much and not be loved in return? She saw him shaking his head, muttering to himself, speaking fragments of this to her, from time to time, as if in brave resignation, yet full of self-pity too and perplexity and the natural worry and concern of a loving father—just because he had caught, through his blanket of streaming fog, through a brief parting of his curtain of self-concern, an actual glimpse of his offspring, had heard through that wild wind of himself always whirling something that struck him

146

at last for exactly what it was, the curt indifferent voice of a child, from a cool and empty face. "Unfair! Unfair!" he would think.

Sometimes he spoke of these feelings sorrowfully, in hung-down resignation, and at other times they fed his ferocious rage and he pierced and blasted her with turning his children against him, with robbing him of what was naturally his, taking viciously away the love and respect due a father who was giving his all, spilling his life's blood up and down the blistering Georgia roads calling on every miserable little outhouse—every little woodshed—of a country store, even on people who had no courtesy or respect, who half the time would not even pay the bill when the goods arrived (so that he would have to go back and load them up), on people that didn't want to see him, who would as soon spit on you as look at you, calling even on niggers, yes niggers—and then to get what he got at home just because (steaming up now, hitting the main highway of his wrath now) his wife, a notorious whore known all over Georgia and Florida for escaping from a crazy house in Jacksonville, did not know a thing about normal children and could not raise them to have any normal respect for their father, even though he was the one all the pressure was on, who was out there no matter what the weather was, in the furnace of summer heat for instance, his back so soaked with sweat he would be stuck fast to the driver's seat, while she was at home taking naps with the fan on her, reading magazines, talking on the phone whenever she felt like it, listening to things on the radio, with nothing to do but turn the children against him! and make up no telling what kinds of lies and exaggerations about him, telling them to hate him ("You must hate your father," yes she could just hear herself) and to always show disrespect for him just because—a working man with no one to turn to if things got out of hand, if trouble ever came—he couldn't stay home all day like she did and play her little games, tell them secrets about *her*, tell them she was a whore (though wasn't he telling them now?) and that she had been raised to be one, deliberately, in Jacksonville, so that her grandmother had had to go get her before it was too late . . . although it *was* too late.

Too bad he hadn't left her where she was, he said, instead of bringing her home off the street (which street, she had wondered) and giving her a home, although of course he realized he had been stupid too, dumb enough to have felt sorry for a whore. Hadn't his family tried to tell him? Hadn't god knows how many people around the dairy, for instance, tried to tell him about Mrs. Culp's granddaughter and what she was and where she came from? What he was getting into marrying a whore and hoping she would straighten up and fly right?—be a normal mother?—raise kids with a normal respect for their father? *Lord god!*

Margaret—remembering—had risen up on her elbows on the couch, stung by all this again. *Leave him! Get rid of him—* she counselled herself, the young wife. *Go ahead! Make up your mind to it!*

And yet—this was strange, oh this was a strange and baffling thing: it was just when his old bad crazed face loomed over her again, streaming demonic rage, his eyes bursting, his monster mouth twitching with blood lust to devour her, swallow her up for her unredeemable evil and vicious folly, her famous whoredom . . . it was just then, as she shrunk once more from the blaze of his fury, that another image suddenly fell upon the first, was suddenly thrown by something, somewhere (*oh where do these things come from?*), taking her breath away every time, making her weep with sudden pity and surprise—the image of his hand stretched out to her in death, his darkly leathered hand held out to her in supplication . . . no, in simple love.

And from behind this image, from lips she could not see now, came a voice, broken . . . no, simply say, a voice not of this world. *Margaret.*

Then the image of herself coming into the room in her nightgown, cold cream on her face and still on her hand when she took his, his voice above the extended hand speaking her name (though *speaking* is not the word): "Margaret."

Then the stricken face, in her remembrance, coming clear—a face in deep-drawn anguish (yet no, there was also something in it of instant resignation), staring upwards to her, lips working, as she leaned to him to say, to speak, lips forming not the terms "Help me, pity me," no, not saying "This death—take it off of me, get it away from me!" No, not that kind of thing at all, those kinds of words or looks, but instant foreknowledge, resignation. And these words— formed with broken breaths, with shredded voice already speaking from the dead, *"Remember.* I loved you."

Then herself and the phone, men arriving. And this gallant word more from him to the stretcher-bearers, being lifted away: "You'll never make it boys." And that the last.

The party of them, she and the ambulance men, in front of the house in the fresh cool night air. The indifference of the evening, somnolent.

Then the silence had taken him. Silence and darkness came for him over the lawn. The houses on the street quiet behind curtained lights, making no outcry. The pine trees saying not a word, barely trembling; the sound of distant TV, image of someone yawning in his slippers, rising to change the channel, an ordinary night. The party of them at the back of the ambulance, her robe unbuttoned, blown gently by a small soundless breeze.

"Sure am sorry ma'am, nothing we could do."

"No."

Silence and darkness had entered and filled him, joining him to the ancient void of history, of all time. *Oh you silence, you stillness, of death—if I could peer after you, even a little ways.*

~

HE HAD been watching TV, a football game. She hated football, had been in the bedroom, putting on cold cream. He had been getting too excited, muttering to himself, jerking forward in his chair, crying, "Get that rascal! Get 'im!"

Not an old man. Sixty years old, no, sixty-one. But his body full of wounds—packed, bloated with wounds; festered, flayed with the sounds of all those inner battles through the years, fear against fear, worry against worry fighting it out inside him; and even pleasure, excitement, good news as well as bad news, any news at all, tightening him up, making his blood, his breath, work and struggle, push and press to flow through his choked, wrung, squeezed body, and the great pyramid of accumulating wound-strains and stress-blows piling over him, snowing him under, mashing his body fuels and fluids into threadlike paths, finally squeezing them shut.

And then this that he had said: *Remember. I loved you.*

Words not for himself, but for her, so that at the bottom of him (was it not true?) there really was something other than self-occupation and concern. In the extremis of death there was not just *Help me, care for me, save me, pity me, me me me,* but this: "I loved you. *Remember.*"

Of course one could take so many views of things, and nothing was ever simple and clear, and one could say, she supposed, that this too was a form of self-preoccupation, an insistence still on the *me* of him: remember *me,* my love for you, don't forget how I felt, that I loved you . . . *I* . . . *I* . . . .

But no. Surely, in the instant of death, it was truly not himself he was full of, not himself he could not let go of, no it was not fear even that seized him, as odd as that was, the one time he was completely entitled to it. Wasn't it true, couldn't she see now, that all along, behind, beyond, all that tension, that worry and agitation that closed him in and filled him up, his eyes, ears, head and heart, so that he could

150

hardly see or perceive the rest of them . . . that beyond, no inside all that, in the inside core of him, was something else . . . .

In their later years together she had already begun to know this, and he had entered what seemed almost like a new period of his life. With the children gone, all that responsibility lifted, with money matters finally smoothed down and evened out, with him free at last of company bosses, working only for himself now and doing pretty well, no longer afraid to open the mail, take out his bank statement; his wife with her own decent job, her little paycheck mostly her own now, with children out of school—with all that, things had begun to be very different, and there had come to be a life between them that the children (it was such a pity) never knew.

Yes somehow, in his later years, his body, his nerves, had let up on him. And in the late afternoons after work, for instance, she would be lying up on her high bed in the back bedroom she had taken for her own; she would be lying up there with her girdle off (thank god), in her slip or perhaps her duster, resting from the day's work at the office, thinking in the back of her mind about supper, reading the *Ladies Home Journal* or some story or other from the library, lying comfortably back with two softly-frilled, queen-sized pillows behind her head (with her Granny-learned love of things that were soft and pretty, clean and comfortable); and he would come into the house from some little errand, or just a little drive down to the Bluebird Cafe, would come into the bedroom and sit down in an offhand, companionable, intimate, husbandly way in a soft chair near her bed, and she would lay the magazine over her stomach to keep her place and they would have a languid, sighing, absentminded talk about the day's happenings, about mail from the children, about the comings and goings of people in the town, or some particular interesting or surprising or humorous thing, or even nothing at all, just sighing and stretching, half-dozing in the late pine-filtered sun through her gauzy windows, letting enough time go by so that something could pass between them that they wanted to let pass.

In those late years they had taken that beat-up old crumpled rag, their marriage, and tried to straighten and smooth it out, and then he had said, at the moment of death, when she was full of terror and he, of all strange things, was not, *"Remember. I loved you."*

So she must try to remember . . . that in spite of everything, one man—though he almost drove her as mad as he said she was—had loved her in his way all his life, had never wanted anyone but her, had died reminding her of his love. And wasn't that, when you thought of it, rather a rare and splendid thing? or was it just common? Oh it was vexing to try to think it through.

If memory were only a simpler thing . . . and did not tie you up in such clumsy tangles, batten down your limbs in such jumbled ropes you never could break free. When today someone said, "I know you miss that old Leonard—I bet you still think of him all the time," she would say yes she did, she thought of him quite a lot. "But I think of them all," she thought. "Every Leonard I knew. I think of them one at a time and all together, and every way you can imagine—so no wonder memory is such a tiring thing."

She remembered the one who came to the dairy, a master of deceit, courted her and married her; she remembered the Leonard who took over from him and ruled her in that vast realm of regret on Harrison Street and even in the new fresh house on Suwannee Drive; then the one who laid down at last his weapons against her, his half-senile rage so reduced he could almost strum it completely out on the soft arm of her bedroom chair.

In the late afternoons she had lain on her high bed and watched the sun's late colors touch her curtains. Leonard would sit way back in the chair.

"Did you think you would fix us anything to eat?" he would say.

"I don't know . . . I don't even know what I want, do you?"

He sighed; he yawned. Time passed. "I don't know-w-w . . . ," he would say, but by the time he answered, he had almost forgotten what the question was.

*Oh it's almost silly,* she would think—*all this ridiculous peacefulness between us, this calm and quiet in the house.*

He would take the keys from his pocket, let them drop in his hand, jingling slightly—as if he were trying to judge by the sound itself whether to take them out to the car or not. "What if I run down and pick us up some barbecue at the barbecue place?"

A little later she had closed her eyes, without even hearing the door bang, though maybe she was just too used to it to hear it anymore. Even with her eyes closed she had been able to see the dusky sun playing still over her pretty room. *Such a good time of day,* she would think, and then almost with surprise it would occur to her that she was not unhappy, that perhaps this was what happiness was. *At this moment at least, I'm happy*—yes that had been her thought.

But it was as if other moments existed too, at the same time, and that she could think, not only darkly back, but forward as well, even to a widow-woman lying alone on her brocade couch at noontime, flattened under a whole fallen sail of memory, thinking of Leonard gone to get the barbecue—and so much else.

## ~ CHAPTER FOUR ~

AND yet as grateful as she was for that brief respite at the end, the winding out, winding down, of his fear-wounded, rage-wearied body and mind, the gradual dispersing, the misting and curling away of that streaming fog of blindness and isolation that clung to him, in the invisible center of which he lived like his own prisoner (yes he was in there somewhere); for the slow lifting and unlocking, in other words, of his quarantine; for the achievement on his part of some semblance of tenderness and kindliness, some recognition of what was outside and beyond himself—of her, for instance, as a separate person, actually alive like he was, with actual worries and fears of her own and a potential not quite completely ruined even now for small pleasures he might actually contribute to . . . as grateful as she was for all that, still those other, earlier Leonards (conspiring with, attuning themselves very shrewdly to, certain elements and people in her early life) had already defeated her, plunged her too deep in her lake of gloom for her to ever quite rise free again, breathe normal air.

When Leonard (the first Leonard) had married her, he had married someone already dream-robbed . . . if she on her part had concealed anything, she supposed that was what it was. She had not told him, after all—though perhaps this was what she had *tried* to tell, on the road to Jacksonville—that she was already a splintered person, her adolescence broken in two by a father full of love, then of betrayal and deceit, by a grandmother beautiful and strong, protecting but betraying too just as surely, leading her into guilty abandonment of helpless people who belonged to her and needed her.

She saw herself driving up a certain narrow dirt street in the old round green humpbacked Ford.

*She pulls up in front of the house and sits in the car to collect her breath, her head bent, frowning, her face in a stiff droop of dread and perturbation. Ruth and Laney are in the back seat. They are little birdlet girls, chirping to get out of the car.* "Out, out," Laney says, working her wee fingers on the door latch. Ruth raps her hand in play, twitting her like she does her dolls. "You bad girl." But Laney is perfectly serious, she wants "out, out," wants to get out and run into Grandma's house, so she can be given as quickly as possible, can be sure it is still there, the particular something that Grandma has which they both have come for.

Margaret hears only dimly the little quarrel of the children, because her own mind is reeling, struggling into quavering focus. She turns her glance to the house, and her consternation is deepened just by the sight of the porch, where the front door is wide open, with no screen, so that any passing stranger can see right into what ought to be decent privacy, can see the old red-brown rug, the ragged worm of its curled-up edge.

"You bad girl," Ruth says, and Margaret reaches back to them. Now Ruth has the door lock pulled up. It is a hard one to lift in this old car, with so many things old and broken and stiff, but she has pulled it up and now released the door latch too, so by the time Margaret has come around to the door, the children are down—jumping, in fact, from the running board. Then they all start out; the little birdlet girls skip and chirp across the high weeds and the rubbish scattered through them. There is no walk, though there is something like an old dirt path, mostly obscured, which they don't even look for, and which Margaret half-remembers is full of sandspurs anyway. Then they reach the wooden steps, which are half-askew and which tilt under them a little bit, and cross the dirty narrow porch to the open door.

In the back shadows of the room there is a rough shape sprawled in a big dark chair, her legs spread wide and her hand between them. *Barbara.* Her hand feels languidly, absently, between her legs; her head is back, in shadows. Margaret pauses in the doorway, with the little girls rustling and peeping behind her skirts now—strangeness, shyness suddenly touching and restraining them. Margaret stands with her stern drooping face, her eyes glaring and yet glazed, gazing fiercely on something which is in the room but also far beyond. She thinks a familiar thought, silly and inept, ludicrously out of keeping with the practical needs of the occasion: "Whoever *did* this, *does* this to human creatures— somebody ought to take him and wring his neck for him." The little girls peep around her legs, venture a step or two beyond the tether of her skirt. Margaret thinks, "I am here, so I must go in now," and she steps forward into the room, and Barbara, her sister, hears her, sees her at last from her back shadows and calls in a damp crippled voice, "Maga, Maga!" and then—in her almost secret language, a dialect known to only a very few privileged persons—"Da-you-eh-it-Maga?" *That you, ain't it, Maga?*

Barbara's words are wet and slippery. She is grown—long since a grown woman—but does not know how to blow her nose, and so most of the time it is so stuffed up she has to breathe through her mouth, so that her mouth is open all the time, and when she speaks she must speak through the thick web of saliva that spreads between her lips. Margaret has thought this before but today she thinks again, "If I could just get her to clear her nose, finally get her to do it before I go home tonight—it would be such a blessing."

The little girls venture to the door of Grandma's room, look inside, look back at Margaret. "Wait till Grandma comes," Margaret says, and they are a little peeved, because they know where the treasure is, the one they have come for. Margaret looks at them in Grandma's door. Ruth is not chubby now, she has been out of that stage for a good while, she is almost skinny, such a pretty little shape in her fresh cotton dress, which is homemade and therefore, unlike most children's clothes, a perfect fit, a perfect length for instance. The skirt flounces just right on her slender thighs. How clean and fresh, pink and decorous Ruth is, how intelligent, how sly and perky her little freckled face. And Laney is in her chubby stage, still has her rosy baby skin, oh she has a darling rose of a face, and she is wearing a dress that Margaret loves, with a high bodice, so attractive, so smart on a plump little girl her size.

So Margaret, looking at her children in this particular house, almost begins to cry, she hardly knows why. Of course even at home, she can hardly believe sometimes how beautiful they are and has to go and look at them, to be sure it is true—but here, in this particular doorway, oh there is a sadness and absurdity and pity and splendor about it that almost makes her cave completely in before she's even taken a look at things.

Yet she moves forward, she gives Barbara a hug and pets her cheek, her head. She pulls back a thick strand of hair, and when pity comes, everything is full of it, even this good thick head of hair that Barbara has.

"How're y'all doing?" she says to Barbara. "How's George and Riley?"

Barbara speaks in her almost secret language, "You puh-ee, eh-you, Maga? You ni-' eh-you?" *You pretty, ain't you, Maga? You nice, ain't you?*

"Where's Mama?" Margaret says.

"You want see Mama, don't you, Maga?"

"Where is she?"

"Ma go ge-you suh-uh." *Mama gone to get you something.* "You want something, don't you, Maga?"

Ruth and Laney are still at Grandma's door, playing a twisting game on each other's hands.

Then they hear a stirring in the yard, and suddenly Margaret's mother is bustling and blustering toward the porch, on a slant across the yard, holding a grocery bag against her chest and crying loudly, absently, to a tall thin man who jerks behind, taking short, rabbity steps, hurrying to keep up.

Then, inside the house, there is great rejoicing, with the grandmother seizing each of the three guests in turn, repeatedly, in at least a triple series of embracings; with Riley hugging too, after his fashion, stretching out stiffly his long arms and clasping the shoulders of the others to shake and rock them; and Bobba as well (with no sense of belatedness), once she remembers how it is done, the two of them working hard to contribute their incompetent noises to the grandmother's carolling song of welcome.

Then this grandmother, a sturdy woman with no fat, made, it almost seems, entirely of strong bone, a person full of goodwill and sociability, her leanness eloquent in a loose print beltless dress, her feet in loose slippers intended for house-shoes, sings and babbles her way into the kitchen, clears a space out of the clutter on the kitchen table, and sets there the Moon Pies and the cold sweating bottles of Orange Crush.

There is a swift, chaotic search for a bottle opener, and it is finally found, not in the kitchen at all, but in an ashtray behind a chair in the living room. Then at last—fat bottles of Orange Crush all around. Laney's bottle is as big as she is—and yet she thrusts back her head and holding it with both hands, takes a long, gulping drink. Margaret is terribly afraid she will spill it on her dress, but she is a careful, competent little girl and she does not spill a drop. And oh it is *so-o good*. For after all this is a grandmother who is not about to forget, who cannot possibly forget, what little girls' favorites are, and who is certainly not going to tender—why goodness no, why never in this world—an old brown Coca-Cola to a little person who craves a big bright Orange Crush. Thus, to these little ones she is naturally a perfectly acceptable grandma—more than acceptable, one of the most cheerful, for instance, and the most admiring. "Why ain't they pretty Maga? Ain't they smart? Look here, Bobba, ain't they the sweetest little things?"

And then, with their nice cold bottles of drink feeling so fat in their little hands, they are taken right into the bedroom, which is just where they want to go, and straight to the dresser—and from the bottom drawer Grandma takes out the fabulous brimming chest, an old dime-store jewel box of coppery metal and studded glass, its legs long worn off to silly stubs. But it is loaded with treasure, and Grandma says, "Oh-h my, look at this, look at what Grandma's got, look what we got here," and then she gets down an old flowery ragged blanket (which is kept way up on top of something tall) and carries on over it too *(Why look-a-here)* as if it is a treasure itself, and spreads it on the dark wooden floor; the little girls sit down politely on the blanket, facing each other, their crossed legs knee to knee, and Grandma takes the box of treasure in her bony hands, and almost singing with pleasure and delight, dumps it in a brilliant pile between them!

Then studiously, with utter seriousness and concentration, the little girls go to work, and hardly move the entire afternoon—feeling and trying, looking and turning, matching and sorting, wondering over, examining like little jewelers, the gems of colored glass and cheap obsidian and make-believe silver and gold. The treasure collection, the jewel hoard, is a kind of mad stew of items long since dissolved into parts and pieces; no doubt not a single earring still has its mate, or necklace its chain, or pin its clasp. Yet this vessel is full of bright, interesting, mysterious little objects and fragments, appendages of this or that, even small stray knobs, of glass or bright metal, buttons even, if there is anything special about them to have caught Grandma's eye, and a great many tiny ceramic figures, dogs and kittens and frogs and squirrels. In fact, a great deal of the collection is of the small-animal world that Grandma loves so much; she loves all wee frisky things, and as always has a little dog or two around the place.

So the little girls play with Grandma's treasure, making finally a sort of design on the old blanket, with rows and circles of items of the same kind—a whole line, for instance, of old tarnished watch-heads, spotted and streaked.

Then, in the front room, Riley, standing by the window, always his favorite place to stand, begins to say, "Nma, nma," in that most mangled of the mangled dialects of Eighth Street, and then something else that even Margaret can hardly understand. So then her mother goes to see, crying, "Gaw, Gaw! Maga! Here come Gaw!" On the porch, then, is big hulking George, and behind him, at the bottom of the steps, Margaret's father.

Margaret goes to the door. She hugs George. She tells him how good he looks and what a pretty shirt he has on. Her mother is beside herself she is so excited about George's new shirt. She says, "Look at Gaw! Bobba, look at Gaw. Maga! Maga, look at Gaw new shirt!" And in fact, wasn't that why? Yes, that was why George had been taken away, even as Margaret had been expected, so his daddy could buy him a shirt, because he had not had a shirt to put on.

Then her father on the walk, and she in the door. Huge George behind her in the room, the idiot melee rising again, sounds of garrulous George—grinning, round-faced, good-natured George, thrilled to the bone with his new shirt, with Orange Crush and Moon Pie, with Ruth and Laney, giving them great fat hugs. Riley's noises too, his thirty years' frustration. The voice of Bobba: "You ga new shirt, Gaw? Tha you new shirt Gaw?"

But as for Margaret, something else. Herself in the door and her father on the walk. She might have done nothing more than stand where she was, spoken to him from there, slightly shadowed. Said, *Yes I'm fine, how are you?* But inside her that day—she recalls it only too well—an emotion flew, made a thin sharp flight.

*Remembering this emotion at noontime, these many years later, she raises herself on her elbows, on the sofa, and it flies again the same flight.* And indeed on that day back in Jacksonville she had done a certain thing. Not for herself, but for him. She had stepped out onto the porch, into the light sun, for no reason but for him to see her clearly. Yes she had done this, had stepped out. Feeling his desire—though she did not want to. Feeling, in spite of herself, how pretty she looked to him in her pale batiste dress (with *all that . . . all that* behind them in the front room), seeing the way he took in, so nearly silently, the clean, summery, delicate swirl of her skirt pressed smooth, the light fluff of her hair. Feeling, in other words, his need (*yes I did feel it, that was possible at certain moments*) that nevertheless he did not press. Her knowledge of his pleasure, his surprise.

So she had made this small concession, which was much more than she needed to, much more than was his father's right, relinquished long ago. Yes she remembered so well walking out on the porch, in the sun, so he could see her clearly, see her face and hair, see her pretty dress, and hear her say, at this closer range, the few things they normally said to each other.

In nothing that was spoken on these occasions did either of them ever allude to any estrangement, any alienation, any conflict between them now or in the past. What they said was of no consequence whatever. How're you feeling, how was your trip, how's Leonard, don't you look good. You too. Well honey—hitching up his pants, always half falling beneath his drooping stomach—*I've got to be getting on back* . . . as if he actually did.

THEN the afternoon going on, and Margaret putting on over her dress not just an apron but an old housecoat she had brought with her to clean her mother's house in. And everything far worse than it ever was—worse, far worse even than in the earlier house on Clark Street. *Thank god I never had to live on Eighth Street,* Margaret thought. *Never had to spend a night there, though I could never have slept, there was no kind of medicine that would have put me to sleep on Eighth Street.* But she put on the duster, and aggravated, grim-faced (if she was going to do something, she wondered why she could not have done it with a little more good nature), with a box of supplies she had gotten from the car (rags and brushes, soap and Mr. Clean or whatever it was), she began to scrub and clean, and to get rid of awesome, amazing junk, like no one but her—surely—had ever even seen before, it seemed to her. Wiping and scraping behind things and on things, in cabinets and drawers. She would go through the whole house like she was on fire—in one afternoon.

Of course later, that night, when she rolled back into her own driveway, she knew she had done it; sometimes, after trips like this, she absolutely wept with fatigue, and from the whole confusing and depressing thing, from a world made that way, where things could *be* that way—and could hardly get out of the car. Yes that was where it hit her; the drive home would take her last breath and she would hunk over at the wheel in the driveway, while the little girls, and later her last-born, her son, would be bleary-eyed, having gone to sleep on the way home, and would be climbing out in the dark, and then the porch light would be coming on, and Leonard would be on the stoop, impatient, blaring at them—*What is it? What's the matter? Come on in!* but glad to see them. Yes, whenever they were gone, even for a day, he missed them, wanted them back, wanted them always to be there, on Suwannee Drive, even when he was not, to constitute his family. By dark he would have been back home from his runnings around the town, a little worried not to have found them home before him, then glad and relieved when they drove up—too relieved to be angry and have a fit, although actually by his reckoning he was entitled to one, since he had always told them to be safely home before dark.

Margaret could see him, still, waiting on the stoop, hollering for them to come in, and herself actually weeping slightly, over the wheel.

Then when they *were* in and the children were being put in the tub, given a snack if they needed it (not of course by him—no matter what she had done, or been through, no matter how dead-tired she was, it never occurred to either of them that he could do anything about it other than stand and watch), he would offer his one line of polite inquiry. —How was your mother? —Oh, they're all right.

She could never be absolutely sure, because most of the time it seemed as if the beast rode him whenever it wanted to ride, but generally speaking—partly because of his definite relief to get them back, not to have them dragged in dead off the highway—this would not be one of his times to go crazy, or to throw one of his fits of blame and accusation over the money she sent her mother, the five dollars every two weeks. Sometimes she would have taken the five dollars with her, if it was due, and no doubt he would be feeling his normal turn about it, and yet something told him this was not the time to go berserk.

Of course over the years she heard plenty about those five-dollar checks; sometimes she seemed to hear almost nothing *but* that. And yet—whether he could actually have been so furious about it . . . or whether it was just one of the vicious things the old devil knew he could pull out to torment her with, she actually could not figure out, but she never got used to it, she never got numb to it, it was a tried and true club to beat her down, and probably that was all he wanted it for, and sometimes she would imagine herself saying—to a lawyer, in case that terrible need ever came—or to the judge himself, "Yes I'm asking for a divorce."

"And why are you asking for this divorce?"

"Because of the five dollars."

"The five dollars?"

"Yes."

"You will have to explain this to the court."

"Well my mother"—here, in her fancy, she clenched her handkerchief and looked away, and it was as if she was afraid she herself was going to be found guilty and given a punishment just for having such a mother to begin with—"is divorced, and she lives alone with three children" (should she say *retarded* children?) "in a small house in Florida. My father still supports her as well as he can"—and that was true, whatever was true or not true, that was true and a fact of the case—"but he is remarried and has *that* wife to support too. So there is really not enough. My mother does not have enough and I am the only one besides my father"—say this without emotion, she counselled herself, if you possibly can—"who can possibly help her out, and even though my husband only makes sixty dollars a week, I feel that we can get by and still send my mother"—*my mother after all, no matter what*—"five dollars every other week. I don't think that's too much to send."

She looked down—she turned all the blurred planes of her glasses on the wadded handkerchief in her hands.

"And you say that your husband . . . are you saying that he does not feel that he can accept the responsibility?"

"Your honor, most of the time I have sent it, but he makes the biggest fuss you've ever seen, *every time*. He never forgets it, he can't get that five dollars off his mind. When things break down. Whenever we go to the doctor. Or when

164

the grocery bill goes up. When one of the children has to go on a trip, or buy something for school. He says we don't have it, we can't do it, we're already behind. We're in bad trouble and we'll never get out of it—because of my mother. *Having to support your mother*, he'll say."

"You mean—he is referring by 'support' to the ten dollars a month you send her? Is that the support you mean?"

"Yessir, your honor."

The judge looks at her husband, and Margaret looks at him too now—through the judge's eyes, and it is deeply satisfying.

Of course he has his hang-dog look. He scowls, in studied seriousness, his mouth drooping so low it seems to drag on his neck. The judge leans forward, to peer the better at him, partly out of simple curiosity. *What sort of creature do we have here?* Margaret and the judge lock him tight in their accusing stare.

So COMING in from Jacksonville, where she had perhaps deposited the five dollars, and even made her mother go right to the store with it and buy certain things other than Coca-Cola and cigarettes, she would think with particular bitterness, and with these particularly vengeful fantasies, about Leonard's old low-down ravings about this little bit of help for her mother; in bed she would be too dog-tired to sleep and she would think about it some more until a fantasy of revenge would come that satisfied her. Yes she would be lying there dog-tired, absolutely worn to a frazzle from the day-long spasm of heavy work. Her shoulders and arms would be stiff, and sometimes her neck would have a crick in it from mopping the kitchen walls.

Not that she was not used to work, she had plenty of her own at home . . . and in fact, Margaret thought, peering into her own young woman's mind of years ago, wasn't it true that for her, work had sometimes been—was, without a doubt, at her mama's on those Jacksonville Saturdays—not just something that had to be done, for the job itself (though god knows it *did* have to be done, and there was no one to do it but her), but also a drug, an escape? She had poured herself into it, driven herself mindless on it, got herself drunk on it, whipped herself so hard and fast that her brain simply filled up with motion and exertion and sheer almost violent labor, and so could not hold anything else, and that actually if there had not been the work to be done, she could not have stayed in her mother's house a single hour, since the truth was that she had almost nothing else to do or say in that house.

Whatever little laughings and teasings, what little talk, gossip, what silly little games and carryings on might have been possible with her mama, her sister and brothers, somehow she had been incapacitated for them by simple weakness of spirit—so that she gave strength of body instead—and by her shame, her self-pity. Wasn't that true?

*Now let me think this out,* she told herself once more, thinking it all over again, years later, at home from the Court at noontime. *Let me take all these feelings and facts and line them up, see what they mean.* It was a fact that unlike certain others in the family, she had not been able to simply abandon them, the ones in Jacksonville. (Mark it down.) But on the other hand, she was not sure she could quite love them either, it seemed as if she could not truly, truly care for them . . . and yet *in a way she did* . . . and George, for instance—why George was a good old thing, he just was, that was all there was to it. And take Mama—wasn't there something, hadn't she honestly always felt that there was something about her, in spite of everything, that was brave and jolly, something that never was, never would be, broken completely down? And when she thought of it, it was also true (another fact of the case) that though people might get terribly discouraged with her, no one actually disliked her; no her mother was actually the best old thing in the world and whatever she had was yours, and she would not have wished anything bad on anybody for anything, and what she mainly wanted was just for people to enjoy themselves.

Margaret considered this closely and she thought, *At least I was able to see this—that this was one of the truths about her (almost a fact, though); at least I could see it and it might not have been possible to see such things without love so maybe there was a certain amount of love involved.*

Perhaps the trouble had been that her pity for them, her fear for them, her fierce anger that they should have been as they were, had to be put up alongside another anger—the two of them mixed in like fire with fire, these two angers flaming, feeding each other forever: her rage, that is, that almost no one should care for them, that their own people should leave them, like Hansel and Gretel, to die in the forest, should not take them and love them and give them all they had and forgive them for what they were . . . and that all these angers, this compound of angers, would not behave (any more than Leonard's would) and went wildly astray sometimes; it was almost as if a heap of angry coals burned her hands until she threw them crazily off in the wrong direction and they landed on Eighth Street itself.

So possibly you could even say, she supposed, that it was love itself (although if it *was* love, it wasn't worth much to the ones being loved) that threw her, at the mere sight of her family in Jacksonville, into such a shudder of emotion that she could hardly bear to be there and could never, no never, simply relax, accept what had to be accepted once for all, talk and tease, laugh and chatter with them, smile and coax, listen to them trying to tell, trying to say. . . . She couldn't—so instead she tore blindly into the filthy house, took her crazy vengeance on the dirt and junk and on her mother's willful negligence, her shiftlessness. She made them all scrub and tote (for what silly good it did), sent her mother down the block to the laundermat with a load of clothes tied up in a huge knot in a dirty sheet—banished her

167

poor mama to the washomat on the sacred day of her daughter's visit. No wonder she had hated to see the basket of supplies come out, but child that she was, another side of her was pleased; and as the day went on, she would be more and more distinctly gratified and pleased with Margaret's labors on her behalf.

When it was all done, things put to rights, the beds clean for once, floors swept, things cleared and stacked, when the place had achieved a semblance, at least, of order and normalcy, and Margaret herself would be leaving, bone-tired, a pulp of battered flesh, her mother would be out on the porch and her voice would be rising lyrically, and she would be inviting the neighbors who were passing by on the street to come in and view the house in its wonderfully transformed state, to stop in and see with their own eyes what her daughter (who loved her so much) had done and how smart she was. But this was a faculty her mother had had, and it was a precious faculty, a faculty superior possibly to any faculty of Margaret's own—that is, her ability to make the best of whatever came along, to turn everything to account. She had not wanted to clean and tote—not on her daughter's visiting day . . . but then if it had to be done, why she did it. When Margaret went right on anyway, why she flew in too and did as she was told, marched off, almost singing, to put the clothes in, her dimes in her pocket ("Careful now—you don't have a hole in it, do you?"), let her disappointment rise into pleasure and pride.

"Maga smart, ain't she, kids?"

"You like things nice Maga?" George would say. "You like it pretty here?"

And Bobba: "You i-ih-pu-ee Maga?"

Margaret saw the road again, saw herself driving home to Waycross, her pain, her anger, glaring out of her as she stared at the dusky road, the little girls lying together on the back seat, getting very drowsy, their hands clutched sweatily on their little souvenirs from Grandma's treasure box, awarded them by Grandma for being so good, so smart, for loving Grandma so much and for cleaning and sorting out her jewelry box for her. *What to think of such a mother—what in the world to think?*

Margaret lay on her sofa, saw gloomily out of the corner of her eye her programs flickering by unwatched on the TV, pondered these old issues once again. To spend so many years trying to figure things out—and not to have gotten any further than she had got! Always trying to start over again at certain natural starting points. To have a mother, to begin with, who was not right, was such a dark, peculiar thing . . . she had not known anybody else who *had* that, who had to come up, from the start, against the fact that the world . . . that at the very core of things something was badly wrong. (Poor planning somewhere, that was for sure.) But of course other people were stronger than she was, would have handled it better, she did not doubt—for instance, they might even have joked about it sometimes. If they had had such a mother, they probably would not have been so defensive about her, so ready to condemn others—so tempted to take hold of others and shake them and make them *see* . . . that such a person must never be blamed for anything, that she could not do any wrong, any more than her children could, that she wasn't capable of it . . . . And yet she, Margaret, with her fuddled old mind had not followed her own advice, had blamed others for blaming her mother while she herself had blamed her too.

"Maga, you feel bad, don't you? You got a headache, ain't you, Maga?"

"This place. The way it is. The way you live. The kitchen. That stove in there."

"You don't feel good, do you?"

"That stove. It's never cleaned. No matter what kind of mess it's in. I don't believe it's ever even wiped off."

"But you know that old stove cooks? It cooks good, don't it, Gaw?"

169

"Not even the grease wiped off. I have to scrape it with a spatula."

"Maga can really clean. She was always good to clean, wasn't she, Gaw?"

Margaret saw herself glaring over the stove, then over the wheel of the car, having to strain a little to see the narrow gray road in the falling dusk, darkness gathering in the woods beyond. She had felt so suspended, so caught between evils, if that was the word. It wrung her, it pulled her body as tight as a rope to look back down the road to Eighth Street, but it wrung her too to look up ahead to Waycross, to Suwannee Drive, to her husband lying in wait in who knew what kind of mood, though generally he did know, even he, that he would have to spare her on the day she went to Jacksonville. As little as he could realize, intuit, about things outside himself, still something worked its way through that dense fog of his stranded self and told him that her limit, her measure of endurance, had been reached.

Of course the Jacksonville trips were something he didn't approve of at all; to him wheeling up and down that particular road was nothing but a waste of gasoline, no good could ever come of it and she was just butting her head up against a stone wall, and to take her own children—*into all that . . .* well he felt entitled to be angry and to go off like a bomb if he wanted to, and so when he did not, he was full of admiration for himself. But she remembered, on that road— mostly a lonesome road through deep pine woods, except where two raggledy towns intervened—the feeling of being caught, of frustration on every side, up the road and down the road, nowhere to turn, no escape from trouble except the road itself. *We travellers between worlds of pain . . . and failure . . . not knowing what to do, where to turn . . . .*

The little girls would be falling asleep on the shadowy back seat, in each other's arms . . . or in later years, with the little body of a sleeping boy snugly wrapped between. *Little children . . .* Margaret thought, drowsily, lying on her sofa, and certain small sliding movements seemed to take place in her mind, and she closed her eyes so she could try to think more clearly, once and for all, about the beautiful trust of little children and how anyone (how she herself) could possibly bear to abuse this trust . . . or even the trust of children that happened to be grown up. She wondered why people failed to see in each other the child's need that never grows up or goes away, that as far as she could tell people still had on their last day on earth and she too would have.

On her sofa, Margaret frowned and closed her eyes tight. She did not want to see the gathering mass of human faces wanting her to look at them, wanting her to acknowledge their pleading looks, she did not want to see their sad staring looks, watching and waiting for someone to trust. *Hey— I'll trust you—OK?* In her mind's eye though, she looked at them, the staring faces, she could not help it, and she saw that the ones that were children were indistinguishable, somehow, from the ones that were not, and they seemed to stare just at her, every one of them, and she looked back at them, and yet she herself was one of them, staring too.


WHAT she needed was a wink or two more of sleep, before she got up to get dressed for the Court, but Margaret's mind could not rest, it tried to go on down these old paths, until suddenly, in one swift motion, she sat up and looked around her in confusion—for the room had darkened, it might have been late dusk outside.

The television was speaking complacently on to no one—the program she had lain down to watch had been over for some time. But outside, lightning cracked, a strange dark had fallen, and she realized that it was the coming storm that had roused her.

Through the closed windows, past the deep drone of the air-conditioner, the drama outside bore in on her. Way overhead things were being broken apart. Great creaking logs of thunder were being splintered and split somewhere.

Back in the bedroom she sat on the bed and reached for her girdle from the back post. The darkness of the room almost alarmed her, and out the back window she could see enormous trailings of massy black—disturbed corridors of flight across the sky. In the yard itself everything was iron still, every tree and shrub trapped and caught, held tight, it almost seemed, in some invisible grip. Nothing out there could move a leaf, but was just waiting—in an eerie, almost artificial-looking, and yet somehow sorrowful motionlessness—for the storm, bloating and building overhead, to break, let fly its animal rage.

So the tension rose, this dangerous suspense, and somehow it was even worse when the thunder began to cease— or could be heard only dimly, in the distance, rolling to a halt down some far rocky slope. For then the stillness and the silence met.

Margaret, standing up, pulled hard on her girdle, thought of the storm waiting to leap, wanting to come without warning (she saw it descending on her in great warping sheets just as she set out for work, saw herself driven off the road, made to wait it dangerously out in the parked car)—yes, it would want to open up on her without warning, with terrible abruptness, like a sudden deadly volley from thousands of hiding guns, something she would have to see, sometimes, on TV before she could get to the set to turn it off. She pulled taut her hose, fastened the girdle snaps.

Then she sat on the bed and looked into the darkening yard, was almost frightened by the tension rising there, and by her own trembling thoughts of other things building and gathering, biding their time, collecting their forces, and she thought suddenly of her husband Leonard in his ascending rage, his face taut and dark, trying, in despair, to go on about some normal business, his eyes almost closed, as if he were listening fearfully to something at work within him, the be-

ginnings of his own fury dimly crackling to life, then burning forward, eating through like a fiery wall whatever he
tried to erect against it, burning on no matter what he did,
growing and gathering, sucking into itself its food of rage
from the air of the house, from every word or phrase ever
spoken there, every look and expression, step and gesture,
all the months and years of eyes looking, heads turning and
bending, of voices quick and languid, demanding, voices
slow and soothing, smooth and assuring—voices and faces
of every kind (no matter what) now profoundly, madden-
ingly goading him, tempting his anger, trying to provoke
him, filling him, stretching and stuffing him, trying to burst
him, his brain, his heart! Until the bomb-burst of his fury
fell, rocking and shaking the little house—oh the shock to
the bricks and boards when his rage came down and he
roared his threats, cried out his curses, his charges and ulti-
matums . . . the others sometimes daring to chime in, Margaret trying perhaps to face him down.

Once Laney had run away, sobbing and crying, all the
way to her grandma's, three miles in almost no time, not
once stopping, apparently, to get her breath—for she was
going for help, thinking her father was going to kill her
mother just because he said he was. She had fled the house
without their knowing it while Leonard in his frenzy
hollered and paced, his face gorged, his mind simply gone
from him. In the midst of it the phone rang, a terrible shock,
its long, high, sharp, cutting ring an immensely surprising
thing, as if at first they could none of them imagine what it
was. Then there was utter silence, as if by this single elec-
trolytic action the air had been suddenly cleared, all sounds
broken instantly into their noiseless components. For a moment no one moved. Leonard's face was still bent toward
hers, they faced each other still, almost head to head, and
momentarily he glared on for the sake of glaring, but his
mad dog was gone, had vanished in that split second in
which the shock of something utterly plain and normal,

sane and familiar (the phone) had come between his rage and him, given him the small advantage he needed to stun the wild dog of his fury and get it down. So while his eyes still glared, just to be glaring, the fire died away in them, and the ropes in his face ceased to move and pull; his lips closed, awkwardly, anticipating that odd, formal, self-conscious, inaccurate set of his lips that they saw during his times of recovery and remorse. Then along with the shrill ring of the phone there was also the sound of Richy crying and snuffing, and Margaret realized he had been crying all along and no one had even noticed him. Yet she herself could do nothing, it seemed as if she could not move, she could not take up her sobbing child. Then Ruth came out of the hallway and took Richy up in her arms, and the phone rang again, and Leonard, standing almost beside it, raised it finally to his lips, answered in a voice subdued, and so completely altered that even his mother had not known who was speaking and he had had to say, "Who in the world did you *think* it was?" Then: "Laney? Over there?" Shaking his head. "Wonder in this world she's not dead in the streets."

And his mama saying, no doubt: *Son what are you doing? What are you doing to these little things? Oh-h-oh son, one of these days, it'll all come back on you. Son son! You never can tell—if one was to get sick (oh Rosella . . . couldn't we have loved her more?) . . . if anything was to happen—every word, every bit of it, everything you did, would come back on you. Son, son!*

And Leonard's eyes, his cheeks, worked and twitched, he stretched his mouth to hold straight his lips. He said nothing, but put down the phone, stood there for a moment with his eyes closed, then strode out to the car and drove away.

Margaret had gone into the bathroom and in the mirror her eyes were like wet glass. She washed them and patted them dry. She said, "Ruth. Call your grandma. Tell her—it's all right."

Then she had taken Richy from Ruth and took him to the

174

rocker in the bedroom. They rocked and she had begun to cry again, and Ruth had stood by her chair, saying, "Mama, Mama, why can't we leave him? We could get along. Why can't we leave the old—bastard," and Margaret had said, "Please," crying, "don't say words like that—is that what we've come to, is that all we are?" Then Ruth began to say *divorce, divorce.* "Get a divorce, because you hate him, you know you do." She looked down into Margaret's face, said, "Mama! We hate him, we all do."

*Oh little children. Is this all? Is this what life is . . . ?*

And what had it been, anyway, that particular time (if it even *was* a particular time and not a scene, as it very possibly was—that she had created out of many hundreds of individual scenes) that had set him off?

She remembered a time after supper, but still light. Leonard sat at the kitchen table doing some kind of task. But what was he doing? She looked closely to try and see. His being there, his doing this at that time of day was already a bad, an ominous thing, for he should have gotten right back in his car after supper. She was in the living room, her face rigid and stern, straightening the room for the evening, picking up papers and books, shoes and jackets, making as she did so as many small regular familiar noises as possible, flapping noises and brushing noises (noises which meant *Everything is all right, life is going on*). Then she stood up straight, with a child's sweater (probably) in her hand, listening hard, because Ruth had entered the kitchen, walking softly, scuffing about in her bedroom shoes almost soundlessly. In fact this was the immediate thing that had sprung the trap of his anger—this little provocative thing: Ruth's more than usual quietness, as if by that she were demonstrating, deliberately making it known, that something was wrong (and because it *was* wrong), as if she were by this light step (absurdly light to him perhaps) and by a certain position of her head, by the holding of it more or less down as she went to the sink, announcing for all to hear (everywhere!) that her father was someone to be careful of, to be wary of, to be feared (though of course he was).

And so suddenly he was screaming out. "Margaret! Margaret! Keep these—keep these damn children out of here, keep them out of here!" As if a whole battalion of children had marched in and surrounded him. And when he hollered, Ruth started and broke a glass in the sink, and then he was off and gone, all afire, racing to the peak of his rage, scrambling, scratching up from behind the table, wheeling up with such a crazy, blundering motion that the tackle box crashed to the floor (poor man), bellowing Margaret's name, damning her soul to hell (oh well), daring her to show her face in the kitchen archway, and then when she did, being driven mad by the sight of it—by her expression hollow and stern, resigned, when he wanted to see her stunned and afraid (but no, that would have maddened him too).

What, in any case, had been her sin? thought Margaret, tracing back through the afternoon, through many similar evenings and afternoons. Was it Friday and the grocery bill due? Each day (having no car to drive while he was on the road) she ordered her groceries on the phone, and then on Friday she gave a check to the delivery boy for the week's bill. So as long as that went on, many, many years, both before and after the war, Fridays were certainly not her favorite days. Even if you weren't sure what day it was, you knew to be tense on Friday. No matter what care she had taken, how saving and ingenious she had been to serve meals that the old thing liked and were also good for growing children and would keep the bill down too (thank god all that part of her life was over)—still about half the time she had spent fifty cents too much, maybe a whole dollar.

So it might have been Friday and the grocery bill too large (and yet, was that the *reason* or just the excuse?)—or was it the end of the month (another special time to worry on, a worse time, in fact, by far) and the bank statement in?

176

She saw Leonard fling down his case and go straight to the mail on the mantle, see the big envelope from the bank, give her, if she was in the room, a dark, threatening, slant-eyed look before he even opened it, then open it loudly—an enormous sound of paper tearing—mutter and scowl as he thumbed through the checks: eight dollars for shoes! four dollars for haircuts! five dollars for cash, five for cash, for cash, for cash (tick them off): *what in the world woman? who in God's name do you think we are?*

But she saw that this time, standing at the mantel, on the stage of this particular memory, looking through the checks, he had said nothing to her but sat down to supper, hardly looked up at her or the children, made no comment on the food, no remark of approval or complaint, bent his head steadily over his plate, eating fast and absently—or was it all deliberate? Was he perhaps trying to provoke her by his silence and sullenness, his refusal to meet her eye? Get her to complain, accuse, give him his desperate excuse to fly in her face?

So the tension rose, as it was rising now, many years later, in the storm-darkened yard, the dangerous suspense, while he fought it out, on check day, with his beast and the rest of them waited for the outcome, the children eating silently too, like little eating machines, Margaret not filling her plate but sitting over a cup of tea at the maple table—where at noon today in fact she still had sat, at sixty-one, the mother alone now at the table, no father, no children, as if they had all been sucked up through the bay window into the powerful light of the south Georgia heavens, or as if she had turned them all into the hanging baskets around the room.

But looking back, she wondered how the kids had swallowed their food at meals like that. And actually sometimes poor Laney could not, and later Margaret would have to take her a saucer to the bedroom. Laney, in fact, even today, could not swallow at *any* table if things were not quiet and calm. This particular child, even in those last years of

Leonard's life when he was a better man, when the worst things he feared (being arrested for debt or just being despised and pitied for not being able to pay his bills, take care of his family) had not come true and he had believed at last that there was a chance they would not, in those last years when the children, grown and gone their own ways long since, had not been caught in one of his table-fits for years, even then Laney, when she came home, could hardly eat a thing when he was at the table, and just picked around at her plate and half pretended to.

But that evening, many years back, the beast had been taking hold of him, beginning stealthily to devour certain secret parts of him, though its victim struggled, tried to battle back. But he was such a little man for such a big beast. And they knew he was losing badly, that the creature would certainly win, when after supper he did not get up and go off in the car, but instead walked through the yard, no doubt not seeing it at all, hardly knowing where he was, and then, when the table was cleared, sat back down (*lord god*) with his tackle box in front of him, waiting for the immense provocation of a child's step—too light—on the kitchen floor.

WHEN the rain broke, Margaret was at her dresser, leaning in to the mirror, her head centered in its pink ruffled frame, to retrace her lipstick. The rain fell heavily, at once, with a sudden rushing sound that at first she thought was the rushing of wind and that made her turn quickly to the window across the room and catch her breath. So the rain startled her after all—like so many things (death, for instance, she could not help but think) that you think you have been waiting for every moment. Hard rapid drenching rain, in fact, was almost always a surprise; your breath stopped for a moment and then it was as if a threat of some kind passed and you thought *Oh—rain. Oh it is just the rain.*

Still, the sound of the rushing rain was not nearly so loud as the silence beforehand, the popping tension of the yard and sky, and there was something in it of relief, release, as if it were washing all the tension back down into the earth, driving it downward with the danger and suspense.

When Margaret was all ready to go back to work, she went back into the living room and sat down on the brocade sofa, looking at a *Good Housekeeping* and waiting for the rain to stop or at least slow down. She had her raincoat and her umbrella ready on the chair by the door. No one would expect her to go out in this, not with her hair just set yesterday and the trouble it always gave her, and the shower to go to tonight (oh that old shower). She did not like to go out in the evenings, being out all day at work was enough going out, when she got home she liked to get out of her clothes, lie on her bed—as dusk fell—and read . . . or work out in the yard a little, then eat her a little supper and turn on the television. Sometimes, she would turn on the strong over-head light in the dinette and cut out a dress for herself or one of her granddaughters on the kitchen table. Other nights she did nothing all evening that was constructive but straighten a drawer. ("Those drawers of yours," Nora would say—"Granny might not love *you*, but she would love your cleaned-out drawers.")

Margaret had turned off the air-conditioner and opened the front door so she could enjoy, while she was waiting, the sound and smell of the rain on the stoop. It battered hard on the brick steps, and two smells pervaded the room—the fresh smell of the rain itself and the steamy, very specific smell that rose off the hot brick.

People all over town would be smelling now this particular odor of steaming wet concrete and brick. In very hot country like south Georgia, you could hardly think of heavy rains without thinking of this smell too. If you were caught, for instance, on the broad sidewalks downtown—if a squall came up all in a minute and you were caught coming out of a store, or running to your car, trying to hold one of your bags over your head . . . then the smell was sharp and strong indeed and you could see the steam off the sidewalks, which in summer would have baked all day in ninety-eight-degree heat, hot enough to blister a child's feet, even to fry an egg on, people always said. She thought of herself streaking through the steaming rain to her car, or smelling it as she waited by a door that opened and closed as people tried to decide whether to run for it or not, her mind spinning backwards for a moment or two, as she waited by Kresses' swinging door, to the dairy . . . not just to the time she herself was there as a young girl, but beyond her own time to when her mother and father were there. This smell of rain on concrete would make her mind fling up confused images of her father meeting her mother when her mother was a girl at the dairy.

For at the dairy there had been a walkway of concrete between the milking shed and the nice damp screened back porch, shaded by two small mimosa trees. This walkway was wide, almost like a patio, and was roofed over so you could get to the shed in bad weather. One day Margaret had been sweeping the walkway, and the dairyman had come up with the cheese press in his hand. He knocked for Granny at the door of the porch, and while he waited he studied the walk that Margaret was sweeping. "That was a good job on that," he said. "Your daddy put this down."

Margaret stopped sweeping—she looked at him hard. "This walk was put down by your daddy. It was his brother and him. Brickmasons. They did work like this, and then this law come along about clean milk and said you can't milk on anything but a concrete floor and so Miz Culp got your daddy, and him and his brother put down the floor in the barn and when they got through they put this down. Good job too."

Margaret had stared at the walk. By that time it was roughened and weathered, and in the main path slightly pitted. Granny came to the door and took the press, and the dairyman went away. By then the walkway was clean but Margaret kept sweeping, very hard, needling the stiff bristles of the broom into the small pits, getting out the least speck of dirt there. She stared and stared into the cement as she swept it, and then she did a foolish thing: she reached down to feel it with the flat of her hand.

She felt it—because it was her father who had put it down.

And when on hot summer days at the dairy a rainstorm would blow up out of the tense, darkened afternoons, snapping suddenly the gray, wire-tight suspension of the yard and sky and the pastureland beyond, where the cows kneeled under trees breathing into their lungs the coming storm, sometimes Margaret would be working on the narrow screened back porch, and in the queer stillness and silence of the brooding storm the sounds of her work seemed to tumble and crash in her ears, to be, in the small room, enormously amplified. She would be washing vegetables for supper perhaps, at the great double sink, peeling and scraping; or she might be cutting corn off the cob, with great wet heaps of scraped cobs at her elbow and her arms splattered with corn-milk. Then, as if someone had pulled a lever or opened a gate, the rain, without immediate warning, would come very swiftly down with a great rushing sound as if of immense relief, like the letting out of breath torturously held, *and there would rise up through the screens of the porch that particular smell of rain on hot concrete, the smell of the rain steaming off her father's walkway;* and standing over her dishpan of corn, her hand resting against the metal sink and still clenching the wet knife, she would stare into the yard or down the rain-drenched walkway to the barn, and conjure up dim pictures—sliding and veering pictures, like one might see on a bad TV—of her father, the brickmason, and the girl he courted on his job at the dairy farm.

"Your mama was a sight, I tell you." Margaret had been told that when she was a girl at the dairy farm. One of the old fat country women from down the road would come to sell Granny eggs, and she would have to rest on the yard-bench under the pecan trees before she started back. "Your mama always had something to say. Her mouth was always open and I mean she would talk to anybody, she didn't care who it was. Her and me always had plenty to say, and I know I'm not the type to care what anybody thinks but me and I liked her. I liked her just as good as anybody else around here—and better than some. She was the kind that never met a stranger and she would come up and take your hand she was so friendly and say *How many babies have you got* and things like that, and what's this one's name and what's that one's name . . . she loved babies—and animals . . . ooh-h I tell you—she would say *Have you got any little dogs at your house? Or Have you got any little dogs you want me to teach some tricks to for you?* And some days she would ask her mama to let her walk me home but she wasn't never allowed—unh-unh! They didn't want her off this place, Miz Culp was real strict about that and wasn't *none* of us going to not mind Miz Culp. Whew! I guess *not!*"

Margaret did not stand close, and when she spoke she frowned and poked her toe in the grass. "But Mama ran off. I don't call that minding, do you?"

The woman had fanned herself with the hem of her skirt. "Well—all I know," she said, "your mama had a bah-rel of fun—and couldn't nobody keep her from it, although some tried, but she went right on and had her a bah-rel of fun . . . and I bet she still does, don't she?" She began to laugh, just thinking about it, whooping for breath and jiggling all the rings of fat around her neck. She slapped her knees—as if they were what was making her laugh. "Lordee!" she said. "And for you to be so bashful and long-faced like you are . . . and your mama to be the way *she* was—and then your grandma"—she looked back towards the house, a mountain of bristling white, and began to sober up. "I never seen the like of it," she said.

~

"Mama was a sight they said." Margaret had said that to Nora and Nora had agreed with her completely. "Don't you know! She was a sight in this world! I would go up to the dairy to play, and starting up from the gate, I would see her way out in the garden hoeing and she would have on these old brogans that one of the boys had probably thrown away, and no socks, and she would be singing like she was getting paid for it—you could hear her way behind the corn; but then if she caught a glimpse of me coming up the path, she would fly out of the patch, streaking down to me in those old brogans, and with this old long raggledy dress flying around her ankles, crying *Noli, Noli!*"—Nora had stretched her turkey neck out and cried it hoarsely, just like Margaret's mother had. It was strange when she sat back— the silence in the house, and this old sound resonating in the silence, and Nora looking as if she had surprised *herself.*

"What did she call you that for? Was that what they called you?"

"Oh no, that was just Emma, I had that name just with Emma, and when Emma was gone, I never had it anymore."

"What did she call you that for?"

"What she did anything for."

Nora studied this over. "Your mama said things the easiest way—if one way was easier than another, then she just said it that way and it wasn't no difference to her. But I know words tickled her, and she loved to giggle and tease about words. And for instance there was this family of Glascocks on the other side of the creek and when she started learning—you know—sex words she thought this was the funniest word she had ever heard and what she would do, she would call them on the phone and say *Who is this speaking?* just to hear them say *This is Mrs. Glascock* or *This is Mr. Glascock,* and then she could hardly get the phone down before she would pop open; she would laugh so hard, she'd fall

183

over in a heap she was so tickled to think of one made out of glass."

Margaret sat back in her chair, staring out into the room, listening, her mouth drawn down.

"They said she was a live wire," Margaret said. "They said she wasn't a child that was sad. They said I was the sad one."

"Oh! The way that girl would holler and carry on! And sing! She could sing any song she heard, she didn't have to hear it but about one time. She didn't sing it exactly in tune and she would sing some of the words her own way but she would sing it all through, every verse, over and over, and she sang real loud. In fact it was so loud that in the house she wasn't allowed to. You know whose rule *that* was. But outside you could hear her up and down the road. She loved to sing and shout and she loved any game—every game—and she could play them all day long, she never got tired. When I think of all that jumping rope.

"Why sometimes that's all we did from morning till night, and Grandaddy Culp made the jump ropes out of calf ropes and one time Emma jumped to a hundred and something, and Grandaddy Culp and I had to swing the rope, and we swung till our hands were dropping off and I wish I had a picture of it—because here was me nothing but a tadpole, maybe five or six, and Emma, in the middle, six years older, and then on the other end this big tall man in his overalls, and him and me counting every jump together in one voice, and then when she finally got caught, all of us would fall down in a rolling, laughing heap on the ground, we couldn't hardly get our breath and then we thought it was the funniest thing we ever did.

"Then Emma would say, *Let us beat you up*, and Grandaddy Culp lay there and let us pound and beat on him with our fists—because this was another game we had, and he would groan and holler and cave in his side and roll his head, and then finally he was dead. And Emma laughed and cried. She just giggled and crowed, that girl, and we would

184

both cry, *He's dead, he's dead,* and he was all flung out on the ground with his mouth open and his tongue out, not showing a sign of life, and then the two of us leaned down, on our knees, over him, just skittery we were so excited, and said, 'Let's be sure he's dead,' and so we would bend right down into his face and say, 'Be sure, let's be sure,' and then he would spring up like a busted spring! snarling like a dog right in our face, and his big hands would leap out to grab us! by the neck! and the way that man would shake us and almost choke us! and make these terrible growls like a monster in the movies and pretend he was going to crack our heads! Every time it was so real we almost thought he would! And we said, 'No no no no, we're sorry, we're sorry. . . .'"

"I'll declare," Margaret said.

Nora coughed, deep in her lungs, from laughing so hard.

"I know they said she was a sight," Margaret said, waiting for Nora to get her voice back.

"She didn't care who she played with," Nora said, "and even when I was just *this* high, just a wee little runny-nosed chicken of a thing, she would hopscotch with Nolan and me—he was just my age—or she would teach us school on the front porch, with little books made out of pieces of newspaper pasted together, probably upside down. Because I doubt if she knew what they said any more than we did. I doubt if she could spell cat. But we just pretended we were reading and if we didn't read it 'right'—you know—we had to get switched. In fact that was the point of the whole thing, and just as she was about to take and switch us because we didn't know our lesson, she would whisper, 'Run!' And we would dash away, off the porch and across the yard, her after us like a wild man, and us running in and out, up and down, around the well and behind the shed and back across the porch again, crying, 'Teacher's going to switch us—help! help!' And her behind us with a big switch, and that was the way we played school."

Nora thumped herself another cigarette, thinking. "Maybe that was the way she thought they did at school."

"But Mama could spell a little and she could read a letter. She must have gone to school at some point."

"Well you know what *Granny* said. She said they wouldn't *let* her go, that there wasn't no place for her but that's not what I think it was, no ma'am. I don't think Granny *wanted* her to go, I think she was ashamed of her and didn't want her off the place."

"I don't know," Margaret said.

"That's what I think," Nora said.

"But she learned to read, somewhere. Granny might have taught her herself."

"Granny?!" Nora was full of scorn for an idea like that. "I can just see that. Granny with little Emma on her knee, teaching her her letters. I can just see that little scene."

"But some way—she learned," Margaret insisted.

"Some way . . . ," Nora said. She sighed. "If anybody— it might have been Grandaddy Culp—but did you ever see him with a book in his hand? Talking and drinking was what *he* loved to do. And walking. He loved to take his jug and along about dusk go for a long walk way down by the creek. Where he could get away from Granny. Because there she would be, with supper cooked and out of the way, still working like two horses although she had already worked like two all day. And he wanted to get away from that mile of tatting piling off her lap—oh busy, busy, we *got* to be busy. Away from those miles and miles of tatting and knitting, those damn clicking highways of white crochet, and those eternal ruffles, about four deep on every window of the house. And from those flower beds and that famous triple row of giant canna lilies at the front of the yard, so beautiful they were dangerous, such a sight that cars on the road—even wagons—slowed down to get a good look. So Grandaddy would just go for a walk—with his jug.

"But Emma," Nora went on, "if anybody taught her, I don't know who it was. One of the hired men maybe."

Nora pursed one corner of her mouth to make a small sneer. "It wouldn't be Granny, I can tell you that. For one thing, this was not the dairy the way it was when you came. Granny didn't have time for all that crochet and Emma too, not to mention Grandaddy Culp. I mean it was already a large nice place and they had plenty of what they needed, but they hadn't made it *big* yet, they were just starting to, and Granny worked like two horses—later she only had to work like one. But there wasn't no naps after dinner, on those high double-mattress feather beds. The beds weren't that high yet. And they hadn't built on the big dining room for the men—in fact they only had about two men, and no negroes, and Granny just fed the men in the kitchen, and she did every smack of the inside work herself and about half of the outside.

"They only had one truck and about thirty cows and Grandaddy Culp took the milk to town in the truck and sold it to the milk company. In fact they didn't even call it 'the dairy,' they called it 'the farm,' and they hadn't narrowed down to just milk, and they sold it to the milk company raw, in those great big cans. Of course Granny could always see two dollars in something where somebody else might not see but one, and it wasn't too many years before she had got her own machines and bottled her own milk and sent it out in her own delivery trucks and called it Culp Dairy—and got rich."

"Not that rich," Margaret said.

"Well it was rich to me—yes ma'am! . . . it was damned rich to plain old good-for-nothing people like us—"

"When Granny died—"

"It was all gone, that's right—but she lived pretty high for twenty-five years after she sold out. She travelled everywhere she wanted to, and the rest of it went for nursing and to practically run her own hospital after she got sick. So naturally there wasn't much left for her to leave—not even enough to fight about . . . and that was the way she wanted it. Because what had anybody done that they deserved to get anything?"

Margaret's frowning face did not move; it stared forward out of her pale-rim glasses to the side of Nora's head. One leg in a low patent heel swung in a narrow arc below her Indian-cloth dress—homemade, cut out evenings or on a Sunday perhaps, on the kitchen table, where there was something pleasant and virtuous in the swish of her heavy scissors through the crisp cloth, her love of good tools, which Granny loved too.

"But anyway—got rich, in my opinion, where at first they had just been doing well."

Nora drew on her cigarette, cocked it by her thin reddish face, still slightly freckled in her old age. "And somewhere in there your father—"

"There was a law passed," Margaret said, "about cement floors."

Her father and his brother had driven into the dairy in the wagon, with all their materials, to start on the barn. Her father was a short stumpy man with a round face and rather strange short arms. Even then he was a fellow that was quiet and moved slowly and did not call attention to himself, but he was an excellent worker and mason—they all said that, yes this was one thing she knew, because Granny would not have had him on the place if he had not been. "Now I think girls had made fun of him," Nora said. "We don't know for sure but listen—when he came out to the dairy, he wasn't no kid, he was a grown man, yet I don't think he had ever had a girlfriend—I think all he just about ever did was work.

"So Emma—she thought your daddy was funny-looking, I remember that. She snickered and teased about him behind his back, and he went on working (oh he was so slow and careful) lifting and hauling, sawing things and measuring things, for those wooden frames for the *ce*-ment. And Emma was a big girl now, fourteen or fifteen, she seemed very big to me," Nora said. "But she still had her same ways, she loved to have fun, and I know she wanted to have some fun off your daddy, and one time she wanted to put something in his tub of cement when he wasn't looking—things like that—and Granny had to keep coming out to get her and try to make her stay in the house. But first thing you knew, she would be out again. And after a while she began to tease your father to his face. She was always swinging around at him from some corner or other—he would just look up, with a board in his hand, and there she would be, grinning and winking at him. Oh that girl was a scamp! Now she was, I tell you. Not his brother, that wasn't the one she teased, no it was always Raymond, and for instance she would tease him about kissing girls. She would say: 'I heard you tried to kiss this girl in town and she slapped your face.'

"Or: 'I heard you can't kiss right,' or she'd say to his brother, 'He can't kiss, can he?' And Raymond and his brother just ignored her; they would just say, *Hand me that saw* or *What did you do with that bucket?* and I don't know what your father thought, nobody knew what he was think-ing. But listen, girls that age are the silliest things in the world; they're all silly, they don't have two cents to knock together, none of them do. No, especially around a man it would be hard to tell one silly teenage girl from another. And your father had not had much practice, he didn't know a thing about them."

Nora went on. "He was so shy—I know Raymond was the shyest thing there was." She stared hard, concentrating, as if an answer to something might come to her; but it did not. She shook her head. "Poor thing . . . is all I can say," she said, "not to know—any more than he did."

Margaret wanted to protest: *But he knew. Granny told him. She told him herself.*

Whenever Margaret thought that, it still took her breath,

189

and then an egg of alarm stuck in her throat. Granny had told her that and she had always taken it to be true. But Nora would say it was *not* true, and she did not want to hear Nora say so—because . . . because surely it *was* true. Because there was this fact, after all: her mama and daddy had run away, they had not gotten married properly at home; they must have done it on their own, without anybody's permission. *Perfect for Granny, Nora would probably say. Don't you see? Exactly the way she wanted it. Nothing to blame herself for, and this crazy child—afflicted—off her hands.* Margaret might say, *She liked my father,* and Nora: *She probably loved your father. A good steady worker, in good shape to support a wife, and ignorant enough—*

But Nora was going on. "Poor Raymond. What he was thinking! But nobody knows that. It's just that when the floor was done, and the law was satisfied, and then the walkway came up and that was finished too—him and his brother weren't gone. They came back. And at first I imagine Granny thought it was to see *her,* or just to sort of let her know they were still around in case any other work turned up, although they were good masons and getting work wasn't something they had any trouble with."

"But I expect Mama herself knew that wasn't the reason," Margaret said. "She had sense enough to know that."

"You wonder who knew it first, her or Granny. I wouldn't put anything past Granny to know," Nora said.

"And in fact the next news you know, who has invited them to swim in the swimming hole? *Granny.* And so the three of them—because there was always three of them— would go down to swim. And so the two of them came out and they came out. And then they started coming out on Sunday—*you* know—courting day! Yes ma'am, Granny knew—*she knew.*"

*Yes she knew,* Margaret thought to herself, *but she had a talk with my father. She said, "Emma should always stay at home with me . . . ."*

190

"They came out on Sundays and took Emma for a ride in the wagon, which must have been a sight anyway because Emma wouldn't put on any Sunday clothes—she only liked old loose clothes and she preferred them dirty. So there she went for a Sunday ride. And your father with his coat on and his brother with his."

Margaret pondered again. "What Daddy was thinking . . . ," she said.

"He didn't think out loud, that was for sure," Nora said. "He didn't hardly *talk* out loud. He had about as much to say as this chair I'm sitting on."

"All his life," Margaret said. "He was always that way."

"And with no expression on his face," Nora said. "Always the same face. So how could you tell?

"I never saw anybody with so little to say for himself," she went on. "And Emma—boiling over all the time, every day, always about to pop open, cutting up and carrying on. In fact—why she even liked *him*. But she *liked* your daddy, from the beginning, she did—nobody knows why. *She* didn't know why."

Nora's gaze drifted to the window. "There isn't any why to that," she said. "Or to why somebody like me . . . why I would start to . . . why Nolan and me . . . ."

Margaret waited—she said nothing. *These old griefs*, she thought. *Hers and mine so tangled up this way.*

"Why anything," Nora said. "Why your father did what he did. But courting ways are the most confusing ways there are. Oh courting ways are crazy to begin with—and listen, your mama was growing up . . . in her way she was growing up like anybody else, and she had *certain things on her brain*, and that—that goes far with a man, right there."

"Yes-s," Margaret said.

"Although I doubt that you could see much of that little old bony bosom under those blousy dresses and skirts. But yet and still—Emma had her ways. And if a person doesn't care what she throws on herself, as far as clothes are concerned, nobody else cares either, and listen, I don't care what anybody says, there was something about Emma that was *attractive*. Don't you know? Even being the way she was. Don't you know?"

"Yes," Margaret had said.


Now Margaret sat on, these many years later, in her living room, waiting for the weather to clear, and closed her eyes. The rain drummed on. Her mind drifted dreamily and it was as if it was raining hard all over Nora's words, driving and sweeping them, blowing them almost away, then suddenly gusting them up again. It seemed to Margaret that behind the rain-screen at her door, behind her memory-screen, Nora's voice was going on whether she actually heard it or not, and other voices too were always going on, heard or unheard, saying over and over again all the things they had ever said. She saw Nora leaning forward. "The thing about Emma—Granny couldn't control her, even with all her rules. And when she couldn't control something she didn't want it around."

Nora had sat back, satisfied, blowing out a defiant torch of smoke. "Now you could work her. She would work. You could work Emma like a mule all day." Nora pursed her lips in a very satisfied way. "Only one thing—you had to stand over her every minute, say *You do this, you do that.*"

Then her words almost faded off behind the screen of rain. "It was not that she was bad . . . or that she would disobey—don't you know? . . . It was just that, for instance, something would catch her attention and she would run away. First thing you know she'd be gone—and that was all for work."

*No she was not bad,* Margaret thought. *And she had no spite or resentment. No matter what happened to her life, or what anyone did . . . what Granny did . . . or me—what I did—she didn't resent it. Not even that she forgave us, no, because she didn't put any blame on anyone to begin with, she didn't think it was her place to blame or forgive. But a person who has no spite or resentment . . . no anger building up over the years . . . what if it is simply that that was not normal, not "right"?*

"Granny knew Emma was not right and should never have left home." Which voice was saying that? Margaret stirred on the sofa. She did not want to think what she was thinking and yet her thoughts went on. *Mama was good. She was a good person, but I could hardly stand to step inside her door. I was a prig of soap and water, and swept floors and cleaned-out drawers. I was a prig and couldn't love her the way I should though I did love her, I loved her,* she insisted, almost angrily . . . to something behind the rain driving on the front stoop, *although my father was the one I loved the most. Daddy, I hated you, I couldn't help it, but I loved you too, I loved you all the time . . . .*

Margaret's eyes stung, she began to dab them, carefully, with a kleenex, not to ruin her makeup. But they stung again, they kept stinging, for she heard her mother singing behind the corn-rows, saw her father driving in at the gate in the wagon, then saw the place empty, the two of them gone, vanished into another world of peculiar trouble and pain. She saw the years passing, and then herself, sequel to that strange union, driving up in amazement through the gate, in the milk truck with her grandfather, home from the railroad station . . . saw herself walking, in a trance of astonishment and yet self-recognition, into Granny's kitchen, saw herself sweeping hard, and then the flat of her hand reaching down, touching her father's walkway.

## ~ CHAPTER FIVE ~

BUT Margaret saw as well—straining over the wheel towards the watery streets as she drove to work through a sturdy rain, no longer violent—glass-smooth afternoons at a dairy of later times (not in fact really a dairy); saw herself sitting pleasurably back in a comfortable chair, on the glassed-in front porch with Granny and Daddy Wallace, so relaxed, so needing to relax, she nearly went to sleep; saw fans blowing gently over them at exactly the proper angle, smoothly whirring fans always properly cleaned and oiled, with no layers of gelatinous dust on their grills, never crawling, never rattling and whining as other fans did on other, inferior floors.

Driving back to the Court, on this wet August afternoon, Margaret saw and felt again the casual perfection of Granny's house bathing her young woman's nerves, saw and felt its airy brightness, its order of pretty, careful things streaming its balm into the bruised pores of her body. Saw Granny herself and her habitual radiance, a picture of well-being and smiling Sunday ease in the splendid costume of her later years: the spotless white lace shoes that always looked brand-new, as if she had just lifted them that morning from the tissues in the box, the soft, beautiful, stylish dresses of white, almost gossamer, batiste, in their slightly varying styles, no longer homemade (this concession made to wealth and advancing age) but bought out of town, in a shop for people of fashion.

Indeed white had been Granny's personal color for many years—wasn't it in white that Margaret, a staring girl, had first seen her, turning slowly towards her in gleams of light from the worktable in the kitchen? In later years she seldom wore anything else, for it afforded, after all, such a splendid harmony with her pure white hair (cropped and finger-waved, later curled and fluffed). In fact, there was this strange thing: that Granny, so eternally strong and ageless, so young even in her seventies, should have had her hair turn white almost overnight at fifty. And also this: that with sublime cunning and daring she had taken no step to stop nature's course, but just let it *be* white, dared to be white-headed in her fifties and won the dare, one might say— looking better than she ever had (as extremely well as that had always been), young and strong, handsome and healthy, winning everyone's admiration once again for her boldness and independence, her stand against colored hair . . . which even so, the other fine ladies of the town and countryside, the missionary circles and garden clubs, did not quite dare to emulate.

But at the dairy Margaret would be sitting, at times, with other Sunday guests, forming with them a pretty circle in the long glass porch, a room fitted with jalousied windows by Daddy Wallace himself—so admirably, so intelligently. Sunday was of course visiting day. And still is, Margaret thought—almost with surprise. *For some people are still living their lives, living out the things that later on they will just think about, almost forgetting whether they themselves are alive or dead.*

But certainly in those days Sunday was the day for visiting, with the younger ones going out and the older ones staying home to be visited. Granny was richly visited, needless to say, and had come not to mind it but to receive it as her due, and even to be gratified and amused by it. For there was Mr. Wallace by her side, after all, a handsome California gentleman, and on a smart low table a much-prized apple cake or orange chiffon or sour cream pound, lying—so rich, so delicious—on a raised glass plate on a crocheted cloth.

So on Sundays there Margaret too would be, trying, however, to arrive too late for the other guests and thus to be able to sit with Granny and Mr. Wallace alone, but sitting sometimes with others nevertheless, often with Vivian, for instance, Granny's youngest child, not very much older than Margaret herself, who in spite of a bad beginning with young people who only wanted to play and do nothing constructive in life, had married rather well, to an industrious and almost prominent man of the town, who was not very good to her but was extremely good to Granny ("Why of course," Nora said).

So Margaret might sit with Vivian and with Vivian's friends, other ladies of the town, more and more of whom had made the discovery over the years of this excellent, this formidable Mrs. Wallace, this *Granny* Wallace, as she was mostly named (and not inelegantly, because no name you could give to this particular person would be inelegant), a grand lady of the countryside with a beautiful house out on the Albany Highway, such a strong person ("Oh, Mrs. Wallace is a stro-ong person, I've always said that"), such an unusual person with such an interesting life, having followed the sawmills with her husband years and years ago, not much past the turn of the century, all the way to the piney coast, then bought a little piece of land down here and a few cows and started a farm and a little milk and butter business, a little dairy business (because some of her people in Minnesota had been dairy people and she had that know-how, you see) and then by sheer work and imagination improved it and enlarged it ("No mention of Grandaddy Culp, notice," Nora would say—"never a word about *his* work, what *he* put in"), and who, in spite of being such an astute businesswoman and as smart as a man ("Oh yes-s-s, Granny Wallace is as smart as *any* ma-an"), made the creamiest cottage cheese you ever tasted and yeast rolls that melted in your mouth (not to even mention her famous ice cream), but anyway a woman who was an inspiration no matter how you looked at it, a person that just beat all for doing whatever she set her mind to ("Look at Daddy Wallace!"), who never let anything get in her way, in spite of many grave misfortunes and the grief of losing her husband and then of having two of her children leave home, practically disappear almost before they were grown. In fact (as it was said) the boy *did* disappear—completely, don't you know? . . . the one that had been married to Nora Hawkes? And you might as well say the other one did too, a daughter that is, a person who was odd in some way or slightly off, yes something decidedly strange about her. But in any case, just consider: neither one of them ever coming back to see her even in her old age ("Can't you hear it?" Nora would say), a grief so great she could not even speak of it; so that for a long time here she was, a widow in a strange part of the country with all her own people far away, with no one to count on ("Why that's too sad to even think about," Nora said), no one to stand by her in times of need, and yet always confident and brave, never asking anybody for a thing—oh for a person to be so strong and at the same time so refined, with such a love of beautiful living, beautiful things . . . .

Thus it was, on Sunday afternoons, that these friends of Granny's, with or without the feelings about her that Nora ascribed to them, would call on her at the dairy, and Aunt Vivian herself called almost every Sunday.

Of course Vivian's visit might be brief, it might be quite

perfunctory, for the truth was it made her nervous at the dairy—she felt there was something reproachful, where she was concerned, in all her mother's ways and airs. Or was it just that strong people always reduced others to weakness, if only by their example? It was as if Vivian felt she was in constant danger of being suddenly found out to be a person with none of her mother's iron, but one who consisted strictly of froth and bubbles of air, when in fact it seemed to Margaret she might really have relaxed, since she already *had* been found out to be such a person years ago.

But how could a daughter who was froth and air have been born to a mother of such high-grade steel? ("What I think," Nora said, "I think Granny made herself—who else could have made her?—with the bricks she had left over after she put up the foundations of her house and barn, for of course she didn't just start a farm and business out of nothing, she put up the buildings too, don't you know? cooked the bricks, cut down the trees for the walls and doors.")

As for Vivian, even today Margaret, once every year or so, paid *her* a call, with very little pleasure in it, on visiting Sunday, and Vivian would be fretful and petulant and sometimes even imagined things and was definitely not completely in her right mind. Of course she had always been a kind of "case," with nerves in a way as bad as Margaret's, not sullen and sealed-up like Margaret was, but a different *kind* of nervous wreck, driven to blathering and babbling, chattering over everybody like a crazy monkey, her own particular stress-case betraying her into long high gulping monologues in a laughing trembling voice, no matter who was around or how many. And as for the friends and acquaintances—the ones who beat a regular path to Granny's door, to express their admiration for her, their delight in her—Vivian, in her way, treasured them, took pride in having a mother so revered, and realized that this parent would always be her only claim to distinction. Yet as Nora pointed out, she probably treasured even more the precious few friends who *understood* that having such a mother might in some ways be an unfortunate and not a fortunate thing, and who would actually let her complain about Granny a little, a practically unheard of act.

Indeed Nora knew for a fact that Vivian on certain occasions had said, in weeping distress of one kind or another, "Sometimes I wish I had a mother that was *not* strong; sometimes I wish I had one that was sad and depressed and cried her head off, and we could cry together and tell each other, and just admit, that everything was wrong and the whole world was a terrible arrangement, designed to make people unhappy, and that life was an awful thing, with nothing but death and death and death at the end, and all of us helpless, utterly powerless to do anything about it but cry and complain . . . ."

Vivian, in any case, was one of those persons Margaret might meet at Granny's in those days, or she might meet Vivian's friends, with or without Vivian, or other sundry ladies and a husband sometimes too, or even a son (although husbands and sons were not obliged to call).

But what she preferred—*yes what I always preferred*, she thought—was to sit with Granny and Daddy Wallace alone, when the others had come and flown, the society people from town (if they even *were* society people), who probably thought she was a sullen and curious person, an individual—in spite of being Granny's granddaughter—of a very indeterminate class, and wondered, perhaps, in secret, how Granny really regarded her.

What she definitely preferred was to sit with Granny and Daddy Wallace alone, in the deep of the slow afternoon, in that settled-down, leftover time of day when dusk was drawing down, and she and Granny, in the quiet kitchen, could put on another pot of Granny's excellent coffee and Granny could cut Margaret (and Ruth and Laney) the last slices of the orange chiffon or the sour-cream pound. And after all Margaret and Granny had this, among many other things, in common: they loved the late afternoon and the hour before dark, and sometimes before Margaret left to go home, to warm up her Sunday dinner for supper and get ready for evening church, she and Granny would walk together in the dusky back yard, and speak of the special nature of this or that shrub or flower, speak of recipes and patterns and the various qualities of miscellaneous cloths and when to do things one way and when to do them another way.

These were, in fact, the only subjects that Granny ever spoke of intimately to other human souls—and then to precious few, and Margaret had been able to think *I am the one that has her, it is me she speaks to*, and the dusk sifted down to them, bound them softly round, spread its transforming net of rosy light over the house and yard and Granny's face, made Margaret think she saw there expressions of special, privileged love, satisfied to have no words but just to peep forth in glintings and shadings in the falling afternoon.


AND YET—if you could ever have a simple emotion, if emotions did not always come in obscene clusters, horribly mismatched—for every year there were certain *other* Sundays when Margaret's feelings were almost entirely different from these, when, sitting with Granny and Daddy Wallace on the jalousied porch, amidst handsome, shiny plants as big as little trees, she received no balm from Granny's house, as rich as it was in courtesy and comfort and good taste, as mercifully free of men on rampages shouting and bulging their eyes, calling people whores and lunatics.

Certain Sundays, that is, stood completely apart: *those four or five Sundays of the year that followed Margaret's Saturday trips to Jacksonville.*

And on these particular *Jacksonville Sundays*, as Margaret came to think of them, opposing them to other, normal Sundays, she could not help but make certain comparisons, indulge herself, let herself slip and slide into fresh anger and resentment; she could not relax, even on the jalousied porch, could not slacken certain muscles in her neck and back but sat stiffly forward in her chair and frowned, and thought about Granny's order and independence, her serenity and security, in negative, irritable ways. The wisest course would have been not to have gone at all, on those Sundays after she had been to Jacksonville, and yet something drew her—perhaps she had not known what it was even at the time. Probably nothing more than this: a ridiculous hope (and a violent need and desire) to bring together, to crush into desperate union, two feelings about her grandmother—and thus, in a way, about all proper people, complacent and secure, with X's scrawled on their shiny gates (No Stopping Here), all people all over the world who are above *other* people, and eat while others hunger, and drink while they thirst; people in houses of blind rippled glass, where the sun rides in on bursting beautiful waves but trouble does not, so that if you try to look outside there is nothing to see but light itself, a splendid sea of glorious glass, though people in distress may be standing in your yard.

But of course the two feelings would not be crushed into one, and it may have been, in any case, that she went out to Granny's on these Jacksonville Sundays just because, having been to the other end of human fortune the day before, there was something in Granny's house she needed and craved and it was the same thing she went there to despise.

But she sat, as on any other day, on the long glassed-in porch with Granny and Daddy Wallace; and Ruth and Laney, in handmade frocks of dotted swiss or pale pique, sat scrunched together on the small settee, pretending to look at the *Saturday Evening Post* spread across their laps, but fidgeting subtly, with an overwhelming preference no doubt (though whether or not, at the time, she had had the presence of mind to know it) for the rummagy, smelly house on Eighth Street, for that other grandmother with the gimcracks and gewgaws, for her loud voice, her cheery cackle and her carrying on, with definitely a preference for Moon Pie and Orange Crush over homemade pound cake (not nearly gooey and sweet enough) and gloomy glasses of milk, served half-full, so as not to spill. And they must have known, without knowing, these tots (in that life before life, before memory has much to tell), that their value for Granny was mainly as decoration, and her devotion to them roughly the same as for her satin cushions.

But in any case the languid conversation of Granny's house, quiet and refined, made them crawl with impatience, and finally they would come and stand by Margaret's chair, smiling shyly, waiting their turn, their fingers curling the hems of their dresses, their chins burrowing into the curves of their bunching shoulders; they would lay little hands on her arm, and when the time came, speak to her softly, almost in a whisper, and she would say, "Ruth and Laney want to go outside."

And then Granny blamed and mocked herself for not having known. For her rude indifference to little girls' wants, said, "The glider, the glider! They want to swing in Daddy Wallace's glider!" And they hung their heads, to show that they did indeed, and whispered, "Yes ma'am." Did they want Daddy Wallace to walk them out? Oh no, they knew the way, Margaret would say, and then Ruth would take Laney's hand and they would walk, very formally and self-consciously, through Granny's rooms to her back door, and the adults on the porch would hear it open and softly close (*oh little girls . . .*). Yes Margaret would watch them go, and then she would listen, with strange concentration, to the crisp flutter of steps through the rooms (*oh little children . . .*) and her heart, from its hateful tangle of wondering grief, would not forget to rise . . . .

BUT AS for Jacksonville—after a time the little girls, growing older, no longer made the trip but stayed home with their grandmother Barker. And then Richard came along and *he* would go, and then he too was too old, Margaret felt. Not that any of them ever complained—no, as tots all the children liked it there, the oddness of the place. (*Lord knows it was odd all right*). Still, Margaret was afraid for them. She was afraid that without their realizing it, without their understanding it at the time, things in that house (that more than peculiar house) would turn out somehow to have been too confusing and upsetting for them ever to explain to themselves.

And after all, it was no fault whatever of theirs—the life lived there. (But then it was no one's fault—a perplexing thing.) There might well be someone or something (something at large out there, something vicious which though people cannot see it they know in fact must be there, some lurking, brooding, never satisfied thing) that would want them to be marked, affected, by having gone there, would want them to worry, for instance, and doubt themselves. "So *these* are my people, *this* is what I come from. This what the ruler of all nature has created for us to worship and admire . . . .") So mostly she kept them apart, and as they grew older she went on this dark journey alone and kept the whole business to herself.

Yet once in a while in those later days, one of them, growing up, a youngster of eleven or twelve or thirteen, would ask to go, rather shyly, almost guiltily, their curiosity having crept up on them perhaps, or perhaps because they even cared a little bit about the old crazy things down there; and so, because the crazy things themselves did care very much, loved to have people come and were always asking about the ones at home ("Where Ruth, Maga? Maga, where you children?"), and because life is always a matter of matching guilt to guilt, once in a long while she made an exception and took one of the children with her. And that child would do the best it could, but now, a different being entirely from itself of five or six, it was much more nervous and strange and shy, and on the drive home the child would not want to talk, it would be thinking as hard as it could, and Margaret would know it was pondering and puzzling, working and picking, as she herself had always done, at this rigid coil of mystery that no one could unwind.

There was one thing that Margaret never needed to explain to them or even mention to them: that it was better that this whole Jacksonville matter (that was such a sword in their mother's heart) be kept entirely among themselves, mystery that it was, touching, as it did, for all they knew— for they were not educated people—on some peculiar, vicious wrong that lay at the bottom of things. She did not say this or explain it, because the children knew—only dimly at first, then more and more distinctly—that it was this very matter, this Jacksonville aspect of one parent's life, that enabled the father to mock and injure and subdue the mother, and that therefore it had some awesome power that must never be allowed to run abroad, never be let loose beyond Suwannee Drive.

And even if they had not known of this power by anything else, they would have known from this: the mother's stern, inward-staring face when she returned from those Saturdays in Florida; and from her look, her voice, on those infrequent times in-between when she spoke of the old crazies on Eighth Street, murmured private murmurs to herself about little things that had to be gotten for them, little messages, inquiries which had to be communicated to them. (*Got to write to Mama tonight—about thus and so, let me put it on my list.*) Yes, simply her look would suffice, so very altered when she was thinking of them, or her voice when she let their names, their ridiculous lives, slip out, swing for a moment, in the surprised air of the house. Thus from all these signs the children knew that the whole matter was something not to be spoken of abroad, they knew that each one of them had, must have—that in fact every person must in some sense be born with—a special cell in his brain for *the people of Jacksonville* so they would not touch on the contents of other cells. They understood that the name Jacksonville itself was a word that in the world outside was best left unacknowledged in every possible way.

So those Saturdays in Jacksonville. An enormous number of them over the years, over twenty years and more, before the war and during the war (though less then, because she had no car and the bus gave her a pounding headache), then long years afterward, up through her father's death (which she could not think about without a severe emotion battering her, beating her down) and then the end of them at last—these journeys to the world below, down to the worst intentions of the universe—with the death of her mother, a death which again she could not think about without a migraine pressure of emotion, without bad images falling mercilessly (though she clenched her mind against them) in a rapid pattern on her mind's screen.

*But all those Saturdays.* Taking the children with her at first, when it did no harm, though of course certain people—Leonard and Granny—believed that it *did* do harm. The way those days drained her. Made her literally sick sometimes, in spite of aspirin and a whole pocketbook of medications, left her a ragged pulp of stunned feelings, of pity and anger churning within her like stubborn chemicals that would not mix and dissolve. And yet she went on, and things were never better. There was no way for them to *be* better—something terribly mean had seen to that. Year after year she pulled up on the dirt street, crossed through the sandspurs to the ugly porch with her basket of supplies. She saw herself scrubbing and wiping, sweeping, mopping, pouring into things smoking streams of disinfectant; standing on rickety chairs to measure windows—for curtains to be sewn at home and brought back next time, when spring would be summer or summer fall; taking the bedding out to air, she and George lugging it through the door, losing their grip on the seams of the worn ticking, trying to decide where to lay it in the ragged yard . . . on and on through the years, bringing nothing but her cheerless face, her toil and ill humor, her distress. *What good it did,* she thought.

She thought too of time going on and what it wrought, her mother growing thinner if anything, though she had always been as thin as a stick, subsisting more and more on cigarettes and Coca-Cola, the old bony hands she might have used to clean up the place or fix herself up a bit entirely occupied with the complex operations of thumping, lighting, smoking, flicking and extinguishing cigarettes, without motion to spare for any useful occupation. And her father growing as stout as her mother thin, aging like many fat people before his time, up until his last moment on earth the main stay and support of two families with, in effect, young children, the buyer of goods and payer of bills, the one competent member of the whole weird little colony, a man with two women to care for (almost equally helpless) and four offspring, three of whom grew older but did not grow up, and so when he died at sixty-eight and should have been free, many years since, of dependent children, were still under five years of mental age. Each morning of his life, including the day of his death, her father crossed over before work from one back door to another, through the two weedy back yards with a basin in his hand, in order to shave the faces of two grown men, his only sons, endowed by nature (the God of love) with no minds but with healthy, luxuriant beards, shaving them from the basin set in the unwashed sink, his first cigar of the day burning down in a saucer on a heap of dirty dishes.

And yet on those Jacksonville Sundays, though it was not wise and though there was needed some false hope or idea to betray her into it, Margaret went out to the dairy as on other Sundays; sat out at Granny's on smooth, immaculate, languid afternoons, amidst fans gently turning and the fragile tinkling of thin, superior china full of delicious coffee; sitting almost as in a florist's shop, among large bright flour-

ishing plants, with Granny and Daddy Wallace, and sometimes for a time with sundry other friends and admirers of
her grandmother's, with business associates of the dairy
days, or the Ford dealer and his wife from town or the clerk
of the county court . . . but sitting, more often than not, in
the late of the day with Granny alone and the husband of
her declining years, a quiet-spoken, large-framed man losing
a little flesh by this time, a West Coast gentleman of polite,
knowledgeable ways, whose California hat of smooth straw
always lay thoughtfully nearby in case he should need to go
out on an errand, for the good of them all.

So it was that they sat together in what passed for earned,
unworried Sunday ease. Yet for Margaret a Jacksonville
Sunday was a transparent day, laid like a sheet of glass or of
Glad-Wrap over the day before, the Saturday on Eighth
Street, and thus not covering or obscuring it in the least—
the two pressed together in a double layer of everlasting
contrast.


DRIVING these many years later over wet August streets
to the Court, in her own late middle age, Margaret viewed,
sternly, not so much the road, but the picture of herself
working at her mother's years ago, all motion, up to her elbows in grease and dirt, wringing a cloth from a pan of something very strong that stung her hands, billowing vapors rising all around her, angry acrid fumes streaming from her pan
of potent solvent (or was it from some cauldron of fury
within herself belied by her sullen face?), the vapors drifting
and clearing sometimes to reveal the queer, still, photo-
graphic attitudes of her mother, her sister and brothers.
She saw this—herself in motion, in frenetic labor at her
mother's—and over this image another of a woman not at
work but utterly still, a guest in Sunday chiffon on her
grandmother's porch, leaning forward on a soft, very clean
recliner of flowery cotton, her elbows bent on crocheted

doilies; a cup of rich coffee comfortably beside her—its lacing of velvety cream rendering it a color of beautiful gold in the white cup; the blinds slightly tilted in perfect symmetry, to refract the flooding light of the waning afternoon.

On most such Sunday afternoons, when she had been to Jacksonville the day before, Margaret would not conceal this information but would wait her chance to impart it to Granny alone, and then things followed a certain path, and Granny would, as a matter of course, express her displeasure, even if only by a shaded look and a knitting and pursing of the mouth. But she would say, "Well how is your mother?" And Margaret would say, "Well how *could* she be?" or "Well you known how it is down there—it's never going to improve" or "Mama is never going to be anybody but Mama—you know that." Or she might go so far as to say, "Mama said to be sure and tell you hello—of course she would like to see you but I told her . . . ," and then Granny would uncross her ankles or move her hips in her chair and Margaret would have the satisfaction of thinking *She wouldn't let on to anyone for the world—but let's see if she doesn't think about this a little bit in her nice soft bed tonight*, and yet maybe she had not thought about it at all.

Once in a while, in fact, Margaret went even further, and reaching down, turning the savage beam of her eyes into her purse, her face flattened with gloom and perturbation, she would pull out of it the folded rectangles of a certain kind of coarse cloth, somewhat wrinkled and mussed, and handing the embroidered pieces to her grandmother, she would say in a stony, bold, unblinking way, "Mama wanted me to iron these for you before I brought them out but I didn't have time." And Margaret did all this (to someone she loved and almost worshipped) with a ruthless, knowing, brutish determination, putting the embroidered cases (crude, labored art of a child for her mother and therefore sacred surely in any house but this one) into her grandmother's hands, waiting deliberately, with blind smug patience, for her to protest and complain, repudiate them once more, refuse sometimes even to take hold of them, as if it was all some obscene trick of Margaret's for which she was full of contempt and disgust.

Then it would be that Margaret, grim and unsurprised, but still full of staring imputation, would, after a moment, take the cases and stuff them back into her purse. And that was all. The visit might go on, in some semblance of Sunday normalcy, or it might not. Margaret might think *It is wrong and bad to even be here* and simply rise to go.

And on other such afternoons, others of these Jacksonville Sundays, Margaret had said nothing, and there may even have been times when Granny never knew that her Saturday trip had been made. If Granny, however, unconfided in, had sensed on her own that Margaret—unable to sit back at her ease in her chair, wearing a brooding, worrying, resentful look—had made that journey to the other side of human fortune, she of course made no inquiry whatever, thinking *If I keep on refusing to ask, maybe she will quit telling me what I don't want to know, even if she has to keep on going down there—when everybody can see it almost makes her ill, and a disagreeable person to be with, and when after all she has these attractive little children to occupy her and keep her mind off things that no one can do anything about and cannot be helped.*

After the war started, and Ruth and Laney were still little more than toddlers (Richard an after-the-war baby boomer still to come), Daddy Wallace, at a certain time, on these visiting Sundays, would go into the house and bring out the radio so they could listen to the war news in sunny comfort on the porch. There would come on the doleful voice of Gabriel Heatter ("There's bad news tonight"), and they would listen in silence, with serious concentrated faces. After Leonard himself was in the war—he had almost been too old to go and was among the last ones called—Daddy Wallace would not go and get the radio until he had asked Margaret, very seriously and with great respect, what would please her more, to hear the news or not to hear it?

If there did come reports of the war in the Pacific, where Leonard, the sailor, worked atop an aircraft carrier, watching a radar screen for enemy planes, they all sat sternly forward to listen the better, and Ruth and Laney, playing perhaps at Margaret's feet, would look up in alert wonder at the studying figures of the adults, their heads lowered queerly to the large elegant square of red mahogany radio on the flaxen table.

*From the bottom of the cleaning basket, under the rags and cans, Margaret had lifted, on one of the Saturdays in Jacksonville, a certain rectangular object of scarred wood.* She had said, "This is for Riley, now this is just for him." Riley had made a noise that no one could understand and reached out for his present. But Margaret held it back, reflecting, and then she said, "Let's you and me go in the bedroom." In the bedroom she looked for the plugs and then the first one did not work and she tried another one and the radio came on, and she and Riley sat down on the sagging bed, on the discolored sheet that covered it, and she turned the dial and music came and Riley made a noise, and she turned the dial again and voices came, and then music and then voices, and Riley made his own sounds too, loud and intense, and much too excited for anyone to have understood, and jerked his arms about in his personal mode of celebration.

She had put the old wooden box on his lap, and he had turned the dial and listened, turned it again, his face strained and sober, the damp room curling his handsome thick black hair over his sweaty forehead. Then he spoke his peculiar noises to Margaret again, with his rough spastic intensity; this time she had understood him and so she had gone and closed the door. He had made noises again, and gestures and signs, and Margaret understood: the others were not to hear his radio, it was only for *him* to hear because Margaret had brought it to him alone; he would listen to it only in this room, with the door closed, so that none of his sounds could get away from him. And thus it was . . .

with Riley and his radio, and it steadied him when his afflicted nerves kicked up and when bad things came to pass, when deaths came, and afflicted fear and confusion and aggravation.

"That old radio," Margaret thought, remembering—so strangely—so many things today, when Riley was gone from Eighth Street and so many were dead, her mother and father dead, her grandmother dead, and Mr. Wallace . . . Gabriel Heatter.

She remembered this: the radio of red mahogany at the dairy had begun to have little spells, little seizures of blurting and grating and bleeping, and had had much careful attention paid to it and the best of care and then attentive convalescence, but had gone on to have yet other seizures of noise and ominous bleep and blurt, and finally been cast away, still almost young, into silence and darkness; whereas the old scarred box of Riley's, its numbers on the dial hardly readable (and not needing to be), not young when Margaret had gotten it secondhand and taken it to Jacksonville, played gallantly on as clear as a bell through the years, issued to Riley (and to no one but him) its silvery consolation. People remarked on it, and the little cronelike neighbor, Margaret's correspondent, a person for whom the Stovall family was a supremely interesting phenomenon, said it for them all: "You just wonder what he listens to. What he thinks it means."

But of course people were addicted to their radios in those days—Riley wasn't the only one. Radios were such nice unassuming friends and Margaret had always kept hers over the sink in the kitchen, which was the room where most of her work was done. She would even iron in there, and bathe the babies, for instance, laying them on a towel on the counter when they were very small, then later sitting them down in a big round pan in the sink. She remembered how when she put them in, they would take a quick breath of surprise and then quiver one sharp quiver—they did not know whether of pleasure or pain—and settle right down to play with their lids and spoons. The radio would be going along on low all the time, always with some little something on it that was interesting or surprising, or just with pretty songs, and she could pay whatever degree of attention she felt like to it though occasionally there would be something that would make her stand staring still for a moment, her hand on the iron in its metal tray. When her favorite songs were on she would absentmindedly sing them too, and sometimes she would still be singing ridiculously on long after the radio had gone on to something else. These days television was a different thing and didn't serve the same purpose at all she didn't think. Of course it was much more absorbing, in a way, but that was just the trouble—it sat people down and kept them down, it changed their ways, their habits of work, for instance, made them slow and stuporous.

When Laney was born, Margaret and Granny had sat in the morning light in the bay window and listened to Amos 'n Andy. Granny would have fed Leonard early and sent him to work, then put out a more leisurely breakfast for Margaret and herself. Perhaps they had finished it and were sitting over their coffee. The new baby (that would be Laney) would be sleeping in the bassinette by Margaret's bed and the other child (that would be Ruth) would be making a house out of little boxes and blocks on the living room floor, and Margaret had been happier than she had almost ever been; it was as if on those particular mornings whatever was dark and bad had crumbled off the sides of her life and now she and her grandmother were sitting on the top of a sunny mountain bay window like Heidi and Grandfather.

Today she could still picture the splendid motion of Granny pouring coffee from the glass pot she had brought from the dairy, to render, after all, these newborn days good, happy, joyful days for her granddaughter, whom she truly loved and who was a special person to her.

"When Granny got back from California," Nora said,

"you were the first one she wanted to see. One reason was she knew you already had your little house and you had kept alive without her so far and you were too proud—or something—to say Gimme, gimme like the rest of us. Because you were one of the few that hadn't written her for a handout while she was gone (Frank and Vivian wrote her practically every day), so you were the safest one she had even if you were the poorest, so she went to see you first." Nora smiled. "Or was it because she just loved you so much?"

*It was all of that,* Margaret thought, *and no telling what all else.*

"But you were down with Laney, pregnant and sick on your stomach, and Granny didn't care too much for that I bet you."

"No she was good to me about that, and she and Daddy Wallace used to bring me things they thought I could eat. And then when Laney was born—don't you remember?—Granny came and spent three days right in the house with me."

"Of course when she saw those windows in your house—those bolts, those highways, of homemade curtain, every little window blowing and ruffling in dotted swiss, or polished cotton, with those little bushy fluffy ties—and those gathered things at the top, those—"

"Valances."

"Those valances. And Ruth in homemade dresses with embroidered roses on the front, and that tatting around the collar."

Margaret had swung her leg.

"I know she thought it was the cleverest, neatest little house she had ever seen, and that everything about you was just . . . charming . . . don't you know? Of course she didn't know, or didn't want to know, that your husband was a nervous wreck and a maniac and beat up on you and treated you like dirt and did absolutely nothing to raise his children but pay the bills, and didn't even do that until he had had a big tantrum over every single one of them—and hardly knew his children were there and when he did try to notice them, couldn't get them to look him in the eye. But she didn't see all that because she didn't want to see it, she just saw all that wonderful work and imagination you had put in on your little house."

Margaret frowned, and her voice was flat. "In the children's room we didn't have any chests and I made some out of apple crates and covered them in front with these flowery panels that you pulled together like curtains."

"Granny loved you to death for that, she loved those apple crates—I can see her purring and mooning over them. And shaking hands with herself for saving you for this good clean uncomplaining apple-crate life. And one thing she loved about those apple crates—since they were so clever and pretty she didn't have to feel bad about not giving you a bedroom suit, or even a down-payment on one."

Margaret had tried to explain something that afternoon. "The thing was, Granny didn't want me to be a failure and to her certain ways of helping people were normal, like being with them when they had a baby, and other ways were not . . . . "

"And so she didn't want to be responsible for people being a failure just by her helping them out?"

But Margaret, on that afternoon at Nora's, had been sitting deep in her chair, gazing across the dusky room to the blurred square of graying window light, as if it were the last light that confusing things, mysterious things, might possibly be studied by. *Who helped who . . . did or didn't help or hurt, love, betray . . . .*

Nora had leaned over her low table to light a cigarette, but seeing Margaret's staring face, she too had turned to the window and gazed deeply for a moment into the frame of darkening light before she reached for the lamp-chain by her side.

## ~ CHAPTER SIX ~

A T  T H E foot of the front stairs, where Margaret paused to collect herself and shake off her umbrella, a strong smell hung on the air, a sour almost mangy smell like that of a wet dog. She spread her umbrella on the floor, then took off her scarf and felt for locks of damp hair; now it was certain, it was no longer in doubt, that at the shower tonight they would think she was a boogerman.

Margaret gazed up the stairs to the Court. The currents of sour wet air seemed to be flowing down from above, and the smell mingled oddly in her nostrils with sensations of pity and sadness . . . at first she did not know why. But this sour odor was almost certainly the smell of someone waiting outside the Court in wet clothes, and she realized that she must have sensed that at once and that the one who would be waiting up there would be the black woman, Lillie Ringgold, arriving before the rest of them for the three o'clock hearing. She must certainly have walked at least part of the way through the storm itself, and no doubt she would have come through a hurricane too if there had been one, for this hearing of her son's, to save him, even though she knew he could not be saved. Margaret could see her with her head down driving forward into the streaming rain, her broad body set against it, on her back an ancient big-knit sweater of her white lady's.

Margaret rose rather heavily to the landing—on this more than peculiar day—and at the top, it was indeed the black woman Lillie who turned to Margaret from the waiting-bench, where she was sitting without visible agitation, her hands folded on her stomach, and beside her on the seat—the source of the stench, her shield against the storm—a wet heap of woolly coat. *Wearing that in August,* Margaret thought.

"How you?" Margaret said.

"Pretty good. How you?" said the black woman.

"Isn't this some rain?"

"Sho is now, I tell you," Lillie said. "Judge ain't here I don't guess."

"No, not if the door's locked." Margaret wiped off her bag with a kleenex. She found her keys, but her damp hands slipped through them when she tried to unlock the door. She realized she was listening for the phone, her missed call from Jacksonville. What if it rang now, before she could get in to answer it? Thinking of Jacksonville, "the people of Jacksonville," the ones elegant people in beautiful houses did not want to have to look at, made her turn—even while she struggled with the lock—and glance at this Lillie again, over her shoulder. Her mind formed a ridiculous picture in which Lillie was opening her old big loose purse. The catch didn't work and she had to more or less fold it together at the top but she reached down in this big old purse and brought out a rumpled brown paper sack, with wet-looking stains on it from somewhere, and said to her son Buddy, *Here you some pencils if this what you want.* It was a sack full of new pencils, a fat handful of beautiful pencils of every color and kind. *If this all you want,* she said again. *So you can come home.*

Inside the Court, Margaret shook some of the wet off her raincoat and hung it up while Lillie settled herself on the divan, presenting finally the same picture of patient stolidity as she had outside. She sat with her ankles crossed on the floor and Margaret saw how her short thick feet bulged over the sides of the worn pumps. She felt that one thing a person should not have to do in this life, with everything else they had to do, was to walk around in uncomfortable shoes. She felt that ought to have been in that bill of rights somewhere.

Margaret went to the window, drawn to the frame of glistening wet. In the lot below she saw Jim shutting his car door. He stood for a moment beside the car, bareheaded in the light rain, in his old black creased raincoat (which probably had not been cleaned since his wife left him), looking up—as if with foreboding—to the office of the Court. *Oh the silly thing—standing there in the rain.* Then he moved slowly across the lot, a disheveled bean pole, his head slightly aslant. Definitely he was nervous today. Anxious about something.

But after all, that last hearing had been such a bad one, and she knew Jim must be thinking about that. A young white boy had been brought to them by deputies. That there were two deputies instead of one, and that they brought him with handcuffs on, was a sign of something, of course, and yet they had had these from time to time, and usually the ones brought this way, with shackles and guards, did not behave any differently from the rest of them. The boy had come in walking as tall and straight as a stick, his head high. No he was not a bit bowed or hunched, he did not drag himself along like so many of them did. What you saw when you glanced his way was a stern, oblivious face and a rigid mouth, and yet looking closer . . . something else very odd: the eyes in the stern face were almost completely shut, you could hardly tell whether he was even awake or not.

So the men had taken this boy with this somnolent face into the room and said *Sit down*. But he had not moved; neither his body nor his lips moved a jot, and so they said again *Sit down*, and then before they could speak to him again or thrust him onto the seat or issue any threat or command, all of a sudden—it was a strange and awful thing—his face moved, the muscles in his face were pulled as if by ropes, he opened his mouth and there was flung forth on the air a roar of overwhelming force, a high steady shrieking yowl, hardly wavering, burning their eardrums, going on and on as if breath would never give out, or did not flow from human lungs to begin with, with time enough while it was still going on for Margaret to look, with stricken face, at the deputies, as if to demand an explanation, and for them to look back at her in helpless perplexity; time enough for Jim to come stumbling, all gawking head and limbs, out of his office, plainly terrified, his arms spread crazily away from him as if he were on fire.

Then just as suddenly—it stopped. Breath broke, and the cry ceased as if snapped in two. The lids closed and the face, somnolent, fell into place again.

In a little while they had had the hearing, inside chambers, with the boy's Court lawyer in there too, and as on most days, Margaret did not go in, she stayed to do the business outside. She knew it would be short. For Jim would just say, his head deep-cocked in fret and consternation, "Let's see," looking in the file, "do we have a—medical report on this case?" The boy himself would not open his eyes and Jim and Fred—Fred was the appointed defense—would look at each other as if to say "Well since he's crazy" (*if he is crazy*, Margaret thought) "we can't do a thing until we get somebody to say he is, so thank goodness they can take him away and there's not a thing we can do about him today. Being crazy." —"Yes."

Or something like that, but in any case it must have been just as they were rising in the hearing room to take him away that it happened again, exactly as before, and there came again the piercing, blistering yowl in a sudden roar from behind the door, and when the door opened on it, this crazed cry (if it *was* crazed) burst then on Margaret's ears with double its high-pitched force, sounding as if it came from some place deeper than any person's lungs could be, or as if it were filled with blood. And yet, stranger still in a way, was the fact that this boy, while this blood-filled cry was coming out of him, was walking, as steady as you please, between the stunned deputies as they led him out, got him through the glass doors.

On the landing, breath gave way again, and in the shaking silence inside, Jim, his arms jerking and twitching like an infant's—as if he hardly knew they were his—looked hard at Margaret, as if to say *Wha-at?! What am I to do or think about this? And why in twenty years, never one like this before? Though others just as bad sometimes in other ways. Lord lord.*

Lillie heaved up from her seat. She had heard Jim's step down the stairwell. When Jim came in he shook her hand, a strange habit for a judge, Margaret had been told.

Lillie did not mince her words. Her lips plumped out. She said, "What this arm' robber?"

Jim began to shake his head in sympathy. "That's what they say. Over in Valdosta."

"And what they say this arm' robber was wif?" Lillie said. Her voice was not loud, her words did not cut and challenge, and yet scorn and contempt were there.

Jim looked away. "They said it was a knife," he said. He was sorry to say this. His head hung to one side, like a preacher's.

"Knife," Lillie said. "If it a knife I bet I know what knife. Old rusty pocketknife he got fum Bradford. That all that is, if it a knife."

Jim shook his head again, said, "I declare."

But then he said, "A knife can hurt somebody though.

That's the problem." He managed to look into her face, and she stared into his. "A knife can hurt."

"Not Buddy though. Not Buddy knife."

Jim murmured sympathetically. Then he started down the corridor towards his office, awkwardly, as if he hardly knew where it was, still in his wet raincoat.

Margaret rolled paper into her typewriter. Lillie, on the divan, settled into herself once more, thinking her own thoughts. Margaret hesitated over her machine. For a moment she had a foolish feeling that if she were typing she would not hear the phone, and as if to prove a point, the phone rang just as she began. It was a grandmother Margaret had talked to before. Recently two rough grandsons had fallen into her care and she could not seem to get any control over them. She wanted to love them and be their granny, but now—she was so sorry to have to say it, even to Margaret—she had reason to think they had been shoplifting. Margaret talked it through with her a little bit. She thought maybe Curtis should go out and speak with them.

She realized when she hung up that Lillie had not even looked her way—she did not care who was calling this white lady today. Margaret could not help but think once more of Buddy and his futile search for a pencil on the night Bradford beat him and he had run away, and so she thought his mother's thoughts: *White people can't get in no trouble over no pencils to write with, cause whatever they need they always got it, fact this is just how low we be—that all this about Buddy can start up with nothing but a pencil and somebody whole life just about ruint over something to write with. Not only white folks always got things and if a pencil what they need they got it but mos' of the time they don't even need one nohow because they got all these typing machines anyway and can't get in no trouble over something to write wif.*

Margaret bent over her typewriter, placed her fingers on the keys. Something was wrong today, which was the trouble with a job like hers. Even when you had been working at it as long as she had. Most things glided past you, very bad things sometimes slipped away from you—it was as if you looked up from your desk and saw them far away, softly falling. Then suddenly, when you had borne so much— everything was unbearable.

If only feelings would ever come by themselves, if ever one thing did not lead to another and things were not always intertwined. For now, sitting alone in the room with this old Lillie, it was as if all her own griefs sat before her in this stoical old black grieving skin, her own misery and confusion looked out of this staring absent clouded face, past the hanging begonia to the wet day beyond. She thought *It is probably just this job, and not all the rest of my life, that has worn me down, and I just have not realized it*. It was as if in the corner of her eye the black woman loomed and spread, expanded dangerously, and Margaret felt trapped and surrounded by her (it was ridiculous), by her heap of massed grief. For after all she was past being fooled by plumped-out lips, or by flaunting passivity and placidness.

Margaret sat drooped over her typewriter and could not get to work. Certain things were determined to coalesce: a message she had not quite gotten today, from a place of pain; then *this* pain sitting with her in the office this afternoon; the pictures she had had, driving to work, of herself sitting forward in a handsome rattan chair—in confusion and grief, in serious mental conflict—at her grandmother's dairy on certain Sunday afternoons of years gone by.

The dark, disturbed day outside her window cast an eerie light over the room this afternoon, and she realized her resistance to bad feelings had become very low indeed. She felt she was about to give in to something—a deep surge of wavery images climbing to consciousness. Jagged fragments of memory no one would want to recall if they could help it, things seen and heard or half-heard or surmised. At first she could hardly distinguish one from another, and yet she knew they all had to do with people who were suffering . . . people not loved or cared for, people grief-torn, rejected and betrayed, people with faces of staring sorrow. Ones who would ask for help but with no one to ask . . . people sick and hurting with no one to turn to . . . all kinds of people all over the world with nothing to call their own and no work to do, being turned away when they even asked for it.

*Where it all comes from,* Margaret asked herself. *What books, what pieces in the papers or on TV—* She would have liked to stop herself but somehow she could not and she went right on and thought, for instance, of people driven by war, bundling each other up in the middle of the night, leaving their houses never to see them again, leaving their old silly loved things that no one even wanted but them, leaving their trees and flowers in the night, wanting almost to kiss the trunk of the old tree in the front yard. *Old tree, old tree, live on to remember us.*

Sometimes when she began to think such thoughts she would stand suddenly up or pace the floor—she would want to run into the street and snatch someone by the throat. But today she simply sat, stunned, at her typewriter, with just barely enough sense to be disgusted with herself—and to wonder where it all came from. You read things, she supposed, and people tell you things (that you do not even want to hear), you dream things, and sometimes you just guess and surmise out of awful little glimpses of life you have personally encountered somewhere. And of course if you work in a court—

She felt that though the scenes and fantasies she had might be gross, they were not a bit grosser than what really went on; no-o . . . when it came to grossness, she doubted that anything you could dream up would hold a candle to the grossness of life itself.

But why was she so prone to all this . . . so fond a prey to these spectres of people's grief and helplessness? Why such a haunted ghost of a person—when others were not? *And is it pity—or fear—that haunts me?* she asked herself.

Did others carry the same nightmares around with them behind their grinning faces, those gurgling voices? ("Well Ma-argaret Ba-arker aren't you looking good!")

But in a way they are not nightmares, she thought again, and we cannot really wake from them. So—she had her pills. All that Sinequan. Her Xanax. She was a very, very weak person.

Of course other people had something too usually. They had drink or dope or nervous breakdowns; in the big cities, crack cocaine; they had crime and the courts, divorce, or going crazy or running away. They became religious maniacs. In fact it seemed to Margaret that normal people were so rare that actually they *weren't* normal and that people that lived cheerful, unhaunted lives, never needing to sedate themselves with a thing—that it must be they that had something wrong with them. *To be miserable and afraid most of the time, and then pathetically happy (because we can be, we cowards, we are capable of that)—that must be normal*, Margaret thought.

The picture came back to her of herself and her father, struggling, in sad perplexity. *Herself and her father together in the kitchen on wash night.* Piling George in a tub of soap. Riley waiting on the stool, naked like a skinned quail, saying over and over, his head tilted in that queer tilt, somberly repeating, as if in never-ending surprise, "Da-ah-oo Gaw Da-ah-oo . . . Daddy wash you Gaw Daddy wash you." Her mother's voice on the phone carrying through the house, cackling, carrying on. She and her father together, struggling.

But she was startled by the phone again. It was the lawyer who was supposed to represent Buddy Ringgold, wanting to know if they were ready for him. Didn't want to get there a minute too soon. Wouldn't even come over and look at the file, talk to Lillie perhaps. Margaret was slightly curt, she was not in the mood for this kind of lawyer today. But she said she would call him back when they brought Buddy in— so he wouldn't have to waste any of his coffee time, his drugstore and newsstand time, doing a little work for somebody who needed him.

Lillie, on her divan, snuffled. She drew out a long sigh, and then another sound—private, low and indistinct—which might have been words or just an expressive noise such as people make to themselves. Sometimes Lillie would speak; on one occasion they had had an actual conversation, but today she no longer even acknowledged that Margaret was in the room. Today was not a day to be made small and ordinary in any way; it was a day for privacy and silence.

*What if I had sat somewhere, waiting and waiting, to see if one of my children would be sent to prison?*

Margaret looked out at the rain, harder now, coming down in warping slants. She thought she might like to work amongst flowers somewhere. Or—how would it be to run a hotel on a beautiful beach, where people were not in trouble, with everyone enjoying themselves, smiling, getting a suntan? Something to change her cast of mind. If only she could do something to increase her resistance to unpleasant thoughts.

Moods—if only someone could find out what caused them, it would be worth a fortune. Sometimes Margaret would be lying on her brocade sofa in the living room reading the newspaper. And she would be reading about something horrible, something that even by itself, without all the other countless things that could happen to people, would be enough to take away from them the strength to live. Yet she might read about such a thing quite calmly, sort of half humming, in fact, to herself, along with the Lawrence Welk show on TV, thinking *But this is not happening to me, here I am as snug as a bug on my nice brocade sofa, feeling pretty good, my duster snugly over my feet.* At such moments she would begin to believe that she had finally managed to seal her pores, just lock the door on things that might disturb her and make her feel bad for no good reason (since she could not do a thing about them). And yet—just when she would think everything was sliding off of her, blowing past like a harmless wind . . . it would turn out that certain things had sneaked in through the back door of her brain and made little secret nests there, for one day something would transpire (a letter or a call, or something seen or heard, some old Lillie, perhaps, in her stern pile of trouble on the divan) and she would have a sensation of something coming loose or breaking down or falling apart, and it was as if all these little morsels of saved-up pain would rush over her in a vast scrambling whirr.

And indeed, today, sitting at her desk in the Court, her hands folded under her chin, half-conscious of a slight odor of dampness, injury from the elements, wafting from the figure on the divan, she thought *All this ridiculous pain people go through, so absurd.* At that moment another little picture crossed over, suddenly, on a back street of her brain, having waited its chance for many many thousands of hours, a little picture that had a kind of comedy in it, and yet no, she was not sure it did: a picture of the hushed despair, the desperate attentiveness, of two very small girls, Ruth and Laney, on her lap in the big rocking chair, her arms around them, holding in front the book in which Cinderella, on the night of the dance, crouched weeping before the fire in her pitiful rags and dirt. Poor despised helpless thing, Margaret thought, and it was passing strange indeed that these many years later, remembering that often repeated scene with her daughters, she would think of this creature, still, as the concentrate of all loneliness, the representative of all outcast people and abject souls, remember her in her limp collapse by the dirty fireplace, in a town that was not, but almost might have been, Jacksonville itself.

Perhaps it was simply that no matter how far she thought along other people's road of pain, she always arrived at herself again, for sometimes she thought of this person too, this Cinderella, as one of *them*, the people of Jacksonville, who also stood (it was all so odd) for all Cinderellas (the same

225

way Cinderella stood for them), for everyone left out and cast aside, people who could not help themselves and whom no one—except a fairy godmother—could help. And she thought again of her own children (the older ones, that the little ones did not grow into exactly, but were shed and extinguished by) riding down the nighttime road from Jacksonville, a town full of cast-off souls, riding home from that most peculiar of little houses, oddest of all little cottages in the world that were real; the children thinking hard, with nothing to say to her as she drove (hunched darkly over the wheel), and yet sliding towards her, under narrowed lids, most infinitely peering looks.

So she recalled their struggle on nights like that. Then the struggle of herself and her father . . . together . . . and then each on their own . . . still struggling, but apart.

But whatever she was and whatever she had come from, she had risen (hadn't she?), in this stretch at the end of her life, from the bottom of a certain kind of pain. She had become a nice-looking woman who took care of herself, a person in clean patent-leather pumps with combination lasts, a symbol of well-being to people in distress coming through her doors of glass, someone with a little money in the bank (something she never expected to have), a house that was paid for and in good condition.

In the Juvenile Court Margaret, leaning with drawn shoulders over her typewriter, but still unable to put her fingers to the keys, listened to the one beyond her on the divan snuffle and sigh her private sounds, and desperately wished she could know what really lay between them (in terms of human grief) but these twenty-odd squares of new linoleum, with a slight, warm gleam to it most days (since they must try to be cheerful here), though today looking gray and eerie, full of curious shadows in the gloomy light.

She turned her head, almost crossly, to the double glass doors through which the lowly rose to this high domain, The Court. Somehow she could not cease to think of them.

*Is it because I am one of them—or because I am not?* On this stormy day, the doors, in their glassy shadows, looked strangely forbidding; but she envisioned an enormous procession of customers for the Court marching through them to her fortified island behind her desk, filing solemnly in as if to a weird graduation. She pictured too the particular somnolent face that had crossed that threshold last week, the wide jaws, the raw mysterious cry flung forth. She thought of him and of all the rest of them marching Courtward, as they had over all these years . . . the confused labyrinths of life they came from.

Men and women angry and sad. Little girls with no one to comb their hair. Old stout grandmas with round faces and braided buns, in washed-out country dresses and old-fashioned coats. Yes especially she thought of old grandmas (because she was an old grandma herself) laboring on the stairs, breathing hard, coming—as often as not these days, when marriages could be such brutal things—to bear their witness in sorrow and shame that daughters, that sons, had abused little children, had injured and abandoned them, kept them shut up and put away like little prisoners, hurt their little bodies and their minds.

Somehow she saw all this darkly mirrored on the stormy glass today, mixing with the frazzled reflection of old Lillie staring forward from the divan, her trouble pulled about her in patient privacy, her lip projected in half-defiance of any rod that might be raised, as she waited for strangers to bring in her child—white men in uniforms, with guns on, bored probably, distracted, with nothing personal at stake.

All these outlandish thoughts pounded her head like a hammer, and she felt as if it were swelling up like some peculiar wound. She wished to her soul she could do something about it all and get it over with, throw herself down for instance, prostrate herself, if it would do any good, before all these grieved souls, every single one she had ever thought about or known, the whole mass of them together;

yes she almost wished she could give herself away, give her blood and flesh a human sacrifice for all human hurt (even her own), and thus at the same time make up for herself, for the safety and separateness of her present life, that she did not deserve, and which no one *could* deserve as long as others were in pain. Why didn't someone just come and take what she had, her nice smooth clothes, her clean little house (hated and loved)?

They wouldn't even have to ask, she would just give it to them and be done with it, give even the brocade sofa, if they thought it would do any good. "Oh just take it," she would say.

IN THE bathroom Margaret hunted in her purse. She took two aspirin and two Xanax, enough to do her some good. She went into the stall. As the john ran down, she could hear Jim in the corridor with Curtis, the court services worker.

Curtis was not a sad-sack like she and Jim were and it always gave them a little lift when he was around. He would be just the person for Buddy Ringgold too, if by any chance the Court was able to keep him and not turn him over to Valdosta. In that case, Jim would probably put him on probation and Curtis would be his worker. But of course Jim said the people in Valdosta were not going to let Buddy go. He said they were going to bring in the man who had been held up, and the knife too, and then he would have to let them take Buddy back with them.

Margaret stood at the mirror over the sink. The lawyers were always telling her how nice she looked, but today she looked like a boogerman. She leaned in closer to the glass. She looked like she had something wrong with her much worse than a headache.

She could tell that Curtis and Jim had gone into Jim's office. But then there was a commotion downstairs and she heard a babble of voices rising to the Court. The colored people. Coming up about Buddy Ringgold she had no doubt. Clambering up here to be with Lillie, although Lillie probably wished they would stay at home. There was a sudden silence, and Margaret knew they had taken the turn to the landing, seen the double doors to the Court.

In the small lounge of the lavatory there was one big chair and now Margaret sat down in it. With all the others in there now she wasn't ready to reenter the room. She sat back and closed her eyes. The people in the room outside murmured and whispered. She could imagine them grouped around Lillie on the divan. Now and then a child's voice piped up and one of the grown-ups would say *Shush now, this the co't*. Margaret considered the phenomenon of Lillie, all the old colored women like her, the big broods of people they had to take care of. Not that Lillie was actually so old, but she was an old-fashioned *type*, an old kind of negro that would soon disappear. All these changes were going on, and yet some people were not affected. History was going past them, going too fast to pull them along; they were still stuck over people's ironing boards, grunting over people's tubs (scouring them, making them shine). Yet more and more, you saw black people working all over the place; they waited on you at the store, at the cleaners; and for instance—sometimes it still gave you a little turn—you might be standing absentmindedly at the bank and then you would be up at the window and a black hand would be reaching out to take your paycheck.

Certainly history was going on—in Waycross, Georgia, and in every other town in Georgia, in this year of nineteen hundred and seventy-nine—and she herself was a witness to it every day. She looked out from her island of cabinets and stands and saw history building and gathering there in the room, accumulating on papers and files, in the new laws and rules and procedures that were coming down, and in the sounds and looks, the gestures and ways of the people—

black and white—that came there. The day would come pretty soon when the younger ones would hardly believe the way things had been and children would giggle and be vastly entertained if you tried to tell them about separate water fountains and things like that. In the history of helpless people (people innocent and absurd), here were some that were finally being redeemed, voices to say, "They have not done anything wrong so stop *treating* them like they have—right now!"

So history was moving on and a certain kind of human suffering was being gradually swept away, and yet Margaret could not help but think—she was such a negative person— that while people were not noticing, new kinds were probably secretly growing, as if there had always been in the world a fixed quantity of human pain and whenever you squeezed it down in one place it was bound to bulge up again somewhere else.

But these old Lillies being left behind. This old Lillie in her old-fashioned kind of resistance, that black people had always had and kept covered over and mostly invisible, except for a few signs that white people had more or less agreed, over the years, to discount. There was a certain kind of petulance, for instance, mumbling grouchiness and contrariness—*that* was OK. Although still, white ladies might say, "If only they could hear themselves, how ugly that sounds." Or: "If only they could realize (but of course they can't) that it doesn't cost a thing to be pleasant. That even if you're poor you can afford to be nice to people."

There was what Lillie had: the projecting lip, the habitually pouting mouth, where you could see the pinkish inner flesh of her underlip; such a phenomenon might be, as in Lillie's case, almost the only sign that she had ever permitted herself of any spirit of rebellion, of less than perfect subjugation. For otherwise she spoke the words, did the deeds, that it was proper and right for a black woman to speak and do, a woman created after all by God in his wisdom to do the scrubbing and sweeping that otherwise white women would have to do. Thus she could speak of her "white lady." —"Got to be to my white lady's today." And the white lady of her "colored woman." —"My colored woman's coming today."

They said Lillie was a good worker, in spite of her projecting lip. Something hard to find these days: a good worker of the good, *old* school. Not a high-class black woman either (you had to give her credit); Lillie was from the bad side of colored town, and yet clean. "O yes Lillie is clean. And honest! Yessir! Oh I would trust Lillie with anything I have, oh I wouldn't insult her by ever putting anything away on her account. She has her pride too you know." But Margaret heard Lillie's voice too. *Now she got a cole and I got to wait on her in bed. So then she gie me the cole and so I sick and she well but she ain't got to wait on me, I still waiting on her.*

Was this what Lillie thought, and all Lillies all those years, living and dying through all the years and white ladies living and dying and for a long time very little outward sign, visible to white ladies, that God's wise little pact, the whole little bargain, was not complete on both sides?

The colored women talked to Margaret quite a bit sometimes. There seemed to be something about her that made them able to say things they might not say to other white women. At least she was not home taking a nap while her colored woman washed out her stockings and pressed her blouse.

She had done plenty of listening, in fact, to both black and white; and in all her twenty years of listening up here (whenever people wanted to talk, and of being quiet when they wanted to be quiet), she wondered how many little tales, how many stories and scenes and small human histories and adventures had entered her brain. She could imagine them dropping like stones into the dark ocean of her mind, the seven seas of her whole plunging consciousness over all the years. What was a miracle, she supposed, was that so many of them survived, that some of all the things she had heard and seen and thought and listened to, had not drowned and been lost but had one day washed up again on the shore of consciousness, sprung up on another day's field of thought, making her stand motionless over the sink at home, for instance, her hands in the dishpan, making her rise suddenly on one elbow and stare into the room from her high soft bed in the late afternoon.

She could not open a runaway file like Buddy Ringgold's, for instance, without a whole bunch of other runaways springing to mind. So many cases of people fleeing, escaping from each other, children running away from parents, and parents from children, fathers from families and husbands from wives and vice versa, boys to join the Army and girls to get married or just to get away, people running, running away, and then others running away from *them* and in Margaret's mind things always mixing and mingling, things from her own life and from these lives up here and the lives of friends and friends of friends and from people in movies and on TV. Everything intermingling—until she sometimes wished she could burst into her own brain and get hold of it all, fly into the whole mess and straighten it out.

This runaway Buddy—and so many others. Had not Margaret herself, in fact, done that when she was young, if anyone actually knew? And hadn't her mother and father run away together, and then her father run away from her mother and then Margaret run away from them both? Of course her Aunt Nora could go on and on about it, and in a way she exaggerated, and yet a lot of what she said was perfectly true.

Voices came forward in Margaret's memory and became other voices, or spoke words that were not their own, queer and ridiculous. The colored people murmured just beyond the door, and her head hurt, thinking of runaways, but things went on intermingling and she imagined something

232

very, very odd—the voice of her grandmother, speaking in accents she could not have spoken in, about the running away of her daughter Emma. She said she would have stopped her but there was nothing she could do. "When a gul get that kind of thing on her mind nothing you can do, not a thing in this world going to do any good. But Jesus know this: I told her anyway—you best to stay here. This the place where you belong, where I always goin to take care of you. You always goin to have the best with me. Wherefore if you go off like you wanting to, out of town where I can't keep no care of you and don't even know what going on wit you, well I tell you this right now—when that time come I through wit you. And you know me dis much: won't be no going back on dat neither. When I through, I through."

WHEN the phone rang Margaret didn't waste any time getting back to her desk to pick it up. She was surprised that before she could speak she had to stop and take a deep breath. But it was just the principal at the high school. Oh he was so slow on the phone she didn't know if she could stand it this afternoon. It always took him forever just to pass the time of day. Even when he finally got started on his business it didn't sound like it *was* business. "Mrs. Barker! Uh-h-h . . . I was over in the new wing yesterday? And-d . . . I believe you have met Mr. Pead, the new gym teacher?"

Thank goodness it was just broken gym lockers again. She buzzed Jim's phone so he could put Curtis on.

Now she had a chance to acknowledge the folks in the room. "How y'all?" she said, and all of them murmured something back. Bradford and Lillie sat on different divans with the others ranged around them. Lillie sat as sternly, as absently, as before, paying the rest of them very little mind. Children climbed over her now and then, and she told them to sit down in no uncertain terms, and they did so without question. Lillie's sister sat beside her and from time to time she would tell one of the girls to pull her dress down or keep her legs crossed, because this was the Court, certain things were not allowed and she was telling them for their own good. The sister was thin and fidgety, the opposite of Lillie in every way; she sat bent forward, her elbows on her knees, smoking cigarettes.

Bradford had his house slippers on. He was a big, loose-limbed man. He smiled at Margaret. "My feet getting bad," he said.

"I declare," Margaret said.

"Standing on that concrete all day at the plant," he said. But he was still smiling, as if this was just an interesting fact.

"They give me one of my off-days today," he said. "To come up here about Buddy."

"Wasn't that good?" Margaret said.

"I always rest my feet on my off-days. So today one of my off-days."

Two of the children sat down on Bradford's knees and he looked like an awkward Santa Claus.

Curtis came out of Jim's room with a handful of papers to put on Margaret's desk. "Miz B. you don't look like you feel too good."

"I've got a splitting headache today," Margaret said.

"Do you think you better take something?" Curtis said.

"Oh I did. It's starting to help me," Margaret said. She handed Curtis a file. "This is Buddy Ringgold's," she said.

All the colored people got quiet when they heard Buddy's name.

"Buddy play in the band," Bradford said, with his broad smile. "I hope he don't miss no more practice."

"Buddy plays the trumpet, doesn't he?" Curtis said.

Then—surprisingly—it was Lillie who spoke, though she did not turn her head or seem to address anyone. "Trombone whut Buddy play," she said. "Now he ain't goh play nuffin. He don't play nuffin now."

Curtis shook his head. He said, "I sure wish that boy had stayed home. I tell you."

One of the little boys said, "Mama, can I play Buddy's trombone when I get home?"

Margaret had another vision of Buddy under the house, crawling over the cluttered dirt, looking for some old something to write with.

Curtis went down the hall with Buddy's folder. Not that there was much in it (and maybe that would help Buddy), nothing but that other time he had run away when he was about ten or eleven years old. That would have been right after Bradford first came. Yes, because—the way Margaret remembered it—he and Bradford had never gotten along. Lillie had told her, at the time, a few blunt, stunted, irritable things about it, and then the little skinny sister would come up to check with them and she would talk to Margaret quite a bit, she wasn't the shut-mouth kind like Lillie was. Lillie had had another husband (though whether he really *was* her husband), but apparently he was the father of all the children. But this *old* husband wasn't much account, and the way the sister told it, he got to where he wouldn't work at all. There wasn't anything actually the matter with him—he just didn't want to work anymore. The sister said some people would put up with that, but not Lillie. Margaret thought: she might want to put up with it but how could she? People like her, those kind of people, can't afford a luxury like that—a big mouth to feed that is just lying around. Margaret knew what it meant to hate a man and care for him too.

So Lillie had run him off, the sister said, had told him he could lay down if he wanted to but it was going to be on somebody else. "You ain't goh lay down on *me*," Lillie had said. "Not with these chilren raising."

Margaret looked at the page in her typewriter, started to raise her hands over the keys, and then did not. Behind her the colored people sighed and squirmed, spoke low desultory

235

words to each other. She still felt in her head a low-level roar, like something moving fast on a track through open fields of brain, but it was smoother now, and the pain was going out of it; in fact something was trying to lull her and put her to sleep. *The pills*, she thought. And also the darkened room, the murmuring voices, the steady plashing of the rain, which had finally struck a pace that suited it and was comfortable. The male voice behind her made a bass platform over which the other voices rose and fell, whined mildly and indeterminately. Bradford rocked children on his knees. *—I'm goh get you some ice cream tonight if this storm ain't still storming. —Ooh-h-h ice cream.*

But it was as if Margaret could hear the *old* husband too. She heard him whimpering and carrying on.

"You wouldn't treat a dog the way you treating me."

"Dog can't get no job."

"Dog wouldn't work for that man I got. Twenty years enough of that."

"Get you something else den."

"I going to, fast as I can. Goo-od Jesus."

"What you said last week, and week before that. I tired too. If I quits one job one day, it cause next day I going to anudder one."

Then winter comes and the children are inside a lot sometimes. One of the boys is playing on a jumping stick. Falls and knocks a gash in the wooden floor. So here is old husband: still no job. And now also he does not find him some boards and nail up the hole. Instead he turns a big tin tub over the gash to keep the air out. *Margaret does not know this—and yet she does.* In places where some people's imaginations are empty, are pink and innocent, unused with nothing more to go on than a baby might have—Margaret's is not. For she knows, she has looked in stern gloom at chairs with sprung coils, at things propped up, things taped together (when they even had any tape). She knows that in

236

the dark next morning Lillie, rising early to do around and cook up some food before she goes to work, falls on the tub and stumps her foot. When she gets home that day, the tub is still there and this is the last night old husband spends in Lillie's house. —*Be gone when I get home.* —*Woman! Run a dog off, run off a snake, but run a man off? From all his chirren? Good Jesus, Jesus help us.* —*Can't even fix a hole to keep the air out.* —*That hole goh git fix, soon as I get a nickel for some nails to board it up with.* —*I got a nickel, I goh fix it myself. (I'll do it myself, said the Little Red Hen.)* —*Goo-od Jesus. Jesus look at this. What somebody will do for a nickel worth of nails.*

So old husband is run off. And first thing you know comes along—Bradford (you have to give Lillie credit). Strong, open-faced Bradford, works every day, the sister says, feet hurt or they don't hurt.

But Buddy and Bradford do not get along. And Buddy—wasn't this the way it was?—didn't want old husband to be run off. Margaret touched her throat; she was surprised that her feelings flooded up this way. *We didn't, did we Buddy?* When he didn't go to work, he was home when we got home. We could sit out on the back stoop, chucking stones at the feet of Lillie's chickens. Borrow two dimes and get some Coke down at the store, drink it on the corner, or bring it home, drink it out under the camphor tree. Telling things. Stories. Things from way back. And ghost things. (Good thing it was daylight.) Me and Buddy out there with old husband. Margaret thought, *Me. Me with my father. Struggling. But also happy. At the plant at night, in the small of-fice with fuel-oil heat. My father the night man. Sitting at his desk, orders and papers to get up. The smell of his cigar. Me with my school books at the table. Me working and my father work-ing. The rest of them at home, washed and fed. My father and I struggling. Then happy at the plant.*

But in this memory a phone was ringing on her father's desk. Or was it at this desk at the Court today? Margaret raised her head, listening, put her hand over the phone. Had it been ringing? Was this Jacksonville on the phone? She picked it up. Nothing.

*Buddy a pretty good boy,* the sister had said. *Crazy about old daddy but sometimes he worked hard for old mama too—off and on. He was an off and on boy, and he could sneak and story-tell too, yes ma'am. But sometimes he was sorry for somebody and he would help somebody out, and about the only one too,* the sister said, *even just ten years old. Carrying water when the pipes bust. Of course things like that—white folks just get on the phone: come on over here and take off these old busted pipes. And then that's all about that. Over there though—over there on Biglow Street, somebody got to do it themself, or start saving up, like saving up for Christmas. Us saving to get the pipes fixed. —Us got a new pipe today. —Well you proud I know that.*

But Buddy runs away. And this is the first file the Court has on any of Lillie's children. This is the first time Lillie labors up the stairs to see the judge.

"First we have to tell the police."

"I tole them. And they said they got it on they papers and not to tole them no more."

"Do you have any idea where he might have gone?"

"I don't think he gone far."

"Was he unhappy about anything?"

"Him and Bradford didn't get along."

"Is Bradford his father?"

"No. His father is not with us."

Then they had found Buddy at R.K.'s Barbecue. There were only two main colored sections in town, and Buddy had run away from one colored section to the other, ended up (hungry probably) at R.K.'s Barbecue and wouldn't tell R.K. his name or where he lived.

*Margaret remembered a certain taste she had not tasted in a long time—it was the taste of R.K.'s hot barbecue sandwiches, flat and thin, pressed almost as thin as a plate, in a lidded grill. She saw Leonard on Saturday morning, coming in the front door* in his hard hurrying step, with the bag in his hand, calling her name almost as soon he opened the door, as if they must hurry, even for this; she saw him at the maple table in the bay window, as she appeared from the bedroom, tying her duster, saw his brown, weathered, corrugated hands lifting the wrapped sandwiches out of R.K.'s bag.

R.K. took Buddy home with him, said *Tomorrow you going to tell me where you live.* They walked in the dark. R.K. looked like old husband, Margaret thought. R.K. was tired and aggravated. He said, *Or if not, tomorrow going to be a new menu: barbecued colored boy.* Probably this: R.K. had more on his mind than a runaway boy. A white man had come. Wanted him to put up his barbecue sauce in bottles with his name on it. Sell them in the store and all over the place. R.K. had the best barbecue and the best sauce, and his name was famous in this town and all around. Of course one barbecue sauce wasn't all that different from any other barbecue sauce, and in fact R.K. didn't always put in the same things twice, he put in pretty much whatever he had—and besides that it wasn't so much the sauce, it was good slow smoky cooking in the cooking shed, and good meat to begin with, but people thought it was the sauce, so they would think that whatever they put R.K.'s sauce on would be good too—no telling what they would put it on—and it probably *would* be good if they thought it would. So he wanted to do what this man said—put up his sauce in jars and sell it for a good price. And yet he did not want this white man for a partner. What he wanted was to steal this white man's idea and let the white man go. *Lots of things white man can do,* he thought, *don't have to put up my barbecue sauce.*

Then the police call. Buddy Ringgold is back home and all the far he had gone was across town to R.K.'s Barbecue. Margaret thinks: probably went home with a big bag of barbecue sandwiches but that didn't keep his mother from picking her a nice stout switch.

⁓

On the divan Lillie is round and stolid, her hands over her stomach, her face abstracted. Her family are ranged around her in guarded, fidgeting motion. Margaret is typing. She has actually typed two full lines across her page. But suddenly silence falls on the room and motion ceases for Lillie has risen from her seat. She stands looking towards the glass doors and then what she has heard they all hear—noise and motion down the stairwell, men's feet.

No words come from the rest of them now and no one comes peering forward to see. *This Lillie job. Lillie the one now. This for Lillie and Buddy to do.* Lillie walks heavily to the glass doors, her weight lurching slightly from side to side. Now Buddy's head rises from the stairs on the other side. He is between two men, and another man walks behind. When the handcuffs come into view, Margaret is startled, she stands up, behind her desk, in consternation, partly because she remembers the other boy last week and hears again his howling wail, on and on at the same pitch, then suddenly cut off, as if someone had pulled his switch.

Buddy and the two men approach the glass doors. They see Lillie staring forward from the other side. Margaret does not see Lillie's face—*I do not need to see it*, she thinks—but she can see the answering look on the face of her child.

And for a moment Buddy's face—his lips, his eyes—open to her, to his mother's look, and something passes between them, through the glass doors, that holds even the deputies still, and holds still, momentarily, Jim and Curtis, in the mouth of the corridor. And in those few seconds before the frozen circles are no longer frozen, and motion answers motion, flickers from space to space, and the deputies open the door, and Lillie, hesitating briefly, steps aside—in those few seconds Margaret knows (*I know what I know*) that in the beam of Lillie's face Buddy reads not one thing or two but many shadings and mergings of things. He reads anger of course. And worry. Love (certainly love)—and pity. Surprise. (*Something in this boy I didn't have time to notice was there.*) Exasperation: *Arm robbin! Where your senses was. To sneak in a window at night be one thing (bad enough). But walk through the front door when the man in there and let him see that old knife.*

Buddy's face speaks, too, its own chorus of shame, defiance, revenge, fear. (Mama!) Speaks—as Margaret can see, even if the others cannot—of betrayal. *The wrong was to me. I'm the one betrayed.* ("I was betrayed," Margaret thinks. "Or did I betray?") And Lillie: *Who betray who around here?* And it is as if they all three say (Margaret too)—*You did!* And Lillie says (but it is Margaret and Buddy too)—*You did and I did and I did and you did but you did first and made me do what I did and anyway, they did too and we did and he did and all us did. Did did did. Arm robbin though.* And also (Margaret knows): grief overpowering—yet no, it is already stirred together with resignation and acceptance of defeat. Lillie believes she already sees down the years, she sees all Buddy's life as clear as a picture, and accepts everything in advance. *Arm robbin, boy. You be gone from me now. You gone.*

*I ain't gone. Mama! I was coming home.*

*You gone boy. Hush! You gone.*


MARGARET left the hearing room with relief; she was so glad she could just shut the door on the whole aggravating scene. The entire shebang were in there, the bunch from Valdosta and the whole crowd of Ringgolds, waiting for Jim to start the proceedings. She had left him sitting forlornly in the middle of the long table, his head cocked downward, trying to collect himself, rid himself—probably—of last week's peculiar fright over the howling white boy. The lawyer, Fred, had been speaking earnestly to Buddy, pretending to brief himself on the case, as if it were any use at this point.

Margaret went down the short corridor and when she entered the main room, she was almost stunned by its silence and gloomy loneliness. On some of their hearing days there were strong reasons for her to remain inside, but generally she came back out here to get something done and to take care of whatever business might come up. Of course today, with the weather, there was not going to *be* any business, and it would soon be closing time. But in there at the hearing her headache would have come back, and she would have kept wasting the little strength she had today by letting it drain out into these other lives that were actually none of her personal concern.

She didn't know why she was that way, she thought it was weakness of character, and what worried her was that her son Richard was even worse than she was. The way he had taken on, for instance, about the Vietnam war.

Margaret stood against her desk and tried to gaze through the curtain of rain into the life of the past. During the war Richard would come home from the university and she would be busy over the stove and he would bring her things to look at just as he had done when he was little. It seemed to her that all her life in that house, whenever she was at the stove, frying and stirring and lifting lids, watching two or three things at once—that that was when the children brought her things to look at ("Mama look—I got 'A' on this"), things to sign even, with gravy on her hand. When they were older, that was still the time they chose to explain complicated things to her, to inform her, with the chicken popping, the rice boiling over, of decisions that would change their lives. So Richard, still, even when he was a very big boy home from college, would bring her things when she was at the stove, a big book about the war, for instance, with huge illustrations that worried her very much. She might say, "I don't want to see that."

"No one wants to see things like this."

"When there is nothing I can do—"

"Think if this were us," he would say. "Think if this were our house, our town. What if it were you, your children?"

She tried not to show her aggravation, but sometimes she would think "Lord, boy. You show pain to *me?* I didn't have to look for it in books. If you have had to look in books for it, thank the lord."

She thought today about these dark matters of people's suffering, right here and in other countries far away, in Vietnam and in the town she herself had grown up in, and she remembered again the phone call that had not come through. She had the ridiculous idea that while she and the phone were alone in here, the phone would finally say what it had to say.

And yet—not a peep. No sound at all but the thinning rain.

She sat down at her desk in the dreary light and reflected again on Richard and his book on Vietnam. It was not to be cruel. It was not that he had no understanding of what her life had been like. She knew that what he wanted was for her to make certain connections and draw certain conclusions. But politics was not something she really understood. Today she pictured again a young mother in Richard's book trying to ford a stormy stream, fire and bombs behind her on the bank, gulping for air as she was raised up on a foaming wave as on a bucking horse, holding tight all the time to two small girls. "What if this were you—and Ruth and Laney?"

"Richard . . . I don't know. . . ."

Her son flaunting his picture. "We are the ones doing this. This is us, our country. Burning up the whole place, killing the people. Is this what you want us to do? Blow up these innocent people?"

"No . . . I don't know why . . . we think we have to do it, I don't know."

Richard held out his picture, squarely, in both hands and stared at it again. "When this is going on—how can people still be happy and enjoy their lives?"

"Because it does not help for them to be *un*-happy. They might as well be happy if they can."

Richy with his books and papers, pictures, magazines, reports. Sometimes she had to say, "Don't let your father see that." Oh the children and their politics, their ideas about things. Of course they had wanted them to go to college, but college changed them, and so for a long time Leonard had not known if it was a good thing or not—he could not make up his mind. She thought of Sunday dinners with one or the other of them going back afterwards to school, Leonard trying to restrain himself from provocations, not being able to. Asking them (whichever child it was) if they were going to church (not that he ever went himself), if they still believed in God (good thing he never asked her). Somehow it was this, believing in God, that was always to him the basic proposition and showed that in spite of everything people were still all right and at least in their right minds and that the other things were just a phase. For if you believed in God, it seemed to him, you were not going to disobey God's word and take a chance on going to hell by being a traitor to your country and your government, or by stirring up the races, trying to get them to mix, when actually the races themselves didn't even want to and knew it was against the Bible and simply a sin to even think about.

All those politics in the house. Perhaps there was a sinister name for what Richard was, and Ruth too, for all she knew, but even if there was, she would not know how upset to be about it. With Leonard gone she could think her own thoughts all the way through, express her own views, and yet after all these years she didn't have that much to express. In the past whenever the children had gotten into something odd or political, or doubtful or worrisome in any way, of course she had not had time to even think what *she* thought, she couldn't waste any time, she had to get ready quickly for what Leonard would think and be prepared to pad things over and plump them up, disguise them a little bit; she had to try to slip some familiar covers over everything in the children's lives that to Leonard would look strange and fearful.

Always saying, *Don't let your father see that.* Then she had a distinct image of Leonard slumped back in his chair in the living room, muttering, as if to himself, but loud enough for her to hear in the kitchen. He had his trousers hiked up around his small bare feet, his socks and shoes tumbled over the rug. To have a son, he was saying, that's against his own country. To work every day of your life, like a dog, for your children, and for this to be what you get for it. For this to be the way they turn out. He knew the answers to give them back and prove their opinions were wrong but of course he couldn't say it in those college words they had, so what was the use? "If someone would tell me why somebody would march in a parade against his own country! Against the President! Of course I never thought a child of mine would be against white people and for the niggers either."

She heard Leonard's deep, frowning, dark sigh, heard him strumming on the chair arm. "But *now*, this with Richard. Lord knows. You don't know what you'll hear next. Could arrest him I reckon—wouldn't be nothing I could do. To be against the whole country, against the government and for the Comm-a-nists. In fact I imagine—Richard . . . I expect he . . . what he is, is a Comm-a-nist himself . . . ." His voice rising now. "Margaret . . . Margaret!"

She came to the doorway.

"Margaret I want you to get used to something." He gave her a dark look. "You are going to have to get used to it, so you might as well start right now. What Richard is—he is a Comm-a-nist. Did you know that? Did you know that was what your son was?"

She was silent.

"Did you know, Margaret, that that was what your son was?"

"You mean—because he's against the war?"

Leonard's anger was not building, this was his moldering anger, as much grief as anger, moldering grief and self-accusation (*If I had been more of a father*) and self-pity (*To work like I have*). But when she spoke, his emotion rose

245

slightly, though he did not move from his slump, forlorn, way back in his chair. He said, "Where would *I* be if I had not gone when they called me? Where would we be if people had said they were against the war and wanted us to lose? You know who would be President of this country today? Adolf Hitler! Hitler would be the President and you and me, sister, would not be nothing."

Leonard had not pulled himself from the chair but his hand shot forward, he fixed her with his finger, his narrow eyes glinting out of that moldering emotion. "You," he said with a sneer. "You would not be standing there in your kitchen putting up your supper, because there would not be any supper!"

Communists. And before that—nigger-lovers. Of course through the years he had gotten over the worst of that, and in later times he had gone with Margaret to see Ruth when there were black children playing on her street and even in the house, and he would put on his happy, yelping, hail-fellow front and settle down and take it very well. She pictured him watching the children at play, his granddaughter and a little black girl with a nest of fuzzy pigtails, putting little dolls to bed, black and white, or drawing and coloring, lining things up. In her memory of him he had a strange, bemused, veiled look on his face on that occasion, his mouth worked, he spoke inwardly to himself in his distracted way, as if he were a spectator to two things at once—the children playing, and something else: an action going on in his mind, something moving and working, laboriously rearranging itself in a back room of his south Georgia brain.

MARGARET sat at her desk, stared at the window, seemed to project these scenes against the light screen of silvery rain. From the hearing, from time to time, muffled voices would rise momentarily. Here was Lillie inside a room with her son today, then tomorrow: apart, bereft of him. "My son," Margaret thought. "I am bereft. Because he is not with me after all." And she did not even have any other children left around here either. Whereas there was probably not a black woman in town that didn't have children and grand-children right down the street, if not in the house, and even if half of the whole lot had gone up north and some more to jail. In this great wasteland of country, jail did not have to take them, or war or death, even colleges took them, and husbands, trips they never came back from, jobs. Suddenly they were just borne away, they went spinning away before you could even cry out, on a crazy rollercoaster, flying out of sight. She saw them on a bright whirling disc, lying flat, spinning off into the black spaces of the universe.

And wasn't this the trouble with most of life? That when it gave, it gave too much, gave in a tumbling avalanche, and then when it took away, took away forever? Years ago, when her children were small, like all mothers she had dreamed sometimes of release, of childless quiet and repose. She would think *Oh to be let loose from this, if only for a day.* Yes, even she, with her shattering love for them. And she would picture herself alone, smiling in an ecstasy of solitude, of si-lence honey pure, see herself in a place where it was a slow and silent pleasure simply to lift her head in languid ease, to sip from a cup with eternal slowness; see herself a large, lone, private figure, leaning against a wall of nothing but lumi-nous air, or reclining on an infinite strand of soft beach, hands clasped behind her head in the classic figure of re-pose, thinking smilingly of something she might think about forever and always be satisfied with, never be dis-turbed by—perhaps of her children, perhaps she dreamed of dreaming of her children in a place that was safe from them.

For after all she had been so entwined with them, the four of them wrapped so inextricably into one. She felt so heavy, so fat and larded over with them, so lined and laced with them. It was as if she wore them on her body and whenever she tried to pull loose from them, to get by stealth a few arms' length away, they caught her at once, came flying back, curled up around her, over her, within her once again. And when she reached or stepped, stretched forward a limb, it was as if there moved also, in unison, all the other limbs as well, so that she did not move with the normal pair of arms and legs but with a whole squadron, a gross set of them at once—she was a monster of limbs and tentacles.

She would think, Oh to be reduced, shorn down, shucked off, to be just myself again. Oh for one Sunday to do nothing but lie up on the bed and read the Sunday paper. When she had needed that Sunday—just one, even once a year, would almost have been enough—she could not have it. Then suddenly she had nothing *but* such Sundays and all Sundays were like that, and now what she dreamed about and craved was to have one of the old days back again, with all of them about her, around her, over her, all mixed up together with her.

*So life is not very well designed*, Margaret thought. *I could have done a whole lot better than whoever planned it this way.*

But those books Richard would bring her—and brought her even now. It was partly because he did not want to leave her behind. Although she had only gone to the eighth grade—to him she was not a lost cause. When he was just a youngster, Richard used to read things to her, from poems and plays and all sorts of things. She would be standing at the stove, or opening the oven in a sudden fury of steam, potholders in her hand, her glasses fogged up. Sometimes she didn't even know what he was talking about, but she would say, *Well isn't that good?* or *Well that's interesting, isn't it?* Or *Put that by my chair and after supper I'll look at it.* Now she thought back: actually the children had almost *had* to talk to her while she fixed supper because after supper Leonard was there. The house changed, the air almost stopped flowing, everything was dimmed and tightened, pressed down, what they felt was curbed and checked.

She pictured Richard and herself sitting in the glider in

springtime, not many months ago, before Ruth had arrived. Dusk was about to begin, the heat had let up and a small breeze had come. Margaret raised her arm. *Oh feel that— thank goodness for a little breeze.* Pine straw under their feet, a great woven mat which covered the whole yard as if someone had cut it to size. Richard was showing her one of his books from the library at the university. A large book, heavy and old. Who would have thought there would be such a book or that anyone would study such a thing?

For all it had in it were stories of Cinderella, or of a girl *like* Cinderella with hundreds of different names. It turned out that all over the world people told stories about a girl that was mistreated and then married a prince—and who was then recognized by a shoe. But they all had their own way of telling it and no two ways were exactly the same, and in fact even the shoe was not always a shoe, sometimes it was a fancy cape or a silver belt. Margaret had thought again of Ruth and Laney on her lap. Little girls, especially, loved this story above all others and could listen to it night after night. They loved Cinderella's anguish on the night of the ball, they loved her rags and tangled hair, they loved their own pity and sorrow—because all of it would be redeemed in the end and the fairy godmother would come in a sparkling cloud (like Jesus from the halls of glory), simply lift her wand. And oh that redemption and that triumph!

Yes, Margaret would think of judgment day and of the preacher in church, crooning *Oh my friends! What a day!* and the people singing of the golden bells, that when they rang them up there—on that wonderful shore—would strike the end of anguish and the beginning of glory. *Don't you hear the bells now ringing? Don't you hear the angels singing? Tis the glory hallelujah Jubilee. In that far off sweet forever, just beyond the shining river, they will ring the golden bells for you and me.* And for this abject child, Margaret had thought, this cinder-girl, who had been sinking to rise no more; say to her, *Rise up! Triumph o'er your foes!*

Margaret had sat, thinking, in the glider in the soft spring yard, looking at Richy's book, and she saw that in some of the stories the people told it was not a fairy that came to save Cinderella—sometimes it was an animal, a beast. Then she had found something that she liked very much, that was a pleasant thing to think about, and which made her think very well of the people who had told the story this way: in some versions of the tale when the beast came to save and transform the poor orphan girl, mistreated and abused, what the beast really was, was the girl's *own mother in disguise*, come back from the dead, simply because she had to and could not bear it otherwise, to save her child and turn her danger into safety and her misery into everlasting happiness and love.

Then Ruth was home too and she and Richard were talking in the living room. Margaret put out the lunch and poured the rose-brown tea.

"She probably gave the prince a terrible time," Ruth said.

"And he was always threatening to send her back to the folks at home."

Ruth murmured. "*Why* people love it so much—people all over, no matter what kind."

"You and Laney loved it."

"Yes."

"Mother says she got sick and tired of it, didn't you, Mother! That's all we wanted to read. We listened like it was brand-new every time—and tried to pretend we didn't know how it would end. And yet . . . why—what it is about . . . ."

"Good winning out over evil, the way it ought to."

"Yes but—"

"The underdog—"

"But still—"

"I don't know . . . ," Richard said . . . "the beautiful, vivid, exquisitely paced, literally unforgettable shape that it has in Perrault."

"Or had already had even before Perrault. But is it one story, spreading all over the world from one place, or do we

250

have a lot of stories that happen to be alike popping up in different places at different times?"

Richard was very happy. He stroked the big heavy book. "They don't know," he said, "and it's too late, we never will know."

"And Cinderella and the prince will never tell."

"Although if the story is right, they are still alive and will always be alive and we could ask them if we knew where they were."

Ruth and Richard laughing.

This was a blessing, she must always remember it, brother and sister laughing, with their mother, in their house where they grew up.

"You mean it is still forever-after?" Ruth said. "In nineteen hundred and seventy-nine?"


BRENDA, from downstairs, opened the glass doors. "Did you ever get that call?" she said. She had on her rain-gear, her plastic scarf pulled tight.

"I really wonder," Margaret said. "They haven't called back."

"It must not have been important," Brenda said.

"You said it was a woman's voice."

"Yes ma'am."

"But did not give her name. Brenda—what did she say exactly?"

"She said, 'I'm calling from Jacksonville. I'm trying to reach Mrs. Margaret Barker.'"

"Mrs. Margaret . . . ," Margaret said.

"And then she just said she'd call back."

"To the office?"

"Yes ma'am. I know she didn't ask for your phone at home."

"Well then," Margaret said, "I guess that's the end of that for this week." Yet something told her it was not the end.

251

Brenda's high heels echoed sharply down the stairwell. Margaret began to pick up in the room. It was after 4:30 by the Court clock.

Somebody had left yesterday's newspaper on a chair. Margaret picked it up. It was folded to the obituaries. She did not read these anymore. When Leonard was alive he used to read them to her every night, sitting in his sock feet in the living room. She would be crocheting, perhaps, or basting a hem.

She might have turned down the sound on the television. Unless there was a game on, Leonard rarely looked at TV—you might *think* he was looking at it, but then he would get right up in the middle of a show and walk outside. In the last years, though, he mainly sat thinking in his chair, or reading along at something, murmuring about it as he read (or possibly about something else entirely), and yet he did not want the pictures on the TV turned off—there was something reassuring about the fact that on the screen people moved, they talked (whether he heard them or not), they rode horses, they sang, the world was going on . . . and something fearful about a screen that was dark. But in the late evenings, with the sound way down, he would read to her from the obituaries in the newspaper.

At their age there was often somebody in them they thought they had been acquainted with. They would talk about whether they had really known the person or not. —"Didn't he used to deliver for the drugstore?" —"No that was a such-and-such but his name wasn't Clyde, I think it was Elroy." —"Says they lived over in Harwood." —"That must be Elroy's brother then."

Sometimes they were simply surprised. —"Well I declare!" And of course at other times it was awful, and as soon as Leonard glanced at the page, he grew pale and his lips worked. She would put down her sewing. —"What is it?" —"My lord, my lord." —"What?" —"My lord . . . here Robert has died . . . he's gone . . . Robert Booth is gone." Leonard would have a whimpering look around his mouth

252

and begin to shake his head. She would lean toward him, say "No! Not Robert Booth!" in an angry, whispery voice. "Not him." Or: "Surely *he* didn't. —"Surely *she* didn't." As if to say, "So! This death—it's true after all, it takes us all. If it takes her, takes him, it takes us all, every one." Or: "What do you mean, Robert Booth?" (*Why didn't anybody ever tell me that he was mortal too? Leonard, what do you mean—how can you sit there and tell me that Robert Booth—* ) Or Leonard: "Margaret. Lord god—look here, look who's dead. Dead!" Accusing, accusing *her* it almost seemed. *What is the meaning of this, woman?*

Now Margaret, standing in the Court, looked at the obituary page in her hand, saw in her mind's eye: *Leonard T. Barker*. And curiously, paradoxically, in spite of all her explicit memories of the afternoon, suddenly it was a terrible shock—Leonard's death. *If it was really true.* For her mind, in spite of everything, still did not really have space for this idea yet and it was as if it had to be crushed down, like a hot coal, into a tiny nest too small for it, no bigger than a thimble. "*Leonard this is you: Leonard T. Barker. Longtime resident of Ware County. Last night at 11:15 P.M. at his home on—*

Then Margaret was seized again by another great, massive, shocking idea, as if it were not something that had been a reality, a known thing, for over a year now, but only an amazing intuition: she had a terrifying image of a tombstone—with, incredibly, Leonard's name on it: *Leonard T. Barker*. For somewhere in the terrible reaches of her mind there was an approach—a road of thought—to this stone that she had never taken before and so she could not believe where it had brought her out. So now she leaned, breathlessly, over her desk, braced herself with stiff arms against it, felt dizzy, almost as if she might fall, felt something mashing her down, a terrible weight pressing against her shoulders, her neck, bending her head, down to a place where she could not help but see again, even with her eyes shut, the engraved stone: *Leonard T. Barker*.

Margaret raised her head and rubbed her neck. She looked around her, took a few awkward, tentative steps on the spangled linoleum. Then she blew her nose and sat down on the edge of one of the divans. She was weak, a weak person, and as foolish as a child.

Good reason not to look at that page of the newspaper. These days, when people died, she wouldn't know a thing about it unless someone she met brought it up. Sometimes Nora would call. "Have you heard about so-and-so?" and Margaret would say, in a hushed voice, "No-o-o!" And yet she would be thinking, "But I'm not that surprised—anymore."

In the hearing-room chairs scraped and so Margaret got up, finished her rounds of the room, straightened up.

The Court clock was moving on towards five-thirty. *Why in the world this hearing has gone on like this*, she thought, but she expected that Jim and Curtis and Lillie and Buddy had been trying to convince the ones from Valdosta that it wasn't a plain normal case of armed holdup. "This is a very, very serious matter, we know that, we don't have to tell you," Jim would have said, "but why not leave it in the hands of the Juvenile Court?"

But now the door was opening down the hall and Buddy's lawyer, Fred, sprang out in a hurry and dashed through the double doors. From the landing he looked back, remembered to be polite, gave Margaret a funny little wave and a quick conspiratorial look of disgust and aggravation, as if to say, *For us to let something like that—people like that—tie us up on Friday afternoon!*

Then the rest of them trooped out in a strange, silent, shuffling parade. Margaret sat down at the typewriter, and Jim came over and bent his long body over her and told her in a scraping, worn-out voice what to put down on the forms. For some reason—even though she was not surprised—she still said, "I declare!"

Near the glass doors Bradford extended his hand for

Buddy to shake, even with the handcuffs on. "Let's don't have no feelings about this," he said. "It still seems like to me—it gon be all right in the end." One of the little boys bobbled his head, like Jay-Jay on television, and stuck out his chest. "I gaw get me a gun," he said, "and *I* gaw shoot they heads off."

The other one said, "Buddy can I have your trombone?" —"You get off that trombone!" Buddy said. He raised his fists in the cuffs. One of the Valdosta men stayed behind while the other one led Buddy down the stairs and Buddy's folks went behind him.

Lillie let the others go first and then Margaret could not help but notice, because today she was noticing so many things, that she paused at the head of the stairs and watched them all descend, her son Buddy disappear in his shackles through the front door. Then she herself, hanging the old furry smelly coat over her shoulders, started heavily down, watching her step on the wooden stairs.

Margaret almost smiled to herself—a silly pained smile, because she was imagining Lillie in a long gauzy dress with something peculiar in her thick round hand . . . *a wand* . . . which threw off a shower of sparks. *Buddy was in his room at the jail, and Lillie, smiling a big toothy smile, touched the door with her sparkler and it opened right away. Buddy walked through it and outside a car drove up shaped like a pumpkin, sort of like the old round-backed Fords of years ago, and took him away.*

Margaret thought, "What if all we want, out of life, is to save each other from every harm, and from the dark domain of the final, last harm, which is very harmful indeed?" For a second her eyes closed and she thought again, calmly this time, of her husband's stone in the graveyard. Perhaps it is just this desire of theirs to save and protect (*Oh did you want to save and protect? I see-e-e*, said a cavernous voice, severe and displeased, sepulchral, out of the great void of all histories past) that people want to seize by the throat, simply be-

255

cause it is so ridiculous, squeeze and torture it until it is just a rag and can't make them feel anything any longer.

It was all too confusing, and she was simply not smart enough to figure it out.

At her desk the forms were filled out, and she separated the copies for the deputy, who had stayed behind, from the copies for the Court. The deputy took them away. Jim and Curtis had put on their raincoats, and Margaret started turning out the lights. "Jim looks so thin and old," she thought. Since his wife and child had left him, years ago, a weekend was no more than a workday for him, and a workday no more than a weekend. It was as if he had fallen off the center of his life and could never hope to reach it again but would always live on its sliding rim. Margaret remembered that on Friday nights he went to his mother's for supper. His mother was quite old. Margaret hoped they expressed things to each other, she hoped they gave each other pats and hugs and did not just blankly sit, staring awkwardly past each other.

But this Curtis was something else. Not that he was not as put out as he could be this afternoon; in fact she knew he had probably put in plenty, more than his share, and kept the hearing going as long as it had, and when it came up in Valdosta they would hear more than they wanted to from Curtis once again. But to look at him now. Even in this sick rainy-day light, his eyes shone in his plump ruddy face, he grinned, his good spirits boiled up in spite of things, he tossed his shock of thick blond hair.

*Oh Curtis you look so pretty in your light summer clothes.* For a moment he and Jim stood jingling the change in their pockets. Margaret looked at them and the contrast was awful and at first she thought *It is just youth and age,* but no, it was much more than that. Some of us never had what Curtis has, she thought.

Curtis said, "Hey! Y'all remember that boy that did all that hollering up here last week?" Curtis, good lord! Margaret and Jim looked at each other with the same incredulous look. My god—on top of all this other. Oh Curtis filled them with affectionate despair sometimes. He said the howling boy had had a session with two psychiatrists, special experts from the state hospital, and when the three of them got together, the way *he* heard it, they finally got the boy to open up and talk, got him pried loose, and they were tickled to death with themselves. Once they got him started they could hardly get him to stop and so there they were, as pleased as they could be, taking notes as fast as they could, looking and listening, speaking and smiling . . . and when they had finished they all stood up, perfectly relaxed, chatting and carrying on, and then they started to reach out to shake the fellow's hand.

The boy had stood back and looked at them and then he looked at the door and at the walls of the room; he looked out the window (at the simple trees outside)—and opened his mouth as wide as it would go. "And you know what came out," Curtis said. He grinned at them.

He said the two psychiatrists were scared nearly to death and had flown like lightning into each other's arms. Margaret could see them, like two of the three stooges, their hair standing up, hugging each other in terror and shock, while the boy's head turned up and he emitted that piteous, high-voltage yowl that rattled the windows and shook their silly bones.

Curtis grinned and grinned—he dearly loved the plight of the two psychiatrists. Jim jingled his change and cocked his head, seemed to stare past both of them as if he hadn't heard. And Margaret—of course *she* said, "Well, I'll declare."

Margaret cranked up her car in the drizzly lot. Backing out, craning her neck around, she saw Bradford's old battered pickup down the street. It was hard to tell but it looked like Lillie and the sister squeezed in front and in the back all the children, holding a big tarpaulin over their heads. Then Bradford came scuffing out of the drugstore with a paper bag. Margaret wiggled her toes as she thought of him squishing and squashing (on his off-day) in his house slippers. They would have to be soaking wet. She thought, *They weren't about to let him forget that ice cream.*

Then she drove slowly home, straining over the wheel. She wished she had not thought about Richard's Cinderella book today, or thought so much about bygone times, and strolling Ruth down to the library, and reading to the children, and Leonard's gravestone and so much else.

As for the fairy tales, she had simply read too many of them to her children, and her brain was affected by them still, even at sixty-one. For though she was staring forward at the wet road, beyond the road was something else—Lillie and Buddy walking up a rosy lane, climbing a hill. They had been somewhere to see about something or take care of something . . . but they had not been able to, and it had not done any good, and so they were tired and worn-out, and aggravated, and they labored and tugged and their bodies simply drooped up the hill. Yet you could hardly see the two of them the air was so full of rosy light; it was full of rose-misted puff-lets of smoky light.

The two of them climbed on, and as they climbed they looked ahead to the unpainted square board house on the top of the hill. Then they themselves began to see how it was enveloped, how it was girded around by the rosy light, and so they went with their eyes fixed forward and Margaret looked closer and she saw that they were not smiling, exactly, and their faces were not full of amazement and surprise, and that yet there was an expression on them that was almost divine—extremely satisfying to look upon. For as they rose to the house, in its cradle of misty light, they saw blooming in the yard, springing out of the ground's fuzzy coverlet of new spring grass, thickly scattered over the breast of the yard, like flowers of every beautiful hue: an

258

acre, yes a whole acre it almost seemed . . . of new *pencils* blossoming forth.

Margaret strained over the wheel. She saw the pencils spread out over the crest of the hill, their radiant profusion. She was about to laugh out loud . . . but instead she stitched her lips and concentrated hard on the road ahead, taking her home through the wet afternoon.

# CHAPTER SEVEN

HERE is a case of true love, Margaret thought, squeezing down her girdle, for truly it was impossible not to feel a deep affection for her high plump bed, such a very personal bed somehow, ready to meet with such familiar ease, on these late tired afternoons after work, all the little sensual need a person like herself could have. She lay back with a sigh and stretched herself down, the whole strained mass of her and all her half-sprung faculties, propped her head on the two broad Granny pillows in their silky ruffled cases. Her cup of tea sat cooling by the bed, and the afternoon paper lay by her side. Today there were pictures in her windows of late rain, slowly thinning away, revealing now in thin foggy light the gleaming black trunks of the pine trees.

This evening, of course, she would be going back out—something unusual for her, since socially she was so nearly a useless person, so alone and withdrawn. But in a few hours, dressed and begirdled again, she would watch for her ride from the living room window.

Meanwhile, she sipped her tea, read in the newspaper

about the Jews and the Arabs. After all those wars, even the old governments were almost worn-out, and the people themselves had been worn to a frazzle long ago. What if there had been some business like that on Suwannee Drive? She imagined she heard Laney's little peaked voice. "When I was nine years old, Mama went out in the back yard to hang the clothes on the line, and somebody ran up with a small bomb, just right for one person, and threw it on her and blew her up." Margaret stared over her newspaper and peered into this little scene, as she had into so many similar little scenes and imaginings through the years, and wondered once more whether she ought to feel slightly ashamed of her safe smooth bed and her pretty room and her fragrant tea—and what her relationship really was to the actual scenes of horror and pain that other people went on suffering—somewhere—every day. Over there in the Middle East, for instance, no matter where you went, it was far worse even than Jacksonville—war and terror was about all people could expect. It was almost a wonder there was anybody left to war *on*.

When Margaret thought the word *war*, it had a raw cruel ring in it, and yet—she always hated, a little bit, to admit it to herself—when she thought of *her* war, the one her husband had gone to and which would always be for them, no matter how many wars came after it, simply The War, it was not a raw, cruel idea at all; in fact she was most likely to think of it when she was cozy and comfortable, or when she snuggled a child up in her arms; and for instance she nearly always thought of it when one of her little granddaughters slept in the bed with her.

When Leonard was in the Navy during the war, and the new air base had brought in the servicemen, she had put a hot plate in the back bedroom and rented two rooms out as a small apartment. They were divided from the rest of the house only by the minute, ridiculous hall, which you could step across with one medium step, even lengthwise. In fact, to think that it was possible, to have renters in this tiny house!—and yet it was. She had moved the double bed into the dinette for her and Laney, and put Ruth on the living room couch. But hadn't it been odd, she thought, sleeping in the bay window? But no, it was not that odd, and actually with all four windows open around you, it was nearly a perfect place to sleep in. There was barely room for the bed and one squeezed-in chest, the room was nearly all bed, and yet there was something clever and cozy about it. Of course Richard was not there, there was not any Richy—he would be conceived on the same double bed after it was back in its place in the front room across the hall, when the house was itself again, stretched tight on its striated nerves again after the war.

She thought of the war times, the three of them in bed at night. She saw Ruth sleeping on the couch, a first-grader (looking forward from then—how big and smart, looking back from now—how amazingly innocent and small). Some kind of something aloose around them, on the lookout for small acts of justice that it could perform without much expense of effort, had seen that having been bald for so long, Ruth deserved to grow a thick head of hair, and so she had, and at night it was a beautiful brown mass on the pillow, kinked from the loosened plaits.

At night, then, Ruth would be on the couch and Margaret would be on the big bed in the bay window, reading in a magazine under a small weak lamp. Beside her the hump under the covers was Laney's little rump, and outside the crickets sang, and from the windows came a fresh night smell that was wonderful—something lost these days when everything was always shut up for air conditioning. Yes in those days there was the fresh night smell, the fresh rosy-skinned children soft asleep, the clock ticking on with such neat, calm regularity in the adjoining kitchen, the clean cabinets full of orderly supplies for simple needs, Bing Crosby ticking on too, it almost seemed, in the radio over the sink, in abeyance for the night, waiting for morning to come to waft over them his crooning crow. *I'll be seeing you* . . . wasn't that it—what he would mew to them, Bing Crosby the serviceman, homesick for his wife, wanting to see her, embrace her again . . . in all their old familiar places . . . *all day long.*

And in their own territory, on their own side of the tiny divide of the hallway, it was a wonderful thing that there was no man, no loud voice to rattle the rafters, to stun and frighten, no little hang-faced man always boiling over, full of trouble and anger they could not fathom (and finally did not even want to). No, the mother read on in the night, the clock ticked, and in that little town it was as if a gigantic windstorm had once swept through and blown all the anguish and anger, the confusion and conflict, past them like so much whirling debris into another part of the world, and left them bare and dry. It was as if all the terror and turmoil had gathered elsewhere, piled up in great fiery heaps in certain terrible, ill-fated places far away, so that there was nothing left for here but serenity and peace and quiet, for the playing of little children, and old people walking slowly on the streets, for women working in homes and offices and plants in their smooth, intimate, feminine, methodical way, without the loud agitations, the sweaty exertions of men.

And yet of course there was at the same time a sense of suppressed crisis, quiet and attenuated but embodied nevertheless in many things—in people at counters scratching in purses for coupons to buy things with (or trade with, with neighbors—gas for shoes, and sugar for meat); in sirens blowing for air raid drills; in children selling war bonds and winning radios and bicycles; in the uniformed men that sometimes walked about the town, strays from the new base on the county road (from which in later years, when the warplanes had vanished and new civilians had come, Margaret herself would fly, on missions to daughters in their cities of northern exile); and also in the Yankee wives, installed about the town by the servicemen in little hard-to-find, makeshift apartments like Margaret's, their metallic Yankee voices always giving them away, ringing sharply in offices and shops.

And of course there were times when the distance suddenly closed between here and "over there," and out of the blind tumult of distant war there would fly a lone swift messenger—to touch with his terrible light cold hand *one of us, some of us*, Margaret thought, *in our twilight world beyond the clash.* And in fact she remembered as if it were yesterday how this dread messenger had come, on a certain day, to lay his cold fingers on her own little house, had chosen—perhaps hesitating on the lawn, his finger on his lips, thinking—the other side where the renters were, said to the pretty war wife from up north, *Plane crash. At the base.*

Margaret remembered calling her to the phone, handing her the receiver (how could she have done that?)—then guilt afterward, her hatred for the phone, her desire to have it out of the house, and later that day her contempt for her own yard, her grass, because two uniformed men had walked over it to present themselves at her door, to rap with a light, mocking rap.

But to Margaret herself no one came—no winged messenger, for instance (swift as the air), to touch her on the shoulder, wait for her to turn with quivering dread, say *Dead. Over there. Your husband. Ship blown up.*

So Margaret had been safe, and even happy (shame to say) while others worried and grieved, or fought in the tumult itself, and while scenes of such horror were being played out in the secret death camps of the enemy that for decades afterward the imaginings of all the world would be horribly fixed on them.

But for now she read on under the small lamp at night, with Laney's little bottom thrust up under the sheet. She read, and the little house hummed, the bed hummed, the walls hummed, the cups hummed on their hooks; and when she turned off the lamp, the crickets, all the night bugs, sang through the windows from the pure fresh night, sang her quickly to strong sleep—sleep that was never better in her life (shame to say) before or since. For there was no man to wait and listen for, no honor and wifely pride at stake in the night, more and more in danger as the night passed again in loneliness, desertion. No one coming home from the pool hall at twelve o'clock or one o'clock or two, stamping under small iron-hard feet as he came her pride, her little girl's dream of man-woman-children-home-love-trust-together . . . at least together, no matter what.

And so for Margaret the war was like a cradle in which the little house rocked, was kept (as strange as it may seem) safe and in peace, and she would think of the little hangdog man rocking too in the middle of the ocean half the world away, of the ship rocking on the waters and yet the little man not soothed, ready to boil over, *refusing* to be soothed; she saw him pacing and prowling, searching, walking the ship, looking up one end and down the other, nosing like an animal along the walls, the sides, up to the bulwarks, down to the waves, never giving up his half-crazed search for some manner of egress, never able to cease hoping for a belt of dry land to open before him across the sea. Since those years, Margaret had thought many times, crouching sometimes at the bottom of bent despair, or in other moods entirely, her lips wrinkled with ironic humor, that perhaps the best years of their marriage were these years of the war.

"I don't see why you can't leave him," the children would say, later on. "He doesn't care anything about you."

"I don't know . . . ."

"He doesn't love you. He *can't* love."

"When he was in the war he wrote me a letter every day."

She hesitated to say "love letter." *Thinking of you honey, tonight, and all I want to be is home.* Home—home, oh lord, let me get back home. Oh wife-family-mother-house-food. Bing Crosby, after all, sang the same thing to her from the radio over the sink as she washed the greens in the dishpan or rinsed things out or scrubbed all their combs and brushes. *You'll never know just how much I love you—you'll never know just how much I care.* And again: she was never as lonely (because this is the way pride is) when Leonard was on the ocean half a world away as when he had been downtown all night at the pool hall (bitter misery and starving need) or out in the fields from dawn to dusk on Christmas Day with his shotgun. For of course you can put up with something, almost anything, for a reason—whereas with no reason you cannot.

So during the war she had had pride. *Which I must have needed even more than a husband*, she thought. Though she was alone, she was not deserted, was not a pool-hall widow or fish-and-game widow, or widow-of-football-basketball-and-baseball (not to mention the stock-car races), but something entirely different: *a war wife*, just as respectable and self-respecting (in a way) as all the other war wives.

And so, more than at any other time since she was a small child, being loved by her father, and having hardly any duty but to love him in return, life was a challenge that could actually be met. She had never been on her own but had transferred straight from parents to grandmother to husband, and even though she had negotiated (almost in secret) the building of the small stunted house, she had never been her own banker or paid her own bills or even signed a check. Yet the war took her, as ignorant as she was, and made her into a legend of fiscal resourcefulness and cunning, of managerial skill. When Leonard went to war there were debts, and when he returned the debts were cleared and there was money in the bank. That had been a great thing for them.

Leonard had not known, until he returned, the full extent of his solvency, and for a while he was almost a happy man, for of course he had had, almost like a disease, a quaking fear of debt—of being driven, inevitably and before anyone even knew the why and wherefore, into keeping an icehouse, caused to sit on its absurd porch while the whole town passed by to enjoy his humiliation. (*Poor old Leonard—bad times—couldn't make it. Those Barkers, his old daddy for in-stance—what they go through.*) So this clearing of the debts, at the unlikeliest of times, was a great thing, and a heroic deed on Margaret's part, something marvelled at by all her family and friends, and which even Leonard himself some-times gave her credit for. Though Mr. Barker had already had his heart attack, was dead before the war began, and could not dissolve at her feet in blathering worship and thanksgiving, Mrs. Barker carried on for them both, prayed and wept in admiration and love—and told the tale ever af-ter to the children: *Your mama—that little thing—with all she had on her during the war, and yet what she did for your daddy while he was gone to serve his country.*

And what had Margaret actually done it on—where had the dollars come from? Margaret enjoyed asking herself that question and then giving herself the answer. She had had, basically, and first of all, her government allotment—ex-actly one hundred dollars a month. Then, by her shrewd partition of the house (as wee as it was) she had had the rent money—thirty-five dollars a month more, and considering, for instance, that the renters had had to draw their dish-water in the bathroom, it seemed like a lot, and yet none of them seemed to mind but in fact seemed to like living there very much and to love her little girls. On weekends the young husbands had mowed the grass and cut back the yel-low jasmine and the wives had taken her to the store.

This afternoon Margaret, from her bed, gazed absently outside at the wet gleam of the pine trees—but actually saw, instead, a scene in bristling sunlight: the old hand mower sitting on the wartime lawn, little feet skimming over glint-ing grass, and young men with sweaty heads throwing little girls in the air, their skirts flying out against the sky like small umbrellas, a wriggling worm of a child stuck through.

In those days Margaret had also taken some sewing jobs making slipcovers, because in certain peculiar ways war was a sane and rational thing, and made it all right for people to do whatever they could, or needed to, to get by—so there was several hundred dollars a year from that.

She had had a very strict budget for expenditures, and yet they had lived absolutely well enough, and with no panic. She had sold the old rattletrap car and simply done without.

Granny, Nora always said, was the one that was tickled to death. —"I don't think she realized how crazy she was about you until you struggled through the war all by yourself without even any way to get around and never asked her for a dollar or any help." —"But Granny and Mr. Wallace did help, and that is when we got the front walk, which Mr. Wallace put in completely by himself (and which I never could have gotten without the war)." —"But that was Daddy Wallace." —"I know whenever they came to visit, before you could even turn around Daddy Wallace would have his screwdriver out and he would be screwing away on something with his hat still on."

In any case they had had their various small incomes and they had had their budget, and by Margaret's devisings it had been cut here and there in so many little inventive ways that there was even room in it for that something that had never been there before—the extra something that was such an enormous relief to be able to do, but which would cause such a long trail of marital grief down the years to come that even now Margaret felt herself almost flatten on the bed to think of it, her body shrink with gloom and despair: she had begun to send her mother, on dirty debilitated Eighth Street, the money order every other week (not *every* week— *lord god*) for five dollars, and so had provided her husband with a devilish little instrument he could use forever after for her torture—whenever he wished to bring her some exquisite pain, he could simply pull out, like a fiendish blade, this little guilty sum, for he considered it to be money stolen from him by people that it was a foolhardy thing even to acknowledge, much less to support. She on her part began to soothe herself with her fantasy: she would envision Leonard

268

being called up in a mammoth courtroom, shivering with shame and fear, his head hung on his breast, while a judge with a great dark face glared down on him in pitiless disgust.

Still she almost thought at first that after the war they would have a new life, since Leonard was in such bliss to be home, and to know—by the happenstance of war—what he would otherwise never have known: that by a wonderful, stupendous coincidence he had happened to be born in the one part of the world (with piney woods and balmy fields), and in the one particular town, where he was absolutely best suited to live, even if at times he was frightened to death of it. And so here he was—united with his family and with biscuits and cornbread. (His mama had actually cried when she saw how poor he was, what the old Yankee food had done to him; she said he was not as big around as a stick of firewood.) But in any case it seemed to him—and in a way of course it was true—that he loved his family with a monumental and consuming love, and if he had ever had a peculiar, dangerous and beastlike way of letting this love be shown, why that was something he simply had no memory of. He saw that life had pleasure to it after all. It was a pleasure for him just to *think* of the three months' severance pay that would soon be coming in the mail, and of the savings in the bank—oh that was good fortune and then some, and the certain proof, these savings, that he was loved in return, and had a wife more devoted than other sailors' wives.

Margaret's memory warmed up and she thought of something else she had saved the money on, something other than the incomes she had already counted up. On ship there were poker games, and so of course Leonard played until he was almost a shark, perhaps he *was* a shark, for after all they were a little bit like the Sunday games at the VFW Club at home, and because in general—he had written her—this was the best way for him to keep from going crazy from frustration and yearning for home, from shit-on-a-shingle every day for breakfast.

When Margaret toted up the whole marriage account, as she was always doing now that he was gone, she had to remember to put this down to his credit: every penny of his poker winnings he had sent back home so his family could get along and hopefully keep his debts down. And so perhaps he deserved to get back and find that it had all been snugly laid away—a warm, lovely hoard that spread a golden glow over his thoughts and plans. "First, a good down payment on a decent car," he had said. "But I sent you that for food and shoes and doctors, for Ruth for her bicycle and things like that." But they had not needed it, Margaret said, and Ruth had had her bike anyway, and all of them had had everything they needed, and so she had just kept the money safe, to help them get started again. *And in case otherwise he might need to murder us in our beds, in his terror that we might starve to death before he could find a job.*

But Margaret, thinking back, reviewing and assessing all these things, the good and the bad of wartime for the ones who were not at the front, getting killed, tried to think reasonably about the whole business . . . and yet one could not think reasonably about it, and it seemed to her that there was one particularly cruel paradox that would always confuse people's hearts—that war, for all its evil, for its floods of woe she could hardly bear to think about, its dragging of heart from heart, for the eternal outrage of little children bereft of mothers, children left crying in the street (*over there*) where dead mothers could not hear . . . that even with all that, perhaps the most horrible thing about it (in a curious way) was that it also did some good, because such a terrible thing should not *do* any good.

Of course, war had a famous reputation for breaking up marriages, but surely it had saved a whole lot more than it had broken up. A man cast abroad in a foreign land or on a foreign sea, amongst danger and enemies, learns to put a certain price on home and kin. And he may go home and plant his first tree in the yard. He may look his children in the eye—actually look at them—for the first time. And his wife's cooking may seem to him resplendent, a sacred art wondrous and mysterious, good cause to respect her all his life. And his bed may seem warmer and softer than he had ever dreamed a bed could be. And as for . . . something else—Bing Crosby had sung it from the radio over the sink, mewed and purred it, for all the war husbands to all the war wives. *Kiss me once and kiss me twice and kiss me once again— it's been a long, long time. Haven't felt like this, my dear, since can't remember when—it's been a long, long time.*

And yet, the fact that war was like that—not completely bad for everyone (*and think of the ones making the weapons,* Richy always said) and in fact for some people a good thing and a happy time even if it shouldn't be—made Margaret close her eyes, hear her son say, "What if this were you?" see him thrusting in front of her his book about Vietnam with its terrible pictures meant to shock and accuse. "What if you and Ruth and Laney—" Margaret saw the three of them tossing on dangerous waves, in fiery exploding air, saw them crouched and bent, clinging in terror to the double bed . . . .

And yet they had not been tossed on dangerous waves, and it was ridiculous to even think of it.


MARGARET'S newspaper had fallen over her stomach. She would have to get up shortly and fix her a bite to eat— make her a couple of patties, perhaps, out of some leftover potatoes. But her mind drifted and it was as if she could hear the voices of her children of long ago. *Wuf didn't eat her smashed potatoes. Mama! Wuf didn't eat hers.*

*Mama, she said smashed . . . and I did eat mine, then you gave me some more . . . she never eats anything, you don't even give her any*

*I don't know, it worries me, Laney doesn't have any appetite and you have such a good one, I don't know*

Laney crying hard

271

*What*
*What in the world*
Crying
*What, what is it, come here to Mama, what is it*
Hushing
*What is it, now-now*
*I want one too*
*Want? Want what?*
*An abbadite like Wuf has got*
*Oh well!*
*But I can't, I can't get me one*
*Yes you can*
*No I can't . . . I can't . . . nobody loves me so they won't get*
me one
Crying softly
*Don't you love her Mama? Don't you love Laney?*
*Stop now listen of course (sighing) my lord*
*Then lying up on the big bed back on the pillows, with a little
girl under each arm, their heads on her breast, kissing and em-
bracing, stroking and soothing. I love they love we love, you she
us love, everything here is love. And even if it is not true (in spite
of Sunday School, singing praise him, praise him, all ye little children) that God is love and if Jesus does not (probably) love little
children and care for them always and every hair on their heads,
at least here I am love, yes I myself was love, mothers and children together are love (and fathers sometimes too, I know once
my own father was love) because that is all we know of it and the
way we know what it is and that there is such a thing, and even a
crazy mother on Eighth Street was love for children that drooled
through webs of saliva. Much more than God a mother (usually)
is love because for one thing she would never groom and train little souls for graduation in the beginning or the middle or the end
of life . . . into the dark domain, never tuck them in bed in a room
of eternal darkness never to wake again.*

Margaret thought backwards to that clever, that resource-
ful time of war and the peace it had brought them; she

272

thought of the thick medium of love and trust they lived in—it was as if they breathed it in through the bay windows, lolling and playing on the bed, and yet they seemed to lie upon it too and to put it on with their clothes and sit down on it to eat; they drank it down in the mornings with their hot chocolate, the children's small hands warming on the cups as they stared absently over the enameled kitchen table to the starched homemade frocks hung ingeniously on a bar behind the door.

And Margaret knew this: a secret catch to her heart which might never have come unhooked *had* come unhooked, and her heart had opened completely, as wide as it would go; and it was only in that wartime, and later on when her son had come and the sacred four of them would be alone together on lovely islands of special time, on days when Leonard was at work or out on the rivers or the fields—that she had been the queen of a kingdom of her own at last, of a small planet made to her own order, strong and good, and something of vast importance forever for the human race, for the very reason that these little beings had love in them put there by her, and would spread it abroad, and it would drip down through the generations and the world would be better off.

Yes she had always wanted to be the leader, the captain of something, however small, and so finally she had been—and she saw the little white house sailing smoothly on a gleaming sea. Her thoughts travelled drowsily on blurred streams and she thought she heard far away her children singing as if in church, in infant voices almost like Donald Duck's:

> Wondrous sovereign o-of the sea,
> Mother, saviour, pilot me.

MARGARET sat in her bedroom chair, pulling up her stockings, fastening them to her girdle. On the shelves around the room were pictures of her children in their various stages of life. She sat back for a moment and looked at them, soberly, reflectively, the way she had so many times. She supposed that at her age she ought to be able to focus on something else—and yet there were always things you could not ponder through to a conclusion, were always there to be pondered over again. No doubt one reason she had loved her children and her child-rearing years so much, loved the small, neat, clean-smelling spaces she had raised them in, was that she herself as a child had lived another way entirely, with profound, unceasing disorder, with odors that you could not even trace and deep and mysterious troubles and afflictions that no one could anneal, and so when she got her chance to try her love-powers out just as far as they would go it seemed to her that she had loved—absurdly— not just what was good and happy in itself but even what was not . . . loved even a child with messy pants, almost loved messy pants themselves because at least dirty pants were within her mortal reach to cleanse and resolve, and certainly it was true that in a way and in certain states of mind she had even loved children's bad tempers and their kicking tantrums on the floor, loved wailing fights and scratched faces, iron-lipped pouts, loved everything they did just because it was they who did it. Oh she laughed to think that yes, in her way, she had even loved chicken pox and tonsillitis, and stitches in the emergency room, harsh teachers at school (since she was *not* harsh), and even her cares and chores, scraping corn and pounding old tough meat, loved, even while she complained, seams to sew up and clothes to fold and sort, dirty ones to feed through the wringer, with no free hand to even rub her back.

But after all, she had loved the things, too, more reasonable to love—children's bodies, for instance. *How beautiful the bodies of children are*, Margaret thought. She loved to look and look at little feet, feel little arches, the slopes of miniature calves, tee-tiny shoulders, she loved to touch the gauzy down on little necks. Sometimes she thought she had been attracted to little children in a preposterous way. She loved all their special gestures and poses and acts yet still loved some with special love—loved a child sitting, for instance, with its hands in its lap, content after its dinner, round-shouldered, still and abstracted.

She had loved for a child to say, "Mama, are you glad you had me?"

Even now she almost arched up, instinctively, from her chair, to frame a reply. Yes there appeared, in a vivid enlargement on her mind's screen, the face of a child with no particular features, a composite child of all children, turning its head slowly and sternly, and then saying—but was it not in pretend seriousness? in mock foreboding? —"Mama, do you love me?"

She thought with pleasure of all the business of pretend and half-pretend, the many gradations of pretend that children and parents could have. She saw herself in scenes where she was truly tired and vexed, and she remembered how she would imagine to herself and her children that she wanted to give them away, sell them or auction them off, put an ad in the paper for them because they were killing her, ruining and destroying her, driving her mad. She saw herself almost reeling, lurching to a chair in which to collapse, her head in her hands, muttering almost like a drunk that she was crazy, crazy, and that she would not even be sorry when they came to take her away—to the crazy house. A stranger might have looked on at this scene with deep dismay and truly believed that she was in earnest, desperately *driven* to these terrible confessions, these humiliating admissions. And yet—the children would look on grim-mouthed, cold, as it would seem, and without pity.

"Yes you *are* crazy—but it's *you*—you got *yourself* that way."

And it was all a kind of "serious pretend," a drama in which they all played their parts with austere conviction, and there was the clearest understanding of this by a five, even a four-year-old. For the truth was it satisfied something in them to speak this way, to say such things in apparent seriousness, for the simple reason that they were not true.

Margaret stirred slightly on the bed. She felt the approach of something, toward the gate of memory, that had to be turned away no matter what, and though her body lay straight, inwardly it was as if she thrashed and turned, twisted her head in suffering agitation, as if there were something that had to be averted, that must be thrown off, and yet it was not thrown off—and then it was as if a light, which had shone on all these remembered scenes, failed, and they were the same, but in darkness . . . .

For though sometimes it seemed that in that separate and special world with her children years ago, she had been happy every day and all the time, of course the truth she was trying not to remember was quite different from that, and in fact there had been times of terrifying darkness and despair, when she had seemed to be walking under a slowly closing lid of disaster, mincing her panic-stricken way stooped over, terrified of stepping inadvertently on the fated place—of wringing inadvertently the fated chord—that would bring the iron lid down on all their heads.

How had such periods begun? She thought they had begun in bad dreams, unspeakable dreams where some vicious intention of the universe (some gracious redeemer, some fairest lord, some lover of little ones over all the world) had cruelly separated her from her children and she had been utterly lost to them, and yet could hear them as if in another room, crying for her, needing her, and could even know that they believed she had deliberately abandoned them and simply gone away—yes she remembered incredible dreams in which her mouth opened with burning fire and yet no sound came and she was prevented (oh wondrous sovereign, oh lover of all our souls) from crying out to them, her children, her body and blood, crying, "No, no, Mama did not leave you, she could not help it, there was nothing she could do. Nothing. Nothing."

And there would follow from such dreams, periods where everything she felt and saw and heard seemed to have some half-hidden germ of disaster in it, and whenever a child had a fever or a mysterious stomachache or she herself had a strange sensation of any kind she was driven to hourly torment and fear that they or she would become ill and her worst fears and nightmares would be realized.

Her mind was a conjuror and it conjured this: a certain Sunday morning of a certain unnameable year. Back in the bedroom the Sunday clothes were set out on the bed. But the children were not dressing, they were making clamorous noises. Margaret was at the sink peeling potatoes. Leonard had already gone off to meet the boys at the Bluebird Cafe and here she had wanted him to pick up some milk. (She could hear the squall of affection from the men as Leonard entered the room. *Hey boy—how you boy—you little rascal—where you been.*) She had to think what to do about the biscuits with no fresh milk. She thought she heard a fly buzz, remotely, perhaps in the dinette. It would be aggravating to have to put down her paring knife and clean off her hands, find the flyswatter—and yet, she did not intend to have flies in the house, not even one. In Jacksonville flies had always buzzed, over all the meals, and that was why there must not ever be any fly here, for this was another kind of house entirely. If flies came, if roaches were allowed to swarm . . . where were they then?

She raised her head and called to the children. Their noise subsided and then it rose again. Running and hollering. Lord god. She washed her hands and wiped them on her apron. Then she was back in the bedroom, grabbing and pulling on the children, saying, *Listen here*, but they wiggled away from her, giggled and squealed, peeped from behind things and made each other screech and laugh. She went back to the kitchen and reached for the switch (from the bamboo hedge) on top of the icebox, and when she did so the tool-crate scraped loudly on the metal surface, and suddenly silence descended at once on the children.

For a moment she hesitated, while the echo of their piping chorus sank away into the walls of the house. When she went into the bedroom, they were pulling awkwardly at their clothes; they did not look up at her and pretended not to notice what she had in her hand. She put down the switch, and sitting on the bed, took Richy between her knees to button his shirt. But little by little they steamed up again; there was something in the tickly, breezy warmth of the spring day that made them unable to keep still, made them snigger at one another with comical sidewise looks, and fling out little tentative limbs, watching her eye, and finally she had to work on each one of them, stuff and stretch them into their Sunday suits.

But then there they were at last, wonderfully turned out, and she saw that oh it had been clever, it had been very wise to have put out, the night before, Richy's new short pants, for it was plenty warm enough for them today, and to have polished his white high-top shoes, for high-top shoes were something that she loved. And the girls—how beautiful their long smooth hair, now that it was combed nicely down with a fine damp comb . . . how pretty their clean pink faces, blooming out from under wide white hats.

Then there was a terrible split in Margaret's recollection, for suddenly they were all of them standing before a very great building. Down from the massive columns, down the slope of steps like a steep hill, came a black figure, and approached them slowly, his arms out like an awkward grandfather. She reached down and pulled each child straight once more in their nice Sunday clothes and patted them down, and even while she was thinking, *Stop now, for a moment do not move, my children, let me look at you,* still she was nodding to them, catching their eye, saying, *Go on,* and so they went, slowly, climbing the steps, and when the old man met them in the middle of the stairs, he did an awesome and yet simple thing: he opened his great black robe and folded it all about them.

Margaret stood watching down below; her arms were at her side and she did not move. But when he raised his head, she turned to him her flat closed face, and it was as if the somber grief of all the planets and all the stars sped in flashing lines toward her face and converged in her eyes, so that—though it was not permitted her to move her lips— she gave him a certain look . . . she gave this dark father a look which she *knew* would burn in his heart forever and to all eternity and more.


MARGARET was all ready to go out. She sat in the bay window of the kitchen, sipping a cup of tea. She had not been hungry enough to actually fix anything, had made do on half a sandwich. Actually she had no appetite at all and she was unbelievably tired. Even her bath had not perked her up. She felt like some old ditto machine with all its vital fluid drained out. She remembered dozing a minute on the bed and having a bad crazy dream about the children that had waked her up. She had had that dream before and she hated it—she wished to her soul she could escape from it.

She also wished she were a person who laughed more, and could enjoy a little more the lighter side of things. She was always reminding herself to watch the comedies on television. Sometimes that cheered her up a little. Nothing had ever made her laugh as much as Lucille Ball. Lord, when she thought of some of the scrapes they could get into, Lucy and Ethel. One night they were supposed to be out of town, they had already told their husbands, and when their plans fell through they didn't want to admit it, and they ended up spending the whole night on the roof of their own apartment building, huddled up in a pouring rain. She had forgotten what had been so funny about it, but she could still see their two faces as they clung together by the chimney, and even now there was something almost hysterical about the pitiful way they looked. These days Archie and Edith were funny too—and Carol Burnett, for instance. And yet—once in a while she would turn them on and it was all so silly it almost made her cry, and tonight might have been like that, so perhaps it was just as well she had to drag herself out, as hard as it was.

The rain had cleared, but the trees dripped and there were wide brown puddles on the lawn. After the rainstorms of the past Leonard would go out back sometimes to grunt worms. Or sometimes he would buy them in a small carton with a wire handle—huge furry caterpillars. Her mind drifted and it was as if it lodged again amongst the voices of the children.

*Wat is a cadapidda?* her daughter Laney was saying.

*A what?*

*She means caterpillar*, said Ruth, holding her book against her chest.

*Wuf won't tell me.*

*Ruth. Ruth. Tell her. What does it say in your book?*

*She can get her own book.*

*Tell her what it says.*

*No.*

*Yes ma'am.*

*No, she can get her own book.* Ruth crying.

*Then give it to me.*

Laney crying too. *Listen now both of you. Stop it, I mean stop it.*

*Why can't she get her own book?*

*Let's see now. Look here. Let's look at it together. Here—it's a poem. Well let's see—this little caterpillar . . . .* (She thought again of the fishing worms Leonard kept in cartons in the refrigerator. That was vile. There was no reason to have put up with that.) But Ruth's poem that she had not wanted

280

Laney to see was, as it turned out, one of the poems that Ruth would never get tired of; she was always reciting it to herself under her breath, or teaching it to her dolls, sitting them all in a row, with a stub of pencil propped in each one's hand. Then Laney had had to learn it too, simply because Ruth had, and the thing was, Margaret could remember it even now, although the children themselves had probably forgotten it long ago:

> Who's that scratching my back? said the Wall.
> It's me, said a small
> Caterpillar. I'm learning to crawl.

It's silly to remember such things, Margaret thought. After all, she considered, her children were not dead, were not ghosts whose spirits had to be evoked by little charms like that. And yet those particular little girls who said that little poem over and over, in such quietly satisfied and yet amazed voices (since they were just finding out about little poems) and had had their dolls say it too with plastic lips in voices which were amazed and satisfied in exactly the same way— these little persons were dead, it seemed to her, had ceased to exist and been replaced by other persons she could never know as well. Or she thought of it this way—now the baby lives of her children had passed into her keeping and belonged to her much more than to the ones that had actually worn them in flesh and blood and then stepped out of them, like undersized skins. She, the mama, standing by like mothers always had, had caught, as they fell, these little worn-out, tossed-away lives, snatched them up for safekeeping, curled them back up in the womb of her brain to be secretly reborn whenever memory bid them to.

She looked through the arch into the living room, out the picture window to the front yard. A light of a peculiar tone was mixing with the rainy film on the big japonica, setting it oddly aglow. At her age some people removed themselves from all these *old* things, from affairs like this aged japonica (and its old friends the bridal wreath and the yellow jasmine), from all this past, from the vanished lives of their children, for instance. Especially in the cities older people almost always, Ruth said, moved out of the houses where they had raised their children and into something fresh and blank, and then they remembered less and lived in the present more.

Margaret sipped her tea. In the distance she could hear the low roar of cars speeding down the through streets, but here everything was very still and she could almost hear her own breath.

*Which is the best way?* she wondered.

She considered this plot of ground of hers, where no human beings, possibly not even Indians, had ever lived before in the history of the world. She remembered how the thick pines had been cut down—ruthlessly, as it had seemed to her—by the builder Mr. McDaniels (who also cheated people out of closets and hallways), so that in those first summers the sun had poured over them a ceaseless stream of scalding flames. In a way it was a sorrow to think of the great big original pines coming crashing down so that a paltry cottage, a low-budget dwelling of four-and-a-half-rooms, could be put up in their place, during the depression when everything was dirt cheap and yet no one could pay the price and Leonard and his father and mother had almost suffocated for fear that if they even gulped down too much of the public air there would be instant retribution, that the earth would open and swallow them up, and the new house too, just because they had had the monstrous nerve to think they could pay off a mortgage on it. Yet this plot of ground, she considered, this house, as small and foolish as in a way it was, was still a ponderous and awesome thing in her mind . . . in her mind it was a very great structure and she had only to look around her and it was as if layers and layers of memory came rippling off the walls, and thick sheaths of it started to fold back off every brick and board.

And so—would it not be better if one day she merely walked out of it, and fumbling on the stoop, her purse on her arm, locked the door for the last time? took one last look at the brocade sofa through the latticed pane of the door and simply went her way?

She considered again the old japonica in the picture window—such a glossy, obese old shrub—in its protective circle of pines. Where no trees had grown for many years, these new strong pines rose now far above the house. This afternoon, in the dusky afterglow of the storm, they were still shedding the leftover rain into little lakes at their distant feet.

In days past people had not gone to nurseries for trees to plant, they went to the woods as they did for Christmas trees and dug up their own seedlings. Margaret had done so any number of times with no success; she had brought the infant pines home in tubs in the trunk of the car and for a time they would seem to live and then they would droop and die. Then after the war, in that period of queer euphoria, of rare hopefulness, that Leonard had had when he first got back, when he was full of thanksgiving and gratitude for the delicious accident of simply having a home to come back to, a wife and children and a house, he had opened his eyes and seen things that normally he could not see through the blind nets of worry and emotion that enmeshed him, and he had actually seen the hot bare yard for what it was, felt the roasting sun cooking the house to a nice turn all summer long. So one afternoon one of his fishing friends had pulled up in a rattling old pickup and he and Leonard went out into fields somewhere and got fresh little pines. They cut them out of the ground in great grassy plates of earth, much wider than Margaret's tubs, so that the little trees would hardly feel, even in their toes, the vibrations of the axe, would not know they had had a change of address.

The trees lived. They grew. And even when other things failed, the trees were a sign of a moment of family hope, of

283

dormant desires—almost forgotten—taking quivering root again, and of something in the spirit of a self-stricken, self-saddled, self-blasted man that even if it were almost never seen, had still been proven to exist.

Yet in the years that followed, gradually something like failure overtook them again; jobs came but they did not pay enough, oh she hated to remember the debts creeping back, Leonard's fear of ruin growing on him again, so that even the smallest debt, the most obviously *manageable* debt, tormented him, frightened him to death, as if it might of itself grow and destroy them. If he himself lost twenty dollars at poker, at the VFW Club, he would come home in a fever of apprehension, and such a blowing rage sometimes that it was a wonder the house had not cracked in two. Then much later on, when he had finally reconciled himself to children going to college—in order, possibly, to make something of themselves, in order, possibly, to live lives a little less frightened than their parents' . . . even when he had finally brought himself, after long travails of sputtering, pacing, and then explosive doubt, to accept the fact of the mother going to work to provide for college bills, to his own possible humiliation . . . even when all this had long since been settled on and agreed to, still he would be subject to awful premonitions, and would suddenly collapse in terror of this calamitous obligation, stealing up on him with such an innocent face, taking them unawares; and he would recoil in absolute assurance of disgrace, in absolute certainty that unless he bolted yowling to their rescue, they would all be stepping out upon a mined ground of awesome devastation.

There were times when his worry, his affliction, was such that Margaret hardly dared to let a dollar drop away from them, hardly dared to spend a quarter for milk or bread or for children's needs at school. There were certainly times, for instance, when he could not even bear to see groceries being brought into the house. (*I know they have to be brought*, he seemed to say, *but don't let me actually have to see them*.) She envisioned him as of old, standing on the far corner of the front yard, leaning almost *into* the road, as if determined not to be kept in any enclosure, his hands in his pockets, talking to himself darkly, answering himself back.

She pictured a Saturday afternoon. The old round Ford in the drive across the yard. Leonard staring toward it from his far corner while she and Ruth loaded the bags into the house. They went back and forth, halting clumsily at the front door, propping the sacks on knees while they pulled back the screen. But Leonard did not move, made no motion to come and help or even hold the door, but only beamed back to them black glaring looks—expressions of hatred and disgust for these great heavy guilty brown bags brazenly piling up on his heap of debt. The shameless, the deliberate provocation of it!

No doubt the half-dozen bags they had carried (perhaps a week of food, after all, for five people who might otherwise be found dead one morning of starvation) had seemed to him to stretch out in an ever-lengthening, doom-filled line, and the huffing and laboring trips of the carriers to be a relentless march to degradation and disgrace. Margaret, pausing momentarily on the path in her low-heeled shoes, in her homemade cotton dress, with her arms loaded, had almost believed he might come tearing toward her from his outpost across the yard—to seize these criminal goods, load them, in frenzied, sped-up action, back into the car, roar away with them before it was too late.

In her bay window, Margaret scanned this picture once again, turned and focused it, refocused it in her mind, attempted to look behind it, through to the other side of it, and to see whether there was not some truth about her life that by some bizarre chance had always been blocked from view.

A neighbor down the street had been killed by a neat little cancer hidden snugly away from the probing X-ray (by the ruler of all nature? by Jesus our fairest Lord?) in a pouch of tissue behind an obscuring bone. No doubt things were hiding too from the probing shaft of her own memory-beam and if they ever came to light . . . what then? What if she had made some gross miscalculation and everything wrong in her marriage had actually been *her* fault and not her husband's? Perhaps it was really she and not he who was sick and afflicted, squeezed so brainless by the fear and failure of her own life (by a child's life, for instance, too absurd to even *start* to trace its effects), that in others too it was only fear and failure she could see, no matter what else was there, and thus saw the whole train of events not only on Suwannee Drive, but at her grandmother's dairy on the Albany Highway, and at the Barkers' on Harrison Street, as well as everywhere else she turned, as conspiracies and nothing else against her deepest needs and dreams, and the needs and dreams of the little girl she had once been and of all the children of the world.

THERE WERE so many dire things to try to explain. Those terrible attempts, for instance, for them to do something as a family, the way families were meant to do. Leonard would not want to do them but would pretend he did, while actually he was as mad as a hornet and they all knew it so that there was no use whatever to begin with and yet they went on with it. Those pretend fishing trips, for instance, where he would take them to some dirty old stream that was just conveniently nearby, which they knew—without much caring why—no fisherman would take seriously for a minute, where there was not even a bank for the children to splash on and where they were scared to go swimming anyway for fear of snakes. Margaret saw them standing in the stickers, eating the picnic lunch at the trunk of the car, staring off into the old muddy river, not even bothering to put a cloth down on the miserable rough ground. She saw Leonard pretending to cast seriously a pole, show the children where fish would swarm. But mainly they would just eat the lunch, get in the car and go home. Then just the relief to be back. But those looks that would be exchanged between husband and wife!

*See, you said we never went anywhere so I took you.*

*See, we went too.*

*But you didn't want to.*

You *didn't want to.*

Awful things juxtaposed themselves. She saw Ruth standing in her jeans and pigtails in a sullen pout by the car, on the old rutted road by the river, full of scorn for her father. Then she saw her as a grown child, almost tall for a family as little as they were, walking in the cemetery with an absent frown on her face, or swinging slowly in the glider under Leonard's pines, with the same expression, saying, "But Mother, you made it all the way, and things got better instead of worse and he loved you—in his way—all his life and could never have lived without you and—"

She saw Richy bending over the tangled bank over the ugly stream, squatting to stare into the water . . . Leonard suddenly wolf down the last bite of his pimiento cheese and throw the crust into the briars. Wipe his mouth with his handkerchief. Then go straight to the car and reach through the window to blow the horn, absently, as if he hardly knew that he was doing it, and without anyone's leave to do so.

Margaret was at the open trunk of the car, her hair in a bandanna, stuffing the trash all into one bag, putting the stopper back on the lemonade, but when Leonard blew the horn, startling her, for the children to collect, in her recollection she knew—yet how had she known?—that Laney had just found something interesting up ahead on the river bank, had come back to get her brother and was leading him by the hand through the briars, stepping gingerly, with caution, raising high each foot before she set it down. When the children heard the horn, they had paused and looked upward to where the car was, half hidden in the brush. They waited and it blew again, and yet Laney persevered, stepped forward again toward the curious thing on the bank ahead.

*Children go on—always—don't let anything stop you.* They had put their heads down to concentrate on the brambly path. But the horn blew. It blew again, and Laney hesitated; holding back a briar, she looked upwards, with a sigh, and then she turned back, up the slope.

*But that is an injustice to him*, Margaret thought, and yet in her memory the horn blew again, and it was so aggravating, she thought *Perhaps not, even so.*

She crossed her arms on the maple table and stared forward through the living room and the picture window. Why *there* was a car, pulled up in front of her house—and it was her ride to the shower, blowing the horn.

Margaret hollered out to the car from the front door, then ran into the bathroom. On her way back out, she picked up her umbrella, just in case.

But when she stepped onto the stoop, looked out into the failing day, she saw that just in that few moments a pale chastened sun had broken through, on a deep slant, just before it was too late. She knew that the peculiar light on the japonica had been the harbinger of this drained, gallant sun, which could not shine over them anything stronger than a damp color of washed-out roses, and yet did shine, nevertheless, even in its storm-weakened state. There was something almost moving about this, something highly pleasing about it, and Margaret paused for a moment on the stoop to admire the misty beauty of this late-coming light.

She had closed the door, and now she waved to the friends waiting in the car, for there were two of them. Did she have her gift? Yes, in her purse. But this umbrella on her arm—no need for that now, with the sun back out, now they had had this amazing change, almost as if, like a small resurrection, the curtain of night had fallen and then been raised again. (That was a wonder.) She opened the door to set the umbrella back inside—*and what if she had not?* Because as soon as she cracked the door . . . the phone was ringing, and probably had been ringing, and muttering and fussing she ran back to the kitchen to pick it up.

## ~ CHAPTER EIGHT ~

THE three women drove on slowly. Margaret sat in the back seat, and the women in front talked about the storm and what they had been doing and how surprised they were when it had opened up on them this afternoon, and how put out they had been to think it might have spoiled the shower.

Then they talked about the bride-to-be. The driver said that the bride had turned into a very attractive girl, and the other woman said she agreed with her completely and that no one, not even the girl's own mother, had ever thought she would be. They said you simply could not predict and that to look at it another way, some children started out well and ended up just ordinary, because for instance their noses had started to grow.

Olive said, "Margaret, what are those three little kids of *yours* doing these days? Have you got all the grandchildren you bargained for?" Margaret said yes she had, three grand-babies was just right—though of course there was still Richard not married, and so you never could tell. *"There's* one that's taking his time," the other woman said; and she always had plenty of documentation to bring forth on any question like that, and she began to name other children who might have been expected to have been married by now and were not.

"They don't all even *want* to get married anymore," she said, and Margaret agreed with her and said it might even be for the best—although really, who could tell?

She was able to say these appropriate things, and this surprised her, and yet when she spoke, her voice scraped and it had a peculiar pitch to it, and though she kept clearing her throat, it simply would not clear.

When she had put down the phone, she had not been able to think what to do, or to think of any excuses to make to the friends in the car, so she went on out, as bleary and dazed as she was, and got in. As they drove away, she clutched at something until she almost hurt her hand, and she saw that she had brought the umbrella along after all. Later, riding along, she realized that she was sitting strangely forward in her seat, with her face stuck into the window like a child's, and it seemed to her that surely the ones in front had been stealing private looks at her, to see why she was staring at the drenched road, at houses and cars and trees, at the red-glinting edge of sky—as if she had never seen things like that before.

Other people could shrug things off, get over things. A phone call like that would not have affected them as it did her, made them weave going through the living room, have to almost aim themselves at the door. When she had answered the phone, a woman had given her name and said she was calling from Jacksonville. Then there had been a slight pause, and in that one second Margaret knew—and knew that she had known, in a way, all day . . . from something, and yet not from anything in particular—what person this call was about.

But they are all dead there, she had thought.

Yes, except—
(Her.)
(Yes: her).
Her.
But surely she wouldn't think that *I*—
She's never had any reason to believe that *I*—
Nearly twenty years have passed and I have not . . . and she and I have not . . . .
That's the way it's been and the way I want it to stay.
Of course.
Yet in the same second that these thoughts had come, certain things in her brain suddenly altered themselves, moved—*at last,* she almost thought—into a certain position, and it was as if her mind, which had been rising like a wall of sharp points to ward something off, shrunk back; as she stood at the phone, her eyes closed and she felt (even, possibly, while she was saying *Yes this is Margaret Barker)* a moment—very grave—of calm and resignation.


MARGARET had a party tray, punch and cake, on her lap. The room was full of merriment. They were all enjoying themselves, teasing and carrying on. A group of them would laugh heartily over something and get all the others to laughing too, they would hardly know why—but it was just that tonight they were *ready* to laugh, wanted to laugh, and were all thinking, together, *This is one of the good parts of life.*

That was the spirit of things. Sometimes, at parties like these, Margaret, when she was in a normal frame of mind, would laugh hard too, until her stomach even ached. Yes something would get her tickled—one of the women, for instance, pretending to give serious advice, and then the silly way it would come out. The whole room would be laughing, and it would occur to them all how silly, in a way, marriages—all human affairs—really were. Yes, there was definitely a comic, almost a hysterical side to them.

Yet at other times they would catch each other in bent, frowning stares, for it was also true, after all, that marriage, getting married, was basically the most serious thing in the world, and in a way one of the most confusing, puzzling things to think about, and so it was possible to fall into a solemn reverie, thinking *These children, these little girls, wanting to grow up more than anything in the world, so now here they are, and they can't wait but are in a trembling stitch of anticipation, popping open with emotion and trust and goodwill. Oh little girls, little girls, we couldn't tell you a thing even if we tried and maybe it's just as well . . . .*

And tonight—tonight, as far as that went, was worse in that way than usual, because she was not *in* a normal frame of mind, and though she was physically present in the room, able to see people laughing and talking, see the bride moaning and exclaiming through the ordeal of gift-opening, smiling and admiring—even though she was here, with all her senses operating as far as anyone could tell, yet actually at times they were not, and for instance suddenly she would seem to go almost deaf and sounds only came scratching through from a long way off, and she would have to struggle to bring them to bear on her eardrums.

Is Laney still in Chicago?

Yes she is.

They seem to like it there.

Of course I know you wish she was closer.

Yes-s goodness, that would really be nice.

John is in Seattle.

Oh dear.

Freddie is in Tucson.

Oh my.

Gloria is married again.

Oh oh.

And she is teaching now, in Birmingham.

In Atlanta.

In Macon.

A little town in Illinois.

Near Philadelphia.

They have bought them some land and they even have some animals.

He's still with the telephone company.

Their first one was born deaf you know.

A heart murmur.

Terrible impetigo.

No asthma in our family, it has to be on their side.

Wetting the bed a lot.

A checkup and they were certainly relieved.

An excellent orthopedist, the best they could find.

Braces on all three, and they don't know how in the world they'll pay for it.

Sometimes she almost wanted to say *Oh fuck,* the way she heard kids say it, half under their breath, or certain people up at the Court. In fact there was a moment when she wondered whether or not she *had* said it, but then no one seemed to be looking at her in any peculiar way.

One of the women stood at a table slicing cake. She said, "Margaret, let me ask you something." Her husband worked in the main courthouse, and she said usually it took a lot to get him upset but this week something really had. They had had a boy that suddenly went crazy and screamed his lungs off all over the courthouse. They couldn't get him to stop and they didn't know why he was doing it. They said he wasn't much more than a kid, probably a juvenile, and so she wondered if Margaret had had him over to her place too.

Margaret said yes she had and it was the same thing with them, and it had been so completely unexpected and such a terrible shock that it had upset them all very much—especially Jim, it just made him so nervous he could hardly stand it; she said they had two psychiatrists working with the boy and for a while it looked like they were getting somewhere but then they found out they weren't.

The woman thought about the boy. She said, "But I just don't see what *could* make a person do like that, do you?"

Margaret was trying to shake her head—but suddenly she had an awful feeling of isolation from everybody else in the room, all her old friends, and she turned such a severe, staring look on the woman she was talking to that the woman quickly lowered her head and went off on another track.

"But you're such a strong person, aren't you," she cooed, "to have stood it up there all these years. You must really be strong." The woman had huge hands and she got up and lifted the whole brimming punch bowl and set it down on the other end of the table.

"Next thing will be a baby shower," someone said, and the bride threw up her hands and said, "Oh-h no ma'am!" Everybody laughed. "Don't even talk like that," the bride said. But of course this little scene was all pretend and just a pleasant relic of olden times and almost everyone in the room knew that this nice child had already been protecting herself for a good many years and wasn't about to get pregnant until she was good and ready.

Margaret thought about the advances they had made in birth control. As far as birth and death were concerned, there had been a good bit of improvement in one but on the other practically none. There were a fair number of ways now to keep people from being born, but no ways to keep them from dying. Death control was still out of the question, it wasn't even discussed.

And then Margaret became aware that a certain voice that she could not place but which had something to do with one *particular* death, had become tangled with the voices in the room, and at first she could not hear what in the world it was saying and then it was as if a little space around it suddenly cleared, and a woman was saying she had bad news. *I'm afraid I have some bad news. Saying Your stepmother is ill. Not expected to live. Wants to see you, is hoping you can come. Saying No one with her very much except the nurse.*

Margaret had an image of herself in the kitchen holding the phone, absolutely motionless, listening in a severe silence. When the woman had said *Your stepmother*, she had not replied, not broken in or made any dispute about it. And yet—she could have said so much. *This is a bad mistake*, she could have said for instance. *She is no mother of mine. She is not any kind of mother to me and never has been. Of course she would say that sometimes, use that term—stepmother—even in my presence. I would just give her a black look and bite my tongue—and she probably did not even notice it she was so crazy, so ignorant.*

"Your stepmother is ill." *I'm sure a great many people are ill*, Margaret could have replied. *I'm sure the hospital is full of them, but this is not any concern of mine. She is the last person that would be. For instance, I had no idea, until this call came, whether she was alive or dead and I had not given the matter any thought in several years. Of course in the past I have wished her dead many times, and if I could ever have killed anyone she would have been the one. But fortunately I had reached a point, where I just felt that the state of her health had nothing to do with me and was simply no business of mine whatsoever.*

*A stranger, of course, could not be expected to understand, but I will probably be ill myself just from getting this call—so it's really too bad because it won't help her a bit and then I will just be sick too and have to start on Sinequan tomorrow around the clock just from hearing her name, from thinking about the terrible fact that a person like her could actually have had an effect on my life, could have made me have to throw away my father's love, for instance, which had always covered me like a warm coat . . . and then be cold ever since.*

THE HOSTESS was helping the bride arrange the gifts on a table where everybody could examine them. The bride was carrying on the pleasant pretense that the gifts were so precious that she could hardly bring herself to even touch them and would do well simply to mate each gift to the giver's card.

Meanwhile the guests had plenty to talk about and conversation did not flag for a minute. The women in the room were mostly ones Margaret had first met at church years ago and had gone to the women's group with, for instance. Now that she no longer went to church she saw them very little. Some of the older, more serious ones worried about her behind her back, and in fact every few years a solemn pair of them would make a formal visit to her house and ask her very earnestly why she had quit the church, and tell her what a very, very serious matter it was to do such a thing. She would murmur and equivocate, would say she was too tired on Sunday to go anymore. They would ask her if she thought she had lost her belief. And of course she could not say, *It's not that I have stopped believing, I never did believe at all, I only went in the first place because of the children—I could tell you certain things about my life and you would know why I could never believe in God, or in a God that was supposed to be a good person and a holy redeemer and a lover of all our souls, and you might not even believe in him yourself.*

Yet looking back, the whole business of going to church was a confusing affair. She still wondered how she could have been so affected by certain things. Whenever Laney had sung a solo, in her frail and lovely voice, standing alone in the choir, so small, Margaret would always weep profusely, and yet when Laney sang at school, for instance, she did not weep. There had been times when she almost felt she *did* believe. Why would she always remember that when Ruth was baptized, they had sung a certain song? *Just as I a-am, withou-out one plea—but tha-at thy love was shed for me.* For Laney they had sung *Take my life*, and after that Margaret had always considered it a very beautiful song and even now she remembered almost all the words:

Take my life and let it be
Consecrated, Lord, to Thee.
Take my hands and let them move
At the impulse of Thy love,
At the impu-ulse of Thy love.

Because she loved children's little limbs, she loved it where the song said *Take my feet and let them be, swift and beautiful for Thee*. Looking around her tonight, deaf from the pressure of her own thoughts, she saw faces opened in silent merriment, and many were aging replicas of faces that had opened around her in song on that evening and on all the other Sunday evenings of those days, and she remembered how amazed she had been, though she had not expected to be, at the idea in the song that her child was giving up all she had, so young, was giving up her will, her voice, her moments and days—that they should always flow in ceaseless praise of her redeemer; she was giving up her heart to the royal throne. Why was she so affected by all this and why was it all so sad? Here were people asking a child to give up its life, to give up its own self, and here was the child saying, in her own innocence and faith, that yes she would, and this was a remarkable and awesome thing, and in a way a terrible thing, because actually people were better than the old mean universe they lived in, they were willing to give up everything for what was true and beautiful ... the only thing was, most of the time they weren't sure there was anything true and beautiful to give it up for.

PUNCH, someone was saying, and Margaret said no thanks, but that it was very good punch.

"You didn't think there was too much ginger ale?"

"Oh no, I thought it was just right."

"Piled on top of her head," one of the ladies said. "And it looks good."

"She has always known how to look her best."

"Not even gray, and y'all may recall that her mother wasn't gray until she was almost eighty."

"That sister though."

"Anna Belle?"

"It's always been too bad—hair that straggly, and to wear it long."

"To have it stringing down her back like that."

*Margaret remembered looking out the window from her mama's house years ago. She was standing on a chair with a crack in the seat, balancing a curtain rod in her hands, trying to raise the whole affair to the brackets without spilling the curtains off the rod.*

Through the open window that day she could see Nomey standing at the back of the yard next door, her hair stringing down her back, her hands on broad hips. She heard Nomey call across a tangled wire fence to someone on the other side. It was terrible language, and filled Margaret with such despair she could not raise the rod to the brackets. On the other side of the fence another woman tossed her head in enjoyable scorn, screamed back, holding the shoulders of a dirty child. It was a question of trash and junk having been thrown in Nomey's yard. But how could Nomey tell it from the trash and junk that were already there? Margaret felt a pulse of some unexpected emotion. Why not laugh at this? she thought. But no, she was not the kind that could.

So it was as if someone had taken a big brush and flattened her face with a thick glaze of despair. Behind her the other ones chirped and chattered, watching her on the chair as if it were the most interesting sight they had ever seen.

"Margaret's putting up the curtains, ain't she kids? Look at Maga now."

"Maga, whah-'ou-puh-up. What 'ou put up? 'Ou put up curtains, Maga?"

～

299

MARGARET felt so bad she got up and went into the bathroom. All that punch, which was entirely too sweet. While she was in there, she found two aspirin in her purse, and a Sinequan. Then she took off her glasses to look in the mirror, so that she wouldn't see herself too well. But when she looked, she knew, even so, they must all think she had some fatal disease. She hung her head, stared through the bathroom tiles to a picture of a dying Margaret, lying face forward on her high bed, a damp cloth on her head.

Back in the buzzing room, she clutched her purse on her lap, waited desperately for a sign from her ride that she was ready to go. She had been tired before, but never, never this tired. The conversations that went on . . . as familiar as they were, were peculiar too and she could not possibly enter into them.

"Oh Helen," she seemed to hear someone say, and yet surely no one *could* say such a thing, "you never told me—how was your death?"

"Oh my death!" (Her hand to her throat.)

"Oh I tell you—didn't I tell you? Oh it was awful, it was really the awfullest thing. Merle Smith died too the same year and she says the same thing—it's something you almost have to experience yourself . . . she and I just look at each other and say *Oh! Oh! Dying!* . . . you *know*. And of course we have so much in common, we always have, but this death—all this death business, I couldn't even begin to tell you all of it, but one day when we can sit down—"

"Well I was thinking about you all the time, you know that—but I knew there wasn't a thing I could do."

"No there really isn't a thing." In Margaret's old sick head the voices went on, and it was the most peculiar thing in the world. "You have to get through it or not get through it, but I tell you, there were times—I didn't think I'd make it. And the worst thing was, everybody getting so nervous and upset—that it just upset me that much more. But then of course (*laughing*) if they hadn't been upset, that would have been just as bad. I guess the thing is, when you're dying, everything upsets you, nothing is ever right or done the right way—there *isn't* any right way. Oh it's miserable, miserable. I told Robert the other day, I said *Listen, if they ever talk about putting me through it again, just tell them 'No thank you, no, no.'* I'm serious, dying again, going through it again, would just be the end of me, I wouldn't even consider it."

IT WAS a blessed relief to be sitting in the dark back seat of the car going home.

The driver squinted forward. "Poor Helen," she said.

"You mean her operation?" the other woman said.

"It wasn't an easy thing for her, the way she sounded tonight."

"I don't think they ever are, do you?"

"God just didn't make us all that strong, I guess he wanted us to depend on him."

"I'll tell you one thing—these bodies aren't worth much when you get right down to it."

All the way home Margaret was silent, she didn't even pretend to have anything to say. When they came to her house, Olive got out and opened Margaret's door.

She said, "Margaret you are worn plumb out, I bet you just wanted to stay home tonight."

She put out her hand and Margaret took it and pulled herself out of the car. She went out at night so seldom that the night air always surprised her; tonight she felt it on her shoulders like a damp cloak. She had forgotten to leave a light on, and the night was so dark the little house was only barely visible. It was almost as if she had been brought home to nothing, to the end of things, just into a big darkness—and yet if she had to be *brought* to it, it must be a particular darkness, just for her. "I *am* pretty tired," Margaret said, and

Olive patted her shoulder so gently that she almost started to cry.

"Good night," they said.

"Good night, you-all."

"Good night."


RIGHT before Margaret got into bed, she took her best sleeping pill, the one that always worked, and in a little while she fell asleep, thinking *If there's anything to think about, let it be tomorrow, not tonight.* Still, she remembered, before she breathed out her last sigh of consciousness into the dark room, that there was someone not expected to live, and she thought *But none of us are, no one is expected to live very long, and maybe all the trouble we have isn't a thing but that. What is unfair,* she thought, *is that dying comes when we're too tired for it . . . sort of like I am tonight . . . .*

*Thank goodness I'm dead now,* a voice said, and it sounded like one of the ladies at the shower. *But listen it's not so bad. I was just like you-all, I said, "Oh I can't, I can't"—and then I did, I got through it, and you will too, when it's your turn.*

*I don't know.*

*You will, take my word for it.* Margaret sighed. She thought of herself replying, not to be argumentative, *I guess so,* although she really couldn't think it through, she could only think so far, and now little points of thought in her brain were winking out one by one, until at last she could not think at all and could hardly even hear herself sigh, once more, or feel herself stretch and then lean mercifully back on the sleepy waters of oblivion.

# Part Two

*Saturday*

# ⌒ CHAPTER NINE ⌒

I T WAS only later in the day, sitting in the darkened room, that she was struck, in retrospect, by the extraordinary brightness of her early morning drive. The sun had come up on a wet land, storm-drenched, with tremendous reflective powers, and the car had seemed to move through an absolute ocean of light, with no banks or boundaries of any kind.

She had not experienced anything like it in a long time. She did not remember when she had struck out from the house so early, with the sun so low that she could drive straight into it. But that was out on the highway, and first she remembered pulling through the mixed, broken light of the town, the sun mostly blocked but spilling violently out from behind things now and then. She remembered making her various little turns, up this way and down that, and the rubbery sound of the tires peeling off the soaked streets. Hardly anyone was out at that hour on Saturday morning. Then, just outside the town, she had come up, at the top of a rise, to the bare, flat narrow highway, and in this unobstructed place, the sun had suddenly burst over her the wild power that she was recalling now so well.

It seemed to burn from a point which lay at the far, far end of the highway and which would eventually block her way. Yet she had turned directly into it, driven almost blindly eastward, over the gleaming wet road into the center of the spreading fan of light. The roadside ditches lay brimming with yesterday's rainstorm, and they too threw up great slanting screens of magnificent incandescence, so that she could hardly see a thing but light itself.

At the time, though, she had not been amazed by any of this; of course the constituents of amazement were there, she had taken them down like shorthand on her sensory record-pad, without thinking what they meant, and only now were they composing themselves into amazement.

But she was hardly surprised anymore that her mind would function that way; she knew that half the time she was mentally absent from whatever she was doing—as she had been at the bridal shower last night—and only later able to think about it, while absently doing something else, so that in a way she never caught up with herself. If this morning she had driven into the morning sun without actually seeing it, it was because she had projected into the damp sheen of spreading light a powerful mental beam of her own—of gloom and glum preoccupation. It was as if her mind had thrust a shaft of darkness into the light and it was only by this darkness that she could truly see.

It was the *old* road she had taken, the Old Jacksonville Highway, as they called it now, and perhaps that had been a mistake. It was the same narrow black tar road she had travelled in anguish so many times in that other period of her life, when going to Jacksonville was one of the regular ordeals of existence, and perhaps she should have taken the new superhighway. Still, she didn't trust these new highways and the way they whipped you along. A simple thing like blowing your nose, or just feeling in your purse for a kleenex, could easily cause you to miss your turn and then there was no way in the world to get back to it. No these new roads were nothing but a headache, and whenever she knew she had to get on one, she stopped first by the side of the road and took a tranquillizer, and usually it was a good thing she had.

Still, on the old road, all those old trips of that *other* time were waiting for her—there was no way to get rid of the memory of them; as soon as she hit the road and headed out, there they were as ready as she was, and they went rolling along beside her all the way. Plus—the little towns on the old road had not improved a bit; no, they had actually gone down; they looked even more glum and bedraggled than they used to. Even in the wake of the rainstorm, they did not look fresh at all. Standing water had steamed up from greasy, buggy-looking potholes around the gas stations, and even around the old worn-out stores, and things just looked hot and putrid.

After a time the citrus stands began and they looked like the same ones she used to see before, except not as prosperous—she supposed most of their old trade was swinging by on the freeway several counties off. The stands weren't loaded with fruit the way they used to be, and what they had did not look healthy. The billboards still said it was the best fruit in the world, but she noted that the signs definitely needed repainting and that the world-famous oranges on them looked almost white.

Still, what she saw had served to fling her mind forward to Jacksonville, where there had been, when she was growing up, a famous orange grove with its own special kind of oranges: Macedonia oranges; in fact it was the only place in the country where such oranges were grown, and the grove had had its own stand, which you got to by driving up a pretty gravel drive, bordered by bushy orange trees and a white slatted fence.

She had remembered her father sitting behind the wheel

in the old crank-car and herself beside him on the seat, going up the wonderful drive of the grove. "Oh father, how restful this is to the spirit!" she had said—not in those words of course, those would not be a child's words, but something to that *effect*, and her father, gazing over the wheel, his cigar in his mouth, would make a fatherly noise of agreement that pleased her very much. When they got up to the stand, he would get out first and hold out his arms and she would jump down to him from the high seat. She remembered the strong, padded feeling of his thick body, her little girl's spidery hands around his short neck, his smell—always—of tobacco, and of something else that she connected with the plant where he worked, although it was not exactly the kind of smell that a fertilizer plant might suggest, no, to her it was not completely a bad smell, it was the smell of machines and of men working, of burlap and rubber and oil. But her father (strange to say—horrible in a way) was such a clean and fastidious man that this odor in his clothes bothered him very much and made him sad and she remembered how many times at home he would get up for no apparent reason and go and change his shirt.

On the back porch on Clark Street there had been a big square washtub and a scrub-board, and her father and mother had had a good many disagreements, they had had the nearest thing to actual arguments they ever had, about this washtub, for actually it had had no function in the family life at all, and she remembered great big bags of laundry waiting on the porch to be picked up by washing services, or piled high in the back seat of the car, and then the fresh bundles of clean paper-wrapped clothes and shirts sitting in the house, and later on, a wooden crate in the bedroom where her father kept his clean shirts and where nothing else was allowed to be.

But as for the orange grove—sometimes the others would come too, but still it would be Margaret and her father who would get out of the car to pick out a big sack of Macedonia oranges. Her mother would stay behind on the high front seat, bouncing on her lap—and crowing happily in its face—one or the other of the sequence of babies with crooked expressions and mild blubbery sounds. At the stand Margaret and her father might get in the refreshment line to buy them all cups of fresh orange juice or coconut milk, and while they waited their turn her father would look back at the occupants of the car, and then at Margaret, and study her very carefully, and perhaps he would feel her long hair, or lay his thick hands on her shoulders, or stroke her thin arms in a satisfied way, and yet in an almost questioning way, and Margaret would stand very still in front of him and simply enjoy his touch, and sometimes she thought it was the most pleasurable way she was ever touched by anyone all her life.

Not far from the orange grove there was a big park, so whenever Margaret thought of the grove she would soon be thinking of the park as well. Radios were just coming in, and they were very costly, it was bizarre, considering that today you could buy one for almost nothing at the drugstore. But in those days no one could afford them, and so on late summer afternoons, people went to this large comfortable breezy park, to sit and socialize under great mossy shade trees and listen to radio broadcasts from loudspeakers set on tall poles. The grown-ups sat together on benches and conversed, whether they knew each other or not, or perhaps they brought their own canvas chairs, or blankets to spread on the grass, and they brought big jugs of things to drink. While the adults amused each other, the children ran off to the swings or romped on the grass, or walked away arm in arm to look everything over far and wide.

The park was one thing that all the Stovalls loved. Even the odd-faced babies seemed to experience their own kind of afflicted contentment there, in the blowsy shade and amongst so many cheerful spirits, though the one who liked it the best was the mother. Goodness yes, and Margaret could hear her now: *Oh Raymond let's go to the park! You want to, don't you Raymond?* If her father even twitched an eye, even tried to give himself a minute to think, the mother knew what to do, and Margaret herself was swept up and thrust in her father's face. *Maga's been begging, she's been begging all day to go ain't you Maga?*

They had a big flour sack they put things in to take with them, and her mother would run around over the house and stuff things in it, right and left, and you never knew what she would put in, and then her father would have to quietly take most of it out, while her mother was in the bathroom, for instance, and put in essential things like diapers and wet rags and big jars of ice water.

When they got near the park, they began to hear the loudspeakers, and Margaret's mother would be suddenly shaken, shocked to the bone with the thrill of it and she would make them all get absolutely quiet so she could hear what song was being played. She adored the popular songs from the radio-speakers, and later, sitting in the park itself, she would try to sing along even if the song wasn't one of the ones she knew, and sometimes people laughed at her and she laughed at herself, and she was simply delighted to be the source of anyone's laughter and fun.

*She loved fun so much,* Margaret thought, *and my lord how she loved to talk.* She was crazy, for instance, about after-supper talk on porches and front steps, and on buses and street-corners, or sitting in drugstores, and so of course she loved the loud, merry, careless talk of the park, where thank goodness no one had any work to do, where all that was simply over for the day. As far as she was concerned, work was nothing but a terrible bore, she wished nobody *ever* had to work and she really didn't see why they did have to, or who wanted it that way.

*Oh that is charming,* Margaret thought, her lips slightly bunched to the side, mildly ironical—*but that was her downfall too. And all our downfalls . . . mine, my father's.* Yes, more and more through the years, this was the way it had seemed to her—that if you looked into the center of their funnel of swirling trouble, you would see this: her mother's hatred of work, her incapacity that way. Because surely, she thought, this is a fact of human existence: that inside us there is always chaos, and so outside there must be something else— a degree of order. But of course Margaret herself was a maniac on the opposite side, a demon for order and cleanliness and routine, and when she saw a speck of dirt she went after it like a crazy person and for instance she would practically risk her life to wipe the dust off the top of her kitchen cabinets.

Still—if she *was* a maniac, perhaps it only proved her point, and was the consequence of her extra allotment of dread and fear, and the extra allotment of dread and fear was the consequence of her mother's incapacity to have ever relieved these emotions, to have set down in people's inner thickets of agitation a few little pathways of order and smoothness and calm.

She saw her mother in the park, swaying happily to the music, her legs, under her long skirts, drawn up on the pallet her father would spread for them. She might be singing to the music the wrong words, and people might be laughing at her—not unkindly . . . or perhaps they were, but she would go right on, not caring at all one way or the other, because the park was a place where she intended to be happy, no matter what, and where anything *but* happiness was simply absurd.

*Of course Mama was ridiculous*, Margaret thought. Yet for her too going to the park when she was three and four and six and eight years old had had a meaning, both then and now, and of course she could not think exactly what it was but it had to do with a certain necessity people had. She saw that it was necessary for people to deceive themselves, that they had to believe, at least part of the time, that they were meant to be happy and not to grieve and brood. In the park

311

something came over them and they were kind, they were friendly to each other, as if to say *Let's all let down and show how good and nice this race of humans really is,* and people would loan each other balls and hoops and cards and checkerboards, and lotions for insect bites; they chased each other's blowing newspapers and swung each other's children, and whoever had food and drink might even offer it around, and for instance somebody might say, in the more formal speech of that day, when the war was over and times were pretty good and maybe people weren't quite so worried as they usually were, *See here, Mr. Stovall, I would be pleased—yessir, I would take it as a favor—if you would try one of these selecto-perfecto (or whatever-they-were) cigars. Now this is a smooth smoke. See what you think of that, sir.*

There were times when people laughed very hard, all together, at almost nothing—at someone's struggling little joke, or another one's inadvertent witticism, or a child's comical antic on the grass, or at squeaked-out or stretched-over voices on the loudspeaker. They laughed very hard and quite sincerely—and why was that? Perhaps they had been drawn there, to the park, almost mystically, for a special purpose: simply to show that a certain kind of decent family and communal life could be carried on. And so Margaret too was drawn. She loved to skitter on the grass until she had skittered herself breathless, then to lie panting on the pallet and feel the breezes that smelled of the sea, stare up into the gnarled plumage of the humongous water oaks. *That was all very well,* Margaret thought, but she saw a picture, also, of herself gazing at the whole scene upside down, doing a headstand on the weedy grass, thinking (even at the time), *This is all very well . . . but the park is such a little part of life and most of life is something else entirely.*

For after all, if she had not quite known it at the time, she did know now that the foundation of life is trouble and dread, and that pleasure and good are only the thin, ramshackledy, fragile structures people attempt to raise out of nothing on this bedrock of grief, and so of course these little structures tremble and quake in the slightest wind, and fall apart, and people were always as busy as little ants trying to put them back up again.

As dusk began to fly, the people in the park began to pack up and to call their children; suddenly they thought ahead to the working day to come—and it came so early in those days. As her father turned the crank of the car, dark would fall on him, and on the way home, there was nothing but the chug-chug of the motor, and even her mother stared and was silent.


IN THE ROOM Margaret was sitting in, thinking these thoughts, a face showed a little dimly on a pillow across the room; the bed listed distinctly, but the figure that lay on it was past any concern, as far as she had ever had any, with listing beds, or with the ragged shades, for instance, which did not succeed in reaching windowsills, or curtains streaked with lodes of dust, hanging by a spell from mouldering plaster.

As for Margaret herself, the sorry room was filled, richly, with her thoughts. It was these thoughts that were her real companions, they had been spreading like fire and nothing could stop them. To have come to this street, after so many years, had simply overcome her with thought, and in a way her mind had never felt so full and abundant, so almost grotesquely strong and alive as it did in this death-room.

And yet from time to time she sat forward in her chair and peered sharply through this cloud of thought to the still face on the pillow.

This morning when she had first come in, she had not wanted to, she had almost gone back home. But when she had entered the front room and seen Nomey in the bedroom

on the bed, in what looked like sleep, she had felt an unbearable desire to go at once and gaze upon her face. *And yet
what on earth for?* she asked herself now.

*But there are reasons for things*, she answered. In any case
she *had* gone—right to the bedside almost straight from the
car, acknowledging only in passing, indeed with almost rude
brevity, the nurse who had met her at the door.

With her purse still over her arm and her face still damp
from the heat of the yard, she had peered and peered at this
figure for the longest time—she did not know when she had
ever looked at anyone so hard. And she did have a sensation, vague, extremely illusory, not really dependable, of old
feelings slowing down in ancient tracks, almost ceasing to
flow; staring down with her darkest frown, she had had a
sense of very subtle alterations taking place on some distant
reach of mind she could not quite get to to examine.

Then the face had stirred, almost as if it had actually been
touched by Margaret's driving stare. The sick ugly old face
had quivered slightly, and the nurse, standing in the doorway, had come and performed certain light ministrations,
and then the eyes had opened, weakly. Margaret, though
she wanted to, had not moved back, out of sight, but had
stood her ground.

As for the patient, breath came up out of somewhere, simply because it had to, and she had said, hoarsely, but really
with rather surprising force, Margaret's name. "*Maga.*" That
old sound, old name. Margaret had swallowed hard and
made a ridiculous attempt to smile—oh that was absurd!—
and it was a wonder that in her confused state she had not
said something absolutely ridiculous like *Well how are you
getting along these days?* But she had said simply *Well. Nomey!*
and then something else . . . what was it? . . . *Rest now*, perhaps. Or no—she had said, *I was sorry to hear you were so sick*,
and when she spoke, she had put out her arm, very slowly,
and she could remember gazing sternly at her own hand before she had laid it, lightly, over the arm of the patient.

When she did this, Nomey had quite decidedly smiled, and the nurse had said *I'll be*—but then it was as if smiling so hard had closed her eyes again.

"DOES SHE talk to people at all?" Margaret asked the nurse.

"Well I'm about all there is *to* talk to—and the night person—but yes ma'am she says a little bit sometimes, I expect she'll have something to say after while, when her medicine wears off. Course she's really going down, she's gone way down, I'm not going to say she hasn't, but I know the other night her and me talked a good little bit one time, and she asked me to sing her some hymns."

"I declare," Margaret said.

"I pulled up my chair and sat right here and I know I felt right cure-yus about it, I mean with just her and me, but I just sung along kinda soft and I sung her *Rescue the Perishing* and, let's see, *In the Sweet By and By*, and something else . . . I can't think what, but it looked like to me she really enjoyed it."

"I declare," Margaret said again.

"I asked her was you-all a religious family but she said not to go to church, no."

*What church would have wanted a bunch like that?* Margaret thought.

"But she said when she was a little one out in the country her grandma taken her."

Margaret supposed she was surprised. She had never had, nor had wished to have, any knowledge of Nomey's grandmother.

"It was like—she couldn't remember her grandma, but she could remember the church."

"Isn't that something?" Margaret said, politely.

"But now she couldn't remember what church it was, she thought it maybe was some kind of Baptist—or some

315

Church of God." Under her breath, the nurse had said, "I hope it wasn't no Church of God." Since now Nomey had had company, this attendant of hers had begun to tuck in her bedclothes, and perhaps without even thinking about it, to hum *Rescue the Perishing*.

Thinking of that now, sitting in the big chair in the same shaded room, Margaret began to hum it herself. *Rescue the perishing, care for the dying . . . .* Of course she had sung this song in church a thousand times, but that was in another life. It would always be odd to her how these hymns took hold of you even if you didn't believe them. *Jesus is merciful,* the hymn said, *Jesus will save,* but—she drew her mouth up—Jesus was not going to save Nomey, he was nowhere around, and had not called on the phone, either, to say he had gotten held up in the traffic. Here someone was going to die, perhaps tonight—Margaret lowered her head and stared at the floor—and of course Jesus didn't *give* a toot.

The stuffed chair Margaret sat in she had pulled in from the living room, as the lesser of the evils available for sitting purposes. Still, she would not have been able to sit in it if she had not brought the things in her big vinyl bag. She had the bag at the foot of the chair, and the valuable items she was already making use of were the clean white sheet covering the chair, and the cotton smock she had on over her dress, a smock very much like the ones she used to wear years ago to clean house next door, at her mother's house.

Of course she had never cleaned *this* house—good lord! She had rarely even seen the inside of it, except from the front door, when she might have to come over to speak to her father, perfunctorily, on one of her Saturday cleaning visits, about some matter regarding the inmates next door.

History, after all, had not ordained that she herself would ever live in either one of these two bereft little domiciles . . . bought by her father when his luck was way, way down on him, about as far down as luck can go on a person, and

316

after he had put his first child Margaret on the train to her grandmother's in Waycross.

Neither house had ever been kept, and no doubt the house she was sitting in today had rarely ever known a clean day. Nomey was just as dirty as her mother was, she didn't mind dirt a bit. That was the great insurmountable, now almost boring mystery of her father's wife exchange—that he would trade in a dirty one and not get somebody clean.

As her father had gotten older and stouter, he got to where it was easier to put up with certain things than to go around and straighten them out when he got home from a full day's work at the plant. He probably got to the point where he would come in—to the little living room Margaret could see from where she sat—and just clear him a place on the couch, and plump down to read the paper, and later on if nobody could get a pot clean enough to cook something in, well he would go out and bring back a bag of hamburgers, and an extra bag for next door. The new daughter of those years, Margaret's half-sister, a thin, shy, snaky girl that liked to wind herself around people, probably came and sat on the floor and tangled herself around his legs and let him stroke her head. Margaret looked into this picture of the two of them, as she had many times, and tried to think once more what she actually felt about it other than anger and simple regret. But even now she hardly knew, for instance, whether she was sorry or glad that this latter-day child of her father's was not afflicted. Loreen swallowed her saliva, you didn't have to wipe it off her face, and she blew her own nose; you could even understand what she said, if you could get her to speak up, and in fact until she quit for good, she had passed all her grades in school.

But she was born out of betrayal—out of wickedness and sin, some people would say—and no doubt that was what Margaret, a child, had felt at the time about the whole business, without applying to it any actual terms. Loreen was born of the enemy, so naturally she inherited enemy genes.

(So she was an enemy too?

Of course.

But what had *she* done?

Her mother shattered my life.

But that was the mother, it's not much reason to hate the child.

It was the reason, nevertheless. And then after a while, no reason is necessary. I might discover perfectly good reasons not to hate her, and still hate her just as much.

You just *decided* she was an enemy?

She *was* an enemy.

Just because her mother was?

Yes.)

Of course the mother, across the room on the crooked bed, no longer looked like an effectual enemy. Her head had slipped downward on the pillow and lodged against her shoulder, so that on top of everything else, it looked as if there was something wrong with the connection of her head to her neck. Margaret frowned. Yes this enemy looked like it had met an enemy of its own that was more than a match for it. Margaret did not care at all for pain, naturally she did not like to be in the presence of it—and she considered that the suffering of enemies was probably one of the most confusing things in the world. (Of course there were so many confusing things.) She felt that somewhere there was probably a secret system, a technical code or program in which all human actions had a place, an underlying logic that humans themselves could not know but which explained all the puzzles and contradictions of people's lives and feelings. We sense that it is there and also that we can never know it. We look at each other hazily, in puzzlement and wonder, absently, and look away, thinking *There is an explanation for all this—somewhere*. If we could know what it was, we would know why it is that when people we do not love, people we have always wished harm to come to, finally have it come to them—we don't always rejoice, and something

318

like pity, perhaps it *is* pity, comes to us and we do not know why.

Of course some people probably had an answer for that: *Well once people have been rendered harmless, once something has come along, for instance, to nudge them over the death-cliff, well there's no reason not to pity them anymore* . . . .

*If you want to put out some cheap easy pity, put it out on the dying—it won't cost you a thing because there's not a thing you can do for them.*

LAST NIGHT Margaret had taken her best sleeping pill and gone right to sleep, thank god, probably snored the roof off the house—and then early, just at dawn, she had suddenly wakened, completely, simply opened wide her eyes, and all drowsiness had left her at once. The bedroom was just visible in the very early light. It had been horrible to think of letting its soft beauty go to waste for a whole day, yet her eyes swept it once, quickly, and she sat up. She was not conscious of "having arrived at a decision" and never thought about it in those terms at all, though perhaps, even in that very sound sleep, she had dreamed things out.

She had gotten up and gone to the bathroom and then sat back down on the bed to put on her hose. She dressed completely, without hesitation, and went to the kitchen to fix her breakfast. Then she had thought through what she might need and packed a bag. She checked the medicine in her purse. Left a note for the laundryman.

All her actions were calm and efficient. Someone would need to know where she was, so she went through the wet back yard to the neighbor's, stepping carefully—since she had on her good heels—around the puddles the storm had left. At the neighbor's back door she rapped softly in case they were still asleep, but they weren't—they had been stirring for some time, because they were about to leave town themselves. During the night the husband's mother had been robbed, in a nearby town, and naturally she was very upset and would be sitting on her porch looking for them constantly until they got there. She had not lost anything of tremendous value, but of course the very *idea* of a robber—coming right into her bedroom—was horrible. Still, the only robber Margaret had been able to conjure up, at that moment, was a small thin robber like Buddy Ringgold and that did not seem so horrifying.

Back at her own house, Margaret collected her bag from the front steps and got right in the car.

Of course then the road itself, though transformed and disguised in a way, by the extraordinary radiance of the damp August light, broke through her mind-gates, and this journey had suddenly made her think hard of the journeys of the past, as they went rolling along beside her—yes it was as if there was a whole fleet of her in old round-backed purple Fords with loud old-fashioned engines, forging ahead together in a massive line like awkward tanks and suffering terrible memory hits from things like citrus stands—which made her mind spin forward to the city up ahead and old times, the *oldest* times, good and terrible. And still there was no actual questioning of the road itself, of *this* journey, *this* road today, *this* more than peculiar expedition to a place she had never expected to see again with waking eyes.

Later she had thought *I will never know my reasons for this, so I will not even ask myself,* and no doubt that was probably very sane, and yet she knew she would not quit asking, and it was horrible in a way to think that instead of taking some *old* questions down, off her question board, all she was doing was putting a new one up.

When she had pulled up on Eighth Street, she had not gotten out of the car right away, for a while she had just sat there. She had not parked the car directly in front of Nomey's—no, she had parked it somewhat closer to the *other* little house that had been her mother's, and she supposed she had done that to show that certain things had not changed and would never change, and that it would take more than somebody getting sick to change them—and also so she could say to herself *I'm here, but I may or may not get out of the car.*

She had studied the ridiculous dirt-poor street, still unpaved *(lord god)* and had begun to reason with herself and *ask* herself what in the world was going on and why she, of all people, should be sitting where she was, in this of all cities, when there was no reason under the sun for her to be here and profound and compelling reasons for her not to be, where there was no vital interest of hers at stake whatsoever, and so had thought again, *I may or may not get out of the car.* And yet she had come seventy miles on a narrow two-lane road and wormed her way over here through the difficult, bad side of town—so of course if it were absurd to have come, it would be even more absurd not to go on through with it.

But damage had been done to her logical powers—first by the highway itself and everything it recalled; then the orange stands; then the road into the city, which forged through thick baking slums, where black men in undershirts hung over Spanish balconies, seemed almost to lean over the car from them, and people darted thickly across the narrow road (though how they *could* dart in this heat) with their cartons of Coca-Cola, so that sometimes the street up ahead had looked simply impenetrable, as it always had in the past.

So this damage to her logical powers. And then the damage from the sea and river smells; from the food smells that she knew but could no longer place; from the Greek names on little stores and cafes . . . from all this, the whole jumping, half-familiar frenzy of the city. Things that had changed and things that had not changed—one thing was as alarming as another, and without a doubt it had all done destructive work on her thinking powers, her reasoning and deciding powers, so that when she had pulled up at last—only

321

these few hours ago—at her destination, it was only natural that she had not been able to get out of the car, but had to sit for quite a little while, as if trying to make, finally, a decision that had actually already been made this morning, in that curious way, without any apparent grief, when she had gotten out of bed.

Then the air conditioning in the car had faded away completely, and when it became necessary either to turn back on the motor or get out of the car, she got out. At the edge of the sandy yard she took a few steps towards the other small house that had been her mother's, as if to show again that it was really to this dwelling, as always, she had come.

She had stood looking at it for some time, having to shade her eyes with her hand, even with her sunglasses on. There were round metal tubs by the front steps; someone must have put them there to grow flowers in, but then someone else, more efficient, had turned them into repositories for soft drink cans and other waste.

Of course the yard itself was a repository too. She had studied the rail around the narrow porch; the posts at one end had sunk into the floor long ago, and the rail dipped now at the same angle it had always dipped at, and somehow this astonished her, took her completely by surprise. She began to murmur *lord me* and to wipe her eyes with a kleenex from her purse. When she looked up again, the little wooden house, its grayish paint crudding and peeling, seemed to her to be suffering horribly in the sun, and she wished she could pick it up in her arms, holding it out from her dress so as not to get herself dirty, and clump away on a half-run all the way to the river—why not let it sink to the bottom of the St. John's and die a cool bubbly death? She had pictured its old slats riding up to knock in the current with other deceased slats.

She had seen some crates on the porch, behind the afflicted railing. The front door stood partly open, and if it was not an optical illusion, there were boxes standing inside the door. This had been a new horror. Very possibly, the house was not being lived in, and if this was true, she could walk right in the door and look around, a frightening thing to even think about, the last thing in the world she would want to do—the very idea of it had made her wish to her soul she were somewhere else.

So what had happened then? She had turned away, struck out across the sandy lot to the house next door, stood collecting herself on the porch, knowing a stranger would come to let her in, and rapped at the door. Then as she had stood inside, looking into the bedroom, certain things in her consciousness receded and other things came forward; she was seized by a sharp desire and had gone straight to the bed—as hot as she was, and with her purse still on her arm—and taken a long, long look.

Then Nomey had recognized her and spoken her name, several times, and she had strained her ugly, dry, hurting mouth into an unexpected and unusual thing for someone in her position—a smile. So then Margaret had taken up her vigil here in the bedroom, in the chair which she had covered with one of the clean sheets from her vinyl bag.

Her children would have laughed at her. They thought she was a fanatic about her little personal effects and her vinyl bags, and maybe she was, or perhaps she just thought ahead more than they did, and was just practical and wise, because her clean sheet and her oversmock were making it possible, right now, for her to feel at least a slight degree of safety and comfort, even here, in this house that was full of special danger for her—loaded with mortal peril of irreversible despair, she did not doubt. When something must be fended off, people must fend with all their might, she felt, in whatever little ways they could.

A cup of tangy sweet tea, for instance, was a nice little fending-piece sometimes, even in warm weather. She would not need to swallow any actual food today—but to make herself a cup of tea in Nomey's kitchen . . . *that* would stand something down, and really she just thought she would if it were possible. Nomey's kitchen would probably not be nearly as awful when Nomey was sick as when she was well. A van from the Health Department was bringing her meals, and the kitchen was more or less kept by the nurse, she supposed; she had seen a big white towel spread out on the sink to keep the nursing items on, and the medicines, all the fending things—though of course their fending powers were practically gone now. She had seen it herself as soon as she had gone to the bed to look. And of course the woman on the phone had told her as much to begin with, if not in just the words she now imagined: *Nomey Stovall can't fend for herself anymore, she's fended out and so are the rest of us and she wanted to let you know. In Jacksonville we have this—this fiend . . . that when he gets hold of you, no one can fend him off and so the doctors just send you home. I guess you have the same one in Waycross.*

Margaret looked again across the room at Nomey, whose head would not even stay up on the pillow, and thought about their common fiend. *People spend their lives being happy and unhappy, half the time they don't know which, and then that's all, and in the end the only one that comes out ahead is the one who gets to snatch them up.*

Margaret leaned her head back on the chair and closed her eyes, in order to see this fiend a little more clearly. Actually, she was a terrible coward, but she liked to think of herself standing up to him, giving him tit for tat. *I want to make every single one of y'all unhappy,* she heard him say and herself reply, "Yes I know you do," and it was as if her temper got the best of her. *I wish I could beat your old hide. Oh I'd give anything if I could just get hold of you—one time. But I'll tell you this—you don't keep people completely down, even so, and even on an old dirt street like this one, I would have to say that people still managed to care for each other. My father loved me to death, for instance, no fiend could keep him from it; in my opin-*

*ion he loved us all and two wives; he loved children that couldn't grow up and never learned to comb their hair and kept him in the poorhouse all his life . . . .*

But really it was as if she didn't know what she *was* thinking and had just managed to confuse herself. She pictured a big graveyard, with an inscription over its frontal arch: *Here lie the people of the earth, the children of the world. They lived, they suffered, they were happy sometimes, they died. That's all.*

But it was as if there was an afterthought that someone had inscribed on the arch's rim. *They were all crucified by the fiend of time and they did not rise again on the third day or on any other day and were not taken up into heaven because there was no heaven.* (So!) You just wonder, Margaret thought, why people thought there was . . . or if it was just that since most of them had been loved by their mamas and daddies while they were alive, they thought they would still be loved—by *someone*—when they were dead.


SHE LEANED over and raised the sick woman's head, bracing her neck the way you would a baby's, to hold the cup to her mouth. Nomey flexed slightly her lips and waited, and in due time it was as if a little bit of strength came up to them, and then she flexed them again and took one small sip and then another.

Margaret thought how ineffably strange it was for her to be doing what she was doing. *To hold this head,* she thought. Nomey tried to say something, but at first it did not sound like actual words. She tried again and the words were down there after all, although they were very weak words: "Maga, you're just as pretty."

The nurse agreed with her. "I tell *you*," she said.

"Her pretty hair," Nomey said.

And the nurse said, "I don't know how she keeps it like that, do you?"

325

Of course Margaret wanted to protest, but Nomey spoke again. "Maga," she said, and Margaret bent down to hear her better. "How's Bobba, how's Gaw and Riley?"

"They're fine," Margaret said. "They're doing real good." But her voice sounded worse than Nomey's. The sick woman's voice trailed off. "Maga's so-o-o pretty," she said, and she tried to keep focusing the half-blind light in her eyes on Margaret's face, but there was very little of this light to focus *with*.


IN THE kitchen Margaret made her the cup of tea. Clean pot, tea bags, sugar—that was a miracle on this street. She could not believe the state of Florida had done something right for a change and actually arranged this care of someone in their own home. In her work she had connections with a number of social agencies, and so naturally she was amazed when anything at all was actually done. Of course for Nomey to be at home like this, there was supposed to be some family here and in charge, and according to the nurse various ones who had been up at the hospital had said they would come and help out, but then they had all disappeared. Of course that was no surprise. Margaret learned that when Nomey had first gone to the hospital, Loreen had come home to be with her, all the way from San Diego, where her husband was in the Navy. But she didn't think she would be able to come back this time, the nurse said. Margaret was almost amused when she thought of this courtship of Loreen's and a Yankee sailor from the local Navy base, the two of them loving it up in Nomey's living room. That anyone would voluntarily connect himself with the Stovalls on Eighth Street was as entertaining a thing as she could think of.

The tea made Margaret warm, and she took her cup and saucer and stood in front of the rickety air-conditioner. It blew a feeble, incompetent stream over her face and chest.

She looked out the top of the window onto the dirt road and the little hot scrubby houses across the way. One of them had lost its front steps altogether and was making do with some mismatched concrete blocks. Over the years, Jacksonville had become, for Margaret, a city of shameful dirt streets and human deprivation; her personal relationship to it made her depict it as a town which, though once a decent place, had suffered a terrible decline until there seemed to be almost nothing left of it but Eighth Street.

When she thought of the things that had gone on around here—and no doubt still did . . . . Her mother would tell her about them quite cheerfully sometimes, until she would refuse to listen anymore, saying, "Don't tell me things like that." After all, it was mostly people who lived on streets like this who came up to her court at home; she knew them well, and she didn't need to know any extra stories about the way they suffered and abused each other.

As for the ones next door—towards the end all their teeth had begun to go bad from so many sticky snacks. Her mother could hardly chew at all, but after all, it wasn't chewing power she needed for Cokes and cigarettes. Whenever one of the household got sick, her mother got some sort of medicine from the drugstore and usually it was the wrong kind for whatever they were suffering from. At the store a steady train of children moved in and out, getting popsicles and gum and Cokes, Hershey bars and pork rinds. Oatmeal pies. They had wonderful nutrition on this street. She didn't see how the children in China could be much worse off.

She thought of the long course of years when she would come to town from Waycross and already Eighth Street had seemed to be going backward while the rest of the town went ahead. It was strange to think that Jacksonville itself had been growing and prospering all that time, and she supposed some people were made happy by the new superhighways that spanned the St. John's, swung tourists out to the beaches of Neptune, Mayport, and Liberty, brought in happy guests in sporty jackets and hats to the Gator Bowl; no doubt some people were highly gratified by the new beach clubs, and the addition of eight beautiful seaside holes to the Duval County International Golf Course; by the new television station, which was what made it possible for Margaret, in Waycross, to catch glimpses, before she changed the channel, of the eight new holes, and the Southeastern Open, of reporters in white shoes interviewing the wives of famous golfers at little umbrella-ed tables, and of the sea-blown, sun-burnished locks of the golfers themselves.

All over south Georgia and north Florida people watched on television the progress of the Gateway City, front door to Sunny Florida. They saw the dedication of the new college and the new airport, and the grand openings of department stores almost as good as the ones in New York; they witnessed newsworthy stages in the construction of skyscraping office buildings, flashing upwards to improve the horizon.

Of course some people seemed to want to stand in the *way* of progress, and just criticize, and the viewers learned about them too and saw them interviewed about the erosion of beaches and the failure of the authorities to build board-walks, much less to improve the schools so people might want to go to them. But no one on Eighth Street, Margaret assumed, had ever been interviewed—except possibly in an aisle of the courthouse, with handcuffs on.

Eighth Street was not assigned by the city to be paved, and in the summertime, dust and dirt, along with the heat, were taken for granted, and no one complained to the city council. Not many even knew there *was* a city council. Of course George and Riley and Barbara did not even know what year it was, and although physically they grew, their personal progress was very small indeed. The news on Eighth Street was that the aging father of Barbara Stovall was trying to teach her to cut up her meat, but of course it was perfectly normal for a person with a three-year-old mind not to be able to.

328

Over the years, not many things changed on Eighth Street, though the washtub, which had come hopefully to rest on Nomey's back stoop, had been replaced later on by a wringer machine for the use of both households; yet the machine never suffered much more wear and tear than the washtub had. Each house came, in time, to be supplied with a secondhand TV. For several months Bobba Stovall was under the impression that the people on the screen could see her, and she covered her face when she walked in front of it. George and Riley carried out a scientific experiment, shuffling back and forth between the two houses to see if the picture was the same on both sets.

George was definitely the most advanced of the three children. That was obvious to everybody, but much later in his life, when Margaret had had them all admitted to Florida homes for the afflicted, she learned their mental ages for the first time: George's tests said he had the capacity of a five-year-old, and the other two were a good bit lower than that. No one knew, for sure, why these children were the way they were . . . though of course they had a mother who was not right; but there was a dark legend among family in Jacksonville that said that at the time they were conceived, and though in each case the mother would come to cherish them and cleave to them, almost fanatically, she had not wanted to give birth to them and had tried to prevent the life progressions in her womb.

George seemed a little more advanced than other five-year-olds, Margaret thought—but after all, he had had a lot of *experience* being a person of that age.

Most mornings Nomey closed up her own house as soon as Margaret's father went to work and more or less moved over to her friend Emma's for the day. It was a close call, but Emma's house was a little dirtier than Nomey's, so naturally that was the one they preferred. It wasn't long after the two women had been established by Margaret's father in their two little separate houses that they discovered how much they had in common and had gotten to be each other's best friend. It was this as much as anything else that Margaret, as a young girl at Granny's and then young wife and mother, had found so absolutely repugnant and outrageous, and in a way still did, she couldn't help it, and yet of course that was not the way to look at it, given all the terrible circumstances.

It was almost a miracle, but it turned out that Margaret's mother had not completely failed to learn from her own brilliant mother in Waycross. She had learned to embroider, after a fashion, and had taught this art to her friend Nomey, so this was what she and Nomey mainly did all day—they applied themselves to their handwork. Perhaps they just did it to keep from stacking up the dirty dishes and taking them to the kitchen, or picking up the Coca-Cola bottles.

*Oh that was a fine pair*, Margaret thought.

She pictured her mother's dress hanging off one bony shoulder, and the pinned-together, yellowed strap of her slip, a garment which also showed two full inches and more below her skirts. Nomey felt right at home with a person like that, because that was the way she herself had always preferred to look, and at Emma's it was perfectly all right. So there they both sat, sewing a fine seam, digging deep for fresh spools of thread in the two embossed paper sacks from the fertilizer plant that held their supplies. Emma had pinned one of her little animal pins on hers so they could tell the difference.

Their favorite colors seemed to be purple and orange, Margaret remembered. Of course Granny couldn't bear to look at this Eighth Street art. Margaret's mother sent her two pillowcases every year for Christmas, and it was almost enough to ruin Christmas. No, Granny was not gratified a bit that her legacy of fine handwork lived on in the slums of Jacksonville, just as it did on Suwannee Drive, where sitting in the bright light of her bay window, Margaret embroidered too, small careful roses and tulips on dresses for little girls.

Margaret's mother, even in this, her chosen art, virtually

her only occupation, was lazy still, or maybe laziness was not exactly what it was, but in any case she had no respect whatever for the integrity of her designs, did not match her colors to her shapes, but simply sewed as far as she could on one thread, the orange of her flowers flowing over into the stem and the leaves, and then she might change to a length of purple or red. Nomey's craft, on the other hand, was much more picturelike. Even though she had learned all she knew of it from her friend Emma, something in her held out against certain violations of reality. Her flowers had the colors of flowers, and her stems and leaves were green.

TODAY, remembering all this, Margaret looked out Nomey's half-shaded front window. Two boys in cut-off jeans and stretched T-shirts walked along the road carrying cartons of soft drinks. This was what George and Leonard had carried, coming back from the store that day, bringing home the afternoon's refreshments. George's round, massive face had stared straight ahead, yet he had been grinning an enormous grin. He had hold of Leonard's hand, and of course Leonard looked comically small beside him, and he was wanting to sink into the ground. Not only had he favored one foot, but he had hunched over as he went, half stooped, hugging himself, trying to pull his old scared, blind skin around him as tight as he could. But George was proud of his new friend and he had not noticed the terrible look on his face.

Margaret had studied hard, that day, this black look of Leonard's—as far as she could make it out from the window. She had *needed* to study it because she had not seen it on his face before, and she was still trying to learn what marriage was. Behind her, in her mother's front room, the others were feeling good. Indeed, her mother was in a merry, wonderful mood, she was absolutely delighted to be making Leonard's acquaintance (*Maga's sweetheart!* she kept saying;

331

*ain't he nice Maga?).* Leonard, for her, was a fine fellow—handsome, friendly, and affectionate—and he had boomed and brayed at her and carried on, the way he could when his nerves drove him on to it. She on her part teased him and giggled and crowed, talked to him a mile a minute about every silly thing in the world; she thought he had a marvelous disposition.

Then Leonard and George had gone for refreshments and Margaret had watched them from the window. She had begun to discern that possibly marriage was not as she had imagined it. Yet she had thought *If people do not get married to dress each other's wounds . . . what do they do it for?*

Still, she had already begun to suspect that marriage was not a dresser of wounds at all, but a *giver* of wounds, like so much else. When she and Leonard had first got out of the drink truck, she had tried her best to convey with her expression something she could not actually say: *If you honestly care for me, bear this with me.* Then later, in the house, she tried again to let him read certain things on her face: *No one can help all this, it's not anyone's fault. They're not to blame for themselves, and neither am I or even my father. They haven't done any wrong.*

When she and Leonard had left Eighth Street that day, Leonard, half dragging his foot across the yard, had struck something in the weeds which almost made him stumble and fall. He picked up something from the sand and held it up to show it to her and they both looked at it in wonder—an old boot half rotted in the earth. A shoe rotting in the yard! That she could bring him to such a place. The shoe no longer had any sex, it was a thing of horror—it might have been something for the foot of a beast . . . and indeed, it was as if there *was* a beast prowling those parts . . . doing its worst on every living soul.

Then afterward—she had not seen him for three days. For three full days he had not come to the dairy, and since he had never failed to appear before, had never missed an evening since he had first come to call, by the third day she had renounced him; she did not expect to ever see him again. She had concluded that it would not be possible for her to marry, for she did not understand how she could be married to *any* person who believed, or wished to believe, as perhaps all potential husbands would, that she had had no origin, but had been driven home to the dairy by mistake with her grandmother's cows.

And then—Margaret stretched her wits to remember— *what had happened?* Leonard and Granny had conspired. Or so it had seemed, even to her—and Nora . . . Nora had assured her it could not have been otherwise. *We who truly care about Margaret's welfare must work together to see that she draws a line of iron between herself and Jacksonville.* "This is the way they would have put it," Nora said; "they would have said, *Margaret has it coming to her not to be held down by all that. She deserves a chance of her own like anybody else.*"

Margaret sometimes thought of it this way: "To give yourself a chance, always betray others, don't ever let them hold you back." What was it the magazines said? "The most important person in your life is *you!* Find out what makes you happy and give it to yourself. It's not worry and stress you need—let's face it . . . so if going to Jacksonville gives you worry and stress, why not go to Daytona Beach this year?"

This is what the magazines said, whereas in church they used to say you had to lose your life to find it, and things like that, and really sometimes the whole business just made her tired. She supposed Leonard and Granny sided with the magazines, and there were times when she had known the two of them were right. What good had it done—bringing her old cross weepy face, her ill-tempered worry and pain down here to Eighth Street all those years? When she left again, it was still Eighth Street.

Tomorrow, for instance, though she would not be looking out this window studying the street, the street would still be here, it would not disappear just because no one leaned over this half-cracked air-conditioner of Nomey's and watched the rusted-out cars go by.

Yet she thought people did things sometimes for no other reason but to defy something in the universe, or just to show (but to whom? to what?) *that man is not a beast,* and she could not think whether this was a good reason or not. From the window she saw another beat-up car go by, churning the Eighth Street dust. Big glossy cars did not come down this way if they could help it. So much of her life she had seen from windows, studying things from afar, seeking out their explanatory elements. At home—all that watching from the window in the kitchen, studying the children playing in the yard, hiding from each other in the bamboo, sprinkling their feet in the hose, trying to shoot the dogs and cats with homemade arrows that refused to take flight. She would watch all that while she was washing greens at the sink, or cutting the corn off the cob, wiping the corn-milk off her glasses so she could see her knife on the rows.

Once, at the window in the front bedroom, she had raised the blind to wipe the windowsill, and had seen something amazing in the yard: a grown figure stumping across the lawn towards her door. She had put her hand on her heart, because it felt as if it had developed a fatal crack. The person she saw had grown very stout, and he suffered severely from a dropped stomach. He had a stumpy, defective gait, as if his belly had pressed on his walking muscles. He stopped to try to hitch up his pants but after a few steps he had to hitch them again.

Margaret, that day, had burned all over with emotion—at first she thought it was simply rage. Later, in fact, she had an image of herself leaning in deep-browed threatening fury out the window, looking larger than the house, shaking her fist at whatever was approaching, like some pitiless woman in a fairy tale. But in fact, and for what seemed like a very long time, she did not move, her brain engine would not go, it was as if all it would do was pop and spit like the old

334

Chevrolet. Time elapsed. How much, she wondered now. She had waited for the doorbell, but it did not ring.

Then—how had she done it?—she had been able to cross the strip of hallway into the living room, advance towards the door, though the temperature of her distress must have still been very high, since she had not even stopped at a mirror to touch her hair. Yet somewhere, in the hallway perhaps, she had come to a conclusion, had decided to say, facing her father across the screen, *What do you mean by this?*

But when she had opened the door, her father was not on the stoop—he was standing at the bottom of her steps, and the awful thing that she realized at once was that he had not intended to presume to enter her house but only to call to her from the yard. So then she was defeated at once and had them all in, himself and the two others in the car, as if they were all absolutely welcome without reservation.

Of course at first her father had demurred. "Honey we've got to get on down the road." He said he was on his way to see a man in Tallapaloosa or Chippewawa or somewhere like that, but then she in her turn urged and insisted and he had listened for a certain note in her protestations and when he heard it—perhaps with surprise—had gone to get Loreen and Nomey from the car, and so that day they had brought their Eighth Street air and demeanor into Margaret's house. As Nomey's old country whine buzzed off her living room walls, Margaret had put her hand to her heart again, been the first to sit down, she was so weak. It was no wonder, of course, that Nomey—a person, as was well known, without any sense of personal decency—had not set out on her trip in anything you could bear to look at. No. What *would* be her attire, if not an absurd dress of drooping crepe, with a furry velvety belt? Lovely with her bare hairy legs.

Then Margaret's children were brought in, and everybody was visiting and carrying on, Loreen letting them fondle her twiny hair, and her father, though he could never recall her children's names, being quite stunned and struck by them once more, for after all they *were* so handsome, and so astonishingly clever and quick. Margaret had steered the whole noisy troop of them into the dinette and set them down at the maple table, which she had to look at twice it suddenly looked so odd. She went to open the refrigerator door, partly to hide her face so she could run a finger under her eye and catch a tear—of sheer agitation, and partly because she was thinking, in another kind of separate anguish, *I must give my father food and drink, no matter how much I despise him*, and then she had believed, momentarily, that there was a providence, yes, because she saw, with shock, something her startled memory had completely let drop away, a plump ham in the middle of the fridge, baked only that morning for normal family needs.

Ripe tomatoes, bread and mayonnaise. Splendid thick sandwiches made with great juicy slabs of ham. Thank god. A pitcher of freshly-made tea. She hardly knew what the others did, but her father ate mightily, though it was not even suppertime. Great magnificent hunger came to him that day . . . just because it was his daughter who brought him food.

And then—their talk together . . . thoughtful, easy and satisfying, almost the only time they ever had talk like that—about the house, about Leonard and the children, about Nora ("I wouldn't mind seeing that girl!"), and Granny—"Well you know Granny, she's just the same, she never even has to have a tooth pulled," and about this new Waycross he hardly knew. Laney had sat on her grandfather's lap, and he had spoken to her quietly and she lay back against him (greatly wondering, no doubt, that there should be a man at this table who did not bark and boom), making Margaret bow her head in pity—for so many things—then raise it to study her father's face . . . calm, with the same calmness it had *always* had, but age-pitted, age-pulped now, rough as a washboard, and with deeply drooping jowls. *Strange, strange*, she had thought, *this whole afternoon*, and

336

when she looked around her, what a wonder it was to see that everything was changed, that she had to study anew her own house, her tables and chairs, stare hard even at her hands in her silly lap, as if they might not *be* her hands.

Then her father was rising, hitching absently his pants, saying, "Honey we've got to pull on out," sighing his regrets—when suddenly the front door seemed to undergo some kind of bizarre assault; at the front entrance there seemed to be an actual collision between someone and the door, then the floor, the walls, the actual airwaves of the house. Thus—Leonard.

He had seen the rattletrap car outside, and come in on his storm, ready to boom and bray at whatever guests he had. He shrieked and cried in her father's face, and then in the faces, each one in turn, of the visiting wife and child—and pleased them very much. *Leonard you're looking good!* her father said, as any father-in-law, with his full rights, might say, even though they both knew that in his case all such rights had been relinquished, and the reason for this relinquishment was standing on her squat, bowed, hairy legs right there on the pine floor. Even while these male civilities were going on, in fact, Leonard had forgotten his mouth and let it sag and droop with something rather different from what he was trying to show; he forgot his eye and let it cut sharply over the maple table, as if to complain very crossly that characters like these, turning up uninvited out of shame and exile, should be given such choice fare, while his own homecoming seemed to have been totally unprepared for, as if *he* were the vagrant guest. *Me Me!* his face beamed—*what about Me? Hungry! On the road all day! Me—completely undisgraced and can at least hold my head up—and now my table looking like this, like the dogs got to it, and my place not even cleared . . . .*

Her father, Margaret felt, had seen this eye of Leonard's and the down-turning of his lips, probably could have seen them with his eyes shut; had read Leonard's booming face twitch by twitch, no doubt, as well as he had read earlier his daughter's different one at the door—and so he did not linger, but brought forward again the man in Tallapaloosa, or Chickewawa, and moved doorward, carward, and Margaret, walking them over the lawn to the car, came to herself, it almost seemed, and her face gloomed over as she made a part of that strange parade, Nomey sidling close to her, showing how friendly she felt, as if Margaret would actually be pleased by that.

Margaret had realized then how extremely aggravated she had actually been, all afternoon, with Nomey's satisfied face, her childish pleasure in being where she was, received like a person of normal qualities. For her to have thought that anyone could actually like her! Possibly care for a single moment what opinions she held about the bay window, the glasses and plates. And now for her to be sidling, hanging near, as if she wanted to impart a confidence. *Oh don't keep trying to speak to me—or I don't know what I'll do,* Margaret had thought. The very idea of this person, of all people, trying to address to her personal remarks, refusing to see that she was being deliberately ignored, as close to insulted as you could possibly come to someone standing in your yard.

Then the three guests had shoved off slowly and heavily in the clanking old drag-bottom sedan, and Margaret had shuddered at the sound of it, and wondered at her father's calm face, not a bit less calm, it seemed to her, than the young man's face in the hopeful roadsters years ago.

She had waited on the edge of the lawn until they were out of sight, thinking that though it was a great temptation, and one she had almost succumbed to this very day, she would not give in—*in this life*—to certain feelings; she would hate her father no matter what, if she possibly could. But in the *next* life . . . (of course there was not any next life) . . . she would have to see.

Turning back to the house, she found that she had let Nomey put something in her hand. A paper sack. She was glad she had not acknowledged it, not given Nomey the pleasure of whispering its contents in her ear. She knew, in any case, what these contents were—walking to her door she opened the bag to be sure and of course it was coarse pieces of embroidered cloth (the joint work of the craft guild of Eighth Street), and this time she felt exactly like someone else always did and almost threw them in the yellow jasmine by the porch. But she was too neat to do that, even in anger, so she took them around to the garbage can in back, then went in by the kitchen door to get Leonard's supper.

She stirred quietly in the kitchen, getting things back to normal as quickly as possible. Leonard was reading the paper in the living room. Thank goodness. That would settle him, give her a little time. Any interruption in his supper routine was liable to set fire to his nerves and then he might burn like a bonfire all evening, completely out of control. She could hardly decide what to do first, but in a moment she lit the oven and got out the breadboard, made the biscuits in no time flat and popped them in.

She cleared the places at the table and when she lifted her father's plate, she saw that he had left behind two of his cigars. It was curious how startled she was. *Oh that's bad luck,* she thought. She just hoped he would have enough smoke to get him home, because he never drove a car without a cigar in his mouth—the car would not know whether to go or not—and it was as if the unlucky cigars jumped forward and connected up in midair with all kinds of other unlucky things in her father's life. For a moment, standing by the oven, almost letting her biscuits burn, she had stared at them absently, her father's sorrowful cigars, and then hid them quickly in the recipe box.


MARGARET turned her back to catch the wheezing flow of cold air from Nomey's air-conditioner and thought again about her father's visit to Waycross and this matter of his bad luck. There had always been days in her life when she had been held utter captive by the firm conviction that there was nothing in the world *but* luck, that everything in life—animal, vegetable, mineral—was really made out of the same thing, pure luck, and that all the blame and credit people gave each other was completely beside the point. Yet on other days it was perfectly clear to her that most of the things people called luck were really their own fault. *She saw her father's luck pass by on the street with a flounce, and her father get up and walk slowly after it. Then there was a spin of the picture and she saw the two of them coming back arm in arm . . . the bad luck looking smug and satisfied and her father beginning to look . . . thoughtful.*

She imagined her father driving off with her mother in the buggy from the dairy, and it was as if they drove right then and there straight to Jacksonville—although that was not quite the way it was—and up to the first house on Clark Street and got down, her mother doing a regular dance in the clean-swept yard, and chattering and hollering as she pulled up her skirts and hopped up the steps to the porch. She went inside and sat in all the chairs and lay on all the beds; she looked in all the closets and cabinets, as if it were a big playhouse and she was going to have a wonderful time. Her father, a pudgy man even then, a roundish, short man with what was already a full face, had hardly had time to pull himself out of the buggy, and yet he came sweating along behind her, taking off his hat, wiping his brow, brushing off his clothes the dirt and soot of the long drive from Waycross, stopping on the walk to take the measure again of this nice, solid, freshly painted house he had bought to start his marriage in, a decent enough house certainly—and yet he had thought of it as just a beginning, and could not know it was the best one he ever would have.

But where was any blame in all this? Margaret thought. In what way was it all his fault? Surely it *was* bad luck that they passed that law—about not milking dairy cows on earthen floors or whatever it was. Was not his fault that Granny had craftily discovered (as she always did discover—by hook or crook) where the best labor was and that he and his brother were the only ones to get because they would actually work, and wouldn't try to get by with a thing.

*That* was not his fault, surely it was not up to him to say *No'm—I can do without your work out there because I hear you have this peculiar daughter and since I am a sort of innocent, unattractive man without any knowledge of women and no girlfriends . . . for all I know I may be ripe for a courting disaster of the worst kind and I just think I better steer clear of that milking floor, not to mention the walkway.*

On the other hand—surely this *was* his fault: not to open his eyes and see what he saw once he got there.

"But courting girls are so peculiar anyway—how could he have told?" Nora said.

"She was so different from him though—you wonder what he wanted her for."

"Well maybe he just thought 'Dear god! If I marry some old poky stick-in-the-mud thing like I am . . .' And I mean somebody that teased and cut up, went around singing and laughing, had some life in her . . . maybe it was natural for him to be interested in that . . . and courting ways are so peculiar anyhow . . . ."

Sometimes in her worst moods Margaret had tried to conjure up that first year before she was born—the first months, or weeks even, on Clark Street, but it was an eerie, fearful thing to think about; she would think up to a certain point and then there would be a bad place she did not want to think over. But she saw her father going along, putting his wife in the new, clean, freshly painted house, with nice big solid rockers on the front porch. He was doing all right and times were good, and Roosevelt—no probably Taft—was President, and he had a new job at Clayton and Rumer, a new plant down on the river, where he was not only a mason when a mason was called for but also a machinist . . . in other words, a skilled person who could do all kinds of things, for after all in the city now there were a great many machines, and people had not only to work them but to repair them and keep them up, and so he was taken on at a very good salary because he was so obviously a good, steady, clean, responsible person.

Yet it was this earliest time, which had seemed so promising, that she thought of with such dread foreboding. *Bad luck starting to tell.* She saw her father, as life on Clark Street progressed with her mother, growing thoughtful, more and more so. She saw him begin to stand and ponder things . . . turning in his hands a pot or a dish or a tool of some sort, or an article of clothing that was oddly misused, or soiled in some unexpected way. She pictured him absently opening drawers and being surprised at the contents. Perhaps one of them was full of little gewgaws, and as her father stared at them, studying thoughtfully, his wife Emma might see him and begin to cry, because (perhaps) she was saving these little gewgaws to surprise him with, and he had to soothe her, hold her and kiss her head; Margaret saw her kiss him back, nuzzle and caress him, and do certain other odd playful little things that she did not need to fully imagine and that she felt her father was fond of . . . in a way, and yet—he had begun to ponder them too, and many other things, all his wife's ways of doing and thinking and speaking. Her childish love of holidays, for instance. *Raymond! What day is it? How far is it to Christmas? Raymond! I wish it was already here—don't you?*

He was thoughtful; he pondered.

At night he had taken to putting on one of his wife's aprons and cleaning up the house. At first, no doubt, he went without that particular accoutrement, but then he discovered that in the kitchen and bathroom, for instance, you made a great splash and splatter, and at first had tied a towel around his waist. This was an attempt to invent, on his own, the apron, and then he found, off in a drawer somewhere, when he was probably looking for something else, a whole stack of big roomy aprons that were exactly what was called for.

In fact Margaret bet this—she bet a dollar that the aprons her father found, and put on to clean up his wife's house in, were aprons *Granny* had packed for Emma to elope with. Still, this was a peculiar idea and Margaret did not like having thought of it, because it required her to imagine Emma not exactly running away from Granny but Granny letting her go and even getting her ready . . . which hadn't Granny always claimed was not the truth of the case? But perhaps this was not what she had claimed—perhaps she had only claimed that she had issued a warning, had duly informed Raymond that Emma ought not to be taken away, that it would be best for her not to marry, and that then when he would not see, she was reasonable, she saw that she was defeated (but when was Granny ever defeated?) and she let them go, and even packed Emma some things, including a few nice, big, homemade aprons. Margaret could see Granny folding them up with a near-smile on her lips, or at least a little ironical twitch, because she probably knew who would end up wearing them—she knew it would not be Emma.

Indeed, while her father was cleaning the house, with Granny's big elegant aprons on, their bibs subtly outlined in pale-colored rickrack, Emma would have been visiting out on the porch or the steps, or on someone else's steps. Or she might be out in back with the chickens Raymond had bought her; Margaret knew for a fact he had made them a nice strong coop and put up a wire fence. Margaret's mother could love anything, she even loved her chickens. They tickled her to death, and when they squawked, she squawked back at them.

Then she began to put in for a puppy—and her husband brought her one home, and if what all human beings need is at least one other human being that they can make perfectly

343

happy—Margaret knew (without knowing) that there had been one day that her father had had what a person needed in that respect.

And yet he had pondered, *must* have pondered, all this.

No doubt everybody was distraught when Emma took the puppy for a long ride on the city bus and it jumped off and disappeared. She herself was so profoundly grieved that she turned against buses themselves and would not get on one for years, but in any case, she had probably seen all the Jacksonville streets she wanted to by that time. Margaret could hear the neighbors making a little fun of her. *If she's not going to ride on the bus all day—what's going to keep her from having to take out the garbage or sweep the porch? Anyway, she still has some chickens she can take for a ride.* Later, her bus rides— with Nomey or the children, or all of them together—would be mainly for replenishing the supplies of the Eighth Street sewing circle.

But in fact, Margaret asked herself, when had her mother taken up her handwork? Certainly long before Eighth Street. Margaret remembered her father folding up blankets in the park and feeling them all over for needles. Yes all his married life, *both* his married lives, he had checked things calmly—beds and chairs, pads and cloths, clothes going to the wash—for embroidery needles.

But as for the lost pup, people said her mother had almost pined away for it (and in fact a certain popular song came along to increase her woe a thousand-fold—*Oh where oh where can my little dog be? Oh where oh where can he be?*).

But one night, weeks later, something whined at the back door and the puppy was back home—with three legs and a stump.

# CHAPTER TEN

NORA had said she was not superstitious but she almost saw a connection. "Your mama and that afflicted dog. And then those afflicted children."

This had made them both smile—yes, even Margaret had had bestowed on her (by whoever can bestow such things) a peep, at least, into a comic enactment of the domestic scene on Clark Street, and she had felt suddenly that it was a rendering that had been going on all the time behind other renderings, but blocked from her view.

Sitting today in this Eighth Street bedroom, on this most bizarre—most afflicted—of all Saturday afternoons, with the room beginning to stew a little in the August heat (which was recovering nicely now from the storms of the day before, and beginning to feel its way around the clackedy air-conditioner), Margaret considered again what Nora had said that day, and how she herself had reflected on it at the time, knit her face, shaped her hollow voice-notes in Nora's old worn-out air. "If Daddy had taken Mama back home," she had begun, "before any of that got started . . .

345

before they had time to start a family . . . the way Granny said he could . . . ."

Nora had made a face of stern doubt, but Margaret had insisted. "Granny told him he didn't know Mama. She said, 'You'll see for yourself what I'm talking about—and when you do, bring her back home.' She said Mama ought to be at home."

"Margaret. If that is what you want to believe. If you can believe it, go ahead."

"And Granny went down there."

"How many times did Granny go?"

"She went at least twice."

"Twice. To her own daughter's. In how many years?"

Margaret frowned, was silent. Her brain did not want to go on, there was something in the way; it was as if she had had to fumble, blindly, for something caught in her mindwheel. If her mother had been taken back home, set loose on the dairy (*here now, run get your hoe and your sunbonnet, you're home now*) before she had conceived . . . . For there was here, surely, a curious fact: in a sense it was the first child, Margaret herself, and not the afflicted ones, that had been her father's worst luck, if you wanted to talk about luck. Men have their little dreams too, surely it was not completely otherwise, and no doubt her father had pondered, had sat thoughtful many an evening, his face in darkness, while he listened to his wife shooting her gab from the porch to the passersby, or handing out Cokes in the kitchen to everybody and his brother, or giving things away to people while they protested, giving someone a red dish, for instance, because they had said red was their favorite color.

But while all this was going on and her father was pondering, and his mind going back to things Granny had or had not tried to convey, and while his life ahead was beginning to cloud heavily over in great gray fog and he could no longer make it out . . . or when what he did discern, of shapes to come, had caused him (even him) to stand sud-

346

denly up, for a moment, in front of his chair, and then sit back down . . . while all that was being felt by her father, *she* had come; she—Margaret—had been born, confused the issue once and for all, and closed off, so to speak, the pass back to Waycross.

Still—what *was* bad luck, and what good? Consider this: immediately after her birth there must have been, on Clark Street, several years of high-grade contentment for all three of them. That period of her life, sealed away in infant brain-vials that could not be completely opened for memory to possess, must have been, nevertheless, the period of life that had built her up and got her ready for everything that followed . . . so that she could at least survive. She had the love of her father and her mother (and the three-legged dog)— and even of a grandmother. Her grandfather Stovall had died in Waycross and her grandmother had followed Margaret's father to the city, and straight from the country had opened up a boardinghouse right there on a city street. That was remarkable, Margaret thought. But this grandmother was strong, like Granny and Mrs. Barker; work did not faze her a bit. Perhaps women *were* stronger back then, Margaret considered; tranquillizers and sleeping pills had not even been invented for all she knew—for the simple reason that they had not needed to be.

But in any case it was just in this era of light that it had come—the explosion of darkness.

(*Oh didn't you hear? About the bad-luck-bomb blowing up on Clark Street?*)

Second child born. First son. Good.

*But—*

Darkness.

Third child. Darkness howling now.

Fourth child . . . .

Her mother's dark womb closed at last.

A surgeon cleaning his hands in satisfaction.

She saw this: her father sitting quietly, to all appearances calmly, through numerous consultations about afflictions. She saw him sitting in a sterile-smelling room, on a high stool of some sort, his thick legs set squarely on the floor, his hands on his thighs, smoke rising from his cigar. The angle she thought from did not allow her to see his face—she would not presume to see his actual look.

But she pictured them all chugging back from the Macedonia orange grove. A back door flying open. Riley bouncing through it. The oranges from the grove flying every-which-a-way, and in fact everything on the back seat— Riley and the oranges, shoes and Coca-Cola bottles— rolling and tumbling down an embankment. Later she had pictured her father rolling too, head-over-heels in a wheel of dirt and oranges. But surely he had *not* rolled. Sprung, yes, from the car—midst her mother's terrible wails. At the bottom of the slope, she had seen her father picking Riley up, his face almost calm even now, looking at him deeply, touching his face. Her mother dragging and slipping in her long skirts on the slope. Sobbing. *Dead. Dead! Raymond Riley's dead. Ain't he? Oh-h-h dead, dead.*

Her mother had not even heard it but Margaret had heard her father say, "No," in what was almost a thoughtful voice. Riley was only stunned and covered with bruises. Soon he was lifting his weak cry, and his mother was taking him up in her arms, the whole loose ineptly flailing pile of him, in an ecstasy of relief and gratification. Margaret looked back to the car. George had pulled himself awkwardly into the back seat and now out the open door, and he and Bobba came forward crying, jerking slowly against each other onto the field.

Margaret did not recall, perhaps she too had wept, but she remembered how the whole field rang with strange lamentations, or thanksgivings or whatever it was—just human noise and who knew what any of it was supposed to say or express; she remembered how her father carried Riley to the car, and how the others had swung crying on his arm,

348

through the broomstraw, and how then the mother had taken the hurt endangered child on her lap in the front seat and begun to croon and moan to him. How Margaret and her father had gone back to pick up oranges. Strange that they would even think of it, and yet how important it had seemed to them to do this, her father carefully holding open the sack and she bending and fetching, depositing in it each and every piece of the tumbled fruit, busted or not; how significant and satisfying it seemed to them to do this.

AT NIGHT at the plant, at Clayton and Rumer's, her father had used his pocketknife sometimes to peel her an orange. She would eat it standing at a window that looked down to the river. The plant had its own landing dock down there, with electricity even, lights for night loading; and barges came up from all over the world and sold them cargoes of spoiled produce, for instance, sold them rotted loads, or loads of fish-heads from the fishpacking plants nearby; while Margaret was eating her orange, catching the juice on folds of notebook paper, or doing her homework at the table by the stove, her father would be out on the landing or he might be inside the plant working on the machines. But actually—what had the machines done? She could hardly think. Ground things up and pulverized them probably, or dried them, mixed them with chemicals; she would hardly have known because she sat inside the office at an old black table and worked in her notebook, and her father came in and out, or went through papers at a great big desk, or looked on shelves for things—pieces of rubber, or little pipes or screws or latches; she did not know what-all.

But she remembered enormous contentment there, in the plant with her father, and it was as if the contentment was there in the room day and night, whether she was or not, and when she got there she only had to crack the door to get a whiff of it.

At home, before they left for the office, they would have put as much order into the place as a place like that could hold; they would have got the others fed and washed, and then it was as if what they mostly did was wipe—not only the bodies of the human beings, but the surfaces, all the furniture. She saw them wipe absently, without speaking, under and over, everywhere at once, then hang up their wipe cloths, stretch them to dry. Turn the wiped handle of the closet, take out their coats.

"Why your father didn't just get out while the getting was good," Nora said. "Since your mother wouldn't let him do anything reasonable. Let him use his common sense. Have the children tested and examined by doctors and agencies and things. No she wasn't going to let a soul get hold of them but her, and she didn't care one little fig what was the matter with them. Of course your father doted on *you*—and maybe she felt like she would just as soon dote on them. The fact that they were completely dependent and always would be—to her that wasn't particularly a disadvantage.

"And your father, even after Nomey . . . didn't throw them overboard."

*Because humankind is not a beast—in spite of everything. Some people have to keep on trying to show that.*

"Of course Granny now. She didn't think twice. When all that trouble was born, that was all, that saw the end of her."

Margaret protested. "*I* didn't though. I didn't see the end of her." She frowned, and when she spoke she did not see how her hollowed-out words would be able to hang even for a moment on Nora's old worn-out air. "I remember the train station, that part comes back. My father and me. He knew I . . . hated him as much as I did." (If she could say now, "Daddy, that was one of my awfullest days"—what would he reply? —"Honey it *was* my awfullest day.") "I don't think I said but one thing—you know—is this the one to Waycross? . . . or something like that.

"Yes, I remember us at the station," she went on. "Standing together . . . looking hard at something across the room, except that there wasn't really anything to look at. The people all around us were so noisy, they talked so loud and we were so quiet. Yes, I remember that day I went to Waycross. I don't know whether my father had written or *called*—"

"Or how many times he *had* to," Nora said.

"But Granny said to come right on—

"Or *somebody* said it—it might have been Grandaddy Culp."

"When I got off the train, Grandaddy was right there. In the milk wagon."

"Not Granny, I could have told you that—"

"Granny was home cooking for the men. If I had not come at dinnertime . . . I don't know . . . I might have been another kind of person. When we got to the dairy, I went in through the kitchen, and it may sound silly but I have loved kitchens ever since."

Margaret had gone on. "I don't care who says what. Granny did *that*—she took me in, her home was my home." And maybe she had done it, Margaret thought, to show something about humankind. Maybe Granny too needed her chance to show it and this was her chance.

Nora studied her cloud of smoke. She listened to Margaret's hollowed murmurings. "Her home was my home . . . ."

"Now if Granny was a person," Nora said, "that a bad conscience could bother her—"

Margaret made another sound of protest.

"I think she just saw her chance for a cheap good deed," Nora said. "And an excuse by taking *you* to wash her hands of the rest of them—although actually, she already had washed her hands."

Nora went on. "Now I don't know if she could actually feel guilt . . . the way you and I feel things like that. And I don't even know—because I doubt if anybody knew—if she actually had any . . . beliefs. Still, I can't say she might not

351

have thought that in the eyes of heaven—you know—she might look like she wasn't saved. *You* know—just look like it. Or maybe that didn't have a thing to do with it, maybe that doesn't do her justice. Maybe she just wanted to show—to herself—that she had always meant well and that when a reasonable-looking good deed came along she would do it just like anybody else. So what she did—she just took you and put you in Emma's place, and that was the last she ever had to do with Emma, you know yourself it was."

Nora paused. "So except for your father, you were about the only one who didn't throw them overboard."

*And I don't know why I didn't*, Margaret thought. But perhaps it had been her turn to give her little proofs, show what she could show. Of course she could not have known she had any such purpose as that at the time, and how could she have believed it was even true that people were not completely evil, that there was some little something to them *besides* evil . . . after her father had done what he did? Perhaps she had thought it was the opposite that was true, that humankind *was* a beast and that everything every single member of this species did, herself included, would just go to prove it over and over again. Maybe it was as if her father had said that to her, in every way but words—had let her see it on his face even, there in the train station. "You see, we are all beasts after all, that is all we are." Or: *Here read this. In my face. No need to say it. Yes, even your father.*


YOUR FATHER, people said—or had they actually said it?—*was a person that seemed to have such good sense, or at least we thought he did. And then—for him to do what he did about that old Nomey.*

Suddenly his wits—just flew out the window. Was that what they said?

I've heard of a lot, but that beats all I've ever heard and still does.

You won't never figure that out if you figure a million years.

To be such a good man.

To work so hard for what he had, then throw it all away.

To be so decent.

Such a friendly, nice man.

That everybody could count on.

In spite of what all had happened to him.

To put up with things the way he had.

*Were those the things people said—about her father?*


"THEN FOR him to say 'Lord! I don't have enough trouble. Give me some more. How about it?'" Nora had sat forward and glared hard in Margaret's direction.

"For him to say: I don't want things to get better, I'd rather that they got worse.

"If he had run away and joined the foreign legion, or shipped out on a boat for Timbuktu. Why there was the ocean, not two miles from his front step, right there ready for him, and who would have said a thing? Who would not have known why? Why there wasn't a soul that would have been surprised, or even blamed him. Look what he had stood. They knew he had stood it longer than they could."

Nora's face was flushed. Her words had come rapidly, as if she had to say them in a hurry before she thought better of it. "Or I even tell you this. If he had murdered them, the whole bunch of them, in their sleep. If he had taken a gun and walked calmly around—your father was always calm— from little old bed to little old bed . . . while they were sleeping—who would have been surprised?"

Nora sat back to consider. She turned her head to blow a jet of smoke. "Well, some might," she said. "But some would have thought it was a blessing. They would not have admitted it but some would have thought it was for the best."

Nora studied a moment. "And actually that might have made some sense," she said.

Margaret had had her deep frown that day at Nora's, her face of despair. She did not know but what her father, in doing the way he did, had wanted to punish himself for something, for the way his life had turned out . . . and now maybe she wanted to punish *her*-self and so she came out here to Nora's—that was one way to do it. A long time would pass and she would not come and then there she would be again. When she would think she was getting away at last from certain things, she would think *But I'm not supposed to get away from them, I ought to always have them with me,* and so then she would go out there to Nora's and sit glumly, frowning, full of hopeless chagrin, and let herself be talked to that way.

"If he had taken an axe," Nora said. "They must have had an axe around the place. If he had taken something like that . . . what would have been the difference?" Nora studied it out, as if she herself were making a plan. "First he could have taken you and put you over at Grandma Stovall's—or if she was dead, she was already dead by then wasn't she?— over to his cousin's, weren't those other Stovalls in town by that time? Then gone back home and put the rest of them to bed. They would be puling and whining. Washed all those old sticky faces. Those old stinky bottoms. Put them in those bent metal beds, plumping them all down . . . with all kind of noises and who knows what-all going on. And when he got through—if he wasn't too worn out—gone out to the back porch and got the axe.

"Nobody would have said that was crazy, all they would have said—"

Perhaps Margaret had turned in her chair, moved her hand from her face, perhaps Nora had seen a look that made her almost desist.

She said, "All I mean is—let's say this, let's say he had had them all put away somewhere. Emma too. Who would have said a word? Who would there have been *to* say one?

354

Now you might say 'Granny'—but I say no, she had washed her hands, as far as I'm concerned. No ma'am. Not a soul.

"Or—the most he would have had to do, he might have had to go around to a few people and say—you know—that a person never can tell what he may have to do in this life or what may turn out to be for the best, no matter how much it hurts you. He might have had to say a few things like that, so people would not think he had not give it plenty of thought or come to a sensible conclusion. He might have had to tell how he had worried it all out. And prayed. 'I've prayed it through,' he could have said. 'I've asked for guidance and this is what I believe the Lord wants me to do—to put them in this good place where they can get the kind of help they need. I know I can't give it to them—I wish I could.'

"Now that would have even made sense," Nora said. "And the way things were, it would have had to be your mama too. You know yourself he could not have kept her and put the others up."

Margaret raised her head to give Nora a sharp look, but this time Nora gave it right back to her.

"You know better than anybody that she was a maniac about those children. Usually Emma would go along with you and in a lot of ways she knew she didn't know much and she more or less expected people to tell her what to do. But not on that. *No* ma'am. You know it better than I do—not on that. If your father had *his* madness, that kept him from just taking off from there like a normal person would, this was hers—when it came to those children, she was as *in*-sane as he was, along with whatever else she was. She didn't care what kind of children they were, they were *hers!* and she wasn't going to let one finger of them get away from her. You know what your father would have gone through—or maybe he did go through it . . . because you tried it yourself after he died. How could he have got them away from her—a strong healthy woman—when *you* couldn't even sneak

355

them off when she was half-dead in the nursing home and had them sleeping on pallets around her bed, and drove everybody crazy, and they couldn't do a thing about it? What was he going to do, if he did anything, but put her up too? I never saw *this*—why he didn't just slip in some little office somewhere and sign some papers, and let them come around to the house and get them. I don't think there would have been a soul to say a word. Especially if they had ever gone to that house and seen the inside of it.

"But no," Nora said. "That made too much sense.

"Of course you think of a lot of things he could have done," she said. "Sometimes I even think of him boarding the house up, with all of them inside, and that big racket going on, all kinds of fussing and hollering, or whatever they did that you could call fussing and hollering—or maybe your mother just playing and carrying on with them, I doubt if even your father could tell which noise was which. But I can see him driving up in the yard in one of the trucks from the plant, the truck full of boards to board it up with. And him knock up the last board and before he drove away, forever, lay things straight in the bed of the truck—because he was so neat. I remember at the dairy he was always cleaning off his tools, and then he would lay them out in a nice row on the grass by where he was working, and Granny loved that, that was exactly the way *she* was, she loved the careful way he did things."

Nora had considered, cocked her cigarette by her face, reflecting. "And then—for him to get interested in Emma." She was getting off her track, going back to the dairy years and years ago. "I don't say that was not a puzzle to Granny at first and she might have had to think about it a minute or two, which was a minute or two longer than she was used to thinking about Emma's welfare. But she was not going to be one of those who was so afraid of good fortune that whenever it came along she was going to take it and throw it out the window. I expect she just decided she had been wrong

356

about something. She had thought that anybody that actually *wanted* Emma couldn't have been allowed to have her because he would have had to be crazy to want her. And yet here was Raymond, not crazy, a skilled mason and a reliable man. And then later when he took up with Nomey—brought her right into the house—Granny probably thought he *had* been crazy all along and that was why he had married Emma.

"Of course, as far as leaving her," Nora said, "to run off with somebody that could put a meal on the table or iron a shirt, make him a normal home . . . that would have made some sense. That wasn't any more than you would expect from a man in a situation like that.

"Don't you remember?" Nora said. "Granny was the first one to say herself that that would have made sense—"

"No, Granny didn't say anything like that to me," said Margaret.

"She was the first one *to* say it," Nora said. "And she said, and I expect we all said, that if he wanted this old Nomey, which was crazy to begin with, but if he wanted her, why didn't he at least run off with her?" Nora bunched her mouth. For a minute she was too disgusted to go on.

Margaret had swung her leg, sat frowning in Nora's deep chair.

"All right," Nora said. "You take a man, and he has got himself in about the worst predicament a person can get into, I haven't even heard of another one that bad, and it is not even all his fault, but anyway he has gotten himself into it, a grea-at peck of trouble, and yet he will not run away from it and he will not take some of these afflicted people without any minds and that would hardly know the difference—he won't even take a few of them and put them away. Nosiree bob, that is not what he does. Instead of getting rid of one or two, what does he do?" Nora slapped the arm of her chair. "He goes out and and gets another one that's not much better off than the rest of them and brings *her* home."

357

It was as if Nora had almost startled *herself.* "I want you to know!"

Margaret had swung her leg that day. She had looked in sullen gloom off into Nora's air while Nora spoke on. Nora did not expect to be looked at. She expected Margaret just to frown and swing her leg—it was a condition she had gotten used to.

Of course, Nora and Margaret were no blood kin, and Nora was no kin to any of these Stovalls or Culps she and Margaret would discuss, and if other people were crazy, in a way surely Nora was too; surely she too was afflicted with some kind of insanity of her own that made her think about them at all, just because once she had been connected to them, lived at the Culp dairy in the time of Emma and Grandaddy, been married for a short while to a Culp brother and called Granny *Granny*, gone down with her once to Clark Street. *She has her madness too,* Margaret would think. *To even concern herself after all these years. And me,* she would think, *part of my own madness is to listen to her since I know everything she will say before I come out here, and in a way it's what I come out here for and that is not right, there is something crazy about that too.*

MARGARET had turned from the window of the house on Eighth Street and gazed once more into the death-room. The crooked bed drew her to it, then the face on the pillow. It seemed like a long way across the small room, and when she had crossed over it to the bed, she felt too tired even to bend her head, too tired to study, as she needed to—*for we must study these things* she thought—the face that had drawn her, and in fact other faces were interposed, the face of her mother, for instance, her almost studious face on the day her father had first brought Nomey home to the house on Clark Street.

Margaret had been sitting at the kitchen table doing some chore; she thought she might have been scraping or shelling something into the big washpan. But she could see into the living room and she had looked up and seen her mother's face, her almost studious look, before she (Margaret) had seen Nomey herself. As Nomey was brought in, her mother had been very quiet, she stood with her lips slightly parted, simply waiting, watching, her face so full of dazed, surprised expectation that she did not even seem to notice it when the three-legged dog got caught in the door and then squirmed through the torn screen, sprang, squealing, at Nomey's feet, raced and plunged at her, yipping at her ankles; none of the others had noticed either, because they too were busy studying, almost like people of reflection, this new arrival and her tied-up suitcase of belongings; they had looked at Nomey and she at them, and her mother had looked wonderingly at her father, and then at Margaret in the kitchen, and Margaret herself looked at all the others in turn, and the yipping and squealing dog went on and on almost without their hearing him, although later Margaret had heard him clearly in her sleep, had been waked from sleep, she remembered, by the dreamed barking of the three-legged dog, trying his best to warn them.

And of that day, and the days before, the days after, the whole crushed-together accordion of days which encompassed the phenomenon of Nomey, there was little else she could absolutely recall. What, for instance, had she known or her mother known, on that day of this person's arrival and during the days that followed? What had they been told? Almost nothing of this time came back—or at least, as far as there *were* events recalled, there was no proper sequence to them and they even seemed to contradict each other. Why and how (aside simply from his incurable disease—multiple bad luck, progressive ill fortune) had her father come to involve himself, tangle himself, with this miserable Nomey, this Naomi-person, or whatever her name was? Sometimes, in years to come, she had come to believe *this*: that it was simply absentminded, pondering distraction.

Somehow he had arrived at a situation where he had made ridiculous, distracted love to her (though love of course was not the word) and hardly known that he had done it. Then her claim on him. That he would not walk away from—since he never *had* walked away from things.

What was known was very little indeed: that Nomey's brother—(no-good)—had worked at the fertilizer plant too for a certain time, and that on payday each Friday, Nomey would appear in the yard of the plant, in her ridiculous attire, that Margaret's father might have thought was pathetic, to get two dollars off her brother.

Then one day—as Margaret had often pictured it—her father had been smoking his cigar and thinking, pondering, in the window of the plant office, when Nomey had come up in the yard for her two dollars. This time her brother did not give her anything, he gesticulated, finally shouted (perhaps he even spat at her feet and she spat back), and Margaret's father, absent, distracted, busy pondering (for all anyone knew) the other childlike woman at home, went to the door, and when the brother slunk off (for he was definitely the kind that would slink), he, Raymond, stepped out a few steps into the yard . . . and then—even Margaret did not know how or why—he was taking two one-dollar bills from his wallet, calm, only half attentive, squinting to see the bills through the smoke that rose, absently, from the cigar in his mouth. And so on and so forth.

So then they began to say, To get rid of a dirty one and not get one that was clean. But sometimes Margaret almost thought, about her father's absurd loyalties (she would not say it to Nora, Nora would think it was nonsense), that a woman who had been smart or energetic or even pretty would not have been chosen by her father, although chosen of course was not the word, for the reason that there would be a meanness in such a deed—in juxtaposing such a woman to the bunch he had at home—that there would not be with a person like Nomey, and to abandon them (and not really abandon anyway) for a Nomey-creature did not really even count as abandonment.

Again, what Margaret had actually known for sure of all this must have been almost nothing, and in memory even less, for her brain had been overheated with too many degrees of feverish pain—memory cells could not survive at that temperature. When had she understood, for instance, that this squat, misshapen creature, who certainly did not look young but was not much older than Margaret herself, was with child? And that her father was obliged (by something or someone) to take her in? When, how, had she understood that he was obliged (by something, someone) to remove one or the other of the two women from the premises—or otherwise organize his affairs . . . ? Made to feel that how he did it was his own business but that it had to be done, that there were those in the world who had not forgotten such a thing as common decency. *This is a Christian street.* Yes that must have been said, not only by the householders of the neighborhood, but, in effect, by family and friends, by various pressure-bringers, including, probably, Margaret herself.

Later she could not recall whether or not she had actually spent any single night under the same roof with her, this vile intruder (known to be so, at once, by the three-legged dog), but possibly it was that first night that she had demanded to be taken, in a state of mind beyond interpretation even then, to—her grandmother Stovall being dead—someone across town, some other Stovall emigrant from Waycross. Where had she been when her father had made the house-trade? Had she already had her personal resurrection, begun her new life at the dairy?

At what point had her father exchanged, with the man at the plant, the house on decent Clark Street for the twin cottages on Eighth Street—already almost squalid even then? At what point had he been severed, officially, from her mother and joined to Nomey, so that—for this must surely have been the way he had reasoned it out—at least both parties would be honest women and their children all legal children with an official father, and so gone looking for two houses side by side, since both households would be more or less equally in need of—not only his fiscal support—but his day-to-day custodial care?

In any case, here was her father utterly disgracing himself, and casting himself (as it turned out) into financial ruin and lifelong penury, by being too weak, too unclever a person to abandon people, to wipe clear from his remaining calendar of days either section of the gang that clove to him, and so betraying the one person he actually really loved . . . earning, that is, by these deeds, the just hatred and contempt of his daughter Margaret.


THESE OLD thoughts raced in Margaret's mind as she stood beside the listing bed—and the eternal frustration of the whole thing pried and pulled at her tear glands until she began to weep from sheer aggravation. When she blew her nose, the nurse came in and thought, naturally, that she had grieved herself into a little mild hysteria, put her arm around her and said, "Now, now, let's take us a little walk," and walked her through the living room into the kitchen and made her drink a glass of water, and said that when the food van came, Margaret must take a plate of supper with her because you had to have food no matter how bad you felt, and that forgetting to eat was probably the worst mistake people made when they were upset. They stood in the kitchen and though the nurse talked and chatted to ease Margaret's mind and get it back for a little while on normal things, and Margaret, standing by the window, listened willingly and even answered vaguely back (*I declare . . . well I do know*), still, windows—windows were her downfall in a way, and from the side window in what passed for a kitchen she could see out to the front of the two lots, where there had stood for a time, after her father's retirement, a certain curious little structure, one of those things that had gathered to it through the years, all the way from Waycross, a great ropy mess of her own outwinding thoughts, yes an object with a tremendous thought-gathering force—her father's store, *Raymond's Foods*, a neat one-room square building of concrete block, straddling perfectly an invisible line that ran directly between the two small houses in the rear, and forming with these little decrepit domiciles a perfect triangle.

She pictured her father standing behind his counter, listening idly to the little radio he kept in back of the cigarette rack. From time to time a person came in and gave him grimy money for cold drinks and Baby Ruths, for cans of Vienna sausage or chicken noodle soup, Blue Horse Tobacco and Three Thistle Snuff. Sometimes, at the back window, he could watch the water streaming ineptly on the panes, and catch wavery glimpses of the grinning face of his son George. In fact the window had very possibly been put in simply so George could wash it every day.

In a house in back, the two slattern women plied their needles back and forth on coarse-weave pillow slips and dresser scarves. Margaret pictured this: Nomey shaking her arm, as she sewed, in irritation, since her bra strap had slipped down through the sleeves of her dress and finally pulled in two. She saw Nomey shake the two strands off her arm—and here she had some good fortune. Her fellow seamstress, the *other* Mrs. Stovall of Eighth Street, was marvelously equipped to respond to her friend's distress, for the bottom of her slip was full of safety pins: when her hem had come undone, she had not taken her needle and thread to it, she had put it back up with pins, because for one thing it was very convenient to have all the pins in the house where she knew where they were.

Emma *liked* to come to people's aid. So she turned up her slip and unfastened a pin. Nomey sat as still as a stone, her embroidery ring at rest in her lap, while Emma stood over her, chattering happily, and pinned together the two strands of the brassiere strap. Nomey said it was certainly a relief— she said she couldn't stand things dangling on her like that. She said she knew people that *could* stand things like that, but she wasn't that kind. "You ain't that kind, are you Nomey?" Emma said.

Her father had put up his little store, *Raymond's Foods,* when he had retired from the fertilizer plant, not much more than a year before he died, huffing, no doubt, going very slow, breathing hard as he sawed and sanded, plumbed and nailed, stirred his mortar—like stiff dough—in a great big tub, set the blocks in place. He was a third little pig, raising a house that would hold up and was even attractive. When it was done, he squeezed himself in behind his cash register, behind his neat rows of cigarettes and keychains and sunglasses, his Milky Ways and Hershey Bars, and probably felt a little bit happy and safe, and would almost have danced a jig (if he hadn't been too obese to exert himself that way), waiting for the bad wolf to peek in and eat his heart out over Oatmeal Cakes and Moon Pies.

Margaret's mind lurched and wobbled, veered way off course, and she recalled that up in the Halls of Glory, way off in the Sweet By-and-By, a year was all they gave him, and so when the year was up, his ballooning body heaved against his heart, churned and mashed it, finally squeezed it shut. Margaret could see a sentence being read on the steps of the Executive Mansion (Bright and Blessed). *Let Raymond Stovall be squeezed by the heart, by his own body fat, until he is dead.*

Of course where Margaret looked now, there was nothing but Eighth Street air, and the ground where the store had stood had gone back to growing sandspurs and palmetto weed. When her father died, the building had been sold by

Nomey and Loreen. Nobody else wanted to run a store on this street, so whoever had bought it had picked it up and moved it off, concrete or not. Maybe they wanted it for a tool shed or something like that.

Two or three times, possibly four times, Margaret, on her Saturday visits to clean her mother's house, that year of her father's retirement, had paid calls on him in the store, breathed the clean respite of his neat, shiny room. On this dirty dilapidated street, where everybody on it was a litter-bug, it seemed like an odd little jewel of a place that did not belong. But what had she and her father spoken of? Nothing. How are you? Well honey. How is this one, that one. I do know. I tell you now. She frowning (of course). And yet—she had said (thank goodness for this) or conveyed at least, if not in so many words: Good. *This is good in here. A good little place. You did good on this.*

He said he knew it didn't amount to a thing. There wasn't much to it at all, and it was just a good thing the plant had had that shed of leftover building scraps . . . those old chipped blocks of concrete, for instance. And yet the chipped parts were turned inside, it all looked beautiful to her. There had been some unmatched lengths of bruised wood, and he had had to piece them together for his walls and his cabinets and things. But when he got through and smoothed over them his silky coats of shellac . . . *my lord!*

After all, he said (or not quite said, either, in so many words), people ate a lot these days and if he only made a dollar a day, why that was a dollar; she knew herself how it was—she had children to feed . . . and those grown-up children in the house back there, why had she seen the size of them? he asked (or seemed to at least). There wasn't much that bunch could do, so what they mostly did was eat; in fact they were normal, perfectly competent eaters and drinkers, he inferred, and they got better at it every year, and George, for instance, why that George could eat enough any day of the week to keep up three mules.

365

The pieced, bruised wood—how exactly had he got it the way it was, she wondered. That honey-smooth finish that drew you to touch it, delicious to feel. She thought of something else he had not quite said: *I really just wanted this little house to fix it and paint it, wipe it off every day and keep it clean, something that I don't have to let a single soul mess up, and in a way I don't actually care if I sell anything or not, because that's not really the point and I've got everything where I want it anyway—I'd just as soon keep it there.*

At home she had a large photograph on her vanity of her father behind the counter in his store. Of course she seldom needed to look at this picture, its image was so sharp in her mind, but it was so full of crystal-clear detail that you could even read the labels on the soup cans. It was amazing that such a photo had ever been taken on a street like Eighth Street, part and parcel now of the white slums of the city, and she had no idea who had taken it. Her mother had kept a copy of this photo on her wall. *This is Raymond in his store ain't it Maga? He loves it out there in his store don't he Maga?* In fact Margaret's own copy had been sent her by her mother, inscribed on the back by the same learned neighbor of years ago, "Your daddy Mr. Stovall in his store."

Her father was so wide a man by then that standing behind the counter made him seem almost grotesquely short, as if he might be missing part of his legs. When strangers walked in, they must have gotten quite a turn—seeing this sawed-off old fat man and his cabbagy, rough-mottled head, his washboard face. Even for Margaret the face in the picture was a startling one, no matter how many times she referred to it in her imagination. It was as if she had never quite *seen* this face until she first saw it in the picture and could study it seventy miles away under her own lamp, sitting back in wonder on her own sofa. A brown, leathern face. Some colored people weren't that dark, it seemed to her. A face almost the color of his cigars—it was as if it had been cured, smoked brown by cigar smoke. Such a mixed and variegated face—full of thick warping folds and deep clefts. Then large wide eyes, and a pulpy, porous-looking, bulblike nose. Deep-drooping, bulldog jowls. A face you could hardly take in all at once. And sometimes she thought it was like the head of some fleshy animal—a hog perhaps . . . or maybe just a big old dog, harmless, not particularly cheerful or cheerless either, looking out at you calmly, without surprise.

This happened to some men's faces, she thought: in old age they started looking like a big old dog of some kind; there were various breeds they might be said to resemble. But here he was, in any case, this old fat man her father, the cigar between his puffed lips smoking to a turn his big droopy-dog face, looking absently into the camera with no desire whatever to turn to it any particular pose or expression . . . this her father in his one-room store that no one ever tended but himself, with a sign on the door that could just be turned over when he went out—Back Soon.

But that was the way, wasn't it, that old men ended up sometimes. Turning up—or putting together—some little four-walled place of their own to be. Mr. Barker, for instance, in the little red icehouse he had run after the depression wiped out his store. Where she doubted if he made a dollar a day and which he went to anyway in all kinds of weather, even when people couldn't possibly want any ice—because it was somewhere for him to be. Then Grandaddy Culp in his woodshed, leaning back in the armless rocker Granny had tried to throw away, his jug between his knees.

She knew a lot of men didn't want to pass their time in houses, because houses belonged to women, even if the women don't care about them and would rather be out on the walks and streets.

In her father's store there had been neatness and heavenly order, everything in its place with other things of its kind. He had great big heavy rags that he wiped things with,

367

and an enormous duster that he kept on its own peg, and there was just no dust and clutter and mess, and she knew—without knowing—that he swept the floor twice a day and picked up the dirt in a wide-mouthed shiny pan and that even the broom and the pan he washed.

At night when her father closed up, she knew this for certain: he got out two brown paper bags, and going around the shelves, he pulled off cans and packages, he pulled quarts of milk out of the cold box, and bread from the bread rack, stopping to set the other loaves straight on the shelf. The bags filled up. He took them and set them both against the wall outside and went back in to turn out the light; he took a last look around, gave the whole room a long reflective look, and pulled the blind over the window grill.

Outside he locked the door and took up the bags, using his stout thighs to help hoist them up against his chest. It was dark. He stumped through the sandy yard towards her mother's lighted house and went through to the kitchen where he set down one of the bags. Then he took the other one to the other house, went through to the kitchen and set *it* down, huffing for a moment and staring absently out the same window she was staring out of now.

*He arose a victor from the dark domain.*

*And he lives forever with the saints to reign.*

Margaret found that she was murmuring an old tune out of the same hymnbook, so to speak, the nurse had sung to Nomey from, and she hardly knew why . . . except that she really didn't have good sense but about half the time.


A HEART ATTACK is a wonderful thing if it's a great big one and does what it's supposed to do.

Leonard had had that kind, and she supposed it was very good luck.

She thought about her *father's* luck, and a whimsical little scene began to play on the stage of her mind. *An official with very long legs was tipping back in his chair and propping his feet on a lower drawer that he kept open for just that purpose.* He scratched on a pad about the case of her father—writing to another official at a similar desk on another floor. "I tell you what," he wrote. "Raymond Stovall has been waiting for some good luck for about"—here he flipped open a file—"sixty-seven years. So I think he's got some coming, and I want him to have a real nice Big 'Un. So tomorrow morning let's let his body fat start to pitch and churn . . . catch his heart in the current and swirl it shut."

Her father died in his store. He was almost bound to since that was where he mostly was.

Margaret strained her mind to picture him with his heart attack on the floor. She saw him raise his head from the smooth, varnished wood, reach forward with something in his hand—*my lord it was his big heavy-duty wipe cloth*—and with a sweep of his thick pulpy hand wipe clean a small pool of blood from the floor and close his eyes.

STANDING in Nomey's kitchen, it was as if Margaret's cloud of thought grew and darkened until it covered everything and Margaret herself disappeared behind it. For a long time she had no sense whatever of her own flesh, of the act of standing, of directing her gaze, of a floor to be stood on or glass to look through. Then sensation stirred against her from somewhere.

Oh. The nurse touching her arm.

For a moment, though, Margaret did not turn to her. She imagined that the nurse might be about to say, "If you think you need to keep staring out the window, like a crazy person, maybe I better at least get you a chair." But of course that was not what she said.

She laid her hand on Margaret's arm and stepped up beside her and the two of them looked together, across a short patch of grassy, yellow-blooming weeds, at the sorry building next door.

"It doesn't look like all that comfortable a place to live in does it?" the nurse said, and Margaret murmured something back to her.

"I guess you knew some of the people that used to live there," the nurse went on, and Margaret took a long breath. Yes she had, she said.

The nurse did not imagine that anybody stayed there very long anymore; she said whoever was in there now was about to move, or maybe they had moved, because the day before she had kept seeing a pickup truck in the yard, backed up to the front steps.

Margaret felt almost like making a certain confession—and yet she hated to say anything this confusing out loud: "Now if you notice me acting strange, it may be because I'm not even sure I'm here. I mean I may be lying at home on my brocade sofa, with the television on, and just thinking about all this, I may just be imagining it, that I am standing where I am standing—because why would I have come?"

She had just begun to think about how curious it would be to say such a thing when the nurse suddenly lifted her head. "Somebody at the door," she said.

The nurse went to see, and then Margaret heard a medley of ill-tuned country voices with severe, rasping drawls (*Nomey's people, lord help us all*) and the nurse giving a report; and in a moment they were upon her in the kitchen, four or five of them. They said it was wonderful of her to be here. One of the women turned to the others. "I told you there were still some good people in the world," she said. Margaret tried to say that she hadn't come to stay—and now that they were here . . . but they were such sorry people. They almost beat what she would see up at the Court.

Then one of them had a revelation. "Why this is Raymond's child," he said.

370

"You don't mean Raymond's girl?"

"Why we been wanting to meet you the longest *kind* of time."

"It sure is a shame the way people don't get to meet people."

A small woman who had said nothing up to now said something very wise and the rest all agreed with her up and down. "Friends are all people have," she said, "and yet it seems like they don't have that many."

"Raymond told and told about you."

"He thought the world of Margaret, or I know he always said he did."

They went on and Margaret tried to protest, and really all she gave them were cross-looking frowns, but they didn't even slow down. At last one of the men put his hands up. "Y'all quit all this gabbety-gab," he said. "Y'all giving this lady a plumb headache going on at her like this and she don't even feel like talking she's so grieved about Nomey."

Murmurs and sighs all around.

"Well this is something to be grieved *about* I tell you," one of them said.

The nurse led them into the death-room in a line and they were suddenly very quiet. Margaret wandered into the front room. Out the window she saw the old wide-bottomed car they had come in, and in the car a sight that was almost funny, and yet it annoyed her very much. They had left an old grandma in the car, in the thick dusty Eighth Street heat; by now they had probably completely forgotten about her, and the thing was she was enormously obese, she had the affliction of terrible fat, no doubt her back was sticking to the car seat; she was sitting with the car door wide open to get some air, and what was almost comical was the way her loose runny fat puddled around the seat and out the bottom of the open door. Margaret was terribly aggravated because she felt a relentless stream of *something* . . . flowing out of her to this old fat woman in the car, drain-

371

ing off a vital fluid of mental fortitude she could not afford to lose.

She could see into the bedroom. The people in there did not look like the same ones she had met in the kitchen. She could see a ring of stern, amazed faces, studying, in silence, the figure on the bed.

BACK IN the kitchen, Margaret found her a good standing place by the kitchen sink. Of course she was an inveterate wiper and cleaner, and before she knew it she had seized a cloth and was stroking the old pitted ledge of the sink. After a while she heard the visitors filing out of the house.

Then the nurse was standing in the kitchen door. "They said to tell you bye," she said. It seemed to Margaret that parts of the nurse's face had moved into slightly different positions.

"She's going way down," the nurse said.

Margaret hesitated. "Are they going to take her back to the hospital or just let her . . . stay here?"

The nurse said that the patient had been duly informed that if this was where she was bound and determined to be, she had her right to it. But she said she had a number she had to call every few hours, to let them know the sick person's pulse and blood pressure and things like that, so they could advise her as to whether there was any extra things that could be done. "Of course, what *is* there?" she said.

Margaret imagined a person at the hospital haranguing the nurse. *If you don't watch yourself, you going to have a bad case of death on your hands, and you know as sure as shooting you can get sued for that before you can turn around and this whole teetotalling hospital can get sued. What you got to remember is that when somebody dies it makes people real mad—and all us in this whole business just got to tighten up and not let things like that keep on happening. You hear what I'm saying to you now?*

372

Margaret and the nurse found themselves staring again at the kitchen window, as if fascinated by a light that was duskier and more diffuse. The stiff shreds of cheap polyester curtain, which attempted, absurdly, to grace the grimy window, were filled strangely with a rich, braided light that made them look almost like the brocade of Margaret's sofa at home. And yet that was ridiculous—nothing here could possibly resemble anything at home.

Margaret tried to consider her course of action. Her legs had begun to feel as if they were composed entirely of pulled muscles, so first she needed to sit down. She ought to go back into the bedroom and sit down in the chair with the sheet on it and try to think what to do. Still, she was not very impressed with her thinking powers today. The hidden parts of her brain seemed to be the ones in control and she did not think she had the strength of character to try to interfere with them. Very possibly she might simply find herself on the highway driving home, frowning intently over the wheel, not knowing how in the world she had even gotten behind it.

There was no reason for her to stay—any more than there had been any reason to come in the first place.

"It doesn't look like she's going to come to herself, does it?" she said to the nurse, and the nurse shook her head.

Margaret started, indeterminately, out of the kitchen, and on the way she picked up from the floor an old tin bucket with its handle half off—she could use it down by her chair as a little waste receptacle, for used kleenex and such. Maybe she *was* a fanatic, that she could be thinking of such things on such a day, and yet she could not help but feel that strange little victories could be won by acts like this—even in the midst of terrible defeats.

She made the difficult crossing of the blighted living room, holding her skirts together to keep them from brushing against the mangy furniture, trodding carefully over the old rag of a rug, which was an absolute danger the way its edges scuffed up. When she got to Nomey's door, she stopped and put her hand to her breast, and it was almost a surprise to find out that she herself was still breathing. She could make out across the room the figure on the bed, and she studied narrowly the limp, afflicted head where it had slipped down on the pillow, and studied too, for whatever explanatory power it might have, the inept, skewed connection of the head to the withered neck, the neck to the breast, the breast to the limbs that rose, haplessly, beneath the covers. Somehow she felt a deep discouragement that beat anything she had felt all day. She thought she had never seen anything so absurd as the white oasis in the middle of the room, her covered chair. On the other side of the bed was the wooden chair the nurse had sat in to sing hymns, and she thought of the nurse's songs trying to resonate in the flimsy, thin-walled room, the singer crooning softly in her old-fashioned voice, falling off tune on the high parts, about the rest beyond the river and ideas like that, about the mansions bright and blessed, and the glory hallelujah jubilee.

What if Nomey should raise her head, in a final excitation? "Maga, don't you hear something? Why that's a bell ringing. *Ain't* that a bell? Wonder what they're ringing it for?"

"Why you old simple thing—that's the *golden* bells . . . can't you tell or are you too silly?" Would that be her reply? "That's the *golden* bells and they're ringing them for you, and all the rest of the human beings that are dying tonight, you needn't to think you're the only one."

Margaret's thoughts kept flying off in peculiar directions like this. *Actually it is not we ourselves that die*, she thought, *it's more the world itself that dies away from us; probably it is simply taken away, in a swift rush, and then since there is nothing left for us to see or feel, we don't know that we still have anything to see or feel with and so it seems as if we do not exist.* Then she thought of it another way—that the last thing people heard was probably a quick little pop, which was the

374

world suddenly going out, never to shape itself again, and then there was just the thin buzz of static infinity. But whether people actually left the world, or the world left them—the result was the same and so it really wasn't worth thinking about.

But in any case there would not be any bells. Certainly no golden bells would be ringing, or any other kind, simply because there weren't any—just as there were no halls of glory, no sweet by-and-by, no beulah land, no rest beyond the river . . . no river in fact. There was no saviour full of wondrous love. She thought of herself standing in church with her hymnbook spread open, her soprano voice rising with the rest, and of how sometimes she had let her hymnbook droop in her hand, lodge absently against the back of the wooden pew in front of her, let her voice trail away . . . until she forgot to sing entirely and would just be looking and listening, alert to something that might come through to her when it had its chance and everyone else was busy with the song. Usually the women's voices would rise fully, while the men's sort of scratched along—it was a comedy that some of them even held up a hymnbook. It was the somber service in the evening that Margaret had mostly gone to. There was no way for her to go with the children in the morning and still put out a big hot meal at twelve o'clock, and not to have done that would have been in those days the worst dereliction of duty you could think of. In fact, she knew women she had always thought had become what they were—alcoholics, or mental cases—because they had not been able to carry out the Sunday practices, and had let their family come home from church, for instance, and hunt and pick their lunch out of the refrigerator. But anyway, in the darkened church, at the close of evening service, there was something else for her to watch besides the singers around her, and she watched it steadily—the lighted cross shining in the fount. She might intone vaguely the slow, somber songs that they sang when the room was dimmed and the cross lit up. *Beneath the cross of Jesus I fain would take my stand—the shadow of a mighty rock within a weary land.* She had begun to realize that all those years she had had her favorite songs, without knowing it, and mostly they were these slow and serious ones, dark and sad, these droopy-dog songs that suited her droopy disposition. *When I survey the-e wondro-ous cross where the-e prince o-of glory-y died, my richest gain I-I count bu-ut loss, and pour contempt on all my-y pride.*

How could things that were not true be so beautiful? She had asked herself that a thousand times. And sometimes, for no reason that she was smart enough to understand, another one of those old numbers that she had not thought about in a long time would come back to her, every word. Standing in Nomey's doorway, she was humming something right along even now, another one of those cross songs. It was a corny old thing in a way and yet it had a power over her that she could not even begin to get the better of. *Lead kindly light, amid th'encircling gloom. Lead thou me on. The night is dark and I am far from home. Lead thou me on. Keep thou my feet, I do not a-ask to-o see—the distant scene; one step enou-ough for me-e.*

She remembered how the song went on and said that the night would at last be gone, and that when the morning came, the singers would see the smiles on those faces—those "*angel* faces," it said—that they had loved long ago in their days on earth.

Margaret frowned. She looked across the room at the sick person. What angel faces did she think they would let *her* see . . . if she got past the shining river into the great beyond? For a moment Margaret saw heaven sprawled out like the big, dim, shadowy, ragged field outside the football stadium, where families hoped to be reunited after the game, milling about trying to spot each other. *She strained her eyes to catch sight of Richy in his band uniform. He was new in the band and one of the smallest ones. She put her hands on her hips and discovered she still had on the big apron she had worn behind the concession stand, making hot dogs for the Band Booster's Club. While she was untying the apron and rolling it up to mash it into her big pocketbook, she thought she saw Laney among the parked cars. A tall, long-necked boy leaned toward her. He was the one who drove too fast and at home would skid right up onto the lawn; it was very rude. She hoped he was not wanting to take Laney off somewhere tonight. Suddenly a hoarse blast from behind her made her almost jump out of her skin. It was Richy, his saxophone around his neck, and she told him then and there she didn't go for that kind of a joke.*

But as for meeting loved ones in a football-field kind of hereafter—even if there was any such place, what loved ones did Nomey even have *to* meet? Margaret thought about this darkly, and of course she was forced to reply to herself that the main loved one of the person on the bed had been her own father. But it was upsetting in the extreme to consider it this way—she preferred to think of the relationship of the two of them in another light entirely.

There was also Loreen of course. And certainly Margaret's mother. All the "children." Yes the whole bunch were all each other's loved ones—she supposed they qualified for that, if not for anything else. She thought of the whole preposterous Eighth Street troop showing each other their ridiculous affection, sticking by each other in their various incompetent ways.

Margaret's legs hurt, she shifted her feet a little bit at the door, and it was a great surprise when a murmur came from the bed, in fact a whole series of murmurs, small ones rising vaguely like little waves, washing up very lightly on a cliff of consciousness they could not cling to and falling back again. Margaret's mental commotion began to grind and haul like a loud internal machine, so that her physical actions were completely swallowed up in it, and she had no idea that she had moved at all until she found herself standing in a new position beside the bed, straining to catch . . . *what?* Possibly nothing more than the echo of her heels on the tilting floor.

377

She leaned forward and eased the pillow upward to straighten Nomey's head. Her murmurs had ceased, but her eyes were halfway open and she seemed to be trying to fix them on Margaret's face. Margaret attempted to station herself in the sick woman's line of vision. *Why here was Nomey actually trying to speak.* "Ma-a-ga . . . ." After a time she began to try again but at first her lips trembled on the words and could not work clear. Margaret leaned over to be sure and hear. "Maga. What you got?"

For a moment Margaret did not understand. Then she was surprised. "Oh! Nothing. This old bucket," she said.

She had been holding the bent tin pail against her chest with one arm as if in an embrace. But now something began to dawn on the old wretched face before her—and though some people would not have known what it was, Margaret knew that it was a look of satisfaction. Nomey seemed to swallow—and then stretch her mouth a little bit. Suddenly she found a little stock of whispery breath. "Maga. What you go' clean up for?" The action of speaking seemed to flutter with each word her half-closed lids. She seemed to turn her eyes to the side of her. "Maga's so smart," she said to the nurse, although the nurse wasn't there.

Margaret set the bucket down on the end of the bed—as if to make something absolutely clear . . . or perhaps it was only because she did not want to hold onto something that might be an impediment to her mental processes. When she looked at the patient again, her eyes were closed, and she looked as if she had entered a dream-world with some peculiar kind of contentment in it. Perhaps it was a place where someone with an old tin pail was putting everything to rights—at last.

*My lord.* Margaret placed a hand around the curve of the bucket as if she needed to see if she was on the right track about something. No doubt she was, but thank the lord, she thought to herself, she did not have to pay any attention to what this sick old thing wanted or didn't want.

# CHAPTER ELEVEN

MARGARET wore her-self out. When she got through she had a very sore shoulder, and she had mussed herself a good deal more than she had meant to, even though she had on her smock and had tied on her head a loose kerchief from the vinyl bag—to keep the dust off without mashing down her hairdo. After all, no matter what happened down here in Florida, in Georgia Monday would still come after Sunday, and she would be back up at the Court, behind her desk, and she didn't want to give all the customers a heart attack as they took the turn at the top of the stairs and saw, through the glass doors, a wild woman with boogerman hair.

As she had worked on Nomey's floor, she had moved the covered chair off to one wall, and when she got through with everything, had sat down in it to change her shoes, enjoying the look of the room—so completely transformed. It was a confusing feeling in a way, but as usual she felt a hundred times better for having stirred around so hard. She supposed she was one of those people who had, in their bloodstream, some agent of well-being that could only be set in action by smelly cleaning salts.

Even though she had definitely re-toned her sagging blood a little bit by this intense spasm of work—as if it were her own house and company from out of town about to knock on the door—still it was one of the most bizarre and ridiculous things she had ever done. (This might be the *most* bizarre.) For years she had put off going to a psychiatrist, but she thought when she got back home, she might look into it. For one thing, when she had first begun she had decided to limit herself absolutely to Nomey's bedroom, but then once she got started she couldn't help but take a few licks at the living room too, and then she had gone tearing right into it, in such a crazy rush she felt like she was getting a fever; after a time she had felt very flushed and a little woozy and yet she couldn't make herself stop, and that was not normal.

Margaret sighed deeply in her chair. The house was quiet, and it seemed even more like a ghost of itself, now that nighttime had clearly, irrevocably arrived. A few weak ineffectual lights had been turned on, and Margaret thought probably the nurse was in the kitchen and had laid her head down on the kitchen table. Pretty soon the night-shift nurse would come on to relieve her. Margaret imagined the night nurse coming in the door and Margaret and the other one coming forward to greet her—and being so startled by her face, *her night face*, that they both let out a little cry and covered their mouths.

Margaret stretched back in the chair, moved her shoulders back and forth so they would not stiffen up on her. She flexed the sore fingers of her right hand—she had used tools she wasn't used to and which weren't really the right kind. The people from one of the agencies had left a small store of cleaning supplies, and there were a few other odds and ends of dilapidated equipment around and about, and she had also torn one of Nomey's old threadbare sheets into a pile of wipe cloths.

Nomey was quite still again, and her eyes were closed. Except for the low erratic whirr of the air-conditioner, her breath was the only audible thing in the house. She was breathing like a wheezy old car that needed a tune-up.

Margaret had been able to tell by a number of very small signs that Nomey had heard and smelled what was going on, and that it was the best death-gift she could have received—just for Margaret to stack and straighten her old junk; to wipe things and fasten them, or bend them back into shape—throw them away, the ones that were that vile; sweep and scour and scrape.

Indeed Margaret had known, by a certain instinct she had that had not been neutralized, abraded or deterged by all the grievous harms and hurts of her life, even by the Old Dutch Hatred she had always felt for the woman on the bed, that if she were going to take a whack (or more than whack) at this terrible room, there was no reason to muffle the noise she made or try to keep the fumes down—there was every reason not to. The smells were pungent ones, but of course Margaret did not dislike them; in fact she had always been succored by these kinds of smells, and believed others could be too. So for a while the air had simply reeked around the sick person's bed, and as for noise, there was plenty of that, and there had been a bad grinding sound which made the patient begin to murmur again when Margaret had pulled straight the old chest in the corner of the room. The chest was missing a roller and Margaret had to prop it with a chunk from a broken lamp base. In fact it was also missing a whole drawer. Later, however, the drawer had materialized at the bottom of a hill of junk and clutter on the other side of the room, and Margaret had lifted from it a great stiff, repugnant wad of mildewed clothes—as well as a caved-in cigar box, where she could still trace the name of her father's cigars.

Inside the box was a thin, irregular packet of old snapshots, half-stuck together. Perhaps the last people to look at

381

them had been children with sticky fingers—the grown children next door possibly, their fingers anointed with Orange Crush. Margaret held the photos in her hands and started to pull them apart. *No,* she had thought, *this will make my head swim and my throat burn, my breath hurt my breathing tubes.* She had looked for the vinyl bag and took the photos and tucked them in. Later, at home, lying up on her high bed, she would study them closely, scowling deeply, trying to see if they had any explanatory value.

In the lost drawer—separated, probably, for years from its brother and sister drawers—there was also an old split paper bag stuffed full of the Eighth Street art. Her face had drawn up in a great knot when she had realized what she had, and yet she surprised herself: she was quite calm as she unrolled the crushed top of the sack and unfolded a stack of yellow folded squares, felt the rough cloth, the ridges of crude embroidery. There was a long narrow dresser scarf that she could use on the chest. The thread had been knotted on both sides, and in the dim light of the room it was hard to tell which side was the right side. Finally she had it laid properly on the bare top of the old propped and straightened chest, which had also been wiped clean all over and succored and anointed with a drop of floor wax.

Then she went back to the sundered drawer, wiped it clean with her wiping cloth inside and out, restored it to the chest. (*Not to be able to make anything well,* she thought, *but an old chest!*) When she stood back to study the effect, suddenly her eyes smarted sharply with anger at herself and her absurd behavior.

But as loony as she was, she had still kept on—as if she had wanted, herself, to see how far she would go. And possibly that was why when she had finished it all up and wrung out the mop, sighing and sweating at the kitchen sink, then set it in the bucket in the corner, and laid nearby a knotted sheet full of terrible rubbish for the garbage man . . . that was why she and the nurse had walked down the crooked wooden steps of the back stoop into the short back yard, gingerly, holding each other's arms for support. By then it had been late dusk, almost tipping over into actual dark—gray motes had seemed to fly around them like noiseless bugs. In the dusky afterglow of the vanished August sun, the jungly yard had looked shockingly transformed, for there was still enough reddish light to gather richly in the moplike heads of the yellow-blooming weeds and lend them an amber radiance.

From the porch Margaret had stepped down into this radiance and it had come floating up about her legs, and when she looked back at the descending nurse, her white dress just touching the sea of hazy gold, she had felt utterly dismayed by the preposterous beauty of what she saw. She felt an awful weakness that was far worse than a stiff back or a sore arm. Still, she had not just stood there scowling but had bent to her task, wielded a small kitchen knife against the yellow blooms.

These tall peculiar weeds—what were they anyway and why did Margaret not remember them? They were a little like goldenrod but Margaret knew goldenrod and this was something else. All down the untended back yards of Eighth Street, it was just possible to see, in glinting after-light, the teeming growth of this uncultivated plant; it hid the litter on the sandy ground, seemed to be fed and fattened, in fact, by this Eighth Street refuse lying at its roots.

Her back had ached, and so she had straightened up, her arms full of the scratchy plant, and turned in the direction she had not meant to turn, towards the *other* little house across the yard.

No lights there. No, there was certainly no life there now. Margaret had heard the sighs of the nurse. "Those folks got out while the getting was good." Margaret could see that the back stoop was half rotted away. The back edge of the roof was ragged and torn, and some of the actual boards of the house had slipped crookedly out of place. The place looked like a small ruin, and yet to Margaret, in her peculiar state, looking at it through the smoky summer dusk . . . it had had a weird softness that was amazing. She had imagined herself on one of her trips to the home for the incompetent. —*George I went to Jacksonville. I saw Mama's house. It's completely worn-out now, nobody can live in it—and yet the day I saw it, I don't know, it didn't look all that bad.* —*Mama dead,* she heard George say, and as she imagined it, he went on to state, very logically, that since his mama *was* dead he didn't want to see her house again and that he didn't want to see his father's house either since *he* was dead. Then he had tried to think a little bit and almost furrowed his brow. —*I want see Nomey,* he said. But in a moment he had changed his mind. —*But Maga don't like Nomey, so I don't want see Nomey.* Margaret had been aggravated, more than a little bit. —*Oh George . . . .*

But out back in the dusk tonight, she had stood gazing over the short yellow field, her arms full of the flowering weed. She had wished they were full of something rare and valuable that she could take and lay on the old broken steps. There was a ringing peal of some kind in the air, and she had thought for a moment the nurse had emitted a rackety laugh. But when she looked back, the nurse's face, in the rosy light, had had an absent, somber look on it. The laugh clapped again—a sharp cackling laugh—and Margaret knew it was nothing but a ghost-laugh; it was her mother's laugh she had thought she heard. *No wonder things were jarred out of place and the house is full of loose boards.* She thought of her mother's stringy neck thrust out the window, her lanky arms clapped on the sill, her merry tickled laugh pealing over the neighborhood . . . and of all that clamor inside . . . day in, day out . . . all that babbling and crying, laughing, hollering, whining, moaning, blubbering. She pictured an inspector from the city coming out, staring up at the ceiling boards. "Why those old sticks have been *laughed* loose," he said—"or cried, I can't tell which, but I know this place has undergone a lot of human noise damage of *some* kind. What sort of folks did you say was living here?"

Margaret had strained forward. She had wished she could reach over the blooming field to the little ruined house. But it did not seem possible to take a single step. For a moment the yellow weeds looked to her like a field of dangerous spikes, deliberately put there to keep her back. She looked at the kitchen window of the rose-shadowed house. Of course it was as bizarre as it could be for her to be standing outside looking in, instead of inside in the thick of it.

*She had remembered shaving Riley at the kitchen sink, getting him ready for the funeral. It was a very cold day for Jacksonville, there was no hot water in the house, and her hand was absolutely numb.* It had felt like an icy claw from rinsing the razor at the tap. Riley was crying all the time and it made the whole thing a very messy operation. Margaret had been silent while he cried. She had quit trying to make any of them hush, and for instance she did not answer at all when her sister Barbara would ask her question. "Eh-ou-puh-my-ma-way-down?" *Are they going to put my Mama way down?* Bobba's question had become just a nervous tick, she asked it over and over again all day.

At home in Waycross one night, Margaret had received a call from the tiny, emaciated neighbor woman. "She don't want you to know but I said I knew you wouldn't want to *not* know, so what I'm calling for's to tell you—that your mama's back home."

"*Ho*-ome?"

Oh Margaret could have wrung the neck of the phone. She had found her mother a decent nursing home, and a person to stay at the house with the children, and she had started work on getting them into the places they should have been put in years ago.

"I don't usually go out to the store at night," the neighbor said, "but last night I went out to the store. And when I went out I heard somebody laughing that sounded just like your mama, and I went on over there and it *was* your mama, as big as you please, and she was out on her porch carrying on like you never saw with some folks in the yard. They told her they thought she was doing real good and they sure were glad she was back home and she said that in the nursing home they told her she was near bout dead and she asked the neighbors if she looked dead to them and they said nosir, she didn't even look sick. All three of the kids were right there on the porch with her, and Bobba kept hold of her arm and you know the way Bobba does, everything your mama would say she said the same thing after her. *Say my ma dead* and things like that. Acourse she doesn't even know what dead is. Well your mama has lost a little more flesh, and sometimes when she's talking, she has to wait to get her breath, but I don't guess she's doing all that bad. She said she wouldn't go back to one of those places for *no* reason, not even if she *would* get near bout dead, but if she did go back, she was goin to take the rest of her fambly with her. Like she did that one time—that it got everybody so upset?"

Margaret remembered her mother in the *first* home: leaning her elbows on her bed like a Roman queen, all her waiting-people around her, lying on rags around her bed in their inept positions, making their noises.

Then a few days after the neighbor's call, before Margaret could get back down there, her mother had died.

The spirit men had come, quietly in the night, and borne her spirit away.

The day of the funeral Margaret shaved the boys and got everybody dressed in their absurd attire. Her father had been dead six months and a lot of his specific caretaking had fallen to her. George was as miserable as he could be, his face was a fat bog of pain, and yet Margaret noticed that he also took care, wherever she went, to stand where she could see him with his tie on. It was a strange day in every respect, but for George to have a tie on was the strangest thing of all.

Margaret had wished she had had time to wipe it clean and press it for him.

Where had that tie even come from in fact? she had wondered tonight, standing in the deep crop of yellow weeds. She had remembered this: Nomey at the front door that morning, bearing a tie of Margaret's father's. *That she could even have thought of such a thing on a day like that.* Margaret drew down, severely, a corner of her mouth. She remembered Nomey coming in the door, the others setting up at once a terrible howl, bumping and lurching, half falling towards her. Their inept expressions of frenzied grief. The blundering of them all together, in a wailing and babbling heap, a wet tangle slipping and slobbering. Margaret standing in the inner doorway with her almost absent frown. Nomey not reaching forward to her with actual hands, but straining towards her with face, with eyes. Margaret looking away, her eyes shuttered. Nomey speaking. "Oh-o Maga, how you holding up?"—or something like that. Margaret murmuring something in reply. Then more or less sending Nomey away. Saying to the others, "All right! You get busy now. You going to see Nomey later on."

But now Margaret imagined a conversation between her and Nomey on the porch that day.

"You still don't forgive?"

"Goodness no. I wasn't used to thieves twenty-five years ago and I'm still not used to them. You stole people's father. And a person's husband who had not done you any harm. I should have got you in court for aggravated burglary."

"But I just thought—that now . . . with your mama being dead . . . ."

"She died her first death the day you walked in the door on Clark Street. You remember how the dog tried to bite your leg arteries so you would bleed to death? And do you happen to remember where *I* was that day? I was sitting at the kitchen table, where my father and I did the clean, orderly things that were our nature, and kept chaos in its place. Then when *you* came chaos busted out."

In Margaret's imagining Nomey tuned up to cry and Margaret pictured her face as she had seen it, in reality, at the service later on—wet and red, her mouth quivering in misery. When she, Margaret, had walked into the funeral room and seen that face, she had taken a seat where she was sure she would not have to look at it.

But when Nomey had left the house that day, Margaret distracted the grieving children by making a big business out of the putting on of George's tie. She recalled that George had had a pat of kleenex stuck on his cheek, where Margaret had nicked him with the razor—at the funeral she would notice that it was still there and would lean over Riley's lap to pick it off.

When she had gotten through with the boys, she had taken Barbara and gone to work on *her*—first she had held her head way back and got her to swallow an Elavil. After a while, the Elavil changed a little bit the configuration of Barbara's question, which was stuck on infinite repeat on one of her brain-stems. It was very cold. The windows were steamed up, and Riley made finger-streaks on the glass. After a while he began to babble, slowly at first, building up a kind of choking steam, and so Margaret went to look out the window.

A huge automobile loomed in the yard, and she knew at once whose it was. A great splendid, rearing, glinting ship of a car was beached high on the Eighth Street shore. *Must* have been as wide as the street, she considered. No doubt when that great tub had come voyaging in these realms, the whole street had had to be closed to the smaller vessels that normally plied there. Inside the car was the warm, spruce, cushiony comfort and safety that Margaret hated and loved so much. She could make out Granny and Vivian, both in beautiful clothes, also Vivian's husband. The owners of the rig had been left behind—a wealthy couple who made Sunday cruises out to the dairy, brought expensive bouquets on Granny's birthday, and wheeled her off in big riggings to a sea-blown house on Jekyll Island.

Margaret had glowered in the window of her mother's house that day. Then stepped back and took the brush to Barbara's bird-nest hair. She had not expected Granny to come, and for a moment she could not settle her feelings or decide what to think. She saw that her guests of fashion were not going to make any move to come inside—they would wait in the car until Margaret went out to leave for the funeral, let her tell them where to go.

She went on about her business. There was no stream of grievers and condolers bringing hot dishes, funeral meats. In fact all morning there had been, besides Nomey, only two callers—an old aunt of her father's and the tiny neighbor-woman down the street. At least these two had come with a degree of sincere confusion and distress, and were even prepared to pitch in if pitching in was called for.

Where were all her mother's *other* friends, Margaret asked the little neighbor. The neighbor said that well, Margaret's mother was the one they were friends with and without her there, they weren't sure they were welcome. "Well *of course* they're welcome!" Margaret had hissed.

She could hardly remember her drive to the funeral parlor. Possibly there was something especially terrible about it—very likely whatever little sac of her brain had been filled with this experience had popped of its own accord, and leaked the whole memory away. She did remember the stout, stumpy, awkward line of bereaved children jostling each other out to the car—and the little elfish neighbor already waiting for them in a corner of the back seat. And she had had one wonderful creative brain-flash that day: she had assigned Nomey and Loreen to ride in the car with Granny.

Granny never spoke of this ride at all the whole rest of her life, but Margaret tasted it sometimes, on her memory-buds, and it had a delicate flavor that nothing else could match.

The funeral was the awfullest thing in the world; she must not have known what she was doing when she had made the arrangements. The service was in a horrible concrete-block addition to the back of a run-down funeral home that just happened to be nearby. The rough walls were painted an incredible aqua and the folding chairs were such cheap, unbalanced things that it was a wonder no one had ended up in a heap on the floor. The preacher had a country twang, he had never met Margaret's mother, and everything he said was ridiculous. Granny and her party sat on the last row and neither Granny nor Vivian had gone up to look at the body. "Well it was only their daughter—their sister," Nora had said, "so why would they want to?

"If I had done like that to one of mine," she went on, "I could not have looked at her either. I don't guess even Granny could stand that." Nora had pulled on her cigarette, thinking about it.

"But anyway I expect Granny just thought—oh I wouldn't know her anyway . . . so to hell with it."

NIGHT FELL, heavily, as Margaret sat on in her sheet-covered chair in the death-room. One weak lamp burned, throwing huge shadow-rings against the walls. Margaret sat with her eyes closed, breathing gratefully the purifying fumes of Lysol coming up from the scrubbed floor, her mind half adrift on the rickety current of sound from the air-conditioner.

But when the sick woman began to murmur, Margaret sat up at once. She went quickly and brought to the bedside, from the chest where she had set it, on the embroidered scarf, the bushy yellow and green bouquet she and the nurse had picked in the yard. In the house it did not look at all the way it had in the rosy yard—it looked like the scratchy mess of weeds it was, a preposterous excuse for a floral display.

Still, she was determined to fix it in the patient's warped line of vision as best she could. She touched her arm and spoke her name. *Nomey look-a-here*, she said. *What we got for you.* The sick woman opened her eyes as far as she was able to; she saw the jar of blooms and something formed on her face that Margaret knew was a smile, and she moved slightly her eyes, opened her lips and whispered. "Maga's so smart," she said.

For a long time she did not say anything else or show any sign of life. The nurse came in and took her pulse. After she had done so, she stole a narrow look at Margaret in her chair, as if to say, *Be prepared—if you possibly can be.*

Later the sick woman spoke once more, and Margaret supposed it was a pity that her mind was so clear. Her voice was almost lost in the thick funnel of breath—or maybe it was blown by strange winds, of a kind Margaret, with all she knew, did not know about yet. *Maga.* Margaret leaned way down to be sure and hear. "Don't forget to tell Gaw and Bobba and them . . . I died."

The night deepened and seemed to Margaret to clutch the house as she sat her vigil in the death-room. Cars with bad mufflers shuddered by outside, and once she heard what sounded like a whole fleet of motorcycles starting up—threateningly—somewhere down the dark street. She was not used to all this, goodness knew, and truly she still wondered at herself. Why had she not started home before dark, while there was still time? Of course for a person as baffled by things as she was . . . she could not see that what they did really mattered at all, could possibly have any meaning or serve any purpose.

She sighed. Oh she wished she had more brain-power, she wished she were smarter and had more education . . . there were so many things that no matter how hard she tried to focus on them would never come clear for her, and all she could do was think along simply on instinct the best she could.

She sat back with her eyes half-closed and thought wearily about her own death. The room around her began to stretch away into a far-off half-glimmering darkness, which itself faded out into deeper shadows still. *Poor old Margaret—didn't you hear? Her life never did work out, and then on top of that—she died.* Tonight she thought too of the death of her husband Leonard, still so fresh in her mind after so much time, still such a surprise. She thought of other deaths she had known and of ones she had only heard about, and there was nothing to explain why they were all, every one, so full of sadness. *What did it all mean anyway?* she asked herself.

She frowned at the patient across from her, cast her net of scowling thought over the listing bed.

There was a certain poem her son had read to her one time and somehow she had not liked it, she had said stop, stop reading that . . . and yet later, lines came back to her . . . *come, lovely and soothing death* . . . and in a way she had come to agree with this poem more and more. But even so, death was sad—that was also true. In this room tonight she saw that there was always *something* wrong and sad about it . . . .

Later Margaret started in her chair. She thought she must have dozed a little bit. She did not know how she knew it, but she knew that time had passed, the night deepened yet again. She sat forward and listened for the sound of breathing from the bed—there was still a scratchy nub of sound from over there.

She remembered that the night nurse had come on, or had she only dreamed it as she dozed? No, a large tall figure had approached her from behind, touched her shoulder and shown her her great dark face, for no reason but just to show it to her.

They had not spoken, though Margaret might well *have* spoken. She might have said, *No need to frighten us—we know who you are.*

HER MIND was not clear—and yet it went on . . . .

"George I went to Nomey's and I don't know why I did but I guess I should tell you she's not doing too well, in fact—"

Is that what she would say?

And what to her own three? "Children, children! I only wanted to tell you—" Margaret sat suddenly forward, braced herself fiercely on the chair-arms. "Oh, it's absolutely urgent that I let you know! . . . that—that we do not understand . . . ." She sank back again.

"Yes I went down to Eighth Street, don't ask me why, just to see things I guess (though what is there to see?), but I cleaned up Nomey's house and then she died and I tried to think it all through again but I couldn't I can't—"

MARGARET slumped backward in her chair and closed her eyes. It seemed to her that earlier, while she had dozed, she must have dreamed also of an old priest, because now she saw him again—and my lord, it was Bing Crosby! It was old Bing in a rough burlap robe, climbing up a darkening hill with a torch in his hand. Some scene from a movie she must have seen a long time ago, and possibly it had not even had Bing Crosby in it, but the way she remembered it, it had. Bing Crosby might have been a priest in some other movie and she had just put him in this one too.

The torch was to light a great big fire with, on top of the hill. It was some kind of primitive religious rite, when people believed very strange things, even stranger than they did today. Every fall when it got cold, they built a big fire so the gods would see it in heaven and it would be a message to them not to let the winter come this time. It was the silliest thing in the world, but they wanted the grass to stay green and the leaves to stay on the trees, eternal summer to cover the earth . . . in other words, nothing to die, not even people. *Let's all just stay like we are.*

Of course it was a ridiculous idea, the whole business, and yet Margaret remembered how sad and tense it was on the screen as the old priest trudged slowly up the hill with his torch. She remembered the grumbling sort of prayer he had said. *All right we will ask you one more time. You gods! Enough of this old death! And hey! Why not let the souls of the ones that are dead come back tonight?* Margaret thought it must be somewhat like open house at PTA ("Oh it's Dead Night tonight," she heard folks say.) *And let those souls just stay with us, and death be no more. What about it?*

Down below, while the old priest climbed, the people were singing in the twilight, and it was peculiar but it was a .hymn Margaret knew from the First Christian Church in Waycross, Georgia. "Rescue the perishing, care for the dying," the people sang, and the old man climbing the hill listened to them in sorrow, in sorrow he rose towards the mound. On his face Margaret saw this: he was deeply ashamed of it but tonight he did not have any hope at all, he had completely lost hope that the gods, watching the bonfire year after year, ever meant to rescue the perishing people. *Or perhaps there are no gods*, he was thinking as he climbed, holding up his burlap skirt. *I would light myself too if that would burn it bright enough*, he murmured, and then he prayed again: "You gods! If you *are* there, see this fire tonight! And remember to save us! Save the people of the earth, the children of the world!"

Of course Margaret's mind played tricks on her, that was for sure, she never remembered things the right way, she remembered them *her* way, but she could see that the old priest was finally reaching the top of the hill; he was approaching the great mound of brush and briars, piled high by the silly hope of those below, hope so strong it almost made him smile . . . but instead the old priest—as Margaret saw him tonight—began to cry, and he cried freely as he waited for the last light to fade. Maybe he was remembering his own dead people of long ago. Perhaps—up there on his lonely hill—it was his mother he thought of, holding his head against her breast, with beautiful hands. Down below, he was hardly ever alone, and he could not let himself be seen without hope—but here, up here on dead night he cried because he *could* cry and there was no one to see that he himself did not believe that death would ever die.

RESCUE *the perishing, care for the dying* . . . Margaret was half-humming it herself, she found, and when she realized it, she almost deliberately changed to something else, just because the darkened room was illuminating—so horribly—the facts of the human case, the death-fact and all the other facts, and because this other song, *Jesus loves the little children, all the children of the world,* was a much more pleasant one to think about . . . even if it wasn't true.

# AUTHOR'S NOTE

THE AUTHOR has had, over the years, extraordinary help and support in the writing of this story—above all, the assistance of a number of close friends, many of them writers themselves, who have had the goodness to read the manuscript in various disordered and indeterminate drafts. I want to thank, especially, my friends Donald Mull of Philadelphia; Ann Kiley of Whittier, California; the late Jean Couch of Watkinsville, Georgia; Austin Wright, Nancy Harvey, Pat Hope, and Carol Rainey of Cincinnati; Janet Groth of Plattsburgh, New York; and Lamar Herrin of Ithaca, New York.

My husband Jerone Stephens has been forebearing and encouraging in many ways during the composition of this work, as have my children Dan, Paige, and Shelley. Shelley Stephens was an acute early reader of this narrative, and my sister Jennifer Parks read and reread the finished work, contributed greatly to my understanding of what I had done, and convinced me that I had gotten some things right.

I also wish to remember with deep gratitude my dear friend and literary agent, Dorothy Pittman of Thomaston, Georgia, and New York, a devoted partisan of this book who did not live to see it in print.

Jim Hall, chair of the English Department of the University of Cincinnati, has been a loyal helpmate of this work for several years, as have two members of the department staff with a high order of technical talent, Kristin Dietsche and Stephanie Starkey. My graduate student friend and proficient assistant, Laura Schneider, has stood by me in this and in a number of other endeavors of the past few years in ways I am especially grateful for. The Taft Committee of the university has provided me time for summer writing without which this story could hardly have been told.

The retreats for artists at Yaddo Colony in Saratoga Springs, New York, and Ragsdale Colony in Lake Forest, Illinois, have made possible for me several stints of completely concentrated work that were of incalculable value.

I wish to remember also a friend and great visionary artist, Tillie Olsen, whose writings have been a guide for me in many ways, helping me to understand that art must try to address itself to all people, and to abet in its own often mysterious way—even in these United States and in this time of discouragement and near despair—the building of a genuinely democratic way of life. Indeed all my radical friends of recent years—far too numerous to name—have helped me take the measure of the social forces that today are pressing us ever downward into the abyss and against which struggle must always go on, in the arts as in all other human endeavors.

I am grateful to the literary critic Sue Kissel, of the University of Northern Kentucky, for an unexpected and generous letter which she wrote about this manuscript during the past year and which eased its way in the world of books.

I must also express heartfelt thanks to my fellow Georgia writer Mary Hood, who wrote an extended review of this south Georgia tale that penetrated more deeply into its purposes than anything I had expected to see.

My fellow writers Gladys Swan and Gordon Weaver I will always remember for the extraordinary care and comradely perspicuity with which they composed critiques of this manuscript. There was hardly a word of their counsel I did not attempt to heed.

My new friends at SMU Press, Kathryn Lang, Freddie Goff, and Keith Gregory, have my gratitude for their patience and intense concentration on behalf of this sometimes difficult work. They are among the people who are today holding open the door for serious writing—and even making of this adventure a thriving enterprise.

Above all, of course, I must remember here the remarkable individual whose life I have attempted in this book to sketch, Evelyn Thomas Wise.

May she rest in eternal peace.

David Logan and Dale Hodges

MARTHA STEPHENS grew up in south Georgia, the setting for *Children of the World* and for her first novel, *Cast a Wistful Eye*. Since 1967 Stephens has lived with her family in Ohio. She teaches modern literature at the University of Cincinnati and is involved in radical movements in Ohio and in Central America around issues of economic justice for all people.